Tears in the Dust

A novel by

Chuck Waldron

*Many stories appear to start at the beginning, but in fact often
start well before the beginning and continue long after the end.*

Also by Chuck Waldron
Remington and the Mysterious Fedora
Served Cold

2011

Dedication

Most of all, thank you Suzanne. We've been through a lot together and through it all you have believed.

My thanks to Henrietta, who gave me the first push out of the writing nest. I certainly can't forget Lorne, whose silenced voice still echoes words of support. To Darcie, my fellow writer and provider of editorial support, here's a special thanks.

Prologue—

A Frenchman named Chamfort, who should have known better, once said that chance was a nickname for providence.

-Eric Ambler: *The Mask of Dimitrios*

Dear Michael,

Was my life preordained, allocated to a certain destiny? Or, was I simply an actor playing a role—a role in a drama where the final act had already been written by some unknown playwright? I prefer to think I somehow managed to throw sand in the gears of destiny with acts of free will.

I was a party to two murders; this is why I do not particularly trust in fate. For this reason, I am writing to you tonight, as my life is fast approaching its end. Sadly, I will never have the answers to the many questions I've had throughout my long life.

Was it fate, my becoming a party to murder the first time? Especially when it was a murder that took place without my knowledge? I do not mean that as an excuse to lighten my guilt in the matter. In 1937, a private detective was murdered with an ice pick on my account. It happened on a railway platform in Montreal. That murder, so long ago, set in motion the entire chain of my life events, events I feel now, I was helpless to escape.

I did not know the man who was murdered, or even that he meant to do me harm. Men I would never know recognized the danger that detective posed to me, and with expert skill and efficiency, murdered him in cold blood, all on my account...

A finely sharpened ice pick is an ideal weapon to slip between the third and fourth rib, finding the heart with lethal accuracy. When the detective's revolver was passed on to me later that night, I knew nothing of its provenance.

As I sit here this very evening, that same gun lies next to a notebook on my table. It stares at me now, accusing and mocking me. That gun has been constant memento of that long-ago murder in Montreal.

A mere coincidence, you might say—I had no real part of that murder, as my hands are clean. I might be persuaded by that argument, but for the fact I was involved in another murder eight years later, on the side of a rain-soaked escarpment in a place called Rattlesnake Point. I was a direct party to that second murder. Some might argue I was acting to save my own life and that self-defense is not murder. That is a point I do not wish to dispute as my body succumbs to disease.

I have given you, my last and only remaining friend, my confession. It is now yours to use, or not, as you see fit. When you write the story, and should anyone read it, I hope it will impart a better understanding of the bond between fate and free will than I had as the events in this story took place.
Signed,
Alestair Stuart Ferguson

❋ ❋ ❋

A cold, late October wind clawed at the window of Michael's apartment as he sat reading the letter. He pulled his sweater tighter, an unconscious response to the bluster of the weather.

He thought back to the time he first met Alec—Alestair his given name. He remembered hearing the story, recounted in a voice that mirrored the haunted face that had quietly told it. Michael had made that man a promise: to write the story whispered in the night. Now, Alec was dead. It had been a promise he could have easily ignored, forgotten. It would have been so easy simply to place it alongside the other unfulfilled promises in Michael's life.

No, Michael pledged silently. He would not go back on his promise this time. Opening his laptop, he sat for a moment, fingers poised over the keyboard as he searched through his memories and began typing out the story he had vowed to write. He would finally tell Alec's story as it deserved to be told, exactly as he had heard it: no more, no less.

Chapter 1

The Story of Alestair Stuart Ferguson

I should have turned back.

I should have turned back that February morning in 1937.

If only I had known then how the story would end. I thought little about fate or outcomes back then.

I walked up a small hill that morning, listening to melting snow crackling under my boots, the unexpected warmth of the morning air flowing over my cheeks. Somehow, I knew it would be a day to reckon with, to hold fast in my memory for some use in the future. My journey—my adventure—was beginning.

Strange, but I still remember something so vividly from that day. Off to my right, I saw a bird; it was a broad-winged hawk sitting on a tree branch, poised for flight. The hawk looked down at me for a fleeting instant with its piercing eyes, and with an explosion of silence, its wings lifted the bird up into the brisk air. As the branch shuttered violently from the hawk's take-off, shedding snow sparkled like myriad diamonds in the morning light. The bird started climbing into the morning sky in tight spirals of increasing altitude; higher and higher it climbed, into the deep indigo overhead.

What drew me to that bird in flight?

I held my breath and watched until it was a small speck in the sky, soaring on lofty air currents, oblivious to the invisible boundary, separating Vermont and Canada far below, needing only the lift of air flowing under its wings. The bird soared upon the warm air currents, patiently waiting for an unwitting breakfast to come out of hiding.

I felt a strong sense of rising melancholy as I watched. The hawk continued its languid circling until abruptly, like the dive-bombers in the newsreels, the majestic bird tilted slightly and began to plunge down, down, down. At that moment, I realized the bird was a symbol of my leaving, of why I was on this journey in the first place.

I remember still my rage and horror watching those newsreels. In their flickering black and white images, I had seen Stuka planes. I recoiled mentally at those images of German warplanes dropping their bombs on an innocent Spanish city, women cradling babies in their arms, looking up in terror and disbelief as those planes circled overhead. It reminded me of my hawk.

I had seen those planes just last night on the screen in a darkened theater. That city they had bombed was Guernica, a name burned into my conscience forever, fuelling this obsession within me to take a stand and make a difference. I had to stop the fascists from bombing undefended cities, to protect the innocents from those murderous hawks.

The hawk would be my totem, I decided, endorsing my journey.

I was leaving that morning to enlist in what I felt to be a great cause: to enlist as a soldier to fight in the civil war in Spain. I was going to join the side of the innocents. I would shoot those hawks out of the sky. I cleared a sudden tear from my eye, wondering, without any particular reason, if there was snow in Spain.

Should I have turned back then?

I glanced back at the life I was leaving behind. Instead of turning back into complacency, I stepped forward on the road before me and marched into the future with sure, certain steps—steps that would take me on a journey littered with shards and broken remnants of right and wrong. It was a beginning full of promise, the beginning of something that would snatch away love, friendships and convictions, spitting them back out as though they never existed.

That morning as I left, I thought I knew right from wrong. I felt I had the ability to discern what was *right* and to stare down the wrong I knew surrounded me. It was such an innocent view I held in my youth. Only now can I see how blurred the line between good and evil can become. That line seemed so clear, so distinct in the beginning; but along the path of my journey, shadows developed to disguise that line, forming gradient shades from black and white and all the shades of gray in between. As usually happens in life, awareness came too late for me.

I snapped out of my reverie. My hawk had disappeared from view. With a sigh, I turned to the west and felt a decided chill. Gathering clouds were growing as though they were alive, turning into a living, breathing beast up there in the sky—an uncertain creature changing its mind as gusts of wind began pushing at the scudding clouds, their shadows chasing me.

The clouds became dark and angry, as though they wanted to claw the eyes out of the blue sky. Was this an omen trying to tell me to turn back? No, it didn't matter. I was on my way, resolute. The band of clouds passed by quickly, and I once again felt the warmth of the sunlight on my face.

I was headed to Canada. It was too dangerous to begin this journey on the Vermont side of the border. The United States was using government agents, police, and Pinkerton's detectives to prowl and surveil all the ports of embarkation, on the look-out for all the "Communists and Anarchists" that were trying to aid Spain. Those of us in that category were viewed as *undesirable*.

They had just passed a new law forbidding travel to Spain as a volunteer for the Republican cause. Visas were denied and people were officially turned back. However, that did not stop thousands of the dedicated from going anyway, or at least trying.

Some of us chose to make our way to Canada, unaware the Canadian government had enacted similar legal barriers. Oblivious at the time, I was on my way to Toronto, to fight alongside the Canadians in the Mackenzie-Papineau Battalion, a proud part of the International Brigade.

I kept walking. I didn't turn back.

Chapter 2
On the Way

I crossed the border; it was as easy as stepping over a fence and I was in Canada. It was a remote area where few people bothered with formalities, crossing the border as freely as the air and water. It was easy to avoid the official crossing from Vermont at Beebe Plain, just to the east.

I wondered if I would ever see my parents and their home again. When I had left home earlier that morning, I closed the door softly, hearing my father snoring away the effects of the bottle we had shared during the night. I knew my mother was lying awake, no doubt whispering her silent good-bye.

I learned last night about the terrible price she paid when I was born. During the delivery, my mother had screamed in pain as a clumsy midwife botched the job. I finally knew why I didn't have any brothers or sisters.

I shrugged. It didn't really matter now, I guess. I had a long way to go, and this was only the beginning. I walked north, skirting the small village of Beebe on the Quebec-side of the invisible border. I felt at home on these trails that were once used by aboriginals. I made my way, turning to walk along Rue Junction, until I reached the railroad tracks. A daily freight train would soon be heading north, away from the border.

I waited where the tracks crossed Rue Junction, staying in the shadows of the early morning light. Off to my left, I heard the whistle signaling a train into motion, an engine and perhaps four or five cars. The train crews knew that locals frequently hopped the train, but they, too, shared the hard times and often looked the other way.

I remained behind a stand of trees until the train began crossing the road ahead of me, knowing it would not be at full speed yet. I judged the speed, timed my steps, and swung myself onto the lower stair of the middle boxcar. I reached around and gripped another handle, swinging my body around between two cars and out of sight. I wedged my pack behind the ladder and reaching into my jacket pocket, I took out my first cigarette of the day, cupping my hand to shield the match flame from the wind.

The train lurched ahead as it reached traveling speed, clattering as it crossed the trestle bridges over various streams, hooting at each road crossing. I counted off each road as we passed: Chemin de Beebe, Chemin de la Riviere, Chemin Le Flamme....

An hour later, I felt the train slowing. Retrieving my pack, I silently timed my next move. At the perfect instant, I jumped down as the train slowed, stumbling alongside the moving train until I could slow my pace to a proper walk.

I had landed on a gravel slope, sliding until I could duck into a culvert, and I waited for the train to pass overhead. The train was slowing for its scheduled stop just past the village of Ayer's Cliff. I could see the small village at the other end of the culvert, and it was easy to duck and walk through.

It was Sunday morning and the good people of Ayer's Cliff were lining up on the steps of the Catholic Church. I waited a bit and walked to the main street and turned north. I paused a moment there at the intersection.

No train for this part of my journey, I thought, and with a sigh, I started to walk once again. It was only ten miles to the depot in Magog and the train to Montreal. In those days, we didn't think anything about a walk like that.

I walked easily until I got to Magog, spotting the train station and the sign over the door that said *Passenger Tickets*. There was an arrow pointing the way, the sign in both English and French. I wasn't entirely comfortable with French, and I knew that my pronunciation would forever and correctly mark me as *l'Américain*. I was neither sorry nor embarrassed about it; it was simply a fact. I hoped it wouldn't draw undue attention, as I pushed money through the window.

The station agent, a surly man as I recall, looked at my money and nodded as he pushed a string of tickets back through the window without a word. I withdrew the tickets and studied them: a string of tickets that would take me through Saint-Jean-Sur-Richelieu and on to Montreal. In Montreal, I would change trains heading for Toronto, and from there, on to Hamilton.

"Call this number when you get to Toronto," father had said, handing me a small note card. "Seth will meet your train in Hamilton. You will be in good hands." He handed me a photograph of the man I was to meet.

Then he warned me.

"The police will be watching," he said. "They hover in places like the station in Montreal, on the look-out for agitators passing through."

I didn't ask him how he knew such things and thought he was being overly dramatic at my leaving. I was still over two hours from the Montreal station where I would change trains for Toronto.

The depot in Magog had the smell peculiar to such places. I sat on a hard, wooden bench in the waiting area, polished by years of sitting. A stove sat in the center of the waiting room, the coals emitting pops and hisses as they settled.

Looking around to make sure no one saw me, I opened an envelope my father had given me.

"Open this once you are on your way," he had said. "And never forget to be vigilant. You never know who is watching you."

That warning made me nervous, as I looked around the station prior to reading the contents of the envelope. When I saw what was inside, I quickly looked around again, but no one was watching me or paying any obvious attention.

There was money—a lot of money—in the envelope.

Then, I noticed something folded within the bills tucked inside. I opened it and began to read. It was a letter of introduction written by my father.

To the Hamilton Committee...the bearer of this letter is my son, Alec. He is to be extended all courtesy. It was signed, *Political Commissar Ferguson.*

I was stunned. I put the envelope carefully back into a pocket on the inside of my jacket. *What else didn't I know about my father?* I wondered.

Chapter 3

Michael sat back in his chair and stretched his arms over his head. He leaned forward again and resumed typing.

✳ ✳ ✳

Alec *was* being watched, however, as he looked up at the departure board. He had failed to notice the ticket agent pick up the telephone and start talking animatedly into the phone.

His ride to Ayer's Cliff had taken just over an hour, and his walk to Magog had taken another four. Alec was impatient; the train to Montreal wasn't scheduled for another two hours.

What's another couple of hours to wait?

He got up and walked to a café across the street. He sat at a table under a picture. It was a painting of a local legend, *The Legendary Buckskin Joe*, the caption said.

Alec sipped his coffee, looking out over Lake Memphremagog and the mountains beyond. He saw two men walking back toward the town on the ice with their catch of fish, and heard a long, piercing whistle as a factory announced the noon hour, even though it was Sunday.

The café was located in an auberge and wasn't busy. "Wait until church is over," the waitress commented.

There was no one to rush him. He asked for a newspaper, and unfolding the pages, saw the front-page story; Spain was beckoning him onward.

Fierce fighting was reported on the outskirts of Madrid as the government's army of volunteers was trying to hold back the advancing army under the command of Generalissimo Franco. Hopelessly outgunned and short of supplies, the loyalists were resisting Franco's elite forces....

It was evident the volunteers didn't stand much of a chance. Alec silently willed the comrades to hold out, steeling his resolve to join them. It was something much larger than he had ever expected, drawing him into its embrace.

Alec put the paper down; it was time. He paid his bill and thanked the waitress. Squinting in the bright, sunny afternoon, he walked to the station, the shrill steam whistle of the train in his ears.

He was oblivious to the fact someone was watching him very closely.

Giles Leblanc was a detective, promoted about as far as he could go in the organization, who quietly accepted his posting to an area thought to be unimportant. He was proud of his job and often pulled out a small, leather case to look at the embossed badge he carried. He worked for Pinkerton's Detective Agency and had few illusions he would ever advance beyond his remote assignment, but there was always a chance. Maybe this was it. He could hear the accolades in his head for being the one who spotted and captured a "most wanted" criminal. He smiled in satisfaction at the thought.

The phone call from the station agent had sparked him into action that morning. He had recognized the opportunity for recognition and reward.

Giles was short, overweight, balding and poorly dressed. He knew these qualities created an air of invisibility, and that was good in his line of work. Few people gave him a second look. He retained his anonymity.

Those who did notice him might comment on his nervous habit of constantly brushing at his wispy hair in a vain attempt to conceal his baldness.

The little man paid quickly for his breakfast, following Alec.

While Alec sat in the café, the balding detective studied him intently, unfolding the communiqué and photograph to compare with his target. He carefully studied the man and the photograph without drawing attention to what he was doing.

Finally, he came to a decision—a wrong one it turned out.

He didn't realize he was looking at a picture of Ian Ferguson, Alec's father, from years ago. The detective was too enthralled with the promise of a five thousand dollar reward for Ian's capture, to realize his mistake.

Five thousand dollars, the pudgy man thought again.

Now, watching Alec walking back to the train station, he started making a mental list of what he would do with all that money.

Yes, looking at the back of the wrong man, *this guy is definitely the one,* he assured himself.

It would turn out to be a mistaken identification that would haunt Alec for the rest of his life.

Something niggled at the back of the detective's mind. It had to do with the age of the man in the photo. It just didn't match up with the man walking toward the train station. It didn't fit. He shrugged and put the picture back in his pocket, pushing the thought out of his mind, and began to follow the wrong man once again.

Alec pushed through the station door, joining a small group of passengers waiting to board the train. He had no reason to notice the nondescript man following him through the door. He didn't see the man walk to the left or enter the ticket office with a knowing nod to the ticket agent. He didn't see the man pick up the phone. He also didn't hear the man quietly talking into the phone.

"I'm sure it's the one. He looks a bit younger than I expected, but I will keep him in sight."

The ticket agent overheard the conversation and smirked as he handed the little man a string of tickets. "Remember who saw him and called you," the agent advised, "I knew something wasn't right about him. I knew who he was right away." He motioned to a stack of *Wanted* posters on the wall. "If there is a reward, I want some of it," he continued, hardly concealing his greed.

The detective mumbled something unintelligible and walked through the door, following Alec to the train.

He was only steps behind, as Alec sauntered leisurely onto the train. LeBlanc walked down the aisle to find an empty seat near his target. He passed Alec unnoticed and took a seat to the rear, where he could watch.

Swinging his pack onto the overhead rack, Alec ducked into a seat and leaned against the window. Alec looked at the familiar mountains of an area he knew so well, wondering if he would ever see them again.

His image of Spain was formed by the photographs and newsreels he had seen, the mountains mostly barren and brown compared to the emerald green of Vermont. He closed his eyes and once again recalled the newsreels of the fighting in Spain. *No*, he thought, *Spain looks nothing like this serene countryside. Spain has olive groves and rocky soil and buildings leveled by bombardments. No, Spain definitely looks nothing like Magog in the newsreels.*

He looked through the grimy window and watched the residents of this peaceful town as they passed by, blissfully unaware of the conflict in the world around them. The train pulled out of the station. He was beginning the next leg of his journey to Spain, a journey he was making so the people of Magog would never have to fight for their lives and country the way those brave souls were doing in far away Spain.

As the train lurched forward, he watched the conductor walking down the aisle towards him, balancing himself against the increasing sway of the train. Alec handed over his tickets and watched the conductor punch a small hole in one, then handed the tickets back.

The conductor braced against another sudden lurch, grabbing the back of Alec's seat, then moved further back in the coach. He passed through the aisle until he came to the small man who had boarded the train at the same time as Alec, who had discretely taken a seat at the rear.

The conductor turned his Masonic ring to face towards the detective, and the two exchanged meaningful looks. The little man nodded and turned back the lapel on his jacket, displaying his own Masonic insignia. He held up his Pinkerton's badge and nodded in the direction of Alec.

The conductor glanced at the back of Alec's head and frowned. He did not like the idea of having a criminal or traitor on his train.

The train made several stops until it was finally racing at full speed toward their destination of Montreal. As the train started to slow, Alec looked out at the expanse of the St. Lawrence River under the bridge. Smoke from the locomotive was swirling past the window, the black, sooty grime taking swipes at the scene outside his window.

On cue, the conductor came down the aisle, balancing against the sway of the car by touching the back of seats to steady him as he walked.

"Montreal, the Montreal station in five minutes!" Alec heard him continue his message into the next car.

The passengers began standing, reaching for their luggage in overhead racks. Alec stood and stretched away the weariness from sitting. He reached for his backpack and slipped one of the straps over his shoulder.

The pudgy man also stood, adjusting his coat to cover his gun and holster, and followed Alec at a discrete distance.

Chapter 4

Murder on the Platform

Michael, totally absorbed by his own writing, looked up from his keyboard, startled to realize the passing time. He sipped on some coffee he had made earlier, scanning his memory for the details he needed. He thought back to one of his interviews with Alec.

He remembered the time Alec had stood suddenly and excused himself, returning with a battered knapsack. He had carried it casually, draped over his shoulder. It had looked old and worn.

"Carried this to Spain and back," Alec had told him in his laconic way. He had peered into the pack, considering something. Finally, he had reached in, pulled out two identity cards, and handed them to Michael.

"You are the only person to see these in many, many years. This is my original Canadian Party card," pointing to a frayed and faded piece of thick card stock. It had his photograph in the upper right-hand corner. The official stamp covered his name, photo and his hand written party number: 8029.

Michael looked at the other card, almost identical except for the lettering, which looked to be written in Russian Cyrillic. Though Michael knew little of the language, one word stood out, *Komintern.*

"Yep, card-carrying member of the Communist Party."

Alec reached in the pack again, and looking at three photos; he handed one of them to Michael. It was a picture of a young woman wearing coveralls. Her hair was wrapped with a bandana and her look of intensity burned through the lens.

"I'll tell you more about that picture later," Alec said quietly.

Alec looked over his shoulder to see if anyone was looking, and once again, reached in and pulled out the pistol, handing it as discretely as possible to Michael.

"It's a Colt, Model 1911, semi-automatic pistol. That's a beautiful high-polish, oven-blue finish. Just look at the finely-checked walnut grips."

Michael held it, looking at some curious nicks on the handle and barrel. The weapon was clean—in fact, spotless. It felt like he was holding hot coals in his hand. He stammered, "Is it loaded?"

"No such thing as an unloaded gun," Alec grinned. "But, no, there are no bullets in the gun, if that's what you're asking. I removed the firing pin years ago. It won't shoot anyone *now*," he said, emphasizing the *now*.

"I've told part of the story to a few." As he said these words, it was like a storm cloud passed over his face. "But, I have never told anybody the *whole* story. Guess it's time I did so."

"Where was I? Oh, yes."

"My train finally belched to a stop at the Montreal station, the locomotive emitting a final sigh, as if it were glad this part of the journey was over. The passengers seemed in a rush for the doors. I took my time and finally started for the exit when the aisle had cleared...."

❊ ❊ ❊

When the train finally stopped, the detective watched intently as Alec stood, stretched, and starting to walk toward front of the rail car. He watched until he saw his target turn and walk down the steps and exit the train. He pulled his jacket together tightly and stood up to follow.

He stayed back at a distance, looking down again at the *Wanted* poster he was holding unfolded in his hand. He had already planned to confront Alec in the station. He tried to shake a morbid feeling, bothered by something he could not quite pin down, the recurring thought nagging at him. The man he was following looked like the man in the old photograph he held, but younger.

Still, he thought, *there's no way of knowing when the photo was taken, and it could have been the lighting*. The photograph of the man was taken at a distance, and distortion could have accounted for the slight differences in appearance and age. The age of the photograph was undetermined.

The man he was tailing appeared younger, to be sure, but he shrugged the thought away again, deciding there were too many similarities for the man in front of him to be anyone other than Ian Ferguson, the name of the man in the photograph. He looked again at the bold letters on the communiqué offering a five thousand dollar reward, refolded the paper and thrust it back in his coat pocket. He fingered the pistol he carried in a holster under his jacket, reassured it was still there.

The station attendant in Magog had wired ahead on his instructions. The detective had been specific in his request: he expected the police to be ready at the station upon the train's arrival. It was a necessary step in order to claim the reward money. The police could assist, but Giles LeBlanc needed to make the actual arrest on behalf of Pinkerton's and then turn the fugitive over to the proper authorities. The police had been instructed to wait and move in as soon as he, the detective on the case, gave the signal.

He was distracted; he started to imagine all the plans he had for spending his reward money. He wanted so desperately to believe the man on the poster was, in fact, the man he was trailing, a man who had been on the run for too many years.

He smiled, knowing the reward was substantial, and it would soon be his. If he was wrong, and he hoped he wasn't, it could all be explained as a simple misunderstanding. He thought no further about the possibility, finally able to push it away.

He watched Alec walking toward the station and scurried ahead to maintain visual contact. The last thing he wanted was to see Alec disappear among the crowd of the station. He had to be able to point his target out to the police. In his haste, he failed to notice the lack of any substantial police presence around the platform. He had ordered them to remain inside the station for fear of scaring off his target.

The little man was the last off the train and the platform was almost deserted. He pulled his jacket tighter and sensed, more than saw, two men wearing railroad uniforms. They were pushing a large luggage cart just to his right. He vented his annoyance, "You're blocking my way!"

The pair separated and one passed behind him.

"Hey there, move-"

Those were the final words of Giles LeBlanc, a Pinkerton detective.

He felt a sudden sharp pain on his left side, followed by a sudden blinding light, as though something had thumped him on the right side of his head.

The ice pick pierced his chest, swiftly and silently completing its deadly job, finding his heart with practiced accuracy. The end for Giles Leblanc was instantaneous.

With a puzzled, puckered look, the Pinkerton man slumped into unconsciousness and took his last breath. He never felt the hand reaching under his jacket and pulling out the pistol. With a slight push from the two men, his body became just another part of the baggage load.

"Dead weight," one of the assassins said with a humorless grin. They pushed the wagon into an unused storeroom, pulled the door shut, locked it, and disappeared down a ramp.

Oblivious to the drama on the platform, Alec walked through the swarming station, noting the unusually large number of police uniforms.

Strange, he thought for an instant, dismissing the notion when he heard the announcement for the train to Toronto. The train from Magog had been late arriving in Montreal, and the Toronto train was already preparing to depart. He had to hurry, pulling the tickets out of his pocket as he straightened the pack on his shoulder and hurried to board the train. He felt suddenly tired and was looking forward to a seat and some sleep.

❋ ❋ ❋

Michael looked up as Alec grew silent, waiting patiently for him to continue his story. He could see the memories in the old man's eyes, and he wanted to reach out and grab them for himself.

"I was looking ahead to some rest on the train. Of course, I wondered about the police and assumed something exciting must have happened. I was just glad it didn't have anything to do with me. How little did I know at that time..."

❋ ❋ ❋

Was it only this morning that I left home? I had walked many miles, hopped a freight train, walked even more, and then finally rode the train from Magog to Montreal. Seventy-five miles and many hours later, I was standing in line to board the train for Toronto. As I watched the line of expectant passengers inching ahead of me, I looked again at the overhead departure board. Yes, 11:05 p.m. All that mattered to me was finding a seat so I could close my eyes. "Don't worry, they won't leave until we're all onboard," someone said with authority.

As I watched our line move forward to board the train, I spotted a man in a railroad uniform walking toward me and waving.

"I know you," the man said, looking straight at me.

I started to protest when the man leaned in and said softly, "Say hello to Seth for me," and unexpectedly, he gave me that hug people often give departing friends.

He flashed a broad grin and his hand slipped something into my jacket pocket. My first thought was that he was a pickpocket. But he hadn't taken anything; to the contrary, my jacket pocket felt much heavier after he passed. I was puzzled, or perhaps astonished was more like it. *If the man hadn't mentioned Seth*, I thought, as my hand brushed briefly against something leathery and solid in my pocket.

When I finally boarded the train and found a seat, I realized it was a holster and pistol that had been placed in my pocket. I didn't know at the time that it had formerly belonged to a Pinkerton detective, the one whose body was nestled safely in a baggage room in Montreal. I thought back to my father's words of counsel, something he told me on our last night together. "You will not always know who your enemies are, but never be surprised by who your friends turn out to be," he had advised.

Taking my hand out my pocket, I started to smile, understanding now what father had meant by those words. Despite the shocking presence of a gun in my pocket, I knew deep inside that some malignant danger had been averted.

I would learn the story about the gun much later, but at the time, I was on a train slowly pulling out of the Montreal station and heading into my future. We were well on our way to Toronto by the time the detective's body was discovered. The police racing about in the Montreal station watched helplessly, as my train disappeared in the darkness, wondering what had become of that detective.

Half an hour later, someone yelled, "Sergeant Peterson, here!" A policeman in uniform ran over to the door of the storage room and shouted to the clerk in the telegraph office. "Send the following signal. Mark it very urgent. Send it to the police in Toronto and to all stops in between:

Man wanted for murder of Pinkerton detective in Montreal. Stop. May be on the Toronto train. Stop. He is armed and dangerous. Stop."

He paused in his dictation to look down at a poster in his hand.

"Name, Ian Ferguson. Stop. Sixty-one years of age. Stop. 5' 8", graying hair and blue eyes. Stop. Last seen wearing dungarees and plaid shirt. Stop. Apprehend immediately, use caution. Stop."

"Did you get that?" the officer shouted at the clerk.

The clerk was already coding the message and nodded *yes*, as he started tapping the key in Morse code, pleased to be a part of the drama.

I knew none of what was happening, of course, closing my eyes to the easy rhythm of the train, as the click-clack sound of the wheels lulled me into a deep sleep.

Chapter 5
Miniatures and Music

The telegram was addressed to Chief Investigator, Samuel T. Harrison, Special Branch. As he sat in his office, Harrison couldn't think about anything but the telegram and phone calls that had taken place earlier. Waves of anger surged over him. He needed something to deflect this rage. He needed to focus all his self-control.

He sat in a darkened room, just a single lamp shining on a worktable. Mozart filled the stillness of the room with a pleasant melancholy, *Number 421*, a string quartet written and dedicated to Haydn. The man hunched over the worktable, considered it his favorite. He nodded to the music, occasionally reaching up to adjust the work lamp.

His large left hand held a miniature he was carving, his right hand expertly and patiently scraping away the smallest slivers of wood. The hefty man was wearing special magnifying lenses over his reading glasses, peering intently at his work, satisfied with the result. He placed the miniature on the worktable and pushed his glasses up over his forehead, rubbing his eyes. He was carving a miniature of Winston Churchill wearing a bowler hat. Harrison would stop occasionally to compare his carving to a newspaper photo he had fixed to the wall.

Samuel T. Harrison was a large man. At 6'8 and weighing 310 pounds, if there had been such a thing as a professional football team back then, Harrison would have been recruited as a lineman. He was an unpleasant man at best, *exceptionally* unpleasant being his main feature. Not exactly a bully, he leaned more toward cruelty. His strength, if it could be called that, was his single-mindedness. His downfall was anger and impatience, except when it came to his carving.

People who thought they knew him considered him coarse and restless, and he tended to make people uncomfortable. Oddly, he was smart and cultured in his own way; he was drawn to classical music, especially the string quartet, and was an exceptional and creative woodcarver. His favorite musical pieces were those of Haydn and Mozart, especially those in the classical quartet form. He was an avid collector of recordings, his personal collection numbering over seventy-five. He knew every hiss, crackle and pop on those records; records he would carefully clean with a soft cloth before returning them to their envelopes.

For such a large man, he was talented with his hands. Few knew his secret talent for carving miniatures, which were mainly military, but also consisted of political and historical figures. His way of relaxing was to fix his magnifying lenses to his glasses and carve with painstaking care, all while listening to his music.

That is what he was doing this night; he needed desperately to relax after the day's news and that awful telegram:

2136 hours/stop/February 7/stop/Montreal/stop/Canada/
stop

To: Chief Detective Harrison.
Please be advised that Detective Second Class, Giles LeBlanc was this day murdered in the line of duty. His last known communication indicated he was following a Most Wanted, Ian Ferguson. According to protocol established for this fugitive, you are hereby notified as the lead detective in the case.

"Damn, damn and damn!" Harrison's huge fist slammed down on the desk when he had finished reading. Papers had scattered in all directions and his assistants wished they could do the same. They were terrified by the glower on his face.

He had been handed the telegram just as he had thought about going home to dinner.

"Get Montreal on the phone, now!" he shouted as he hammered the desk again. "I want to talk to those assholes, now." An aide scurried out the door, glad to have an excuse to leave.

Harrison sat and reread the telegram and focused on the name. Finding and arresting Ian Ferguson had been his final exam assignment when he was training to be a detective with the Agency. He had failed to capture Ferguson, and it still ate at him all these years later. Ian Ferguson had become a name that represented failure to Harrison, and failure was a hard dose of unpleasant medicine for the large man to swallow.

He had come to think of Ferguson as a ghost, a spirit that would appear in the corner of one's vision, only to vanish while blinking. Ian Ferguson was a name that would appear and disappear over the next thirty years of Harrison's career, rising during his training and continuing until the end, a name floating like a phantom through Harrison's career.

He had called Montreal and pieced the details together. Some second-rate stringer of a detective had spotted Ferguson and followed him on a train to Montreal.

Montreal, wondered Harrison, *What the hell is he doing in Montreal?*

He listened to the details, how the detective wanted to set up some elaborate trap to capture Ian Ferguson and collect the reward. Instead of simply arresting Ferguson on the train, he organized a large squad of uniformed police to capture the man as he walked into a crowded train station.

It hadn't worked, obviously.

Imbecile, he thought, *Far too complicated for a man of Ferguson's abilities, and the detective's obvious lack thereof.*

"I need to get to Montreal and fast!" he yelled out to his staff, and another aide was glad for an excuse to leave, hurrying out the door to make the necessary arrangements. Harrison did a lot of yelling, but it didn't mean his staff would ever get used to it.

Harrison tried to calm his voice, but it rose to a shout despite his efforts, "When I get there," he said into the phone, "I want answers!"

This time, Ferguson, I am going to find you, he vowed silently.

Chapter 6
Coote's Bay

I awoke as the train slowed, approaching Port Hope. It was the final stop before arriving at the Toronto station. The latest conductor walked through our car announcing, "Ten minutes to the station, have your tickets ready," and exited through the rear of the car.

I reached in my pocket, feeling the leather of the holster again. Looking around at the mostly empty car, I carefully pulled it out of my pocket, keeping it from prying eyes. I had just put it away when the conductor returned.

"Tickets," the conductor said as he passed by, punching a hole in my ticket. It was becoming a familiar routine. The conductor pushed through the door and stepped into the car ahead.

Once he was gone, I again retrieved the pistol and opened the holster flap. There was a note tucked alongside the gun. I hadn't noticed it before.

For Spain, the note read. There was also an old pair of glasses tucked in with the gun. *Wear these and do what you can to change your appearance. Ditch the gun if you think you are going to get caught.* It was unsigned.

I still had no idea of the gun's history, as I tried to measure the meaning of gun and the note. I heeded the note's advice, however, opening my pack and taking out a pale blue work shirt. I slipped the gun deep inside the pack, well out of sight.

Getting up from my seat, I balanced against the sway of the car, walked to the end of the car and pushed open the door of the lavatory. Squeezed in behind the locked door, I changed shirts, shoving the old one down into my pack, not caring that it would wrinkle. On impulse, I reached back in and pulled out my ditty bag. I opened it: shaving soap, razor, toothbrush. Looking at the contents, I eyed the small box with shoe polish and brush. I wasn't sure it would work, but I had heard about someone using shoe polish to change hair coloring; it had been on a radio show story, I think. I brushed the shoe polish on my hair. Looking in the mirror, I knew it wouldn't hold up to close scrutiny, but it was better than anything else I could think of at the time.

Stepping off the train in Toronto, I was shocked once again at the number of police uniforms in sight, even more than I had seen in Montreal. They were intently watching all the passengers but didn't seem to notice me, having transformed into a slightly stooped man with dark hair and glasses, the limping gait coming to me in a flash of inspiration.

I saw them looking at photographs they were holding, trying to match them to passengers streaming off the train. Even in those hard times, there were a lot of people on this train from Montreal.

There was one man, I remember, who drew their attention. They were quite rude with him and pushed him hard against a wall. I recall walking by and looking back as they released him. They finally seemed convinced he wasn't the man they were looking for. I knew without knowing that it was me they were looking for, and I wondered if all this activity had something to do with the pistol in my pack.

Once the passengers had cleared the train, the police seemed to realize something had gone wrong. A man, obviously in command by the air of authority he possessed, issued stern orders, and officers swarmed the empty train.

As I left the scene behind, I looked up and had to admire the marble arches and high ceilings of the station. It rivaled

Montreal, but I had been in such a rush to catch the train to Toronto that I didn't have time to even consider that station's example of architecture.

Ah, I remember thinking, *neither really compares to the view of Grand Central Station in New York.*

I looked at the departures board. My train to Hamilton wouldn't leave for another hour and a half. I had plenty of time and walked around the station, my footsteps echoing on the marble floor. After a few moments, I found a coffee shop and stepped inside.

I had to be careful with my money, but I used some of the money my father had given me to treat myself to a nice meal, enjoying the quiet of the moments before my train to Hamilton was ready to depart. The food I had packed at home for my journey had long been used up.

I finished my meal, enjoying the bitter taste of the black coffee, grinning at the waitress for some unknown reason. I knew this was hard work for her and made sure I left her a generous tip. I remember it was four bits that I left her, quite a tip in those days. She waved when I left, and I remember feeling very much alone suddenly.

I absently rubbed my hand through my hair and looked down at my hand. The black of the shoe polish was starting to gel in the heat of the station. I rubbed my hand on my pant leg, cursing, and hurried to the train, hoping my thin disguise would hold up to examination for just a while longer.

Ahead, I saw two police officers in uniform. They were looking at a picture and watching each passenger walking toward the boarding platforms. I was sure that one was paying particular attention to me, but he turned away as I approached. I stole a glance back over my shoulder and the two officers were laughing at some joke. My hands were sweaty and my lip trembled as I passed by.

Once on the train, I craved sleep again. I couldn't recall ever being so tired. I thought better of giving in to sleep and urged myself to stay awake, as the train finally pulled out of the Toronto station. Too soon, it lurched to a stop at the Port Credit station, exposing me to another possible round of police scrutiny.

I looked out my window at a small group of passengers waiting to board the train, while some people in my car were standing and walking to the exit. The conductor was standing just outside my window yelling, "All aboard," and the engine grunted. I could hear the wheels spinning as they attempted to gain traction. I realized I was holding my breath and let it out as we began moving. I looked at the schedule in my hand. There were two more scheduled stops between Port Credit and Hamilton. One was Oakville and the other was Burlington.

Unfamiliar landscape flashed past the window and I caught glimpses of scenes alternating between factories and empty spaces. It was unimpressive to me, just ugly and functional. Rain began to splatter against the window and created grimy streaks that did nothing to improve my mood.

Something had been bothering me. It was the note. I withdrew it from my pocket, looking at it again, turning it to the other side. That was when I realized there was more on the back. I hadn't noticed the reverse side before and saw the instructions just in time.

The train will slow down as it crosses the bridge over Coote's Bay. Jump off on the other side of the bridge. Someone will meet you.

There was just one problem—*where the hell is Coote's Bay?* I wondered.

I looked up at the latest conductor walking back through the car, joking with two of the passengers he apparently knew. They must have been regulars.

As he passed my seat, I took a chance. "This train goes to Hamilton, right?"

"I sure hope so," the conductor laughed.

"A friend of mine mentioned Coote's Bay," I said. "I'm not from around here. Where is Coote's Bay? There isn't a stop listed on the schedule," I was talking too much but couldn't stop myself. "He said it's quite pretty and I shouldn't miss it."

"There's no stop at Coote's Bay. We pass right by it. You will see Hamilton Harbor off to the left and Coote's Bay to the right. It's a pretty place. I used to take my lady friends up there," he smiled at the thought. "Ah, but I'm a married man now," he finished, shaking his head.

"How will I know when we get there?" I asked.

The conductor thought for a moment. "We make our last stop at Burlington. Then, we pass through a station at Aldershot. We don't usually stop there, we only slow down. Only a few minutes more, just three miles past, is the bridge over Coote's Bay. We go pretty slowly over the bridge; you can't miss it."

"Just curious," I said, "Thanks."

The conductor nodded, "Looking for work in Hamilton, eh? Hell, who isn't looking for work these days, I guess."

I nodded my head. "Yeah, who isn't? I've got a lead on a job in Grimsby." I don't know why I said that. *Keep your mouth shut,* my father had said, *Don't offer too much information.*

I felt the train slowing and watched the sign as we passed Aldershot station. Like the conductor said, the train only slowed as we pulled alongside the station platform and then started to regain momentum as it passed out of sight. The conductor looked in my direction and touched the bill of his cap, smiled, and moved on toward the rear car.

Following instructions from the note, I waited until the train started moving again before I looked around and stood. "Need a stretch," I said to the two men behind me. They didn't even pause in their conversation as I picked up my pack and walked to the rear of the car, hoping no one was paying any mind.

Glancing back, I eased to my left at the rear of the car and lowered myself down three steps to the door. The door window was partially down and I leaned out and felt the air on my cheeks, fresh and surprisingly warm. I realized we were going very slowly now, and the train was practically inching its way over the bridge. The inlet to Coote's Bay yawned far below in the semi-darkness.

I felt the car shudder as we finally crossed the last of the bridge, and before the train could gather speed again, I pushed down on the door handle. Feeling resistance, I pushed harder until the door finally gave way and I fell out the door more than jumped, clinging tightly to the handle. Even though I had hopped on and off a lot of trains, I wasn't prepared for this jump.

I tried to judge the speed to start running, as my left foot hit the cinders. Instead, my foot twisted under and I felt excruciating pain jolt up my leg as I let go and stumbled to a halt. It felt like I had stepped on a live electrical wire. I had felt worse pain before, however, and simply gritted my teeth, willing the pain away as I heard a voice calling out from the night.

"Alec? Alec Ferguson?"

I stopped, frozen, my mind racing with panic.

"C'mon lad, this way," someone said.

A big man with a wide grin stepped out of the darkness. He looked ready for a good scrap, just like the picture I was carrying, the one my father had given me.

"They're looking for you everywhere," the man with the grin said. "We have to get you to ground, now."

"What's...what's going on," I stammered, confused and scared by what was happening to me. I was hungry, frightened and my ankle hurt like hell. I began to wonder what was wrong and why I was even here.

"You have the gun?"

I nodded, deciding to put my faith in this man my father had recommended.

"There's a dead Pinkerton's agent in Montreal. Somehow, they think that used to be his gun," Seth laughed. "I can't imagine where they got that idea." Seth rolled his eyes and hurried over to a waiting truck.

He laughed suddenly, roaring with delight. "We're on our way to Spain, you and I. Then you'll be using that gun to kill some fascist bastards before we are through." He slapped me on the back and I got into the truck, too hurt and tired to care about anything beyond the fact I didn't have to walk anymore.

Chapter 7
Samuel T. Harrison: the Beginning

Unless you happened to be one of only two men with the privilege, you never called him Sam, Sammy, Samuel, Harrison or Mr. Harrison. You never called him detective, Sergeant or anything other than Samuel T. Harrison. That was what his mother had carefully written in the family Bible, and that had settled it for him. He was curious once what the "T" stood for, but she was gone from his life before he could ever ask. Curiosity was not a strong suit for Samuel T. Harrison, and he was satisfied to leave it at just "T".

He always carried the Bible with his name recorded next to his date of birth: August 4, 1880. It was his habit to open the book each night, letting the pages open at random. He would read it for precisely fifteen minutes. His religious grounding was equally random. His theology, if it could be called such, was recorded in his true gospel–the Field Manual of the Pinkerton National Detective Agency. He would run his hand lovingly over the cover page and the agency motto: *"WE NEVER SLEEP."*

Samuel T. Harrison had grown up in rural Kentucky, watching his father carefully. His father was a mean cuss of a man. If he ever admitted it to anyone, let alone himself, he was terrified of the man. His father was the major influence shaping the future Harrison's character and personality. When his father would return home after his many absences, he sat on the porch of the modest family home, a cabin really, drinking.

While his father was away, his mother provided another important early influence—a time when the cabin would be filled with music, recordings played on a hand-cranked roller drum. She kept it hidden when her husband was home, pulling it out from behind the laundry tub when he left again.

The player was an awkward affair that was more a revolving cylinder than a drum, per se. The sound was primitive, but the music it provided touched a primal nerve in him. While he may not have appreciated its mathematical precision and the perfect matching of instruments, he did recognize there was beauty in what he was hearing.

Arias, string quartets, and other classical music filled the mountainside air, reaching a remote part of young Harrison's senses. He honored her request to keep it a secret from his father. He often wondered at the faraway look in her eyes when the music was playing, a look of being transported to a better place. But, the beauty they shared would be hidden away each time his father returned. Harrison eventually found a special part of the barn where the gramophone could safely escape his father's notice.

At home, his father would spend most of his time in a rocking chair, smoking a cheap cigar and sipping bourbon. His gravelly voice would call out his son's name, often cuffing the boy on the side of head when he answered. He would yell at him to fetch the bottle when it was time for a refill.

Filled with enough bourbon, he would quietly get up, go into the house, and start beating the mother of Samuel T. Harrison—his father's notion of foreplay, he would come to understand later. When he was finished with the beatings in the kitchen, he would drag her into the adjoining bedroom. Harrison would sneak into the house and stand quietly at the wall between the bedroom and kitchen. He would listen to the animal sounds of his father's rutting grunts.

When his father finished, he would walk out from the bedroom, pulling the top of his pants together. Harrison looked past him more than once, his mother behind on the bed, curled into a ball and whimpering. One time, Harrison had seen her clamping a towel between her teeth to keep from screaming.

Samuel T. may have had some form of love for his mother, but it was his father he truly idolized. Watching the beatings, he convinced himself that she must have done something to deserve those pummeling fists. It was a lesson Samuel T. learned well, much to the regret of many women he would encounter later in life.

Harrison's father was a strikebreaker in the employ of the Pinkerton National Detective Agency, one of many rough and ready men the agency recruited—men with a penchant for violence and intimidation.

"We just call it 'Pinkerton's' for short," his father said. His father hated strikers, lawbreakers and anarchists. He was convinced they were out to destroy the American way of life and had to be stopped at all costs, up to and including threats, beatings and other mayhem.

His father had been very busy, indeed, hating strikers on July 6, 1892.

Samuel T. was 12-years-old when his father returned to tell of a special adventure. Sitting on the porch step, he listened closely to his father talk about the violence and mayhem he had witnessed that day. The boy was surprised at his own growing erection as he listened. He never connected the stories of violence to a secretly growing sexual awakening. Incurious about it, he simply sat in awe as his father seethed.

His father didn't bother sipping his bourbon that night, as he slurred the story, gulping down large swallows of the liquid in the telling.

"There were over three hundred of us called in. We came from all over, mostly New York and Chicago," he said between swallows, "It was something, I tell you, meeting all those other Pinkerton men. We taught those strikers a serious lesson."

His eyes were glowing, "They were holed-up in old Henry Clay Frick's mill, just like it was their own. They locked themselves in and erected barricades. We heard you could see some of them pacing back and forth with guns at the ready."

"It was up Pittsburgh way, Carnegie Steel, it was called. Old man Frick himself spoke to us, his sleeves rolled up, and he told us to crack some heads. Damned if he wasn't impressive. He sure looked tough. And then, someone started handing out batons, iron bars and baseball bats. We just looked at each other and grinned. We knew it was going to be great fun."

His father glanced down at his empty glass with a puzzled look and suggested with a nod and a belch that he needed some more. The boy was caught up in the excitement and raced to the kitchen and back, carrying the bottle with him, careful to hide his erection.

His father slopped the drink out of the glass as he lifted it to his mouth. "Someone started to whisper that some of the Chicago Haymarket rioters were there. We wanted those fellows, let me tell you. They had killed one of our Pinkerton men in that riot. It was six years back, but we never forgot."

While his father talked, they both looked up in surprise as a covey of quail exploded between the rows of corn in the small garden.

His father belched and continued.

"Now, this is important." His words were slurred, but his intensity was plain. "Someone passed out posters with pictures. This guy, Ian Ferguson, was the ringleader in the Homestead mill. I first heard about him being one of the ringleaders at the Haymarket Riot." He stared at the boy. "You remember that name, boy."

"Did you get him, pa?" the boy asked.

"Fuck no. Wish we did. But I want you to remember that name, son." The boy nodded a silent vow to his father.

"Other men were in on it, too. They were all on our Most Wanted list from the Haymarket day. There was a huge reward if we got 'em. But, Ian Ferguson was the one we wanted most of all."

His father lifted up the front of his undershirt and scratched his belly. "Those steel guys like Frick are pretty slick, boy. They said one thing to us and something else to the reporters. Carnegie and Frick stood in front of the newspaper reporters and said that no steel plant was worth spilled blood. Their people told us just the opposite—in private, of course."

The boy stared at his father and waited.

"We all gathered together alongside some dam on the Ohio River. I don't know where for sure, but it was somewhere up near Pittsburgh. Some of Frick's men handed us rifles and we all stumbled our way onto barges. It was dark as hell. We could feel the barges thump as the towing cable stretched tight and they towed us upriver."

"Part way up the river, we heard whistles blowing. You know—the kind of whistles that plants use. It was early in the morning and so dark we couldn't see our hands in front of our faces."

"Then we started to hear shots. We looked over the side and could see gun flashes, and that damned plant whistle was screaming like a bitch in heat. I have to tell you, I was getting more than a bit nervous at the sounds of those gunshots, but I was feeling possessed."

Samuel T. Harrison sat enthralled, his sexual excitement growing to a peak as his father went on.

"Finally, when it was starting to get light, we could make out crowds of people on the bank of the river. Women and kids were all running along the bank, keeping pace with us and yelling and pointing at us."

Samuel T. Harrison watched as his father belched again and walked to the edge of the porch. His father unzipped his pants and let fly a stream of piss onto the graveled walk below. He walked back to the rocker, scratching his buttocks, and sat back down with a thud.

"Where was I? Oh yeah, then all hell broke loose. We could see the crowd, the plant workers on the bank, tearing down the wire fence, and they were all shoving their way into the plant yard. We were trying to get off the barges fast as we could and stop them. Frick wanted us to take over the plant. That was when I heard a shot close by. The fucking papers later said us Pinkerton guys shot first, but I knew it was them—those fucking strikers."

"We fought back and forth for what seemed like an hour. Man standing next to me said it only lasted maybe ten minutes. Our captain, Fred Heinde, was wounded—shot in the leg. We heard one of their guys was wounded, too."

"Then it was time to let them really have it. I remember someone yelled to open fire and we all just started firing our rifles, not aiming at anyone in particular, just firing into their crowd. We heard later that we had killed two of the bastards and wounded a lot more. I tell you son, it was exciting." He shook his head, grinning like he wished he were still there.

"Then it turned bad for us. We kept fighting, but it was hopeless. We were out-manned and out-gunned. There must have been a thousand of 'em before it was over, and only three hundred of us. They even had themselves some cannon, if you can believe that."

Harrison was fully aroused, his erection becoming painful as his father went on.

"We did our best. Finally, the next day we raised a white flag and tried to surrender. We heard them calling us murderers and worse. While we were trying to leave, they started throwing stuff at us and spitting at us, especially the women. They marched us to a place they said would serve as a jail. That didn't stop the crowd from trying to beat us. They marched us to a train and said we were being taken to Pittsburgh and charged with murder."

Harrison's mother opened the door and walked down the steps. She looked disgusted at the pool of piss on the walk as she went to the pile of firewood. She carried some wood for the cook stove and made no attempt to hide the hideous bruising on the side of her face. The boy saw a vast blankness in her eyes. As she passed through the door, it snapped shut behind her.

He turned back to his father, still in awe.

"Luckily," his father went on, "feelings were different back in the city, and they just released us. We all looked at each other knowing that Carnegie or Frick had pulled the right strings for us. I'm telling you; after I was released I didn't waste any more time in that part of the world."

Samuel T. Harrison sat in rapt attention, and he couldn't control his breathing. The excitement of the story was palpable to him. He closed his eyes and imagined his hand on the family Bible and silently pledged an oath to become a Pinkerton man, just like his father.

With the thought of swearing that oath, his sexual excitement was finally released, and he felt the spasms of ejaculation, the warm and sticky feeling wetting his underwear. He looked up guiltily. His father was barely conscious. He was finished with his story and paid no attention to the boy at his feet.

Later that night, he was lost in a fantasy about being a Pinkerton man just like his father. Harrison barely noticed the sounds from the next room as his father slapped and punched his mother. Young Samuel T. Harrison covered his head with a pillow and closed his ears to her pleas and cries, as his father roughly mounted her and plunged into her—once, twice, three times—until he rolled on his back, finished with his pleasure.

✳ ✳ ✳

On his birthday in 1897, Harrison turned seventeen. With a letter of introduction from his father, he boarded a train for Chicago. He marched with a straight back into the office of the Pinkerton National Detective Agency, stopping briefly to admire the sign that said, *We Never Sleep.*

He demonstrated his lack of subtlety by loudly declaring to anyone within hearing, "I'm here to break some union heads."

A man standing to the side of the room looked up lazily from some documents he was scanning but immediately recognized a special talent in this young man standing before him. The agent wasn't particularly tall and was slightly balding. He would pass most people unnoticed, and that quality was a gift to a man who spent his life as an undercover detective. He handed the stack of papers back to a woman standing next to him, walked up to Harrison and took him by the arm. With that simple gesture, the man became a life-long mentor to Samuel T. Harrison. *This is just the boy I have been looking for,* he thought. *Yes indeed, and with some training and my guidance, we will smooth out the rough edges.*

He directed Harrison to the desk and instructed the woman there to help him fill out the application form. While she helped him, she stole glances at him, looking up in awe at the huge young man looming over her. When they finished with the application, she called the balding man over. He came out of his office and looked over the forms, nodding his approval.

"I am sending you immediately to our training camp," handing Samuel T. Harrison a ticket and directions.

"Tell them to send you back here as soon as your training is over. You and I have some very special work to do."

Chapter 8
Samuel T. Harrison: Training Days

Harrison truly enjoyed the discipline of his training days. His only inner doubt was whether he would measure up and pass. He wanted his detective shield.

One day, towards the end of his training, an instructor admitted quietly to the others that he was afraid of the new recruit, Harrison. The other instructors, sitting around the table on a break, nodded their agreement.

"All I needed to know," one said, "was that he was the special candidate of James McParland, director of the Chicago office." The others shifted uncomfortably. There wasn't a single Pinkerton man who didn't know the reputation of McParland. He was a man to be respected and feared. If this was McParland's man, well, that would be the end of any questions.

"Son of a bitch did *this* to me," one man said, pointing to the bruises on the left side of his head, "and it was only in practice."

The others nodded sympathetically. They had to admit, if Harrison could do that to this instructor—one of the best judo men in the agency—he must be some kind of mean.

"He's not dumb, that's for sure," said one instructor, so quietly the others had to lean in to hear. He was the instructor responsible for training recruits in the art of being a Pinkerton detective. "He's never going to blend in, though," the man laughed. "Imagine being 6'8", weighing what—close to three hundred pounds?"

"Size fifteen shoes," another instructor added.

"Yeah, imagine him trying to blend into a crowd," and they all started to laugh.

Another man walked into the room, overhearing the conversation added, "He can blend in when he wants to and he sure as hell is going to impress those bastards on strike, though."

They all roared their approval and went back to newspapers and coffee, a couple of the men quietly slipping cognac into their cups to brighten the day.

What these men really didn't appreciate was the unwavering determination of Samuel T. Harrison. They would have been astounded at how easily the man *could* melt into the background when he wanted to, and what a dominating presence he could be when he chose to be seen.

Harrison had paid special attention as he listened carefully during the class on stalking your prey. He would often surprise one or another of the trainers during practice by stepping silently out of dark shadows, quietly saying, "Could we have a word, sir?"

"How the hell does he do that?" one of them asked.

"As big as he is," someone agreed.

"And when he takes you by the arm..."

"Have you ever seen him on the firing range? I saw him put four shots out of six into the bull's eye. The other two were only out by half an inch." The others nodded that they had heard the same.

"It doesn't make any difference whether it's a hand gun or rifle."

"I told him to beat up another man in my class one day," another trainer said in a whisper, the rest angling in to hear the story. "It was only supposed to be practice, not real. They kept it quiet in the front office, but the poor man he beat on ended up in the hospital. They had to send him home in casts, that's *casts*—plural—his career with Pinkerton's over."

They all agreed that they did not want to be on the wrong side of Samuel T. Harrison.

✳ ✳ ✳

For his final training test, Harrison was sent to New York City. They gave him some information about a real man on Pinkerton's Most Wanted list. His name was Ian Ferguson and he was supposedly living in a small rooming house in the city while working on the docks.

It was a name burned into Harrison's memory from the story his father had told him that night long ago, and he was eager to close the books on the case; to do that for himself, and for his father.

But, that wasn't the only appeal when the assignment was handed to him. All Harrison needed to be told was that Ferguson was a man who organized strikers and was probably an anarchist or socialist, or worse. That information was like the scent on the ground to a bloodhound. The connection to his father's story only sweetened the deal for him.

"This is money for the assignment," the instructor said, handing him some bills. That instructor later told his colleagues that the assignment to send Harrison after Ian Ferguson had come directly from McParland himself.

"Imagine my surprise when the man personally walked into my office to tell me," he said, "I just about shit myself."

After he received his assignment, Harrison left the classroom with a wallet containing two hundred dollars, a fortune in 1897. He checked his personal weapon, a small pistol, and put it back in his pocket. It was a colt caliber .38 called the *Frontier Sheriff Special*. When he had chosen it, he had admired the barrel and the inscription, "PT. F.A. MFG. Co. HARTFORD CT. U.S.A." Turning it over, he saw the date—1880—etched on the other side.

That's me, Harrison thought, *the new frontier, the new sheriff in town. And a five hundred dollar reward,* he turned that over in his mind more than once. That was the reward for catching this man, Ferguson. Harrison wasn't that interested in money. What he needed to know was that his reputation as a Pinkerton man would be complete when the arrest was made. He was determined to make that happen.

He noted the comment on the communiqué he was given: *Dead or alive.* He grinned. It really didn't matter to Harrison which way it turned out. He patted his colt and felt content.

While Harrison was large by any measure, there wasn't an ounce of fat on his body. People would gasp audibly at his girth. His chest measured 50 inches, maybe more. His arms were as large as some men's legs. He wasn't particularly good looking, but he often caught women looking at him in a certain way that had nothing to do with fear.

He touched his hat; he always wore a bowler hat, as was the custom of the day. Until his end, Harrison would always say he admired Winston Churchill, especially for Mr. Churchill's choice in headwear—a bowler, of course. But, that was still a story yet to be told, as he stepped off the train that afternoon in 1897.

Harrison walked up the marble stairs from Grand Central Station and immediately decided he hated the crowds. He stepped out onto the street.

Harrison was impatient and he was counting on finding Ian Ferguson. He began the search immediately. He called on the New York City office of Pinkerton's as instructed and presented his credentials.

The receptionist gasped when he walked into the offices and whispered to a friend. "He is so big," she said with a knowing wink.

As Harrison was leaving, she called out, "Do you have a place to stay?"

He looked down at a paper he held in his hand, "The Roosevelt," he replied.

"What about dinner?"

"What about it." he said.

"Well," she smiled, "we both have to eat, and why not together?" Her voice was surprisingly throaty.

Harrison stopped and appeared to be considering something. He had never been comfortable around women. They seemed so weak to him, and something else—undeserving, perhaps?

He was no stranger to sexual arousal. His usual response was to causally relieve his sexual stress by quietly masturbating, a habit he'd had ever since his father's story that day on the cabin porch. It wasn't something he particularly enjoyed; he more *endured* the exercise in order to relieve the mounting tension in his groin.

Now, standing before him, he viewed this woman in a strange way and felt a stirring. It was a first for him.

"What do you say big man? My name is Louise."

Louise would later think back to those words and the memory would not be pleasant.

They agreed, dinner at seven at the restaurant in his hotel.

It's alright, he thought, *I haven't spent any of my allowance yet.*

By the following morning, Harrison would no longer be the innocent when it came to women. Louise was to become the first of many unfortunate women who would regret sharing a bed with Harrison. He had learned well from his father, and Louise remembered screaming in pain more than once while he slapped her and sipped from his bottle of bourbon. It was a memory she worked hard to repress, without much success.

Louise was not without experience with men, but when Harrison entered her, it was with a crude roughness she could never forget—her genital area was torn and would forever have a scar as a reminder of her night with Harrison. She left the hotel during the dead of night, terrified and humiliated. It was difficult to walk, and she turned her head away from the curious desk clerk so he wouldn't see the cuts and her already blackening eyes.

She sent a note to work the following day: *I'm sick. I think it's the flu.*

She sent the same note for five days in a row.

Finally, she sent in her resignation. The bruising grew darker and uglier by the day. She borrowed money from her father, promising its return as soon as she could.

"What happened-" her father started to say, then thought better of it. He recognized the signs and was a kindly man who loved his daughter and could not bear to see her humiliation.

That night, she took a train back to Buffalo and knew she would never, *ever*, return to New York City again. She would never work for Pinkerton's again. And, she would absolutely never see Samuel T. Harrison again.

While Louise was dealing with her demons, Harrison realized it wouldn't be as easy to catch Ferguson as he thought. His brief encounter with Louise had not given him any real pleasure. He wondered why men bothered with sex. He had looked at her with disgust afterwards and thought she deserved what he had given her. He wasn't sure which was best—the beating or the sexual release. In any case, he had simply rolled over after it was over, and within an instant, he had fallen asleep. He didn't know when Louise had left and really didn't care.

His mood turned even uglier when he realized later the next day that Ian Ferguson had skipped town. Harrison, his gut instincts working overtime, suspected something was wrong and started to imagine that someone inside Pinkerton's had tipped Ferguson off. He would have been astounded to know how right he was and that it was McParland himself who had leaked the information to Ian Ferguson through a double agent.

All Harrison knew was that Ferguson was gone, and he sensed his failure to pass the test.

"He heard there was a giant after him," an informant told Harrison. The information wasn't volunteered; he coughed it up while being threatened with a beating. He had 'volunteered' that information while Harrison held the man's neck in his hand, squeezing ever so slightly.

Harrison still had most of his allowance when he boarded the train back to training camp. He sat upright in the passenger section rereading a telegram. An assistant from the agency had handed him the telegram as he was boarding the train. Now, Harrison reread it again.

We regret to inform you that your father died in his sleep last night. Your mother is being held in the Harland County jail.

Samuel T. Harrison set his eyes on the future. *Let her rot in hell*, he thought. All he needed from his mother was the family Bible, which he always carried with him. Closing off the memory, he reached into his pocket and pulled out a small piece of wood. From the other pocket, he took out a carving blade and began carefully carving a new miniature.

Chapter 9
SAMUEL T. HARRISON: A Pinkerton Man at Last

Harrison often thought back to that aborted training assignment. Convinced he would be kicked out of Pinkerton's because of his failure to capture Ian Ferguson, he breathed a sigh of relief when they gave him a badge instead, and told him to keep the gun and the advance money.

His expansive chest filled with pride at the ceremony when they handed him the badge and identification card. He was one of them now. He knew his father would have been proud. He was a head-splitter, now, just like his old man.

Unfortunately, his father was in a coffin. The undertaker had written that they couldn't get the knife out of his ribs without doing enormous damage to his body, so he was buried with the blade broken off from the handle, still embedded in his chest. It was lodged solidly in place. *How that little woman could have enough strength to do that, we are not sure*, the mortician had written. The undertaker didn't add that his father's penis and testicles were nowhere to be found on the day they had carried the body back to the funeral parlor.

Harrison put the memory of his father in a hidden compartment in his mind as he continued to review the files about Ferguson. The exercise may have concluded as far as Pinkerton's was concerned, but it didn't end for Harrison. It was a practice he would continue over the next several years. *If I ever catch him*, he told himself repeatedly over the course of his career.

No. Harrison's career with Pinkerton's definitely did not end with that fateful trip to New York City. To the contrary, his career was like a flower in bloom, bursting with color. His mentor, Jim McParland, welcomed him back to the Chicago office. He had called Harrison into his private office, an invitation he seldom extended to anyone other than superiors or very select colleagues.

McParland preferred to mingle with the ranks of his squad in the communal office. He used his own office as a sanctuary, a place for scheming and contemplation. His office was used to tease out those leaps of logic that helped him find a solution to the myriad of puzzles that many of his difficult cases presented.

What few people knew was that McParland's squad was an elite team, hand-picked by him and assigned only the most difficult of cases. It was also a secret unit, skilled in covert operations. When the squad was spoken of—rarely above a whisper—it was with a combination of awe, fear and respect. The very existence of the squad went unnoticed outside the walls of Pinkerton's senior management. Men who were unfortunate to be caught in their web would be handed over to the local police, with no need for McParland or his covert squad to be in the spotlight.

"Ah, I heard you did extremely well," McParland said to Harrison, once the door to his office was closed.

Harrison was not a man of words, but he knew that his mentor was not to be ignored, and excuses were futile.

"I failed," he replied simply.

McParland tilted his chair back and belched an uncustomary laugh, more like the throaty roar of a lion. "Do you know how long we have looked for that man Ferguson? Do you realize how many good detectives have met that same fate? No, you didn't fail. You got closer than anyone else. You were at least in the same city with the man."

"Let me tell you what. Someday, when we get a lead, and we *will* get a lead, do you want to be the one to try again?"

Harrison's smiling face flashed his answer.

"Until then, we have some serious work to do, you and I," McParland said. "Go make sure the door is closed."

Harrison got up, checked the door, and returned to his chair.

"I need a special man with a special talent, and I want you to be that man. Together, we can shape a formidable team. We can use my brains and experience. But, there are places I can't go, and many of them are very dark places. These are dangerous places, as well. You may be asked to do things that others would find impossible to do. There is a need for a man who can do things that can't be traced back to me. There are certain ways of talking to people..." he trailed off, looking at Harrison pointedly. Samuel T. nodded his head.

"I hear you have a way about you. We can take advantage of your...methods. Some detectives are able to cause panic and fear. You, my friend, go beyond panic and fear. You can affect abject terror; one look from you, I hear, is enough to instill absolute dread."

He paused, looking at Harrison closely. "Do you know what I'm getting at?"

Harrison considered that question for a moment. He was smarter than most people gave him credit for, but he knew he was treading in very deep water with this conversation. "I think so," he finally said.

"There's more," McParland said, nodding in satisfaction, "When you get to those dark places, you are going to meet some evil men. They are evil in ways even you have never experienced. Are you prepared," he paused, "to take extreme measures?"

"Like what?" he asked, but Harrison had already guessed.

"If I don't tell you, then we can both deny we ever had this conversation," McParland said after a long pause.

Harrison carefully adjusted his tie and checked the cuffs on his shirtsleeve. For such a big man, he was very particular about his clothing. "What conversation," he said, looking over McParland's head and watched him smile. It wasn't a question.

There were two men in Harrison's life he would take orders from without question, without flinching. One was his father, now dead. The other was Jim McParland, and for the next eight years, he followed McParland without a second thought.

His assignments were never written down. The two men would meet at a pub on the north side of Chicago, The Tap Root Pub. It was a popular gathering place located in a building dating back to 1862. Not even the great Chicago fire had been enough to close its doors. The two men would sit in a booth in the rear, drinking mugs of beer and chewing on the pickled eggs from a dish on the table.

One night, McParland told him, "I know how you feel about unions. Just like your father, eh?" He kept his voice barely above a whisper, and Harrison had to lean forward to hear him in the noisy bar.

"I fucking hate 'em," Harrison snorted his disgust.

"Well, you need to change that. Get to love them," his teacher said with a sly grin. "Learn and earn your way in. Can you learn to pass for a working stiff?"

Harrison waited until McParland left The Tap Root that day. He wolfed down two corned beef sandwiches, washing them down with several mugs of beer. He didn't know how to deal with inner conflict; he wasn't equipped for it. He thought in black and white, preferring a direction that led straight to his target. He felt uncomfortable with detours. *What was McParland really expecting?*

He belched out the carbonation from the beer and looked up at a woman sitting at the bar. She had turned at the sound and didn't turn away from Harrison's icy stare. It would have been better for her if she had. Her broken arm would later take several painful weeks to heal.

The following day, Harrison began his research. He took the streetcar to the Stockyards. He hated the smell but knew the organizers were hard at work. They were trying to sign men to the union.

Harrison watched the gates for several days. He found a place across from the employee entrance that served coffee and a simple menu. It was a place where working men felt comfortable. Harrison would sit at a stool, reading the newspaper and listening to the conversations around him. He developed a taste for the pig's ears and snouts on the menu.

The waitresses worked hard and seemed to have a special bond with the customers. Harrison noted that bond did not extend to the owner, a squat, sordid-looking man who sat behind the counter in a dirty shirt, sucking on a cigar all day. Harrison was glad the man wasn't the cook.

Sitting in the eatery, Harrison was surprised at the languages he heard around him. The stockyards were like a magnet for men speaking Italian, Bohemian, German, Polish, and a host of other languages he couldn't even identify. He took note of their dress and eventually bought work clothes on his way to his rooming house on the north side of the city.

Finally, after a week of observation, he walked into the plant office across from the coffee shop and said, "I'm looking for a job, you hiring?"

The man behind the counter took one look at the huge man standing in front of him and said, "For you, I know just the job."

Chapter 10
SAMUEL T. HARRISON: Union Man

Harrison was not a man to avoid work, hard or easy. Now, working in the slaughterhouse, he was learning what *truly* hard work was. His plant bosses took one look at the huge man and he was instantly assigned to the killing ramp. There, a man with a thick Bohemian accent showed him how to hit the cattle with a precise, lethal blow. The hammer used was not unlike a sledge. It almost looked like a toy in the hand of a man as large as Harrison.

"Humane" was not a word they used on that slaughterhouse floor. Done correctly, one blow was enough to stun even the largest beast walking down the ramp. Once a cow, still breathing, fell to its knees, a second man would step in and tie a rope around the hind legs. Men standing to the side hoisted the cow overhead, suspending it on a hook trailing along a conveyor. When the carcass of the cow finally stopped swinging, a man would reach up with a sharp blade and slice along the neck, severing the jugular. While they worked, the men stood in a continual river of blood, their rubber boots stained. They stood among the stench of the life-giving liquid, once part of a living thing.

The men around Harrison gave little, if any, thought to such niceties, as they continued the dismantling of the carcass while the conveyor kept up a relentless pace.

The men around him talked in many languages. If he had been able to understand, he would have heard them talking about similar work they left behind in their homelands, somehow thinking it would be better here in Chicago. They had long ago accepted the fact that people wanted meat and this was how it got to them.

Harrison started his shift at 4:00 a.m. every morning. His hammer would swing continuously until 2:30 in the afternoon. There were few breaks and exactly thirty minutes for lunch. During his shift, a cow stumbled down the ramp every two-and-a-half minutes. If he kept track, which he didn't, he would have counted over 240 animals in one shift that he had help convert into prime rib dinners.

It was hard work, even for Harrison. He often rubbed his aching muscles as his crew showered and changed. The change room was a huge, open shower accommodating fifty men at a time. It was not uncommon for personal items to disappear during a shift, and Harrison soon learned to leave anything of value at home. No one touched his family Bible in his locker, however. Everyone always gave a wary look at the huge man and it would have taken a truly brave man to steal anything belonging to him.

It wasn't long before he finally heard someone discussing a meeting (in English, for that matter), and he heard the mention of organizing a union. A small, balding man with expressionless eyes and a Slovak accent whispered to Harrison as they were leaving one day. "We're all thinking about getting together. We need to deal with bosses. Is not reasonable to think about an eight- or eight-and-a-half hour working day? And who gives a shit about our safety?"

Harrison looked at the man and didn't say anything. He simply grunted.

The man waited until the following day and once again approached Harrison. This time, asked if he might be interested in attending such a meeting, Harrison said, "Maybe."

The third day, Harrison said he was interested.

"Someone will contact you," the balding man whispered, and abruptly walked away. The man joined two others, and the three quickly shifted to a language that Harrison had come to learn was some kind of Slovakian.

It wasn't that easy for Harrison to gain acceptance, however. All new men were treated with suspicion. Outsiders who were not friends of trusted workers had been known to infiltrate organizing attempts. Someone admitted they worried especially about agents from Pinkerton's. They wanted to make sure Harrison wasn't a provocateur.

Harrison had to learn how to control his rage when the men talked about Pinkerton's. He quickly learned that the agency, *his* beloved agency, was hated and feared by these men. One night, while drinking a beer in a tavern near work, he overheard three men who were talking about the Carnegie Mill riots near Pittsburgh. His ears were sharply tuned to their conversation.

"Fucking Pinkerton men got away with murder that day." The other men grumbled in agreement. He knew it was the same mill riot he had heard about from his father so long ago, and Harrison couldn't abide anyone showing disrespect for his father's memory. His fury welled inside of him, threatening to spill over.

One of the three men, the one who had talked the loudest about the mill riot, had his head smashed in on his way home from the stockyards that night. Two nights later, his brain shattered, he never even remembered the beating, and certainly never could have been able to identify the man who took his mind away forever. He never heard his attacker saying, "This is for my old man, commie prick."

Harrison waited patiently, and finally, he was rewarded with an invitation to an organizing meeting. He was greeted carefully, many still wary of him. These men had good reasons for their suspicion of strangers.

The mood changed when a man walked into the room, obviously the leader. There was a surge of men to the makeshift stage. Everyone wanted a glimpse of this man. He walked over to a box and picked up a megaphone, pointing it out over the crowd.

"Men!" he was drowned out by the roar of approval until he held up his hand for quiet.

He waited for quiet and began, slowly at first.

"Are you tired? Are you sick? Are you sick and tired of being treated as bad as those animals you slaughter?"

"Yes," roared the men as one voice.

"My *brothers*, my *comrades*," he emphasized both words, "it won't be easy. They tell you that you are earning over $18.00 a week."

"Bullshit," a man in the back yelled, "I ain't ever seen anything close to that."

"Then they take out money for my boots and other things. One week, all I had was $8.00 in my hand on the way home," yelled another.

"They told me I broke a hammer and took it out of my pay," said yet another and everyone laughed. They all had similar stories to shout.

"My wife, kids and I are starving!" A murmur spread through the crowd at that comment, everyone commiserating with the voice who had spoken.

The man on the stage held up his hand for quiet and looked out over the restless crowd, judging the appropriate moment to begin again.

"I know, my brothers, but hear me out. We want to stop that and you deserve the same pay for eight-and-a-half hours a day that you are now getting for ten hours a day."

"Damn right," someone yelled. The crowd was restless, like a living and breathing animal sensing prey.

"They will yell and scream," the man shouted into the megaphone. "The bosses will tell us how much it will hurt them to pay that. They are telling you this even while they are making record profits."

"What can we do?" some yelled.

"We strike, brothers. We close the slaughterhouse down. Talking to them is getting us nowhere. Now is the time for action. They only understand action."

Harrison watched as several men walked through the crowd handing out leaflets, *The Time Is Now*, emblazoned across the top of each one. There was an uneasy stirring in the room.

"How will we eat if we don't get paid?"

It became a conversation of give and take, a conversation that Harrison would hear over and over in the time that followed. Meetings similar to this one went on for weeks, as the workers slowly came to the conclusion that nothing would change unless they took a stand.

They needed a local leader, and an extremely large man suddenly stepped forward, taking his hat off saying, "Enough! Now we strike!" Stunned, Harrison heard his own voice shouting those words out to the crowd, his hat suddenly in his hands.

Harrison was a union man.

That night began his career as a chameleon; he became an undercover agent for Pinkerton's in the skin of a union man. His rise through the union ranks was rapid and sure. Soon, *he* was the man walking on the stage and picking up a megaphone to rally the crowd. His commanding size alone was enough to capture the attention of those around him. He developed an unexpected speaking facility and could easily talk about the evil of Pinkerton's and inspire men to strike, much to his own surprise.

Their first attempt in the Chicago stockyards wasn't successful, but others were. There was a movement slowly taking shape and gradually, the men started to see improvements.

McParland sat waiting for Harrison in the Tap Root Pub one night. He was eager to hear the latest news from the stockyards. He was startled when a shadow passed over him and a huge man slid silently into the seat across from him.

"How do you do that?" McParland asked. "A man your size shouldn't be able to sneak around like that."

Harrison had changed clothes after work and walked to the elevated train, taking it to the stop nearby. Now, sitting across from McParland, he reached in his pocket and pulled out a paper, "Here's your list of agitators. Those three at the top are the ones we need to worry about the most."

McParland looked at the list of names and urged Harrison to drink his beer while he read. He put the paper face down on the table and looked at the giant sitting across from him. The two men finished their beers in silence. When they pushed the empty steins to the end of the table, McParland leaned over, motioning Harrison closer.

"It might be a good idea if those three men, the ones you mentioned, met with an unfortunate accident of some sort, don't you agree?"

Harrison swiped the paper up and crunched it into a ball. "I was hoping you would say that," an oily smile spreading across his face as he slid out of the booth. He left without so much as a fare-thee-well.

Life's direction can indeed be curious at times. Harrison actually felt sympathy for the hard-working men on the plant floors. He still knew how to hate the people behind the scenes, the ones who sent the striking men out to do the dirty work while they hid behind their cigar smoke in dingy back rooms.

McParland felt no offense at Harrison's abruptness as he put on his coat and left soon after their meeting.

The year was drawing to a close. 1898 ushered in the union career of Samuel T. Harrison and solidified his covert role with the secret unit inside Pinkerton's.

The three unfortunate labor organizers on the list he had shown to McParland did not see the end of that year. Three accidents, several weeks apart, drew no unusual notice. With no family and no real standing in the ongoing life of Chicago, their deaths didn't even rate an obituary or notice in the newspapers.

Chapter 11
Assassination of Governor Steunenberg Wednesday, June 14, 1899

Most men would have been exhausted after a ten-hour shift at the packinghouse, but not Harrison. By now, his huge arms were used to swinging the killing hammer. In the shower after work, he held no illusions the water washed away the stench of the blood and his manual labor.

Now, stretching out his legs in the streetcar, he lowered the window to breath in the cooling air.

"You have to close..." the driver started to say, but when he looked back at Harrison, he rolled his shoulder and decided he wasn't paid nearly enough to face him down.

The day before, June 13, 1899, it had been hot and humid, darkening skies soared in evil majesty to the west of Chicago. He had heard about a tornado the day before, somewhere in Wisconsin. One of the men at the packinghouse had stumbled off the floor keening, "They say it was horrible in New Richmond. My family, my family, they have all been killed!"

Hard-working packinghouse men turned away from the man, each of them thinking about their own families left behind somewhere.

That was yesterday; this evening, it was time to meet McParland for another report on his union activities.

Harrison got off the streetcar and made the familiar walk to The Tap Root Pub. It would have been more convenient to take the elevated train, but it was a warm evening that summer of 1899, and Harrison felt like a walk.

People were already starting to whisper about a new century just ahead. He passed a street corner preacher predicting that God would destroy the world the moment the clock ticked past midnight on the last day of the nineteenth century. He was shouting to his congregation of strangers passing by to repent their sins and prepare for the rapture. His "congregation", however, consisted of a singular elderly man with crutches, who seemed unable to leave. Other walkers simply ignored the preacher and raced by as quickly as they could.

Harrison paused and listened for just a moment, then proceeded on. In the next block, he pulled open the door to the pub and let his eyes adjust to the cool, dark interior. Spotting Jim McParland at their usual booth in the rear of the pub, Harrison walked back and squeezed onto the bench and grunted his hello.

"Fucking guy out there says the world is coming to an end," said Harrison, almost laughing. Humor was not an emotion he often allowed, and it was an alien sound coming from his throat.

"For some, every day is an end," replied McParland and waited to see if Harrison got the point. He didn't, so McParland leaned forward, "You are quite the union man now."

"Hmmmph," Harrison spit out the sound.

"Do you have anything new to report?"

"I think we are getting ready for another strike," Harrison said, not realizing that he was including himself now, using 'we' whenever he referred to the union workers. "Men are pretty ready, fired-up, really. Truth is, most of them don't have that much to lose."

"And you?" McParland asked, "What do you think?"

"You know I don't have any love for unions, not one bit." Something about the conversation, however, made Harrison start to squirm, an uncustomary display for him.

"They do have some real gripes and I can understand that. The guys at the stockyards are hard workers. We stand up for each other," Harrison again using the 'we' word.

"One guy, Jakub is his name, starts to cry every time he talks about his wife and two children. They are still back in Bohemia. He starves himself to send money back home, hoping to save enough to bring over his family eventually. I watch him losing weight. He's skin and bones but still works like a bull." Harrison had a face that was unreadable to most, but McParland detected a flash of sympathy there, though his voice remained matter-of-fact.

McParland realized he had to say something. "It's not the working men we are after, Samuel. They have complaints, to be sure. No, it's the organizers that are the dangerous ones. Socialism, whatever you call it, is their goal. They won't be happy until all the wealth, as they see it, is equally divided and stripped from the rich men of this world, who work as hard in their own way as the workers themselves. Who would invest in factories if it were that way? The men who risk their fortunes are entitled to a larger reward, don't you agree?"

Harrison nodded but didn't speak.

"If the anarchists and socialists and shit disturbers weren't stirring the pot, the owners would be more kindly toward the workers."

Harrison was still a believer, still a Pinkerton's man through and through. But, something was edging into his consciousness. He was not too sure anymore that the owners felt all that kindly about their workers and all the other Jakubs of the world.

"Like always, I keep a list of the organizers we want the most," Harrison finally said, turning the subject aside. "There are two more names I have at the top of my list: Rudolph Schnaubelt and Ian Ferguson. They were at the Haymarket explosion. It was one of them I'm sure, who had our man, George Menge, killed. Assassinated is a better word," Harrison added and went on, "Burned to death in a fire? That was a cover-up. George was a Pinkerton man, one of us. They killed a Pinkerton's detective and they will pay for it."

It was a long, vehement statement for a man of such few words.

"I've heard whispers," Harrison said, "Schnaubelt is supposed to be somewhere in Canada. Nobody knows where Ferguson is. He is a ghost that appears, does some dirty work, and disappears as just as quickly as he came."

McParland jumped as Harrison slammed his beer mug down to emphasize his words. When the big man was quiet and under control once again, McParland said, "You have my word, if we ever get a tip on either one of them, you will be the one we send after them. But that's not why I brought you here," he continued, waiting for the other man's full attention. "How's your geography?"

"Kentucky, Chicago and New York City," Harrison answered blandly. "What else is there?"

"Idaho," McParland answered. "Unionists are hard at work there, and they are like dynamite with a short fuse. It's an explosion waiting to happen. The governor is some guy named Frank Steunenberg, and he's heavy in the union's pocket. He calls himself a Populist. He's from Iowa originally, land of corn...and populists, it seems." He coughed and went on, "Might as well be socialist for all the difference it makes. Anyway, he has all the mine owners running scared. They are worried he won't back them if there is a strike. He started talking about increasing wages," he paused and took a long drink of his warm beer and knew that Harrison was listening carefully now.

"We just got word that one company refused to give in and decided to stand up to the union, to call their bluff. The bastards destroyed his mill at Wardner, a small mining town. I hear it's a squalid place, not far from Spokane. It's in the Coeur d'Alene Mountains and close to a region where there is intense excitement among the mine owners. Gold-bearing quartz and argentiferous galena, whatever *that* is, have been discovered in several places. Whatever it is, there is no doubt it's valuable and worth risking a lot of money."

"They claim the Sullivan and Bunker Hill mines are loaded with the stuff. At first, when some geologist discovered it, employees were not even allowed to enter the mines. Someone said all you have to do is scrape it off the floor of the tunnels, it's that good. People back east heard about it and are ready to invest in the stock of the Sullivan and Bunker Hill mines."

Harrison had, in truth, only been half listening. He came awake. "They destroyed mill property," Harrison said flatly. It sounded like a question, but it wasn't really. In Harrison's mind, that was the worst offense of all.

"But the best part is," McParland tilted his beer mug and drained it before continuing, "the governor finally had enough of the unions. He knew the investments needed to be protected from the anarchists and declared martial law. He sent a telegram to the president. I tell you, the unions are now furious with him."

"Sounds to me like a man who knows how to do the right thing," Harrison said, "just like Frick in Pittsburgh. My daddy would be smiling right now, if he could."

"I want you there, Samuel. We can use a man with your talents on the inside. We need to know what the organizers are planning. The mine owners are paying Pinkerton's plenty for information."

"We need our union man there," McParland finished when Harrison remained quiet.

Harrison and McParland said their good-byes and Harrison decided to walk to the library. It had been a long but pleasant walk he didn't mind. The library was crowded that evening, but he used the time until closing for his research. He located an atlas and studied the pages on Idaho with great care. He wouldn't need to look at the map again; with one look, the image was permanently locked in his memory.

As he was leaving the library, a young woman bumped into him in the crowded lobby. She looked up at him and smiled. He was disgusted by her drab clothes and hairstyle; both reminded him of his mother.

Her reward for meeting Mr. Samuel T. Harrison was a smashed jaw and two broken ribs later that night. She was more than sorry she invited him back to her apartment, a walk-up over a corner grocery store. Later, when the police asked her how it happened, she was too terrified of her attacker to offer any useful details. The last thing she remembered Harrison telling her was, "Say anything about this and you're dead." Earlier, she had felt the pistol in one of his jacket pockets and didn't doubt his word for a second.

❋ ❋ ❋

Harrison forgot her as soon as he left the apartment.

Active in the stockyard union, he was now a trusted member of the inner circle of union organizers. He learned to call them his *brothers* and *comrades*, and they had no idea he was systematically sending all their thoughts and plans to McParland. They continued to be amazed, however, at how their organizing efforts were thwarted at every turn.

"We have a traitor among us," someone would say. But no one seemed to connect that to Harrison.

The organizers would show up at their meetings, expecting men to listen to speeches about improving their working conditions. The organizers wanted to issue a call to action. They would find out that not-so-friendly visitors from Pinkerton's had already been there before them.

One of the loudest voices expressing his outrage toward Pinkerton's belonged to Harrison. All the while, he smiled at the truth of the situation on the inside.

Harrison easily transferred his undercover skills to Idaho; a dedicated union man hiding a dedicated Pinkerton's detective on the inside. It worked to his advantage to have his credentials as a union man verified by the Chicago union leadership.

Mining, he quickly found out, was hard and dangerous. Harrison never adjusted to the claustrophobia of being underground or to compressing his huge frame into the elevator car to get there. Still, he kept up his union activities as the world slipped further into the twentieth century.

It was long and slow work, and Harrison inched toward a fateful day. He had no way of expecting it, but Harrison said he would always remember the day it happened. It was cold and snowing heavily.

1905 was nearly over. He was thinking about an invitation. A young woman, new in town, had suggested he go to a New Year's Eve party with her. He was thinking about it when the door to the union hall burst open.

"Someone killed him!"

"Who?"

"The governor! Well, ex-governor, I guess. They killed Steunenberg!"

Confusion was the order of the day as men gathered around, eager for details.

"It was a bomb."

"Did you hear the explosion?"

"Was that what it was?" someone shouted. "I thought it was odd to be blasting on a Saturday."

"No, it was a bomb, tore his front gate and the front of his house off and killed him dead as a doornail."

Harrison guessed correctly that something huge was heading his way, and he was right. By that evening, he was re-reading a telegram: *I'm on my way. Let's meet at the Tap Root Pub,* signed, Edward Rucker.

The message was plain and in code. Harrison knew exactly what the reference to the Tap Root Pub meant, it meant top secret. He admired McParland's choice of cover names. Rucker was the original partner with Allen Pinkerton. But by 1905, only the insiders at Pinkerton's would recognize or remembered that connection. Harrison looked forward to seeing his boss again and almost started to whistle as he walked back to his rooming house.

❋ ❋ ❋

McParland was the man in charge of the investigation, although only Harrison knew his real name. The local and state police were no match for the investigative skills needed for this case. McParland was, and he had access to the latest technology. Pinkerton's head office told him he had an unlimited budget to find out who killed the governor.

"We need an example," the telegram from New York had demanded. "It's time to show the politicians just how dangerous these agitators can be."

But, McParland really didn't need all the resources and technology. He had his secret weapon: Samuel T. Harrison.

The two men met on a train between Wardner and Coeur D'Alene. They took separate seats, as if they were two strangers. The train was slow and covered the thirty-six miles in just over three hours. An hour after they arrived in Coeur D'Alene, they got off the train. After Harrison had a glass of beer at a nearby tavern and McParland had a meal at the hotel, they were on the train back.

They boarded the train separately and when the train was underway, both men walked to the rear open-air platform and spoke quietly together, despite the wintery weather. It was February 1906.

"Orchard," McParland told Harrison. "Harry Orchard. He's near Boise. He lives in a cabin out on Rocky Canyon Road. He's the man."

Harrison had no trouble locating Mr. Orchard. After his arrest and a few minutes with Harrison, which seemed like hours to Harry Orchard, he confessed. Harrison promptly wired McParland, who read it and actually *whooped* his excitement.

Mr. Rucker wants you to meet the 8:30 train, his return wire said.

"Now we need to have another conversation with our Harry Orchard," McParland told Harrison as they walked from the train station. He whispered further instructions to Harrison, his secret weapon, walking alongside.

Harrison had the police sergeant bring a hunched-over Orchard into a small interview room. There was only enough room for a small table and four chairs. Constables in the outer office heard shouts and a scream, but they had been told to take no notice of it all. When the sergeant returned for the prisoner, Orchards' face was bloody, ugly bruises forming around his eyes, and one of the chairs was shattered.

"It appears he hurt himself when the chair fell over," McParland said, standing to the side. He handed over a written confession signed by the unfortunate Mr. Orchard. His statement implicated the notorious union organizer, 'Big Bill' Haywood, as one of the assassination conspirators. After all, he had played a central part in the activities of the Western Federation of Miners. The union president, Charles Moyer, was also named in the confession.

They were distractions, however. The real target was identified in the statement. The agency had long had their eye on George Pettibone, as early as 1892. Orchard conveniently confessed that Pettibone was involved in the assassination as well, and probably was the ringleader.

Later, Harrison sat in the courtroom at Pettibone's trial. It was amazing to see the famous people, reporters and photographers. They were all trying to claim their moment of fame.

The celebrated Clarence Darrow, himself, came to the defense of Haywood. Pettibone was later acquitted and the charges were finally dropped against Moyer. He didn't even have to stand trial. That left poor Mr. Orchard. The famous lawyers and the reporters had left town by the time his trial was finished. No one cared about the unfortunate Mr. Orchard.

He got the death penalty.

That was enough to satisfy Harrison, who didn't care much about the legal realities; he simply wanted to see unionists in jail, or worse. Even though the death sentence was later commuted to life in prison, Harrison was pleased with his role in putting the man away. Harrison had convinced himself that Orchard was not innocent. He didn't trouble himself with the vagaries of guilt and innocence.

He had gone about his business of methodically compiling a dossier on Orchard, whose real name was Albert Horsley. The records showed he was born in Canada, some place called Wooler, in Ontario. He was a miner sure enough, but he was a radical unionist and long-time troublemaker.

That, alone, was enough for Harrison, who believed such men respected no borders or boundaries. If he weren't guilty of something, why else would he have a string of aliases: Goglan, Hoga, Dempsey, and Orchard, just to name a few. He was a card-carrying member of the Western Federation of Miners and Harrison had helped bring him down.

❊ ❊ ❊

From that point on, Harrison's career with Pinkerton's National Detective Agency was never in doubt. He was finally sent to be in charge of Pinkerton's Pittsburgh office. He would often drive over to the mill plant, the Carnegie Steel Mill, his father had told him about. Here, he felt a connection to the man who had taught him so much.

That was where he was in 1937, when got the telegram about his old nemesis, Ian Ferguson. A Pinkerton's agent had been killed in Montreal and Ian Ferguson was in on it somehow.

Ian Ferguson. The name his father had told him about so long ago, a name Harrison never forgot.

He had learned to control his legendary temper, but as he looked at the photograph of Ian Ferguson in his hand, he felt the old anger building up inside. It pounded at him as he drove back to the agency and blew like a storm through the outer office.

Same age as me, he thought. Then he picked up a typewriter and hurled it through the window, as startled agents, sitting at their desks, simply looked at each other in amazement.

Throwing the typewriter didn't make him feel any better, however. He returned to his desk and for some reason thought back to the funeral of Jim McParland, an Irishman and longtime mentor. McParland had died on May 1st, 1919. Had it been that long now, almost twenty years?

He remembered telling McParland's widow, Mary, that he would someday dedicate the capture of Mr. Ferguson to her husband, one of the two men who had been permitted to call him something other than Samuel T. Harrison.

Now, he had his chance. With access to all of Pinkerton's considerable resources, he made a phone call and was soon packing for the trip. He was flying to Toronto to take charge of the investigation. He was going to honor McParland's memory. He was going to get Ferguson, dead or alive. It didn't matter to him whichever way it went. In fact, dead was probably preferable, if it meant Harrison were the one to accomplish the task.

He pushed back the curtains of the twin-engine plane, looking down on Lake Ontario passing below. *I've got you now, you bastard.*

Chapter 12
Alec and Seth in Hamilton

It was getting dark when I jumped off that train and met Seth. I remember limping up the embankment to the waiting truck.

Seth sounded urgent, "Hurry it up, we can't hang around here."

The driver was standing off to the side in the dim light, the ember of his cigarette cupped by his hand. He didn't say a word, simply lifted the tarp on the back and motioned for Seth and me to hurry. I almost gagged at the stench and reached up to pull back the flap for fresh air.

"This truck is used to carry waste from the meat rendering plant," laughed Seth, "but, you're better off with the stench than the fresh air, trust me. Close the flap."

"Awful smell," I said, trying not to vomit.

"I'm telling you, better keep that flap closed."

I took a deep breath and reclosed the tarp. We were sitting on a metal floorboard that was slippery, and I tried my best not to notice and ignore the slime. The truck, a seven–year-old International, lurched into Hamilton on York Boulevard. I lifted my head, peeking through a slit in the tarp, and could see the street sign just past the head of the driver in the cab. There was a second man on the passenger side who kept moving his head from side to side. The ember of his cigarettes was glowing in the darkness.

"They're keeping a sharp eye out for the coppers," Seth said, watching me. I didn't need to ask why.

We felt the truck suddenly brake and make a sharp turn to the left. Seth kept his balance, but I sprawled across the slippery floor, slamming into the side of the truck. I didn't want to think about what I was sliding on. The window behind the driver on the back of the cab opened.

"There's a road block ahead at Queen Street. Lucky we saw one of the cars. I'm heading left on Locke down to Barton Street. Maybe we can get around them."

I figured Seth knew all those street names. He helped me sit back up and we held onto the sideboards with both hands as the truck made a sharp right.

"Dammit," the driver yelled back, "another road block at Bay Street. Hold on, we can try Stuart. It's a usual route for us anyway."

The driver stopped just short of Bay Street, and the second man got out of the truck, walking ahead. Seth and I bumped together as we pressed our heads to the glass, each trying to watch.

Finally, we saw the man on the road swing his arm and wave. The driver let out on the clutch and the truck shot ahead with amazing speed. As the truck struck out across the intersection, the passenger jumped back on the running board, holding onto the side mirror while the truck gained speed.

"I think they've done this before," Seth laughed.

Once past the intersection, the truck moved on without incident until the driver stopped in front of a three-story house on Catherine Street, just off Barton.

"Be quick, you two," the driver shouted back.

Seth picked up my pack and motioned me off the truck. I didn't have to be told twice. I pushed open the tarp and jumped, immediately feeling the pain shooting up from my forgotten ankle. Seth jumped after me, as I willed myself to keep quiet.

"This way," Seth said as he motioned towards a darkened lane.

We walked up to a door. It was a warm night and the solid inner door was open behind a screen door. I saw a bare light bulb hanging from a wire in the hallway, the only illumination to be seen.

"Not the Ritz," Seth said ruefully, "and you haven't even seen the best part yet."

The screen door opened with a slight squeak, and Seth muttered a soft "damn," as he had forgotten the spring. He let go of the door and it slammed shut too quickly. It made a loud *thwack*ing sound, and we both grimaced at the noise echoing in the night. We stood quietly, waiting to discern if anyone had heard.

Finally, Seth whispered, "The landlord's a nosey bastard. Can't let him know you're here. Not supposed to have two in a room."

I was glad Seth was carrying my kit for me as we climbed the flights of stairs to the top floor. My ankle was throbbing like all hell, and it took all the willpower I had left to climb behind Seth without complaint.

There was something about this man ahead of me on the stairs. We had never met, and I didn't really know much about him, but I took an instant liking to the man. He acted like he knew what he was doing, but something–I think it was his sense of humor–kept him from coming off as a know-it-all.

There were two doors on the third landing. Seth stood for a moment, listening. I remember I could hear the sound of a radio program from the door to our left. It was Amos and Andy; odd how I can still bring that memory back after all the years that have passed since that night.

I watched as Seth quickly unlocked the door straight ahead. We both slipped quickly through the door, and I think I dropped to my knees and sat breathless on the floor. Had I even taken a breath since I jumped from the train? I wasn't sure.

I unlaced the boot on my twisted ankle and took the sock off.

"My God that looks ugly," Seth said with a low whistle, looking down at the purple swelling. He opened the door to the ice compartment. There was still a large chunk from a block of ice remaining, and he used a pick to shave off a handful. He took out a handkerchief and wrapped the ice, handing it to me. "Here, take this. That should help some."

"Thanks, it does," I sighed, holding the ice to my ankle.

"I have something even better." Seth reached up to a cupboard and took down two glasses. He reached up to a shelf and pulled out a bottle with no label, filling both glasses generously.

"Here's something for your pain," he said and handed me a glass.

I looked at the glass and the flaxen liquid. I held it for an instant, and then drained the contents in one long swallow. I gasped and sputtered, covering my mouth with my hand to stifle a cough. It didn't help, and I started to cough and laugh until tears ran down my cheeks.

Maybe it was the relief of feeling safe for the first time in what seemed like weeks. It certainly felt like weeks—though it had only been days. I couldn't stop laughing in spite of my pain.

It was infectious, and Seth soon joined in.

It helped for a while, but when the pain returned, I somehow felt better able to cope with it. I knew it was just a sprain, though it hurt something terrible.

Seth finally stood up and pointed to his bed in the corner. "Take it," he ordered.

"I can't."

"Like hell, it's been a long day for both of us." I watched Seth roll out a blanket on the floor. Before I could protest further, Seth had dropped down and was snoring. He was curled on top of the blanket, his jacket rolled up for a pillow. I let myself fall back on the bed and the next sound I heard was the shrill whistle from the nearby steel mill, calling workers to the morning shift.

I sat upright, remembering the still, quiet mornings in Vermont.

"Don't pay the whistle any attention. I'm not going in today. I made arrangements," he said, his voice coming from the corner kitchen. Seth stretched out a cup of coffee to me, the steam rising in the cool of the room's interior. "We have better things to do today."

Waiting by the door, I heard the neighbor in the next room as he left for work, grunting his way down the steps, feet sounding like lead weights pounding each riser.

"Now," said Seth, nodding to the door.

We set aside our coffee and Seth opened the door slightly and peered out. We slipped silently out of the doorway and down the stairs to the landing below. There was another door there I hadn't noticed last night. It didn't look like it was used much. Seth slipped out into the hall, unlocked it, and motioned for me to go ahead. The steps rose steeply and led up to a musty attic.

The attic was an unfinished area with cobwebs shining in the sunbeams, motes of dust dancing in the light. There were some old boxes, wires running in all directions, and the attic was thick with dust. Some of the wires had obviously been gnawed, mice or rats most likely.

"I hate spiders," Seth shuttered, brushing at the cobwebs. Seth reached for one of the older appearing boxes and opened it. It wasn't covered in dust like most of the others. "Maps and pamphlets," he said, tilting it over for me to look.

"We have a job ahead of us. A week from this Saturday, there's a rally. We think the steelworkers are finally ready for action. I could sure use your help."

I gave him a grim nod and rubbed my ankle, willing the pain away.

"I'm the main speaker. Have you ever done any of that?"

"Not much for speaking," I responded with a shrug.

"When I hand you the microphone, just say what comes from your heart. We–you and I–carry the blood of our fathers, Rudi and Ian."

The mention of my father sent an unexpected jolt of loss through me. He was always away a lot during my childhood, and I was accustomed to his many absences, but it was surprising how far from him I felt just then. Yet, at the same time, I also felt so close, standing here plotting in this dusty attic.

"We always have to keep a look-out for the police. They would love to bust some heads. Worse, there is word that Pinkerton's is sending in some strikebreakers this time. There will be hell to pay if anything breaks out. The steel men are looking for a good brawl. Are you up for a good fight?"

"What was it you said to me back at the train?" I asked. "You know, about Pinkerton's looking for me?"

"There was a Pinkerton's man following you on the train from Magog to Montreal. You didn't know that, eh?"

"What? How..."

"Your father sent word and alerted us you were on the way. A porter on the train tipped us off that you were being followed. He watched the conductor and some detective making arrangements. The porter knew the man, Giles LeBlanc, growing up together. He knew LeBlanc bragged about working for Pinkerton's. That detective never made it from the train into the station. They weren't supposed to do anything more than rough him up and delay him, but one of the men in Montreal hated Pinkerton's so much, he slipped an ice pick into him. Not that I really care," Seth added with a nonchalant shrug. I paled visibly.

"Is that why the cops were all over the place?"

Seth nodded, "That's his gun you have. What do you think about that? One of our guys has a sense of humor, I guess. What do you think they will do to you if you are ever caught with it?"

"I don't really know," I whispered, but I knew damn well what would happen. Seth just looked at me and moved on.

Brushing at more cobwebs, Seth continued, "Strange thing is, though, when the alarm went out to all the police and train stations, they said it was Ian Ferguson, your father, who'd done it. We can't figure that out. How could they make a mistake like that?"

"Is he alright?" I asked. I suddenly feared for my parents.

"Oh, yeah, Ian's fine. But now we hear that there's a hotshot detective being sent here to head up the investigation. He is one of Pinkerton's top men, some guy named Samuel T. Harrison."

"But, what about my parents?" I asked.

"We got word to them, already. It's funny what a name change and a vacation to a warm climate can do," laughed Seth softly, "at least until this blows over. Our fathers have always been a couple of slippery old buggers. That's how they managed to last this long, to avoid capture." I heard my father made a visit to Vermont personally, just to help them pack for their little vacation."

"How do you know all of this? I feel like such a novice."

Seth put his hand firmly on my shoulder, his look growing serious, "Not for long my brother, not for long."

❊ ❊ ❊

To avoid problems with Seth's landlord, I found a room nearby where we could meet at a small park midway between our flats. Sitting on a bench, the two of us would argue, agree, debate and disagree. Our bond was forming like forged steel.

One evening, I recall, as spring was drawing to a close, we sat and enjoyed an unusually warm evening. I always liked it when the leaves were first forming on the trees, turning a dark green. The near-fullness of the trees created shadows under the streetlights that night.

"Feel like a beer?" Seth asked.

Without answering, we got up and walked the four blocks to a corner bar frequented by the steel workers. I liked it. It was a rough place, with a long bar running the length of the room, from just inside the door, to the very back. The furniture was roughly constructed and often victim to brawling steel workers. Much of it was patched back together and looked as if it were about to fall apart. It was the type of bar where men just stepped out a back door to piss their beer away. It wasn't a pleasant sight or smell, I tell you.

The bar was crowded that night, and Seth volunteered to muscle his way up to the bar, yelling to the barkeep, "Two drafts," holding his fingers up to show the money.

The barkeep nodded. Like many men in that neighborhood, he knew Seth and slid the two glasses between the men hunched at the bar.

"What the fuck," someone muttered.

"Pays to have friends," someone else added, "Maybe you should try it sometime."

"It's for Seth, so shut up," the barkeep said, ending the complaints.

The two of us found a vacated table against the wall and sat down. My eyes were starting to burn from the smoke hovering thick in the air. I watched as Seth reached in his pocket and pulled out two cigars.

"Care to join me?"

We shared the ritual of lighting the cigars, stogies really, low grade at best. The flavored tobacco emitted a foul aroma, but we both leaned back, exhaling smoke and scanning the crowd like two men who belonged there.

A loud argument broke out in the back of the room.

"She's called *La Pasionaria* and her name is Ibaria something." Such strange words coming from the low ranks of this society.

"Delores Ibarrurri," another man said. "I saw her on a newsreel, begging for volunteers to come to Spain."

"It's getting worse. The fascists are getting help from Germany and Italy now."

"I heard there are Germans in German uniforms. They don't even try to hide it anymore."

There was a hush as the rest of the men in the room now listened intently to the conversation. The Spanish cause that year was a much talked-about thing.

"Is that all you Commies can talk about?" someone said, and with those words, the fight began.

It wasn't a fight; really, it was more of a beating. The unfortunate man who called them commies didn't have anyone to back him up, and it was a giant mistake for him. He was soon poked and prodded and shoved out the door to lay unconscious in the street.

"Why would anyone come here and talking like that?"

Seth looked apprehensive.

"Why would he do that?" I asked.

"Maybe," Seth paused, looking up from his mug, "he did it on purpose."

Then we heard the sirens, police cars screeching to a stop in front of the bar. The window was cloudy, but I could see several men in uniform, some pounding their nightsticks into the palm of their hand as they walked towards the door.

"Quick. This way," someone said, and we slipped out a back door. In the alley, we could see the lights of the police cars at both ends of the alley. We should have expected it would be blocked.

Seth had used this escape before and knew a short cut. He reached and yanked back the wooden slats of a nearby fence, and the two of us crawled through and ran. I was panting and trying to catch Seth and my breath at the same time. We were soon sitting back at the park bench, breathing hard.

When I finally caught my breath, I said, "It's time. I know that the union work is important, but what I really want to do is get to Spain, and I don't need the sideshow of this place distracting me from what I should be doing."

"Agreed," Seth replied, and I was surprised he agreed so readily. Seth was a man, I had come to learn, who always argued six sides of any debate before he would agree.

"Then what are we waiting for?" I urged.

Seth pulled out a letter. "I meant to tell you this anyway," he said. "We need to go to Toronto. Why not tomorrow? How soon can you pack? There's an office on Queen Street there. We have to go for an interview to see if they will take us." I looked over the letter he passed to me. The letterhead said, *Committee to Support Spanish Democracy.*

That letter finally set everything in motion.

Chapter 13
A Curious Encounter

I was restless and realized sleep was hopeless. Seth and I were leaving for Toronto in the morning and I lay on the bed, shrouded in the oppression of the unusual heat on that summer night. I turned over and over in bed, the sheets sticking to me. There was no way to find comfort and I finally gave in, sitting up and letting my feet drop to the floor. I sat for a moment on the side of the bed.

We were leaving in the morning, and I had moved in to stay with Seth that night. I didn't have much to carry; my belongings were in a heap at the foot of my bed. I didn't want to wake Seth. I could hear him snoring lightly in the bed.

Wiping the perspiration from under my arms, I slipped on my shirt and trousers and picked up my shoes. I carried them with me and quietly closed the door to the room behind me. I crept down the stairs and out to the front stoop. I leaned over, tied my shoes, and straightened up. I rubbed an ache in my back as I glanced at my watch.

Close to midnight and not even close to sleep.

I started walking south toward Barton Street with no particular destination in mind. The heat gave emphasis to the drabness, and continuous smoke from the steel mills draped over the grimy houses. I looked around at the modest homes; boarding houses mostly, places where the mill workers slept without any attempt to make them pretty. I pulled a handkerchief from my pocket and wiped the sweat from my face, feeling no relief.

As I walked, I thought about the next morning. We planned to take an early train or maybe even a bus. I was finally on my way to Spain, with this distraction in Hamilton behind me. Tomorrow, we would pass our interviews and our acceptance would be the last hurdle, or so I thought at the time.

My impatience acted like a clamp on my stomach and I forced myself to keep walking. I turned right on Barton where the lighting appeared brighter. As I walked, I looked without seeing, sneaking brief glimpses into various shop windows.

I passed an open door of a tavern and heard the shouts and arguments inside. At this hour, with that much beer flowing, it was only a matter of time before one of these "debates" turned violent. Steelworkers needed to let off steam. It was the one small part of a life where they were free to make a choice, even if it resulted in broken bones and blood. Bones would mend.

I was thirsty for a beer, but that wasn't really what I needed that night.

What made me stop in front of the small store on my right? Maybe it was the sign. Maybe it was just fate.

At the time, I didn't believe fate had my life mapped out for me, but I looked again at the sign. *Fortunes Told. Do you want to know what's in your future? Let Madam La Belle tell you.* I silently mouthed the words on the sign as I read them.

I hesitated for a moment. I looked at the sign again and started to walk on before I stopped. *What the hell*, I thought, *it might be fun. It can't really hurt anything.*

I didn't believe in fortune telling. I didn't think my future could be predicted. *But it might be amusing,* I thought. I checked my money and turning back to that store, decided to pay for some harmless entertainment.

A bell jingled as I opened the door and stepped into a small lobby. I drew back at the sight of an old woman sitting in a large, overstuffed chair. It dwarfed her. Her small eyes peered out from a withered face. Her skin looked as flimsy as tissue paper, each wrinkle prominently featured. Her silver hair glistened, and the color seemed to change to gold as I watched. I shook my head. *Was it the lighting?* I wondered.

"I've been waiting for you."

"Me?" I said and laughed. "How could you?"

I tried to figure out what her gimmick was and didn't know what else to say.

"Troubled souls have a hard time sleeping," she said, as she held a shawl and pointed.

"Back there." I pushed through a curtain of hanging beads and stepped through the doorway. I heard her struggle to her feet behind me.

The room was dimly lit, but it was the coolness I noticed. I felt it immediately as I crossed the threshold into the back room. I turned and saw her wrapping her shoulders with a woolen shawl. It was a hot summer night, yet it felt cold here in this room. She pulled the wrap tight around her shoulders, walking with a surprising agility, and sat behind a small table.

The only light in the room came from a thick pillar candle on the table and a smaller candle to the side. The lighting gave her the appearance of a much younger woman and her eyes glistened like diamonds.

It must be my imagination, I thought. *How does this work?* I was convinced it was all an elaborate illusion she used to earn her money. *At least she doesn't have a crystal ball, I mused.*

I grew even more skeptical, and an inner disquiet slowly leached into my mind. She handed me a paper. It had the price of a reading. I looked at it, nodded, and handed over the money.

She didn't say anything. She didn't thank me or ask my name. She picked up a deck of cards and handed it to me. "Shuffle."

I mucked the deck and handed the cards back to her.

"Tarot cards," she murmured in a throaty voice and began placing the cards in a certain pattern. "I'm using the Celtic Cross Spread," she explained, *as if I would know what she meant by that.*

I had been sweating profusely in the summer heat and now my shirt felt ice cold clinging to my skin. I jumped when the candlelight flickered briefly; my skeptical mind blamed it on my lack of sleep.

I watched her turn a card and pause, looking at it intently. Turning another and then another, she finally broke her silence. "I see a small cabin, in ruins," her eyes were almost closed.

"I see a bad man standing on a hill. He is pure *evil*. Your parents...you will never see them again," sadness clouded her face.

"What are you saying?" I stammered, unable to believe what she was telling me. I hadn't paid for this kind of a story. I felt the harmless amusement from earlier slipping away like an figure disappearing into a thick fog.

She turned another card and shuddered. She scraped up the cards to rearrange them. I stared at her and waited. It was all I could think to do.

"A long life is ahead for you and adventure is around the corner."

She stopped suddenly.

That was more like it, a long life; I waited for her to go on.

I thought she was falling asleep and I was almost ready to stand up and slip quietly out the door. Her head snapped up and she opened her eyes. I had to turn away from the intensity of those eyes as she looked at me.

After a moment she looked down at the cards again.

"I see dust and blood," she began to tremble, "I am sensing pain, more pain than you can possible imagine. It's your pain, the pain of loss."

What did I see on her face? It was pure awfulness. A card with the picture of the Devil lay beneath her trembling fingers. She went on, "There are men in leather coats with guns. They are truly evil men with evil guns."

She waved her hand over the cards and I could see her concentration. "There is the body of a woman, a young woman, covered in blood. She lies in a church and there is a cross on the wall, but it is upside down. I see your tears dropping to the dusty floor..."

I didn't know what to do and waited, stunned and nervous. I was suddenly afraid of what more she might say.

"I can't go on," she moaned, "Such pain I see!"

"Here, take your money." She picked up the money I had given her, flinging it on the table in front of me.

"Take your money and leave, now! I don't want your money."

When I realized she was dismissing me, I left with the money still on the table, shaken by what had happened. I heard the door behind me opened and slammed closed. My money was scattered on the sidewalk. Behind the locked door, I could hear a terrible keening.

I walked in a daze and climbed the stairs to our room. *Damned lady must be a lunatic*, I thought. I lay in bed listening to the ticking clock and waited for the alarm. Sleep never did come to me that night.

When the alarm began its rude ringing, I was already packed, just sitting on the edge of the bed, staring out the window. It was time to leave for Toronto, for Spain. I put the memory of the fortuneteller behind me.

❊ ❊ ❊

"What was..."

"Enough," Alec held up his hand, palm out. His voice carried a roughness that Mike hadn't heard before.

"I can't go on, right now. I need time alone," Alec said, and waved his hand in dismissal. He walked away until he disappeared past a turn on the trail by the lake.

"What about tomorrow?" Michael yelled after him. There was no answer.

Chapter 14
The Committee Interview

Michael felt uneasy, wondering if Alec would return. When Alec had walked away earlier, Michael knew that he was troubled by the memories, especially the detour the story seemed to take when Alec had talked about the fortuneteller. Alec hadn't stormed off exactly, but Michael was sure the man's shoulders were trembling as he walked away.

Yet, Alec did return.

"It touched a nerve. I have spent a lifetime trying to forget the bad parts. The only problem is that forgetting the bad things also blocks out the good."

"Back then, it wasn't enough to say you wanted to go to Spain and fight for the loyalists. They were very careful, worried about infiltrators and informants. There was a committee in Toronto that vetted all the men who wanted to go. You'd best turn on your recorder now."

※ ※ ※

We were both awake when the alarm clock began clamoring, each of us with our own private thoughts and doubts. The bond between us had grown strong over the months. It was forged from a shared belief we inherited from our fathers. Seth and I talked about growing up listening to impassioned discussions about social justice, socialism and the need to find a more equitable way to share the wealth. I lived with the doubt, wondering if I could ever live up to my father's expectations. I was afraid that I didn't have the conviction; I was more like a leaf blowing wherever the wind happened to send me.

I wondered if I should share my doubts with Seth. Seth said he often heard his father quoting Abraham Lincoln, the words Lincoln used in his debate with Douglas. Seth would imitate his father's voice. "It's about the eternal struggle between two principles, right and wrong."

He said his father was convinced Lincoln's truth was ahead of the times when he had talked about the wealthy saying, "You toil and work and earn bread, and I'll eat it."

Lincoln had added, "It didn't matter what shape it takes, whether from the mouth of a king who seeks to bestride the people of his own nation, and live by the fruit of their labor, or from one race of men as an apology for enslaving another race, it is the same tyrannical principle."

Lincoln had been talking about the eternal struggle between those who have and those without, and the injustices in the space between them. I had grown up hearing words like that as a life-long call to arms, and so did Seth. We were the sons now awaiting a date with our own destinies.

"You awake?" I heard Seth say.

"It's time, I guess, isn't it?"

We took turns at the kitchen sink, brushing our teeth and splashing tepid water in a vain attempt to wash away grime that seemed to prevail in this neighborhood. We took turns sharing the toilet before we finished dressing.

"Ready?"

"Let's do it."

It was a conversation of few words but filled with emotion.

We packed our kits the night before, backpacks really, in the style of packs worn by the International Brigade in Spain.

I worried about carrying the Pinkerton's pistol in case I was stopped. It would ensure a long prison sentence. In the end, I wrapped it carefully in a shirt and stowed it among my clothes.

Carrying our packs and a small suitcase, we walked hurriedly to the central bus depot. To be careful with our cash, we walked past the train station and the panting steam engine that invited us on a quick trip to Toronto. We were being cautious as well as frugal. We were warned that the trains especially were being watched closely for 'agitators.'

I remember it was an old bus that rattled its way out of Hamilton that day. It had seen better days on more important routes, was my guess. The bus snaked along the north shore of Lake Ontario, passing through numerous small town centers and stopping at each one, reaching the outskirts of Toronto hours later.

Seth was looking out the window and saw something. "Here, he said, and picked up his gear, "we get off here."

We stepped off the bus. It was still early morning, but the summer heat was building, and the two of us found a small pocket of shade. We were the only ones waiting at the transit stop as we watched the bus drive off, belching dark clouds of diesel fumes.

We heard and then saw an empty streetcar lumbering to the turnaround, bell clanging its arrival. The streetcar made the turnaround and finally stopped in front of us, the door opening with a *whoosh*, the driver looking at us expectantly.

Seth pulled out two denim berets before the streetcar arrived, handing one to me. They were the type of berets favored by the Brigadistas in Spain. We were wearing them as we stepped up, ready to deposit our coins. The streetcar operator smiled his appreciation, as we started up the boarding steps and waved us away from depositing our money.

"Fuck 'em," the driver said, "the ride's on me brothers," he said, laughing as he pushed the handle forward. I remember grabbing a strap to balance myself against the surprising jerk as the streetcar accelerated again.

As the car picked up speed, the driver said, "I know where you guys are going," and reached up to give the bell a couple of rings, "For luck," he explained, as the car slowed to a stop where a small group of expectant passengers were waiting. Most were carrying lunch pails and wearing the hats and vacant looks frequently worn by working men everywhere.

"When I give you the nod, get off at the next stop," he said. "The Committee offices, right?"

"Thanks," we both said in unison, nodding.

"When you get off, all you have to do is walk back on the same side of the street, not too far down. The office is on the third floor. You won't miss it, there's a sign on the door."

The streetcar plodded on. At each stop, a few people got on and a few would get off. Finally, the operator nodded and the car slowed to a stop. "No pasarán," he said quietly, as we waited on the steps for the door to open. *They will not pass.*

As I stepped off, I looked back to say something, but the door had already closed and the car moved on. The two of us looked at each other, deeply moved.

Seth grabbed my arm and urged me on. Halfway down the block, he turned and smiled, pointing at the hand-lettered sign: *The Committee to Support Spanish Democracy.*

Inside the door, the hallway was dark and grimy; a single light bulb hanging from a tilting wall fixture was the only source of illumination. There was a bank of mailboxes to our right. Most of them were damaged, with the doors removed or hanging loosely.

A sign directed us to the third floor, complete with an arrow pointing in an upward angle. We looked up at a steep rise of steps and we were so excited, we started up them two steps at a time, each of us racing to be the first to the top. As we rounded the first landing, we stopped abruptly. A long line of men were waiting on the flight of stairs ahead.

Seth tapped the shoulder of the man ahead. "How long have you been waiting?" he asked.

"Close to half an hour."

Suddenly, we saw two men coming down the stairs with wide grins, thumbs up. "We're on our way," they whooped.

The line ahead of us started to move more quickly, until we could see the doorway on the third landing. Men were going in through the doorway and then coming back out a few minutes later. Each time a man came down the stairs with a smile, we would all cheer and pat him on the back as he passed.

Just as we were getting to the top of the stairs, the door opened and a man walked out who wasn't smiling. He walked down, turning away from the line as he descended the stairs. No one knew why he had been turned down, but we didn't want his luck to rub off. Those of us in line backed against the wall and gave him a wide berth, as he slowly slumped down the stairway.

"This is the committee that decides if you go or not," someone said quietly.

"Yeah, they want to know if you really believe."

"I heard there have been infiltrators."

"So did I, and what about the new Foreign Enlistment Act?"

"What's that?"

"Canadian government," the man spit, "says it's illegal to go to Spain now, no passport for travel to Spain."

"Heartless bastards," someone said. Others nodded in agreement.

"I hear they are using Pinkerton's for infiltrators."

I heard that and felt the hair on my neck bristle. It felt like a chill wind blowing across me and it wasn't comfortable. I thought about that gun buried in my backpack.

When talk on the subject finally petered out, we all grew quiet again, each with his own thoughts and fears. Then, I was at the head of the line, and the door opened and a man motioned me in. He led me down a narrow hallway and into a small room.

I glanced back and saw that Seth was being led to a different room. We exchanged glances before the doors closed.

I was nervous, but I knew why I was here. *Let them ask whatever they want*, I remember thinking. I looked at the people in front of me. Three people–a woman and two men–were sitting behind a table. The woman pointed to a chair. They were wearing khaki caps with a red star on the crown. One of them whispered to another, and I overheard the word *comrade*.

"Your name?" The woman sat with a pen poised over a notebook.

"Alestair...Alestair Ferguson. I go by Alec."

"Another eager young man from Hamilton, eh?"

One of the men, an older man, looked at Alec for a long time and held up his hand for the others to wait. He rubbed his chin and finally spoke, "Ferguson..."

I could hear a watch ticking, the room was that quiet.

"Can't be, but I know a man named Ferguson. You look a lot like him."

I had been taught to carefully guard our family history, but something made me reconsider. "Ian?" I finally asked. "Are you talking about Ian Ferguson?"

"That's the one," he said, curiosity obvious in his eyes.

"We're related," was all I admitted.

"I knew it the second you walked into the room." He turned to the others and waved his hand. He was clearly in charge.

"This is Ian Ferguson's son."

"Let me see your birth certificate, some form of identification. Show us something that proves who you are."

Alec had worried about this question. He reached into his wallet and handed over his baptismal record.

"It's all I have," he said.

"I knew your father in Seattle," said the man with silver hair and a scruff of beard in need of shaving.

Alec made his decision and handed over the letter of introduction from his father as well.

"That's him," the older man said after reading the letter. They all nodded in approval, and the woman picked up an embosser and stamped *APPROVED* on a booklet that looked like a passport. She pushed it across the table to me and smiled.

They asked me more questions about my motives for volunteering until they finally were satisfied they had more than fulfilled their duties. They couldn't afford to show favoritism.

"Before you leave, I have to ask," the younger man said, "You have a slight accent, almost American. Why enlist with us?"

I had grown up close to the border in Vermont and I knew the sound of my voice was a blend of Canadian and American accents, with a touch of Quebec French occasionally. People always heard what they wanted to hear, and Seth had assured me that my accent would pass muster.

When I didn't answer, the man across the table said, "It doesn't matter."

I could have easily slipped into a lie about my nationality. Instead, I told them how proud I would be to be a part of the Mac-Paps, the Canadian battalion that was an element of the famous Lincoln Brigade of volunteers.

"Good luck, comrade," the older man said, eyeing me with a knowing look.

Before I left the interview, I was given further instructions. In two weeks, I was to go to another address. There, my papers and travelling money would be provided.

"Talk to no one about this, comrade. It is getting very dangerous for us and for you."

I stood, and for some reason saluted as I thanked them, and then turned to open the door. Seth was waiting outside the door, a wide grin on his face. He was holding his beret in his hand, then placed it on his head and we saluted each other.

He realized I was not smiling and suddenly became very quiet. "Fuck man, didn't they...

I had him fooled until I broke into my grin, one that matched his.

"We're in," I said as we bounded down the stairs to the cheers of the other hopeful men waiting in line.

"No Pasarán," one shouted.

"No Pasarán," we shouted back in unison.

❋ ❋ ❋

"Doesn't it seem like it's taking forever," Seth said impatiently over a glass of beer. Two weeks had passed at the pace of a worm crawling through maple syrup. Now it was two weeks later, and we were sitting across the street from the address we had been given. We were early and sat enjoying a cold draught of beer while we waited and watched through the window.

"I know slugs that have moved faster," Seth snorted.

We looked at the clock and nodded. It was time. We finished our beer and walked across the street, showing our identification to the two men guarding the door.

"In there, comrade." One motioned over his shoulder and whispered his directions, while the other glanced carefully up and down the street.

"Clear," he finally decided. The door shut with authority.

"We're hearing rumors of a raid by Pinkerton's," he explained.

Seth and I walked through the door and into a small lobby, with the two men, acting as guards, following us. They stood quietly behind us until a buzzer sounded and another door opened.

"Good luck, comrades!" they said and left, their job finished.

Seth and I were inside a large room with a long counter and several rows of shelving behind. The man behind the counter was the same man at the interview, who had been curious about my relationship to my father, and he laughed at my startled recognition.

"Do the two of you do everything together?" He laughed until he started to cough. "No matter...friends and family, that's what matters. I knew Ian Ferguson had a son about your age. But, it's like I said—no matter. I was proud to work with your father. The two of us are too old to be out in the field now, eh?"

He pushed two cards across the counter, and as I picked up my cards, Seth did the same. I felt I had joined something larger than myself when I looked at the identity cards. The first one had my name and volunteer status. I had been accepted and assigned to the Mac-Paps, as I had requested.

The second card, printed in a mixture of English and Cyrillic lettering, was my membership card. I was now an official member of the Communist Party of Canada.

The man behind the counter placed a passport in front of me.

"It isn't official," he laughed, "but it is as good as a real one and will work just the same. We know—the RCMP has set up a new unit to look for forgeries, but these are still good enough to pass the test."

Finally, he gave us each a leather envelope. I opened mine and looked. Inside were money and tickets. The tickets would get us to New York by train and from there, passage on a boat to France.

The man saw me looking at the boat tickets. "It won't be a fancy cabin, comrades, but we make do, eh?"

On the street, we looked at each other and knew this was the last moment we could turn around and walk away, and yet, we both knew we could never do that.

✳ ✳ ✳

Michael turned off the recorder and suggested a stretch. "You were on your way to Spain. Was it difficult getting there?"

Alec chuckled, "If we only knew how tough it was going to be..." Alec shook his head. "Still, I would have gone even had I known. I have to tell you, I never expected to tell anyone this story. I never expected anyone to really give a damn."

Chapter 15
Harrison Sets a Trap at Montreal

It came to Harrison like a thunderclap. *Ferguson isn't in Montreal. He didn't stay there. How could I have made a mistake like this? What was I thinking?*

Harrison, in bed, forced his eyes open, quickly adjusting to the dimness of the room. Rubbing his forehead, he glanced at the woman on the floor. She lay curled in a ball with a sheet wrapped around her; she looked back at Harrison with blank eyes, not realizing how lucky she was to be alive. He wondered absently why she was still there.

He showed no further interest in her, closing the door behind him as he left. She was just one more woman who would not be reporting him to the police, appreciating the threat he projected with his eyes.

He never fully appreciated the reason for his choices in women—vulnerable women—all bearing a resemblance to his own mother. He only knew that once he was through with them, he discarded them like yesterday's news. They deserved their lesson, the same lesson his father had taught his own mother. It was a lesson Harrison had heard regularly, as he lay listening in his bed in the dark.

He had much more important things to think of as he walked briskly back to his hotel room, still reeking of the night's sexual encounter. Not bothering to shower, he went straight to the hotel restaurant, much to the dismay of his waiter.

"Man smells like a pig," he whispered knowingly to one of the other waiters.

Harrison was ravenous and angry as he waited for his breakfast. The two emotions often went together for him. He gulped back the hot, steaming coffee, black as usual. The waiter returned with two plates heaped with steak, potatoes and five eggs over easy, all on one plate. The other was piled with five pancakes oozing butter and syrup. It was not an unusual breakfast for the big man.

When he finished, he pushed back his chair and yelled for a newspaper. The waiter responded by rolling his eyes toward the ceiling and shrugging his shoulders. He brought two newspapers, one from Montreal and one from Toronto. "More coffee, sir?" his voice dripped with sarcasm.

Harrison held the waiter's eye until he saw the sarcasm slip away and nodded his yes, watching the waiter pour his coffee and retreat quickly to the kitchen.

If Ferguson isn't here in Montreal, where did he go? He picked up the Montreal newspaper. The front-page story reflected the unease in Europe. He didn't bother reading past the first page. He picked up the Toronto Star and straightened up. *That's where he went.* Harrison threw the paper down on the table, rattling the dishes; a water glass tipped and the liquid seeped into the tablecloth.

He ran into the lobby and didn't wait for the elevator, taking the stairs two steps at a time, up to his room on the fourth floor. He didn't notice the woman was gone. Instead, he grabbed the phone and shouted the number to the operator, "Give me granite 4344, and do it now!"

He saw his reflection, his reddening face in the mirror, blood pressure soaring, and he listened to the ring tones, waiting for someone to answer the phone.

"You know who I am," he said without any preliminaries. "Put me through to Johann."

He picked up the pen next to the phone and started writing a note until his call was answered.

"Listen, asshole. You blew it. You're wasting my time and he's making his escape. He's not in Montreal, I can feel it." His excitement was palpable.

"We need to leave a team here in Montreal, but we can concentrate some of our efforts in Toronto." The voice on the other end seemed slightly disinterested.

He held the phone out, squeezing his eyes tightly shut to keep from crushing the phone in his hand.

"Do you know who the *fuck* you are talking to?" he shouted. "This isn't a suggestion, fuck head. In fact, I want *you* to stay behind with your lame-ass team that missed him at the station!"

Harrison fumed, thinking about the detective that screwed up and was killed for his ineptness. *Still, he was one of ours,* he thought. That made it personal for Harrison.

"What you do now is telephone Toronto and make the arrangements to have an office ready for me when I get there. I need the best men they have, do you hear me? Make your call and then have a ticket waiting at my hotel desk when I check out, in..." looking at his watch, "exactly 58 minutes," and he slammed the phone down. *Dumb fuck,* he thought, as he headed for the shower.

As expected, his tickets for the next train to Toronto were waiting at the front desk. It was an express train with only a few stops. It would be a fast trip. He paid his hotel bill and hailed a taxi. It was a short ride to the station and his train was leaving soon.

At least I can spend the trip in the dining car, he thought, laughing at one of the rare light feelings he allowed himself.

He stepped off the train in Toronto, a redcap following with his luggage. He walked up the marble stairs to the street level, his footsteps echoing each anxious step. At the taxi queue, he was about to raise his hand for a cab.

"Mr. Harrison, sir?" It was a young man's voice.

Harrison turned, "Yes."

"Everything is arranged, your office is ready. My name's Wilson, Dave Wilson. There's an apartment on the floor above the office, nothing fancy, but it's furnished. You won't need a hotel." He paused, eyeing Harrison's luggage. "Here, let me get that," he said to the redcap, and placed Harrison's luggage in a waiting car.

"I know I look young," Wilson continued, "but I'm in charge of the Toronto office. I know your reputation. It will be an honor to have you with us, sir."

Hmmm, I already like the way they do things in Toronto, thought Harrison, as he ducked into the back seat of the waiting car. Wilson opened the passenger door to the front seat and nodded to the driver, who pulled smoothly into the traffic. As the car drove down Queen Street, jockeying over the streetcar tracks, they passed a group of men, factory workers probably, standing in line.

What a bunch of losers, he thought, as he looked at their threadbare clothes. *The depression has given us more of them than we can handle.*

Queen Street, he read on the street sign. Passing a door, he noticed a sign about some committee that was supporting Spanish democracy, whatever that was all about.

He checked his impatience as the car moved slowly in traffic. The driver expertly avoided an oncoming streetcar, turning corners twice, and finally stopped in front of the Pinkerton offices on King Street.

Harrison had to admire Wilson's style. The young man was sure of himself and crisp at directing other men, despite his youth. He personally led Harrison to the second-floor office where the luggage was dispatched efficiently to the floor above by some anonymous clerk.

Harrison took time to look around. Wilson had made sure Harrison had a window office overlooking the street. A streetcar rattled by and the brakeman seemed to enjoy ringing the bell. As Harrison watched, an arc of electricity jumped from the contact between the wire overhead and the arm reaching up from the car. The streetcar finally departed from his sight to his left.

"There is a box of my personal effects. It's clearly marked," Harrison said. "I need it right away."

"At once, sir," and Harrison heard young Wilson's footsteps hurrying up to the apartment above.

Again the 'sir'; don't overdo it boy.

When Wilson came back, he handed the box to Harrison, who opened it and started to set out his belongings. It wasn't much. Harrison didn't have a need to display his own self-importance. These were mostly the tools of his trade. He carefully arranged his notebooks and pens alongside the place where Wilson had left three carefully sharpened pencils and a brand new notepad.

The last items he lifted out of the box were a photograph and small booklet, the only personal keepsakes he carried with him.

Was it only last year?

※ ※ ※

The previous summer, Pinkerton's had sent Harrison abroad on a fact-finding mission to study police methods. On his visit to London, he had expected to be impressed with Scotland Yard, and he was.

The true goal of his trip, however, wasn't Scotland Yard and the obsequious detective who gave him a tour of the premises. His real reason for coming was a side trip to Berlin. He had been asked to take a look at police methods in the new Germany. He'd been told the agency was interested in recent developments in Europe, and he found Germany ablaze with color; flags and banners the color of blood, with spidery symbols in black on white.

He observed children with milky complexions and rosy cheeks. He watched the German people walk with a certain assuredness that impressed him. It was their pride at being German that awed him the most.

People kept asking, "Have you seen *him*, you know, *Hitler*?" It was a question he always seemed to be asked by voices filled with reverence.

At the end of his week's stay in Berlin, Harrison was invited to a reception. It was a gala affair in a room that seemed painted in gold, and the walls reflected the lights from huge chandeliers overhead. Magnificent wall hangings and paintings hung in every direction he looked. He was dazzled by the myriad of uniforms of all colors, mostly black, replete with medals and insignias. The men all seemed to love raising their right arms in salute to each other at every opportunity. Some women even joined in the saluting.

He was so taken by the uniforms, in fact, that he later wrote a report about them. When he returned to the United States, he recommended the agency consider adopting uniforms and a form a private militia.

"Interesting," someone had laughed after reading it, "but, no way."

Toward the end of the reception, Harrison was led into a small, private room. Sitting casually on a bench was a man with his arms crossed, peering intently at Harrison through rimless glasses, projecting a look of total insouciance. The man's uniform was austere, but Harrison recognized the man immediately. It wasn't difficult; the man's photograph was plastered in every police station in Germany: Reichsfuhrer Heinrich Himmler, the head of Germany's police and security forces. Harrison had been told this man was very close to Herr Hitler himself.

Himmler held a cigarette holder in his hand and languidly waved smoke away. He stared at Harrison intently through his rimless glass until he looked as if he had made some sort of a decision.

"Germany is always pleased to welcome your agency's representatives. I trust your visit has been, um, informative." It wasn't a question.

Harrison feared few men, but his instincts all warned him to be careful with a man of such bovious power, a man to be reckoned with.

Himmler suddenly stood up, and with his cigarette holder dangling from between his lips, put a hand on each of Harrison's shoulders. "I have a personal favor to ask of you," he said, looking directly into the detective's eyes.

"When I leave, please listen to what this man," his head gestured to his right, "has to tell you." With that, he strode to the door and was gone.

The other men in the room, watching the departing back, were all standing in starchy poses, their right arms sticking high into the air in the popular salute.

Harrison looked down at the photograph of Heinrich Himmler, remembering that night with a smile. He admired Himmler's autograph. Someone handed him the signed photograph as he had boarded a flight back to London.

Next to the framed photograph, he placed a small booklet on the desk. He glanced at it but didn't have to open it. He had it memorized and knew what it contained. He mostly agreed with the race policies outlined in the booklet, but he was most interested in the German police policies toward the Communists and Laborists.

He thought back again to Germany and the night of that reception.

"We've noticed your work," an aide to Himmler said with a silky smoothness after the Reichsfuhrer had left.

Harrison didn't respond, but waited for more.

"We are quite interested in certain people from your country, people who share, how would you say it...our beliefs." The words were hanging over the two men as he added, "We have supported the forming of a Nazi party there. It is called the German-American Bund."

Harrison realized he wasn't expected to speak and simply waited for the man to continue.

"We have a leader identified, Fritz Kuhn. Do you know him?"

Harrison nodded yes; he knew the man.

"We want you to be his deputy. We can't officially recognize him, of course. Certain international issues are at stake. He is an ass, to be sure. We are asking you to be the real person to get things done; we want you to be the true force behind the American Nazi Party."

✳ ✳ ✳

That was some night, he thought now, sitting at his desk in Toronto. Harrison smiled to himself. His career with Pinkerton's was secure and his secret job with the *Bund* filled him with pride. He had wondered if it might even help him catch his nemesis, Ian Ferguson, somehow. *The Germans hate the fucking commies even more than I do.*

Now in Toronto, he picked up the phone, "I want our team together in one hour." He hung up without waiting for any response.

With the team assembled in the outer office an hour later, Harrison gestured for Wilson to bring out a special photograph he had requested. It was a three-foot tall photograph of Ian Ferguson.

"Great work, Wilson," he praised, looking at the photograph propped against an easel. It was rare praise indeed, coming from Harrison.

Using a pencil, he pointed to the oversized photograph. "This is the man. Each of you will carry a pocket-sized photograph of him at all times, on duty and off. In fact, there is no such thing as being off duty until we catch this Commie bastard."

"And if we see him?"

"I want him," was all Harrison said. They nodded their heads in understanding.

Wilson followed Harrison. "I have given each man a direct assignment.

"Good. We go all-out until this is over, understood? We are sending some men to Hamilton, just in case he has joined the agitators there."

"It has already been arranged," Wilson calmly replied.

"But," Harrison said thoughtfully, "there is a place..." he said, waiting for their full attention. "If he is thinking about going to Spain, we need to watch one particular location very closely."

"Spain?" was the puzzled reply.

"It's the latest cause for a man like Ferguson, and I noticed a sign on the other street. It was something about Democracy in Spain. What do you know about it?"

"We've been watching them."

"Well," Harrison snorted, "watch even more closely."

One team was given a special assignment to watch the offices of the Committee to Support Spanish Democracy.

I knew there was something about that sign, Harrison thought.

"Wilson."

"Sir."

"Good job. Now, I want good men for that Hamilton assignment." Harrison walked over to a window, his hands clasped together behind his back.

"This guy Ferguson is in Toronto, I can feel it. But I'm glad you are sending someone to Hamilton. It's not far, and where workers are organizing, you can just bet you might find Ferguson. It's the kind of thing he specializes in. It won't be obvious; this man works best in dark shadows."

Harrison watched as the team of men picked up their folders and transferred the photographs to their pockets. *Yes,* he thought, *Wilson has done a good job, but this Ferguson guy is slippery.*

But this time, we are setting the trap!

Harrison *thought* the trap was set. Although he was sure of it, he still harbored an uneasy feeling. He focused his memory back on the drive past that Spanish Committee sign. Had he recognized one of the men walking out of the door as the car passed the committee office?

Could it have been him? he wondered.

Harrison had long ago learned that many cases were solved by small hints and clues that seemed to lie just outside human consciousness. Were these senses alerting him?

He watched his men as they took up their stations across the street from the committee offices, each holding a photograph of Ian Ferguson. Each man was determined to be the one not to disappoint the new, very large man in charge.

"As soon as you see him, we make our move," Harrison told the group of men now assembled around the corner. Most were carrying axe handles, the preferred beating tool for knocking heads. "I want this guy."

Chapter 16
Travel Plans

Seth and I were warned not to go back to the committee office. After picking up our documents at the warehouse several blocks away, we were told to go back to our room, gather our belongings, and head straight away to the train station.

"We're really going," I said excitedly. I kept looking down at the leather envelope in Seth's hand.

"It's going to be easy," Seth answered with his usual optimism. "They have taken care of everything, eh?"

We were both quiet as we walked to a nearby streetcar stop, each with our own thoughts mulling through our heads. We sat on a retaining wall and resisted the urge to reopen the envelopes in public.

"My big worry is the U.S. border crossing at Niagara Falls. I hear they are stopping men our age from entering the country, afraid we will take away one of their precious jobs. What if they find out my real identity, that I'm an American?" I asked.

"Same thing on both sides of the border," Seth added.

"What the hell," I said, "let's get a beer and celebrate. We can worry on the way."

We walked across the street. The tavern was a dingy place, but the beer was cold and there was an empty table away from curious eyes.

"Gents," the barkeep said in a booming voice. "What'll it be?"

"How about two cold beers and some privacy," Seth said without sarcasm.

"Look around," the barkeep laughed as he waved his arm around, "an empty bar and a half-blind barkeep who can't hear much," he chuckled amiably as he started drawing our draughts.

"Take that table back in the corner and I'll bring these over."

Seated at the table, we didn't say much, if anything. We each opened our respective wallets, laying the contents on the table. There was the money. It wasn't a lot, but it was more cash than either of us had seen all at one time. For some reason I could never explain, I kept the money my father had given me a secret from Seth.

We examined our train tickets from Toronto to Niagara Falls. There was a note instructing us to get off the train in Niagara Falls and walk south to another bridge crossing into the United States.

Closing my eyes for a moment, I imagined the water cascading over the falls, roaring and thunderous in my ears. Once across the bridge, we would be questioned. When we were through the border-crossing kiosk, we had to walk to the train station on the New York side. We were to use the additional tickets to take the train into New York City.

It sounded straightforward enough.

We covered the contents of our packages as the barkeep walked over to set our mugs on the table. He picked up the money and walked away without even a flicker of curiosity.

"I wonder what this rusty bucket is like," Seth said, looking at their boat tickets. "It's not a name I ever heard of."

"Don't much care as long as it gets me there," I replied.

Once again, we reread our instructions for crossing into the United States. We read about the boat that would take us across the ocean to France, and from there, we would cross over into Spain.

We were told to memorize the instructions and then get rid of them. The barkeep didn't notice—or more likely didn't care about—the small flame Seth put to our instructions, holding the paper by a corner until the flame gradually consumed the entire piece. Seth shook his fingers at the heat and dropped the curling paper into an ashtray, until the dish contained nothing but ashes and a small curl of smoke rising above.

I held up my fake passport to examine it. "These passports sure look real to me."

"Let's hope they look real to the border guards," Seth laughed. I noticed it was an uneasy laugh, and it made me cringe inwardly to hear it coming from the man who was always so sure of himself.

We looked at our two party cards, one in English and the other in Cyrillic. Seth started to softly hum *The Internationale.* To our surprise, the barkeep began to whistle the melody along with Seth. He yelled over from the bar, "Sorry boys, can't afford a jukebox," began to laugh, and turned away to wipe down some more glasses behind the counter.

The door opened, bright sunlight spilling into the bar. Seth and I quickly scooped up our documents and stuffed them back into the leather pouches. We couldn't see the man who was standing in the doorway, sunlight directly behind him turning his face into a mass of shadows.

I was on edge as the man walked quickly to our table.

"What the fuck," Seth said as the man sat next to him. "Who are-"

The man held up a hand. "Relax comrade, I'm a friend. We had someone following you. It's now standard practice to make sure no one is trailing you. Sorry, we do it for everyone until they are on their way. We took extra care for the son of Ian Ferguson," he said, looking directly at me. "And the same goes for the son of Rudi," turning his attention to Seth.

We relaxed some but were still wary. What if this man weren't a friend?

Another burst of bright sunlight came as a second man walked in and quickly moved back to our table. He was carrying our two backpacks and two suitcases. He placed them on a table next to us, turned and left without a word.

"That's our stuff," Seth said, a little piqued.

"Change of plans," the stranger said. "We have someone on the inside at the Pinkerton's agency. They have a new special man in charge, Samuel T. Harrison. We think he is starting to put everything together. It won't be long until he realizes it's you and not your father."

"What are you talking about?" I asked, confused.

"Near as we can tell, Harrison is convinced it's Ian he's trailing. Some guy on the train from Magog to Montreal, one of their stringers, was hoping to claim the reward on your father's head. Only thing is, it was you he saw and not your father. He was killed for that mistake."

I sat quietly for a moment, digesting this information.

"I still don't get it," I said. The stranger looked pointedly at Seth, obviously waiting for him to speak up.

I noticed a funny look on Seth's face: discomfort.

"I couldn't tell you the whole story before," Seth said, "I wanted to tell you, but I had my orders. Our fathers had it all arranged. We had someone watching your back the whole way here." He looked down somewhat guiltily at his beer before he went on. "We realized that man in Magog, mistaking you for your father, had arranged to make an arrest at the Montreal station."

I sat in silence, stunned.

"That gun you have in your pack," the stranger said, "yes— I know you have it."

I held up a hand in useless protest.

"The man from Magog was a Pinkerton man, small time to be sure. That was his gun. Harrison has a personal vendetta against your father, Ian. A big old hard-on for him, it seems. It goes way back to when he took charge of an investigation and Ian slipped the net."

Suddenly, some of the events of the past few weeks seemed clearer to me. It was no accident I ended up with Seth, and I felt an unfamiliar urge to hit something, to get angry. So much had been decided for me without my knowledge. I felt like a puppet.

"Now, Harrison is starting to ask questions. He's noticed the difference in age, but I'm not convinced he's put it all together—yet. It won't be long until he makes the connection and knows it's Ian's son he is after. When that happens, it will be damned dangerous for you. You two have to move quickly."

The stranger flicked an anxious glance towards the door. "Right now, they're getting ready to raid the committee office. It's miles away, to be sure, but..." he trailed off, leaving the implication hanging to dangle in the air like a noose.

He explained the change in plans. "Harrison has ordered all the crossings at Niagara Falls and Buffalo covered. He has sent extra teams to scour the docks in New York."

"Take this," he handed over some additional money.

"You have to leave at once. Get to Galveston any way you can. Take the money and buy tickets to Windsor. Travel separately, and when you get to Windsor, walk over to Detroit. They aren't as worried about that crossing and don't watch it as closely. It just might work. Here's an address in Windsor for you to contact."

"Galveston?" Seth and I asked in unison.

The stranger didn't say anything more and stood up, nodding to the barkeep. The man behind the bar smiled and nodded back.

On his way out, the man leaned over to say something to the bartender. The man behind the bar laughed and waved him on.

We got up from the table, our nerves as taught as garroting wire. We picked up our kits and headed into the sunlight, careful to look both ways before we started walking.

"No Pasarán," the barkeep said, as we walked past him to leave. We nodded in understanding, no longer surprised at the silent network of believers that surrounded us in our journey.

Before we could pass through the door, the barkeep called to us and gave us a final suggestion. "Take the streetcar and bus to Port Credit. They might not be watching that station so closely. Wait and buy your train tickets there," and then he went back to wiping the grimy glasses on his apron, as though we had never even walked through the door.

❊ ❊ ❊

I was angry and seething. On the train to Windsor, I refused at first to talk to my friend. Finally, I started to relent. It wasn't his fault, really, that he had been forced to withhold details from me. I knew that party discipline had been imposed in this matter. Soon, as the train was racing at full speed, we were back talking, locked in our didactic debates and re-cementing our bond.

When we dismounted the train at the Windsor station, no one seemed to pay any attention to the two of us, even though we had ignored the advice against travelling together.

I could see a magnificent bridge in the twilight to the north as we walked to the address in Windsor the stranger had given us. There, a young girl answered the door. She was nine, perhaps ten.

"Follow me," she said without further comment and led us between the houses to a lane in back. She held up her hand for us to be quiet as we followed her through an adjoining yard to a truck waiting under a streetlight. Without a word, she turned and walked back into the darkness.

"Hop in brothers," a man behind the wheel said, startling us. "No, not the front," and thumbed to the truck bed behind.

He got out and showed us where to squat down and sit behind several large crates. We had to pull our knees up to our chins and I knew it would soon be uncomfortable as hell.

We felt the truck lurch into gear, surprising for an old truck. Indeed, it was an ancient truck and if there was any suspension left, it had long passed beyond usefulness.

We listened as the truck wheeled into a tunnel. "This here's the tunnel under the Detroit River," he yelled back. "My daddy worked on this here tunnel when it was built." The driver had to shout to be heard above the wind racing by as he sped through the night. "It's about seven years old now. I hear it's the only tunnel in the world between two countries."

When we realized we had reached the American side of the river, we unconsciously held our breaths. But the driver seemed to be a well-known fixture at this border crossing. We heard a muffled conversation and a laugh, and once more, the truck was in gear and moving.

The driver drove for maybe ten minutes more and pulled through a gate and into a huge rail yard. At his insistence, we got out and pulled back a section of another chain-link fence so he could drive into the darkened rail lot.

We jumped back on the running board, Seth on the passenger side and me on the driver's side. We followed a road for several more yards, maybe a quarter of a mile at most, when the driver yelled at us to jump.

"You guys are on your own now," he nodded, as the truck coughed and roared into the inky darkness away from us.

Standing in the Detroit rail yards, we considered our destination.

"Galveston," Seth said. "How the fuck...?"

It may as well have been the far side of the moon they had asked us to find. But, the depression was a time when rail yards were train stations for men like us. We called ourselves Depressionists—we were men who had learned well a new way to travel. We 'rode the rail' using empty boxcars for passage.

"Over here brothers," someone yelled from the dark. It seemed it was going to be a night for people jumping out of shadows.

It was a summer night, but we could see them huddled around a fire barrel as the temperature was taking an unexpected plunge, unusual for this time of the year. We huddled together, warming our hands over the fire, then turning to warm our backsides.

We asked some questions and worked out our plans on how to get to Galveston. Spain seemed like an unreachable goal. But, we were determined, and if it had to be Galveston, then Galveston it would be. Neither one of us seemed to ask how the hell traveling to Galveston got us any closer to our ultimate goal. We just followed directions and trusted to the party, the powers that be.

"This here is what you need to do," someone told us.

Chapter 17
Oklahoma Dust

I can close my eyes and still remember the day I arrived in Sweetwater. I didn't know until someone told me, that I was in Oklahoma. I just knew it was hotter than sin. It was unlike anything I had ever seen before. As I looked out at the passing dry, dusty countryside, it seemed to me Oklahoma was desolate and God-forsaken.

Seth and I had barely made it out of Detroit that night. We realized we couldn't travel together any longer. They were looking for two men like us, travelling together. It was a reluctant decision for us both. He jumped a train heading south, and mine was headed west through Chicago.

Peering out at the bleak landscape, I lost my balance and let out a soft "damn," feeling my backside scraping against the sandpaper-rough wood siding. The boxcar rattled underfoot; it gave a sudden lurch as the train rounded a curve. I felt the swaying ease as the train slowed.

How long has it been since Detroit? I was losing all track of time and I missed Seth. Still, we both knew we made a larger target traveling as a pair.

I felt like I was in a furnace. I braced myself in the open door and looked up, watching dark clouds gathering against the afternoon sun.

There's Heaven, the thought of my mother's voice echoing in my mind.

Heaven, my ass, I thought, *unless heaven is somewhere over West Oklahoma. How many more days to Galveston? All I can see is sagebrush and sand. Damned close to Hell is more like it.*

The only difference between Hell and Texas, I had heard somewhere, was Oklahoma.

I knew Seth had to—just *had* to—get to Galveston, and I prayed we both made it.

I tugged on my sweaty shirt, trying to pull it away from my body, gauged the moment, and pitched my kit out first. I can still see it turning over and over in the air and tumbling over the sand, all my worldly possessions rolling down the embankment.

I hesitated until I spotted a soft-looking ridge of sand, then jumped. I felt needle-like pain over my body. I rolled, quickly brushing away hot coals spewed out by the engine. Willing the pain away, I focused my thoughts on a spring-fed stream somewhere in Vermont until my heart returned to its normal beat.

I heard a curious ringing in my ears and soothing words telling me everything would be just fine. *Where is that coming from?* I wondered, and suspected my hunger and loneliness were playing tricks on me.

Grabbing my kit, I checked to make sure the gun was still there, sprinted past mesquite bushes, over a small rise, and ran deep into a copse of cottonwood trees.

That was when I heard a man shout.

"I knowed I saw him, there he goes. Hurry up, dammit, we'll never find him if he gets in those trees."

"Wh...wha...wha'd he look like?" a second man wheezed.

"Damn, this chasin' sure don't get any easier."

I hunkered down and smiled as I heard them sucking for breath, winded from running in the baking 107 degree heat.

"Blue shirt, tan pants, medium tall and dark hair. Looks just like all those other bums we chase off."

I sure as hell flinched when one pulled a pistol and fired in the air.

"They musta' heard that back at the depot. We can say we took a shot at him."

The other one said, "Chet has some coolies on ice, let's get out of the sun and get us a beer. No use now, this'n's gone for sure."

I heard their footsteps through the underbrush and gravel, retreating toward what served as a town. I carefully stood up and glanced around. No, this was more of a junction than what might have once been a town.

They weren't locals, I knew, recognizing their accents. I had heard the railroads recruited guards from the dismal intestines of cities like Chicago and Pittsburgh. *Thugs*, was more like it. *Probably stupid Pinkerton's men*, I remember thinking.

My 'free' ride from Tulsa is behind, Galveston and the rest of my life stretching ahead. Don't know exactly where I am, but it sure isn't Vermont. I pushed the melancholy thought away. The two guards were nowhere in sight when I started walking.

How many nights lately had I sat around a fire, sharing rations with other bums like me? We had a lot in common—despair and little hope. Lots of rootless men sat around small fires in those times, and our conversation covered politics, philosophy, food and railroad schedules, all things that were truly important in this kind of life.

When it was my turn to talk, I told them my story using few words. I told them about the war in Spain, how I had to go. Some nodded in understanding, but most were too hungry or fearful to know or care about what was happening in a place so far away.

"My brother is there," a man said one night. The night sky was filled with stars.

"Yep, I have a cousin who went over there, too. He sure as hell ain't coming back from there," said another with a bitter sadness in his voice. "Just a letter saying he was dead."

There was a strong quiet as grown men tried to figure out what to say and in the end, decided to say nothing at all.

"I have to get to Galveston," I said. "I'm meeting a ship there. There's a lot more than me going," I said, thinking of Seth. I had been advised not to talk about any of this in case there were infiltrators from Pinkerton's or the government hanging around. But, I remember looking around; the ones who weren't showing a face of despair were wearing masks of false hope. These were the men the world didn't want to see and tried to forget. There wasn't a Pinkerton's man alive who would play a role in this kind of life.

As the fire was dying, one man pulled me aside and told me about a train to Sweetwater.

"Tomorrow, get up early and take the early train and lay-over there overnight, then, jump the southbound," the man said, "Takes you straight into Galveston. It stops right near the docks."

Now in Sweetwater, smelling the lingering train scent mixing with the mesquite, I rubbed a headache and stretched out on my back between two fallen trees. The guards reappeared in front of me, walking up a gradual slope from a dry streambed. I ducked under some cover and watched the guards walking away until they blended into unimportance. Turning over to ease contact with sand that felt soft and hot, I patted a shirt pocket. *What the hell*, I thought, withdrawing a cigarette.

I struck a match, shielding the flame with cupped hands, and felt a rush of nicotine. A pungent whiff of disinfectant mingled with mesquite as I tried to shake my head clear. I admit that I took pleasure in the heady sensation and watched the clouds transforming overhead. The sky, just moments before, had seemed filled with a promise of rain. Now, I watched the clouds break apart and scatter.

"Politicians calling this here a dust bowl," a man said to me.

It sure looked to me like an accurate description. I rolled on my side to spit and watched dust rising in a puff. The only other place I ever saw that happen, was on a dusty hill in Spain. But, that gets ahead of my story.

Standing again, I picked up my kit, looked around, and started toward town.

*What a God-forsaken...*I hesitated in my thoughts. *No, God didn't forsake Sweetwater, he just doesn't even know the place exists.*

I saw a faded sign ahead; crude lettering welcomed me to Sweetwater, saying it was "the best little city in Oklahoma." I smiled. If this was the best, I'd hate to see the worst. No one bothered to change the population on the sign. Some joker had chalked on a number, long faded, and then crossed it out with a large *X*.

I walked into the dusty cow town on its one and only street. The real street corner was the meeting of two intersecting rail lines south of town. There wasn't even a railroad building at the intersection, just a watering tank with a long spout like an elephant's trunk, outlined against the sky.

As I walked, I spotted a pair of rusted trucks and two dust-covered cars, vehicles that hadn't moved in ages. There were three, maybe four people. They all seemed to walk in slow motion. They came out of a dilapidated-looking dry goods store and walked to what I guessed passed for a barbershop.

Patting some coins wedged into my watch pocket, I squeezed out two quarters and turned toward the sign for the Sweetwater Saloon. It promised beer on ice.

Maybe I can get a job for sleep 'n eats, I wondered, wishing Seth hadn't taken most of our money. What money I carried had been frittered away on something 'frivolous': food.

I pushed through a swinging door and paused, reacting to the sharp contrast between the room and the glare of the late afternoon sunlight. This place felt and looked dusty to me. I peered into the duskiness and waited for my squinting eyes to adjust. I tensed at the two men sitting at a table, wearing uniforms of railroad cops. Would they guess? *Found their iced beer,* I thought.

They didn't pay any attention to me as I walked up to the bar. The bartender stood behind the counter, wiping his hands on a dingy apron. A grimy mirror stretched behind the bar looking like it hadn't been cleaned in twenty years. An assortment of half-empty bottles stood lonely vigil over uneven shelves.

I blinked and thought, *this could just as easily be a bar back in Toronto. How long ago has that been now?*

To my left, a young woman sat at the end of the bar. I remember thinking, *She looks like a fixture; some interior decorator must have designed her to fit in with this place.*

I looked at her plain dress. *Lucky to have one,* I thought. *I bet she only has one and has to wash it every night and wear it the next day.* I knew no one would be unkind and mention a little patchwork here and there. Her hair was done up in no particular style. A half-empty glass of unidentifiable liquid rested in her hand.

I looked at the man behind the bar.

"You must be Chet. How about a coolie? Make it a cold one." I had been told that if you wanted a beer in Oklahoma, you ordered a 'coolie' in these parts.

"Right up," the bartender said, lowering his voice beyond the hearing of the guards.

"Don't recall you hereabouts, and I never forget a face. Nope, I never laid eyes on ya 'til this-here time. An' ever-one in these parts knows a coolie is a cold one."

I had long ago learned that the men who worked behind bars were men who were close with secrets. I decided to trust this man, a little at least.

"Name's Alec," I said. "I heard a man named Chet had some beer on ice. Saw your sign." I shrugged nonchalantly as I stared him in the eye.

I watched the glimmer of a smile form as Chet looked over at the sweating railroad guards. "Don't want to drink with those two, huh?"

I watched the bartender size me up, and without waiting for me to ask, he leaned over and said in a private voice, "I could use someone to clean up tonight," his calloused hands placing a bottle on the bar. "Hot meal and a bed in it fer ya."

Keeping his voice lowered past the hearing of the guards. "First train's outta here at seven," he nodded. "Before them assholes even think 'bout wakin' up. I'll knock on yer door early enough. You can be on your way."

I nodded back and watched as the bottle in front of me gathered condensation, water drops challenging the heat. A fan turned tedious circles overhead.

Yes, I thought, *that will be just fine.*

"I could use the bed and I'm not afraid of some work," I replied.

"Who's the dame?" I asked after a moment, swiftly downing a cold swallow of beer. "Related?"

I saw the bartender shrug.

"No, not related, and her name's Lily. She just showed up one day and can't seem to leave. A lot of people just run out of money and energy in unlikely places."

Drawing the cold bottle across my brow like a military salute, I turned to her, "What kind of a name is Lily?"

With an inscrutable smile she answered, "Pa wrote it in the Bible when I was born. Ma named me Lanette, but Pa said I was pretty as a lily, I was his Lily."

When she asked, I told her my name.

"Where'd you get the name Alec?"

Alec smiled back, "Fair enough. I've been on the road a long time, and it's longer still since I saw the folks who named me. Never thought to ask 'em what deep meaning it had for them."

The guards were walking with an unsteady gait when they left. Several empty bottles of beer littered their table. I didn't wait to be asked and moved to clean up. There wasn't much to do, but I cleaned until Chet raised a hand.

"There's some chili in a pot out back. I think the three of us can enjoy some fine dining," and laughed at his own joke.

We ate mostly in silence. It was impolite to ask probing questions in places like Sweetwater, Oklahoma in 1937, questions about where from and where bound.

Not much more was spoken between me and Lily, or even needed to be. The clock behind the bar had turned to half-past eight when Chet turned and started to rewind the clock's spring. With an understanding as old as humanity, I finally stood up and offered Lily my hand and we walked together up the stairs. I looked back and Chet looked at me for a moment, then turned to move some bottles. I wondered how much he cared about Lily, knowing this was the only survival skill she had left.

She helped me into a tub. It was one of those large porcelain ones with four claws—you know, four feet—one on each corner. Then, with a unique but reassuring dissonance, she told me to be careful and helped me in.

I leaned back and fancied my soaking in the tub. I enjoyed the soaking almost as much as the anticipation of the pleasure of a soft woman. I rested my head back on the tub's edge. My last cigarette had nearly burned away; it draped from my mouth, and a long ash fell with a *plosh* into the water.

"Heard there's a war," I said languidly to Lily. I was having a hard time keeping my eyes open. "I need to get there, to Spain, that is. People are afraid to help, to take sides. As always, it's some little guy who's really up against it. Me, I can't run away from it."

I told her about Seth and worried about the telling. I had been warned. I don't know why I was telling her all this.

I was tired when I said, "I have to catch a boat in Galveston a few days from now. It's hard to think about killing someone, pointing a gun...but I have to go."

Later that night, I dreamed and imagined pain, nurses and death. I had a disturbing image of the old fortuneteller. Night images exploded like kaleidoscope patterns until some internal alarm sounded, and Chet's soft voice was at the door. "Seven o'clock train. It's on schedule."

Slipping quietly from bed, I pretended I didn't hear Lily crying. I pretended I didn't hear her quiet, "See ya, Alec."

Even at sunrise, it was already beastly hot as I raced toward the southbound train. It had slowed at the crossing of the two lines and was now picking up speed again. If only it had stopped, but it had only slowed at the crossroad. *Damn, it's not going to stop. It's barely slowing*, I thought and started to sprint.

I ran faster until I could reach up for a grip. That was when the dust storm hit. I remember making a desperate lunge as a fierce blast of hot air and dust battered my eyes. I made it, however. I was on my way to Galveston and stayed in the empty car through many short starts and stops, until I felt the train make its final stop, recognizing the noises of a busy rail yard.

I pulled the door back open slightly and peered out between the slit it created. I didn't see anyone, but I saw the sign indicating I was deep in the crowded yard of Port Galveston. Gantries were swinging overhead, some swinging cradles of cargo from shore to ship, some swinging their cargo from ships to waiting arms on the dock. Train cars were slamming together as my train was finally shuttled to another track in the yard. I looked out and saw that my car was hidden from view, and I could hear no sounds of activity nearby. I jumped from the car and scurried along a weedy fence until I spotted an opening. I ducked through some broken links and started down an un-paved lane. When I was well away from the yard, I walked up to a man standing at a bus stop.

"Know where Digger's Bar is?" I asked. It was our agreed-upon meeting place, the place Seth and I had been told about. I could only hope we would both make it to Digger's. Someone had told Seth about it back in Detroit, and it had sounded like the perfect place to meet.

Here in Galveston, I could tell my question made the black man uneasy; he was evidently not used to white people talking to him. I had heard about such things. Jim Crow was alive and well here in the South. I watched him thinking about it for a moment, and then he nodded and pointed, "its near half a mile, that-a-way, suh."

He seemed to be genuinely surprised at my thank-you, as I turned and started to walk.

Digger's, no surprise, turned out to be yet another work-ing man's bar and was crowded with longshoremen and rail yard workers. *Not much different from bars for working men anywhere*, I thought.

It held a welcome familiarity for me, and I wasn't sur-prised at the noise of men shouting beer orders and arguing politics, all in equally loud voices.

I jumped when someone tapped my shoulder, "I thought you would never make it. What kept you?" and I turned and embraced Seth, to his embarrassment.

"Our ocean liner awaits m'lord." Seth bowed low and couldn't stop laughing. "We are travelling first class and I can't wait until you see it, or should I say *her*? She ain't no dame, that's for sure, but she's a pretty site for these eyes." Seth tried his best to imitate a Texan's drawl.

✳ ✳ ✳

Michael turned off the recorder.

"I have an idea," Alec said, "All this talk about cold beer is getting to me. What do you say to us going into town for dinner and beers?"

Walking to the car, Michael turned and smiled, "I know just the place."

Chapter 18
Harrison's Fast Plane from Toronto to Galveston

Harrison was furious and seething. Seated in the back seat of the new De Soto Touring Sedan, he was glaring at the back of the driver's head, urging him to hurry. The car had a Pinkerton's sign painted on the doors. It was brand new and hummed quietly over asphalt pavement, until they reached a gravel construction road and passed a sign for the new Malton Airport.

Harrison thought back. He had been in the office in Toronto when the teletype started clicking, an alarm bell clanging to indicate an urgent message being sent. It was from the New York office. Harrison had stood by the machine, and in his impatience, pulled the yellow ticker tape through his fingers as it was coming in.

Galveston? What the fuck? He ripped the rest of the message tape from the machine and read further, getting angrier by the moment.

Urgent to Det. Harrison/stop/Ferguson sited/stop/Galveston, Texas/stop

He continued pulling the ticker tape and read further

Two men seen waiting to board ship/stop/further information coming/stop

He bristled as he read the final words:
Aircraft chartered/stop/Malton airfield/stop/Your immediate departure ordered/stop

Harrison resented the imperious tone of the words and was furious he had missed Ian Ferguson in Toronto. *What the fuck did they think I was doing, sitting on my ass?*

He was confronted with an awful reality: Why was someone at headquarters now questioning his ability? Catching Ian Ferguson should have been an easy task. He knew his first mistake was leaving it to someone in the field at the beginning, instead of immediately going to Montreal himself to take personal charge of the apprehension. He alone realized just how dangerous and clever those Haymarket Rioters were, especially Ian Ferguson.

He replayed the phone call in his mind as he neared the airport.

"I almost had them in Toronto," he had said into the phone earlier, realizing how lame it sounded.

"Almost...isn't, well...good enough," came the reply from his superior. Harrison was stinging when he returned the phone to the cradle. It had been weeks since the last sighting here in Toronto. Too long.

How did they get away? And...Galveston? The last place I would have imagined.

Refocusing now, he looked over the shoulder of the driver ahead and watched the gravel road spinning past the headlights, until the car slowed, and they turned into a large, grassy field. A freshly painted sign declared this was the home of the new airfield for Toronto, due for completion in 1939.

There were signs of construction, and dump trucks were hauling large loads of crushed rock. To the side of the construction area, there was a crude set of runways and perhaps two dozen assorted planes. One of these was sitting on the grass, separated from the rest, and a man waved Harrison's car to a stop.

"Are you Harrison?" he asked, as he leaned in the rolled-down window.

Harrison held back a nasty retort and simply nodded, exiting the car. He looked at the sleek-looking plane awaiting him.

"It's a Lockheed Vega 5-C," the pilot said, holding open the door under the wings, just behind the struts. "It's the latest model and extremely fast."

"Our only worry is the weather," the man explained as he signaled to the co-pilot, and the motor immediately began an impatient whine as the propeller turned slowly. Then, with a hitch, it started spinning faster, until it reached a deep-throated roar. The blades of the propeller were soon turning so fast they were individually invisible to the naked eye, forming a solid blur.

"Sit back and enjoy the flight," the pilot said. "We will be cruising at a hundred sixty-five knots, but we'll get up to one-eighty-five if we have to." He made his way through a narrow door to his seat in the cockpit.

"We have to," Harrison yelled up to him. "We have to get it up to one-eighty-five. You have no idea how important this is." The pilot turned away from the dials and nodded back to his only passenger.

Harrison settled back in the leather seat and fastened his lap and shoulder harness. He waved away the offer of a thermos of coffee, as the co-pilot made sure the boarding door was closed, and returned to his seat in the front of the plane.

The engine roared with promise as they bumped over the grass until they were poised at the end of a runway. The pilot spun the plane into the wind and started down the runway. As it neared lift-off speed, it started to bounce, once and then twice. With the final bounce, they were airborne. Climbing at 1,330 feet per minute, they reached cruising altitude in just under twelve minutes, according to Harrison's watch. He felt the plane make a shallow bank and turn toward the southwest, and Harrison knew all he could do now was pass the time.

He suddenly started to grin as he thought about Galveston. *This time, they don't know that Samuel T. Harrison is on the way.*

"We should make it on one tank. But, we have an extra tank for the trip just in case," the pilot came back and was leaning down to yell in Harrison's ear over the engine. "I figure it's just a bit less than a thousand miles as the crow flies..." he looked down at his watch, "10:42 now, we should be there by... let's see...maybe six hours, give or take." He seemed sure now, "Take away an hour for Texas time, we should be landing at 3:47 local time."

"If that's the case, I don't think we have to push to one-eighty-five then. I'll take that coffee now," Harrison said with a smirk, remembering there was serious labor unrest in Galveston, too. *Ought to be some heads to break. I could use some recreation after I make this arrest.*

The plane flew at an economical one hundred sixty-five knots, cruising at just under 15,000 feet. The sky was clear, and soon Harrison glanced out the window to watch the Mississippi sliding under the Lockheed Vega. He looked at his watch as he sipped his coffee, *Won't be long now, my friends.*

Harrison sat up with a start. Had he been asleep? He shook away the cobwebs from the fleeing memory of his dream. It was a curious dream, his mother plunging a carving knife into a watermelon, a demonic grin on her face. She was plunging the knife in again and again. As the memory of the dream faded away, he felt his tension ease.

"Fifteen minutes," the pilot shouted back. "Looks like there might be some rough weather ahead. You'd best buckle up."

Harrison was always buckled in. He would never admit to anyone, even himself, that he was afraid of flying.

"Storm front coming. We need to hurry," the pilot shouted.

Sure enough, Harrison looked out at a bank of black and very angry-looking clouds off to the starboard side as they circled over Houston. The pilot didn't waste any time and made a fast approach to the Galveston airfield, tires screaming in protest as they bounced several times before finally making solid contact with the concrete.

Harrison looked at his watch: 3:45, early by two minutes. He reminded himself to thank the pilot, thanks being something he rarely offered to anyone.

The pilot kept the plane at a fast taxi, his head out the window, yelling at the ground crew to get the wings tied down, just as the wind and driving rain hit full-force. Harrison felt the plane straining in the wind, the rain pounding on the window.

Then, as suddenly as it started, the storm passed over and a brilliant ray of sun broke through. It hadn't been a cooling rain, however, and Harrison watched steam rising from the concrete and the fenders and hood of a waiting car. The driver ducked out of the coolness of the car and into the heat, waving for Harrison to hurry.

"Welcome to Galveston, sir. Actually, it's Houston, but Galveston is not very far-"

Harrison held up a hand. "Enough, I have a killer headache. Just drive."

There was a look of chagrin on the driver's face, but few men ever debated with Harrison, good mood or bad.

"There's a bar in Galveston," the driver said. "That's where we learned the agitators make their special arrangements, you know, to get men on board boats without anyone knowing. A lot of them sail close to Spain or Portugal or France. A man,, Willis is his name, is our contact there and he will point out the two men you are looking for."

Harrison snarled. "How can you be so sure?"

"Willis called last night. The two men were there drinking beer when he called."

Harrison smiled to himself.

The sedan made several turns, passing warehouses and gantries swinging nets of cargo onto waiting ships. Harrison couldn't help but notice that most of the ships looked well past the need for paint and repair.

The driver made a sharp turn to the curb and braked in front of a tavern. Walking under the sign of Digger's Bar, Harrison pushed open the swinging doors and stood in the frame of the doorway until his eyes adjusted to the poorly lit interior. Men looked up from their drinks, sizing up the newcomer. Most, if not all, recognized something sinister about the man and soon turned back to their drinking and desultory conversation.

Harrison walked up to the bar, and without so much as a hello, he held up a photograph. "Seen this man?"

The bartender pretended to look and shrugged as if to say *who cares.* Harrison reached over the bar with a lightning move, grasping the bartender by the head, smashing his nose down onto the bar. He straightened the bartender back up and ignored the blood gushing from his nose.

"Seen this man?" Harrison asked again.

"I...I...I don't know," stuttered the bartender. "Lots of guys come in here," and Harrison knew at once the man was lying.

"I will ask you once more, my friend."

"O.k.," the bartender said reluctantly. "It was weeks ago, I'm not exactly sure when."

"Yes you do," and the man froze at the menace in Harrison's voice. "How about last night? We can make this hard or easy. It's all up to you."

"The Oreposa, they are leaving on the Oreposa."

"They?" Harrison glared. "Give me names!"

"They don't use real names. But," Willis paused, "I overheard them one time. Alec and Seth they called each other." The bartender paused, not sure if he should spill the rest. "They get on that boat tonight, the Oreposa, in the early hours of the morning."

Alec? he wondered, *Who the fuck is Alec? If Seth is using his real name, why is Ian calling himself Alec?*

Harrison reached over slowly and patted the man on the shoulder, as if to say thanks. Then, he grasped the man's left arm and slammed it down over the edge of the bar. The snapping sound of broken bone echoed throughout the bar along with the man's scream. No one volunteered to come to his aid.

Harrison, still in a foul mood, walked out of the bar. The driver would later attest to that. Harrison sat in the back of the car and contemplated his next move.

Harrison's mood was even worse as the next few hours passed. He had his team in place, and they all raced to a warehouse and the wharf alongside. They drove in and ran to the dock to find nothing but empty water alongside.

A security guard walked over to see what was happening. "You're too late, that old rust bucket sailed at high tide," and looked at his watch. "That was 'bout two hours ago. That ship's on the open water by now."

Harrison could only stand and look at the inky water lapping at the pilings, his guts twisting.

The day got even worse, as he anticipated another plane ride.

"You failed again. I think it's time for you to come to headquarters in New York." Harrison was stunned when the caller continued, "We won't be accepting any more of your excuses."

The slippery Ian Ferguson had eluded him again.

"Drop me off at the hotel and make damn sure you have me at the airport in time tomorrow." Again, he wasn't asking, and the driver understood that.

Looking for a way to vent his fury that night, Harrison left the hotel. After a few blocks of walking, he met an unlucky prostitute working the street. She wasn't particularly pretty, dressed in a filthy dress. But, she was desperate for money and that fit his purposes that night. She needed money for food and she needed it for the booze to help her forget her pitiful life.

While Harrison was heading for his plane the next morning, a police officer walking his beat discovered her body behind a dry cleaning store. She had no more need for money, food or booze, her pitiful life finally at an end.

Chapter 19
Mal de Mer

After dinner, Michael and Alec walked through the small Vermont town, taking advantage of the pleasant weather of another day.

"The French have an expression, *mal de mer*," Alec said, ready to continue his story. "I know it means seasick and feeling like you want to die. That old bucket, our ship, was called the Oreposa, named after a town in Spain. It was old, crewed by a bunch of misfits, and even in port in calm water, it would rock something fierce."

Alec continued on, "Still, it was our ticket to Spain and we didn't complain, even though I was seasick and vomiting before the engines even started."

As we walked, Alec paused. "Now, where was I?"

✳ ✳ ✳

"We sail in four days, just enough time to get into trouble." Seth did have a tendency to go on when he was excited. "It's a sorry old steamer, The Oreposa, whatever *Oreposa* means."

I knew that more was coming and just waited for him to continue, enjoying the feeling of the cold bottle of Lone Star in my hand. I thought briefly back to Sweetwater and Lily. But I set her memory aside.

Seth reached in his pocket and took out two pieces of paper, handing one of them over to me, "These are our seamen's papers; you are an assistant radio operator," he said, laughing until he coughed.

I think I just looked at him.

"Me? I'm a cook. Sure hope I don't kill anyone with food poisoning."

I looked at my seamen's papers, shaking my head.

"You sure this will get us past inspection?"

"We board at nine at night. The real cook will meet us at a warehouse and help get us on board. We'll hide in the cargo hold until we get to Spain. The guy said the captain doesn't have a clue and spends most of his time drunk anyway. The first mate is sympathetic to the Spanish cause. Apparently, he's a Catalonian."

"I understand from the cook that most of the crew are Afrikans and barely speak English. They won't pay any attention and spend a lot of time drinking some homemade liquor."

Seth raised his bottle of beer, "Cheers. Sounds like a vacation, eh?"

We were not the type to spend our time just sitting in a bar. As we had when we arrived in Galveston, we spent our time talking to the longshoremen about the working conditions in the port of Galveston. It was obviously a major shipping port, and it was equally obvious that the black workers were working the hardest, for the least pay.

"It doesn't sit well with me," I said, and told Seth about the man who had given me directions to the bar when I got off the train in Galveston.

"Me either."

"Same story as Hamilton, eh," I said. "Cops are ready to bust heads. Anyone wanting to get a fair deal gets a broken head instead. I'll bet there are some Pinkerton men helping out with that."

We had helped the workers while we waited for our ship to sail, but we had a voyage ahead, and finally it was time to slip on board. Even at this hour, it hadn't cooled at all, the temperature still hovering around ninety-three degrees. Seth and I walked through enveloping fog where the breeze from the water met the heat of the shoreline. Our footsteps echoed far too loudly for my comfort. Twice we stopped, thinking we heard voices.

The second time we stopped, we stepped back into the darkness as two coppers walked under the street light, one slapping his night stick against his leg rhythmically as he walked. "Like to use this tonight," we heard him say, watching as he raised his baton in front of him. "Sure would like to bust me some nigger heads open."

I closed my eyes and tried, unsuccessfully, to shut the comment out of my mind. I was just about ready to step out and confront them when I felt Seth's arm on mine.

"Not a good time now, my friend. We have bigger battles ahead of us."

Finally, the cops walked out of sight, and the two of us scrambled along a side street as the mist slowly turned into a dense fog. We felt our way along the street until we reached the door of a warehouse. Seth knocked.

"Quiet," a voice said, "I hears ya."

A short, stocky man stepped out from between two buildings, holding up a hand for silence and motioning us to follow him. I felt a slight chill as we reached the edge of the wharf, the water lapping the dock in the darkness below.

"Are you the cook?"

"Quiet. Do you want them to hear you asking fool questions? I'm just showing you the way to the boat. This way, and keep yer yaps shut," our guide whispered.

There was a four-foot gap between the wharf and a small platform on the side of a freighter. Just past the platform was a small opening. The man pointed.

"You have to jump. Time your jump when the wave brings the ship up highest."

We watched the freighter rising and falling slowly. When it reached a high point, Seth jumped with a "what the hell?" as he hit the side of the hull with a thud, but landed on his feet on the ramp.

I jumped soon after, when the ship met another high point. Neither one of us was graceful about it. Jumping while we were trying to hold on to our kits without dropping them into the water wasn't easy. Once on that slippery platform, we ducked into an opening into a dank room.

"Just wait here," the man said behind us. He had followed us to show us the platform and now darted off into the foggy mist. Moments later, we heard footsteps, and the cook appeared from inside the opening. He was obviously nervous as he motioned for us to follow. He was carrying a torch and kept sweeping the beam from side to side enough to give a faint illumination to our path.

We finally came to an opening to a large, makeshift room. It was sheltered on three sides by huge crates, and what looked like a pallet formed a roof overhead, with a blanket stretched over the pallet. There were three stained mattresses on the deck, and near them, two buckets.

"One's for drinking water and one's for your shit," the cook said, pointing to the buckets. "Don't get 'em mixed up," he laughed.

"There are three mattresses," I observed.

"One of 'em is for me, I guess," a man stepped out of the shadows from behind a crate. "My name's Antonio," he said, grinning widely. "I'm glad for some company. Cookie here keeps disappearing and I get lonely." He looked at the insignia of the maple leaf on my cap.

"What's that?"

I paused, wariness instilled in me after such a long journey, but still far from my ultimate destination. I looked him up and down, judging him cautiously.

"Joining the Mac-Paps," I finally said, touching the insignia.

"The Lincoln Brigade for me," Antonio said. His strong accent plainly laid claim to growing up in Brooklyn. "I don't blame you for being cautious. Damned government and Pinkerton men are all over the ships leaving New York," he said. "A lot of us are getting sent all over to places like this until it cools down up there."

Seth and I relaxed, almost.

Seth pointed to the maple leaf on his hat and said simply, "Canadian."

Antonio suddenly rushed to embrace Seth and me, filled with unexpected emotion. It was a bone-crushing hug and there were tears in the man's eyes.

"No Pasarán," he said, his voice throaty.

"No Pasarán," we responded in unison.

The cook slowly shook his head, sharing our emotion. "I'll make sure you guys don't get hungry," he promised, as he set a small lantern on the floor, then turned and left.

I was starting to be worry about food. The slow motion of the ship was creating an uneasiness that was my introduction to *mal de mer.*

"Think I'm feeling kind of sick," I finally admitted with a grimace. With that, I suddenly reached for the shit bucket and vomited violently until my stomach was empty. I wretched some more as a foul smell of the bucket drifting up to my nostrils.

"Wait until we sail," Antonio said seriously. "It gets worse. This old tub was built in 1920. It's sure seen better days. I've worked on boats like this. Let's pray for good weather."

"What do you mean?" Seth asked warily.

"We haven't even left the dock yet, and if it's moving like this now, wait until we meet some real ocean."

After eleven days, I knew exactly what Antonio meant. The smell of our room became almost poisonous. We tried to empty it often, but the fumes emitting from our collective shit bucket was enough to gag all three of us.

The ship pitch-poled and slopped the contents of piss and shit around our feet, the result turned catastrophic. I can still feel each wave pounding against the underside of the hull. Even though it was steel, we sat and watched the hull flexing. I was certain it wasn't supposed flex that much.

"Try not to think about how deep it is under us," Antonio tried to joke. It didn't work.

Even Antonio, who had been to sea, was barely able to take nourishment without vomiting. Seth and I weren't nearly as lucky.

As soon as I ate something, it would start coming back up almost at once. The only thing that helped me was some stale soda crackers the cook brought down. When he looked at us, his face showed genuine concern, as our voyage entered the second week. I watched Seth losing weight and he said he saw the same in me.

Just when we felt at the end of our tether and it seemed the ocean was at its worst, it started to turn calm. I almost felt hungry one day when the cook appeared. "Get ready," he said.

"I'm not sure I can even walk," I admitted. The constant vomiting had left me with a serious weight loss and extreme weakness. With a surprising suddenness, we felt the forward motion of the freighter change. We were definitely slowing down.

"The captain's so drunk he won't even notice that we're stopping," the cook said. "First Mate said we have maybe five minutes to get this dinghy out the ramp and into the water," he said, pointing to the ragged-looking boat at the door to the ramp.

We all eyed the dilapidated raft dubiously.

"It floats, don't worry. There will be a signal light coming from the shore. Look for a light that keeps swinging in an arch and just keep rowing towards it," he stopped and stepped out of the shadows. "You do know how to row a boat don't you?"

To our surprise, we saw that the cook was wearing a beret and olive jacket. He was grinning widely. He noticed our startled looks, explaining, "Guess this fucking crew won't be complaining about my cooking anymore," and laughed.

Several minutes later, the four of us were all paddling hard, if not efficiently, into the inky night toward shore as the whistle of the S.S. Oreposa blared out three angry blasts of the steam behind us.

"Guess that means they are mad about missing breakfast," the cook laughed, and we kept rowing.

Seth stopped rowing for a moment, his breathing labored. "Where are we?"

"The village ahead is Calafell. We are south of Barcelona. That's where the Oreposa is heading."

"Why couldn't we-" I began, but the former cook stopped me.

"Too dangerous in Barcelona," he grunted, breathing heavily into his rowing.

We soon heard the sound of waves breaking on the sand. It was a gentle sound, and we were able to run the boat far enough up onto the sand to step out into ankle-deep water.

As our eyes adjusted, we could see the young girl who had been waving the lantern. She extinguished it quickly and helped us pull the dinghy up onto the sand. She had surprising strength for such a waif.

I looked around and realized I was finally on Spanish soil. At least, I hoped I was. The girl, Estrella—*star* in Spanish—opened a wicker basket and handed each of us a sandwich wrapped in butcher's paper and poured each of us a cup of steaming coffee. I remember being amazed at how quickly my appetite had returned with my feet on dry land once again. I sipped and savored the strong, black coffee and wolfed down the food. I was ravenous.

"Hurry," she said in Catalonian-accented English, "leave the boat. Someone will take care of it later."

The four of us picked up our kits and followed her up the slope toward a road. I felt my legs cramping, but I didn't complain. It was the first time in days that I didn't feel like vomiting.

❇ ❇ ❇

As they finished this part of the interview, Michael was reluctant to stop, but it was getting late.

"What did it feel like? What was it like to finally be in Spain?"

Alec sat there for a moment without speaking. Finally, with a sigh, he said simply, "I have a lot to tell you about Spain."

Chapter 20
The Fortress

Before Alec continued his story, he displayed a handful of envelopes. Looking through them, he pulled a letter out of one of the envelopes, yellowed with age. It looked like it had been soaked in water and the pages were curled and stained. The faint odor of smoke still lingered on the paper.

"This is a letter I sent so long ago."

September, 1937
Dear Ian,

I hope you and mother are well. Finally, Spain! I know you must wonder about my silence. The weeks since we left Toronto have been difficult, but worth the sacrifice to get here. The Pope has just recognized Franco's Nationalists, and we hear the Germans and Italians are sending even more arms and men.

I can only hope I am in time to make a difference. Why doesn't the world wake up to what is happening? The people here are remarkable. I have seen hard people pulling fish from the sea. I have seen hard people tending farms. And the olive trees are spectacular. I can't tell you much, but I am well and truly tired. We have trained endlessly, and I need to close this and enjoy some valuable sleep.
Yours, Alec

Mike finished reading and waited for Alec to continue.

✳ ✳ ✳

We spent the night in a small copse near the road. We tried to sleep after the girl, Estrella, had left. Unable to find meaningful slumber, we talked in low tones, often lapsing into pauses of silence. It seemed very dark. I can remember the vivid display of stars overhead.

I woke up—well, mostly awake anyway—and I stood and stretched, my back aching, as I watched the sun rising. There was a tip of light on the horizon that rose, slowly at first, and then with an amazing speed, as a brilliant orange globe emerged from the bowels of the ocean. The sky was a lesser orange around the fiery ball, in stark contrast to the deep indigo blue behind. It seemed majestic rising from the pitch-black water to pierce the night and startle the day into existence.

A warm, onshore wind brushed the weeks of my travel and uncertainty aside. It felt right to be here.

I heard a young lad, perhaps ten or eleven, as he came whistling down the road. He was pushing a small cart, looking to his right and all around, and then he walked over to me with a broad smile, holding up his hand in a sign of goodwill.

He retrieved a large wicker basket, which he placed on the ground. Then, he reached inside and turned, handing me a large mug of coffee, the steam rising over the liquid. "Coffee, Señor," and he pointed up the hill to a small wagon.

"Wake up your friends."

"No need to," a familiar voice said, as my three companions joined us. We walked up to the wagon. On the tailgate were bowls of breakfast cereal next to a plate with large slabs of bread.

"A feast," said Seth, walking out of the brush, zipping his pants. "It's almost too good to be true, eh?"

"Sure beats my cooking," Feldman said, and nobody argued with him. We had learned last night the cook's real name.

Antonio, who had been down by the water's edge to clean himself, had walked back to rejoin us. The boy waited patiently, watching us finish our breakfast—wolfing down being a more accurate description of how we ate.

I turned to look at the mountains in the near distance. They weren't particularly high, but looked forbidding all the same. I couldn't help but compare them to the ones back home. Unlike the green hills and mountains of Vermont, I remember thinking that these looked angry, perhaps angry at what so many men were doing here.

"Tenemos que ir. Los hombres, los nacionalistas, son cercanos," the boy said with some urgency in his voice. He acted as if he had seen a signal. Antonio, Seth and I looked at the boy, puzzled and not understanding what he was saying.

"One thing about working on a boat," Feldman said, "you have to learn many languages." He began hurriedly gathering his gear together, "I think he said the Nationalists are close and we have to leave, now."

The boy started stuffing the bowls and utensils into a large box and pushed it all into the cart, covering the contents with driftwood.

He somehow guessed that Seth was our natural leader and handed him a note and crude map. It pointed the way over the small range of mountains rising to the southwest. I looked closely in that direction and saw a faint trail barely visible in the distance.

We each stood in silence for a moment and gathered our belongings.

"I guess this is it," Feldman said.

We all nodded and started the walk up the long winding trail. This was the trail, I suddenly realized, that was likely leading me to a very dangerous place. Still, I barely hesitated.

We walked in silence, planting one foot in front of the other. I managed to sling my belongings over my shoulder. I did it in the manner of the way backpacks were carried by the men in the newsreels—the Brigadistas—the men I meant to join.

I did my best to adopt a military style as each step took us higher into the mountains. Soon, the weight of my pack caused the straps to cut into my shoulder, but I would never admit my discomfort or show it to the others.

At last, we reached the crest of a small hill.

"Look at this," Seth said, pointing to our location on the hand drawn map, "Montaña?"

"Not like any Montana I ever saw in the movies," said Antonio, looking over Seth's shoulder at the map. "In fact, I've been to Montana, and it ain't nothing like that," as he pointed to the dusty ledges above, cropping out from the mountains.

"Jackass," Feldman laughed, "*Montaña* is Spanish for mountain. If the map says that the mountain is a mountain, then it sure as shit must be a mountain," and he couldn't stop laughing. I looked around at the rocks and stubby growing things that I guessed were small trees.

As we walked, the next montaña looked far more formidable, rising much higher overhead. How long had we walked? The sun was disappearing behind the crown.

I didn't realize how high we had walked until I turned back, sucking in my breath at the view stretched out below. The Mediterranean stretched like a vast blue platter in the distance, heat waves shimmering about the undulating water. I shielded my eyes and pulled my cap out of my kit.

I saw a movement from the corner of my vision.

"Look," I pointed to the others.

Far to the north, we watched the outline of seven planes coming towards us. Then, on some signal, they all turned away from the water and headed over a mountain range. They all had the characteristic shape of the tri-motor plane favored by the Germans.

No one spoke at first.

"We need to hurry," Seth finally said, "I don't think there is much time left. Just over this next mountain," breathing with difficulty.

"It looks like it might be easier going after we get over this little hill," no one laughed at his understated humor, not even he himself.

It was easier going after we crested the mountain. We could see a plain stretching ahead with more mountains serving as a backdrop. Not high mountains, more like hills. Then we started to pass small farms as we walked.

"Toma algún agua," a man shouted, as we passed the gate to his farm. He handed us an old wooden bucket and the water was surprisingly cold.

"Gracias," Feldman said, and I understood what it meant without asking. It was my first lesson in Spanish.

"De nada, señor," the man answered through a toothless grin. We could see that it really was something to him, our being here. I turned back and watched the man still waving to us as we walked away. In many ways, it was more of a welcome that often would be offered on our trek.

Later in the afternoon, we were taking a much-needed rest and leaning against a rock wall. Over the top, I heard a woman's voice calling, "Ustedes tienen que comer, paran aquí, paran un ratito."

We automatically looked to Feldman for translation. He shrugged and said, "I'm not sure, her Spanish is too fast for me. I think she is offering food." We took the food she offered without further question.

"No Pasarán," she said, as we picked up our kits to leave. The taste of savory stew lingered in my mouth, a sweet mixture of rice, sausage and chicken. The slogan we had heard all along our way took on special meaning the closer we got to the war.

Her words were accompanied by a salute, her clenched fist thrusting into the hot, Spanish sun. We saluted back in kind, turned, and walked on.

Our tension and excitement grew the closer we got to Figueres. This place on the map was our destination. The gentle slopes and level land made walking easier as we passed many small farms and olive groves. We called out the names of villages as we passed: Fortia, Villa Sacra, and others. Anyone like Feldman, with even a smattering of the language, would laugh at our pronunciation.

Then I saw the giant shape of a building in the distance. I saw it—it was a gigantic fortress looming on a high hill, dominating the entire landscape. It was the Castillo de San Fernando. Even if I had known it was our gateway to hell, I wouldn't have turned back that day.

Seth, our leader-in-waiting, took a deep breath. "This is what we came for," and he pulled his belt tight and started walking again, faster now.

Antonio, Feldman and I fell in obediently behind him, grim looks on our determined faces.

✳ ✳ ✳

"We were there for real," Alec told Michael. "You need to see the place to really believe it," he said. "My God, but it was *huge*. I have to tell you it scared me."

Mike turned off the recorder and checked the batteries. Just to be sure, he replaced them with fresh ones.

Chapter 21
Basic Training

They resumed the interview, and Alec waited for the nod from Michael. Once the recorder was going again, he picked up his story where he left off.

"You were telling me about the fortress," Michael said.

"Yes, it was our training camp. Ill-mannered sergeants and loutish political commissars shouted bullshit as loudly as they could, trying to convince us we could make do with outdated equipment. That was especially true of the rifles," he said, and paused.

"I sometimes expected my rifle to blow up in my face. It didn't, but it was known to happen to other men."

"And the politics," Alec said, "sometimes it seemed as if any two or three men could declare themselves to be a party, each man with a different view of how things should be run."

Alec struck a match and said, "There were some dangerous men there, Russian agents who seemed to have unusual authority. They liked to wear leather coats, even in the Spanish heat. "Odd," he said, "they all seemed to favor fedoras. One man, with a name...I think it was Vladim, was the one in charge."

Sadness washed over his face, "I learned later how evil he really was."

He waved smoke away from his face.

"Let me tell you about the training.

✳ ✳ ✳

I tugged at the collar of my shirt, feeling the perspiration pooling under my arms before it started to trickle down the inside of my arm. My mind wandered briefly back to the cool hills of Vermont, and I imagined standing in the cold water of a fast-moving stream with a fly rod, flicking the fine line over my head.

We still had some distance to cover to get to the fortress, and I blinked myself back to the present and walked along with the other three men, one foot in front of the other until we came to a crossroad. We had walked to the top of a small hill and looked at it again, the distance closing.

"Jesus, Mary and Joseph," Antonio said, and I half expected him to make the sign of the cross.

"If Jews had saints," Feldman said, "I would add them to your list. Look at that," he said, lapsing into a stunned silence as he looked at the huge building looming in front of us. I tried to think of words to describe it, but I knew it was impossible. It was a structure that defied human description.

The four of us stopped and tried to take in the reality and make sense of what we were seeing. A series of hills fluted like ripples ahead, and at the top of the last one was an astonishing sight. The outline of the building stood contrasted against a small mountain beyond and the stark blue, cloudless sky beyond.

"Figueres," Seth said with awe, looking down at the hand-drawn map he held. "I thought it was a place, a town." Seth stopped, and was, for once, at a total loss for words. "What in the..."

From our right, a column of several men were walking towards us. It was obvious we would meet at the crossroads. The men were marching in an unorganized manner and trying to swing their arms in a military way.

"Halten," someone shouted as they approached. Their footsteps created an uneven pattern of stopping.

"Wir sind von Deutschland, jenes ist der Ausbildung-slager gekommen?"

I immediately turned to Feldman, who simply shrugged his lack of understanding. Seth, hearing the language of his father, filled us in, "He said they come from Germany."

The man who seemed to be in charge changed to heavily accented English. "Ve come to train, ja. Ve vere told to go to de castle," he said, pointing to the west, "Castillo de Sant Ferran."

Now we all turned our full attention to the apparition on the hill in the distance. It had a name now: the Castle of Saint Fernando. It was an architectural marvel, on a hill rising just past the town of Figueres. It was a structure unlike anything I had ever seen or imagined. The Castle of Sant Ferran was, we were told later, the largest fortress in Europe. The dimensions defied any mental imagery we could bring to bear. It was, in fact, the largest fortress in the world.

We eventually learned first-hand its many dimensions and comparisons. But, for now, as we gradually started walking again, we felt drawn to it as if we were iron flying to a magnet.

Seth started first, followed by me, with Antonio and Feldman falling in behind.

"Marschieren," we heard shouted behind us. Slowly, the collection of footsteps joined ours, those men chattering in German, much to Seth's delight. I couldn't understand what they were saying, but I understood the excitement mounting in their voices. Seth fell back to join in, at ease with the language.

One of the men began to sing, and the melody of the *Internationale* floated over the countryside. His lone baritone voice echoed over the fields and bounded past the olive trees. Other voices began to join his German, the passion unmistakable.

Feldman joined in, his tinny voice adding a French version, blending in without effort. Antonio began to sing in Italian, his language of choice, a language of his neighborhood in Brooklyn.

Seth and I looked at each other beaming, as our English joined the international collection of languages. At that moment, we knew what it was like to be a part of an International Brigade of warriors. Our steps quickened almost to a run, and as one, we began thrusting our arms into the air in salute.

Turning a corner, we came to yet another crossroads and suddenly, the road stretched out to the castle just ahead. It was a road crowded with men. We must have looked like a ragtag bunch. There was no unity of dress to the group. I spotted some men walking without shoes, some with threadbare pants and shirts. We were all carrying our meager belongings in an assortment of bags, boxes and knapsacks. What passed for suitcases were mostly the cheap type—cardboard.

But we all seemed to be walking with a shared purpose.

Something amazing hit me. What I had assumed to be columns of all men, actually weren't. There were women walking alone and in groups, the purposefulness of their stride matching those of the men. I also saw young boys and girls marching towards the castle. I saw many older men, men my own father's age. *Maybe we both should have come,* I thought.

The leader of the German group ran up alongside us, his breathing labored in the hot Spanish sun. "Hans—my name is Hans," his breathing returning to normal as he slowed.

"I didn't know there would be Germans on our side," Antonio said from behind.

"Ja," Hans said, shaking his head emphatically. "Where do you think communism started? It was Germany, ja. And we know firsthand how dangerous the Nazis are." He turned and pointed back. "Every single one of us has experienced arrest and the torture that passes for interrogation. See the tall man there, that one?" he pointed, "He was arrested because a neighbor man didn't like him. His name is Carl. Carl was sent to a camp and the neighbor man now lives with Carl's wife. It's a good joke, ja?"

No one laughed.

"Carl doesn't have any fingernails left."

"How can that happen?" Antonio asked.

"The rest of us are Communists, all the reason they needed for arresting us," Hans said.

Feldman had been listening intently. "And the Jews," he said, "I hear terrible things are happening to the Jews in Germany."

"It's even worse than you have heard," Hans replied. "All of us stayed low after we got out of the prison camps. They were watching us. Have you heard about the Gestapo, the secret police? They watched our every move. Anyone suspected of being a Communist is an enemy. And to be a Communist *and* a Jew..." his voice faded to nothing.

Someone else spoke out, taking up the story.

"When anyone had a chance to make it out of the country, we took it. We did it one by one and agreed to meet at a small town just over the French border."

Feldman waited, needing to hear about the Jews.

Hans continued, "There were three men that we knew back there, back in the camp. They were Communists like us, but also Jews. They never came out of the camp. We finally had to leave without them."

Listening to that, I was even more convinced of my need to take a stand against fascism, and this seemed like a good place to start.

The men fell silent as we kept walking toward the towering castle. It looked even larger now, but remained distant.

"The fucking thing looked so close back there. How much further is it?" someone muttered. No one had an answer.

We walked on.

When we finally reached the outskirts of the town of Figueres, we saw tables set up at intersections. Behind each table, there were men and women wearing uniforms and looking very official. Signs in several languages were now directing us towards the castle. Seth and I stopped and presented our Canadian identity cards issued in Toronto. We saw men without identity cards moved to the side for further interview.

"See you inside," we yelled back to Feldman and Antonio, waiting to be interviewed and approved. Seth and I started walking through the narrow streets of town, cobblestones uneven underfoot. A hill sloped ahead to the northwest. We saw a sign identifying the road: *Carrer de Castell de Sant Ferran*, and we guessed it was the road to the castle.

We walked faster and came to an incline leading up to what we would come to know as the 'advance entrance,' and walked through it to the main entrance ramp beyond. I looked up at the main entrance with its display of intricate carvings, each of the carvings reflecting the long history of the fortress.

Men and women lined the walkway, sitting or standing. Some were alone. Some gathered in small groups. Most of them ignored the presence of the newcomers; the ones that did turn as we approached understood the excitement Seth and I were feeling. They, too, had felt the same emotion upon arrival.

One or two even waved and smiled a sort of welcome. We noticed that everyone looked very serious. I heard the din of many languages in arguments for and against. For what and against what, I didn't know, but I would soon find out.

The two of us finally walked through the arch of the main entrance and were met by a man and woman wearing blue coveralls and red berets. Behind them, a column of men were marching past. I stopped and admired the peaked caps on the marching men; their dark shirts looked like denim and their heavy pants were tucked into high boots. Leather straps and belting supported the packs on their backs.

"I don't see any weapons," Seth whispered aside.

"Comrades," the woman said, sounding official and holding up her hand. "Show me your papers, please."

She and her companion seemed to take a long time in examining the papers and she finally said, "Follow those signs," pointing. "You will come to a large room where you will be examined by a doctor. They will point the way after that."

She turned away, no further interest in us, the two young men who had traveled so far to be here. I didn't realize until later that her apparent disinterest was likely masking a heart that was aching for all the young men and women passing her on the way to a war that no one completely understood. It was more likely she was quietly shedding private tears for the hundreds she already knew would never pass this way in return. I knew none of this at the time, and eagerly pulled on Seth's sleeve, urging him ahead.

We undressed and stood with a group of men. Most of us tried our best to cover our pricks and balls while we waited. Some seemed oblivious. When the medical exam was finally over, we were taken to a room and sprayed with a disinfectant powder. Finally, they told us to dress and directed us to an even larger room with countless tables stretching into the distance. Each table was crowded with men sitting down to their meals, the din of voices like the hum of a giant swarm of bees. Seth and I grabbed metal plates and cutlery, and once through the line, we sat and enjoyed our first hot meal in days. We both agreed it was better than the finest restaurant we had ever eaten at, laughing at the thought. Fine restaurants were not part of our experience.

After the meal, we followed the other men in rinsing our plates and realized we had no idea what to do next. As we stood and looked around, a young woman walked up to us.

"I have been sent for you. This way, comrades," and she led us on a puzzling tour of hallways and rooms. Finally, she stopped at a window where we were handed a pillow and blanket each. Then, she led us into a large corridor that branched off to our right. The corridor held what seemed like hundreds of bunk beds. She stopped at two that were empty and said with a slight smile, "These are yours. I assumed you two wanted to be together."

We nodded our thanks and later admitted we were sorry to see her leave, each sharing our own version of an erotic thought of spending time with this young woman, without her uniform to cover her luscious body.

Before leaving, she told us to go back to the same window where they issued blankets. "Tomorrow, you get your uniforms there," she said. "Be sure and be there right after breakfast, before all the good uniforms are gone."

Then she was gone.

I was sure I could never sleep in my excitement. To my surprise, I was aware my face was rubbing on the rough fabric of the blanket as I woke up suddenly. There were few lights on at this hour, and as my eyes acclimated to the dark interior of the fortress, I turned my head, looking down the long corridor of bunk beds. Men were in various stages of dress and undress, and most gave the appearance of having a place to go. My mind was clouded with sleep and anxiety, and I suddenly remembered we needed to report for a uniform.

"Hey there," Seth was walking back with two metal cups with steam rising in the coolness of the room. "They know good coffee in this country. And, I met the prettiest young woman," he sighed. "Oh well, we have someday ahead of us, eh?"

I never did understand how Seth could start a day so un-expectedly, but I gratefully accepted the coffee.

I felt grimy. My customary start to the day usually included showering or a bath, both luxuries too often denied since leaving Hamilton. *How long has it been now?*

The din of conversation in scores of different languages drove away any thoughts I may have had about toileting. Stepping out of our corridor with its many bunks, I realized it was only one of many corridors branching off a long central corridor.

Seth, as if reading my mind said, "Have you ever seen the likes of this? There must be thousands of guys here."

"Over seven thousand, old chums," someone said in passing with a clipped and very British accent, laughing as he walked away.

I was trying to comprehend the full nature of this fortress, as we started walking in the direction of the window where we were supposed to get our uniforms and equipment.

We had just started walking when we were accosted by men urging us to join their particular political party. The array of positions and coalitions was dazzling. We had assumed there was a common commitment to the cause, even though we had heard about all the different factions.

"This way," one man said, pointing to a sign for the popular front, "Join the UR," whatever that was.

Another group of men held up signs and urged us to join the Antifascista party. Two of them tried to block our way until we agreed. There was another group under a sign proclaiming *Mujeres Libres*. I stopped and looked at the group of determined-looking women gathered around the table. Someone, in passing said, "Mujeres Libres means *free women* in English, that's an anarchist organization for women."

I stood there looking at their table until someone said, "They don't want you, comrade," and walked away laughing.

Seth and I were excited as we walked on through the din of voices, hearing languages from around the world. Two men, with a strong Irish lilt were arguing, and a voice in plaintive Cantonese drifted past them.

So, this is the International Brigade, I thought in wonderment.

We stood looking at the floor plan. The corridor we had been following came to an intersection with corridors going in all directions. We made our decision and turned a corner until we were standing at the uniform window. We learned later just how lucky we were to be first. Many of the men who arrived later in the day found the quartermaster out of uniforms. They were told to pretend they had uniforms, a group that came to be known as *el ejército de fingidores,* the army of pretenders.

There was a sign above the uniform window, *oficial de intendencia* and in English below, it said: quartermaster.

I went first and was directed through a door to a long counter, where I was given an official pack and told to transfer all my belongings to this new backpack. I was careful to look around as I moved my pistol unobserved. As hot as it was, I was issued a heavy woolen greatcoat. I placed it on a table next to the window, with my new pack on top. Next, the commissar handed me a tri-peaked hat. I remember smiling as I placed it on my head, adjusting it to the side in a slightly jaunty manner.

The quartermaster instructed me to hold out my arms and the he placed pants, a dark shirt and high-topped boots in a pile on my outstretched arms. Balancing it all, I somehow managed to pick up my greatcoat, pack and blanket, and stagger away. I was directed to another room where I could change and get everything organized. I stumbled past Seth, and he said I needed a burro to carry my load. He laughed at my progress until he stepped up to the window. He stiffened and looked very serious, listening to his instructions.

I carried everything into the next room, where I became a soldier. My old clothes went into a heap on the floor. "They will go to someone who needs them," a man said. "There are a lot of people, especially in Madrid, who can use these clothes."

That, somehow, made it easier to say good-bye to them.

Seth walked in carrying his issue and we were both laughing and saluting each other, until we were ordered to strip naked to be doused again with a disinfecting powder and told to dress in our new uniforms. We watched as our discarded clothes were thrust through a waiting window.

My new pack felt harsh against my back. I had wrapped my coat in a roll over the top of the pack. Still, I was unaccustomed to the way the pack poked my shoulder blades. I willed away the discomfort and with a firm step, walked to the next room just as Seth followed, balancing his precarious load.

The two of us looked at each other and nodded.

We were directed to yet another room and walked to yet another window, wondering if the warren of rooms ever ended. I was brought up short when I heard a sharp clacking sound and a woman came to the window and thrust a rifle at me. It didn't take an experienced military eye to tell that it was an old, old weapon. Turning it in my hand, I read the inscription: Moisin Nagants M1891.

Another man came in as I was looking at the rifle. He had an unpleasant and gruff voice, "I will be your trainer. We start at the break of dawn tomorrow. You had best get your rest tonight."

I nodded my understanding.

"That rifle you are holding was out of date years ago. Hell, it was out of date at the turn of the century. The Russians call it the 'Vintovka Moison', the Moison Rifle. They don't refer to it kindly, I tell you."

I turned it over in my hands and looked at the bolt.

"It will take all you strength," he said, "to pull that bolt back, especially if you're in a hurry. And we usually are, sometimes a life and death hurry. It may be an awkward beast to carry and maneuver, but it can save your life if you know how to use it properly."

I hid my skepticism as best I could and kept turning it in my hands.

"If you have any time before dinner, you might want to walk around the yard and see if you can get used to carrying it." He laughed. "You will likely see others trying to do the same."

Seth walked through the door to get his rifle.

"Your comrades can fill you in," the trainer said, gesturing in my direction. He was still chuckling. "Don't let this laugh fool you two men. I will be a bastard in your eyes before your training is over."

"How long will it-"

"Not nearly long enough," the trainer interrupted, walking out the door. We saw him pulling a bottle of some sort out of his pocket, taking a deep swallow and coughing.

"It starts now," I said.

Seth and I looked at each other for a long time and finally Seth said, "What do you say, comrade, can we find our way back to our bunks?

✳ ✳ ✳

Michael sensed this part of the story was over and turned off the recorder. He looked at Alec.

"God, I wish I could live that day over. I wish I could change the outcome," the old man said, softly, his eyes squeezed tightly shut.

Chapter 22
First Battle

As the interview resumed, Alec passed another letter to Michael and said, "It was true, there was never going to be enough training. It was over too soon, as we were rousted out of bed one dark morning and roughly ordered into a truck."

Alec passed him a folded piece of paper. Michael read the letter stained with dirt and years.

August 25th, 1937

Dear Ian,

No one sang me a happy birthday today, but I knew you and mother were thinking of me. There was no cake with candles. Instead, there was a loud clanging and we all stumbled out of bed. Orders were shouted, directives issued; everyone was shouting at once. There was a sense of the urgent and unreal as we hurried through breakfast, toileted and lined up for ammunition.

Sad eyes surrounded us as we walked in file down to a courtyard. The tailgates of waiting trucks yawned at us. We climbed aboard. I have to tell you, we were all quiet. There was none of the usual joking and philosophical debates. I believed that our training felt altogether too short for our needs, but it was finally over and we are now on our way to battle.

Love, Alec

When he finished reading, Michael turned on the recorder and waited for Alec to continue his story.

✳ ✳ ✳

We rode in trucks bumping over some of the roughest road I had ever seen. The driver did the best he could, dodging bomb craters and potholes. I heard something in the voices of the other men; there was muted anxiety in those voices. It matched the way I was feeling right then. The rumor mill was working overtime, and their anxiety was a mirror reflecting my own.

No, not anxiety, it's downright terror. The other men tried their best not to look afraid and tried to act indifferent, but I knew they were as afraid as I was.

"Does anyone know where we are going?" a man asked.

"Who the fuck knows, but it must be important," someone replied, "to wake us up at this ungodly hour."

"Does anyone even know what is going on anymore?" another man asked.

"It's terrible, I tell you. Franco gets anything he wants from the Germans and Italians," one man said, as he tried to spit over his shoulder through an opening in the canvas flap. In his nervousness, the man could only manage a spray of spittle that ran partly down his chin. He hurriedly brushed it away with the back of his sleeve.

"And the French government," his buddy said, "if they had their way, they wouldn't let anything across the border that might help us. Fuck the frogs," he said, in a cockney Liverpool accent.

"That sure leaves us in a fuckin' pickle," the first man said, shaking his head.

"Stuff it," someone said from the front of the truck. I recognized Seth's voice. "We do with what we have." He was being unusually quiet this morning.

I was sitting at the back, cupping my cigarette from the wind, watching the changing scenery on a journey that, many years later, would take a mere five hours. But, this was 1937, and there was a war. So, our truck crept along with the rest of the convoy, at a pace that a snail would have envied.

Another man tried to cheer us up. "Russia won't let us down." It sounded hollow to the men in the ancient truck, sputtering its way along in a convoy of other ancient trucks. Our vehicle didn't feel very military to me, and I wondered what it carried before being drafted into the war.

Mostly, then, we rode in silence.

Suddenly, I heard a voice with an unexpected pitch, and we turned and stared at the woman speaking. "I was assigned to the information office," she said, immediately confirming her authority in matters of military intelligence for all the men in the group.

"Franco tried to take Madrid," she said. "He tried in January and again in February," she added. She took off her cap and tossed her auburn curls. It was a sight that stayed with all of the men in that truck for a long time, I tell you.

"Tell us something we don't know," a man spit out his disgust.

She stared back at him. "The League of Nations banned volunteers by foreign nationals like us but the fascists keep sending Franco more and more arms and men."

The men leaned in to hear her now, over the roaring of the truck.

"The Italians sent their troops along with their flowery hats, and the Spanish men, wearing their fezzes, came from Morocco. Well, it's giving Franco all the edge he needs," she said, "and only the Russians are still standing up for us with tanks and guns and even planes."

"And what does our side do?" one man snorted, "We start fighting each other."

"Did you hear?" another agreed, "The Soviets couldn't tolerate Nin. They had him assassinated!"

No one responded, knowing it could be perilous to openly discuss the political factions and rivals. You never knew who would be listening. Meanwhile, the gears in the trucks were whining as they were forced to cope with the twisting roads and steep hills.

"The Germans sent their airplanes and pilots. The *brave* German airmen bombed the women and babies in Guernica. April, it was. Women and babies, mostly..." I saw tears in her eyes. "As if I didn't need any more reason for riding in this damnable truck..."

The quiet returned. We knew the situation was getting desperate for the Brigadistas–the loyalists–and that was exactly why we all had made our journey to be here, to be a part of this history. But suddenly, we all felt unprepared.

We suspected our training was not up to the task of going up against the rebel Franco army, and we knew our equipment was damn near obsolete. But, no one told the driver to stop or asked to be dropped off. Everyone just sat there, heads looking down as they scuffed their boots on the floor or stared at their hands.

I looked at Seth sitting in the front of the truck. Seth, who was always the man in the center of any conversation, was leaning back, a cigarette in his hand, staring at nothing. *What's wrong, my friend?* I remember wondering, and tried to recall what we had talked about the night before.

"I'm getting worried," Seth had confided in me. These words coming from a man who never showed any signs of worry bothered me more than the outdated equipment or the fear I saw in each of the other men surrounding me.

"I thought it was clear," he continued. "I came here to fight fascism. I heard about the Popular Front and we knew they were lefties first. But, you and I talked about standing up for the common man, the people..." He paused to light a cigarette; he seemed to be chain-smoking these days.

We were standing in a corridor close to our bunks as we talked. He looked around to see if anyone was listening. "I've been talking to some men, Alec," he told me. When he saw me starting to ask, he interrupted, "Its better you don't know who."

"But," I shot back, "why are you locking me out of this— now, when we are on our way to bleed and maybe even die? We are in this together, right?"

"The Soviets," Seth said after a moment, "sure, they are sending in arms, planes and fighters. And they are sending something else, too—a mandate on how they think things need to be. They made sure they sent in special men—dangerous men. It isn't anything like the communism our fathers taught us to believe in..."

Seth shook his head as he stared unseeing over my shoulder. I had never seen this side of Seth. His uncertainty worried me.

"The NKVD," he continued, "started infiltrating the Popular Front groups. They arranged to have POUM outlawed. The Workers' Party can no longer function in the open. I'm telling you, Alec, these are evil and very bad men."

I nodded. I had heard the whisperings too, but as usual, Seth was a step ahead of me in his thinking.

"You and I," Seth went on, "were so proud to get our party cards and Russia seemed like a beacon of hope. But, Stalin isn't Russia." Seth spit name out with venom I'd not seen before. "There are a lot of people 'disappearing' in Russia just because they disagree with Stalin. It's frightening."

I started looking around as we talked, worried someone might be listening. We had been warned to keep our political thoughts to ourselves.

Seth lowered his voice to a bare whisper, "The NKVD had Andreu Nin arrested in Barcelona. Word leaked out even though his arrest wasn't made public. He was taken to a secret prison. Some say it was Alcala de Henares near Madrid."

"We shouldn't be talking like this," I said, stepping back slightly. I was getting very nervous with this conversation.

Seth wouldn't stop, however, "Alexander Orlov himself conducted the interrogation. Interrogation?" Seth snorted, "Some interrogation indeed—torture would be a more likely description from what I've heard."

There was sadness laced with bitterness in his voice, as I wondered how he could know all this.

"Four days later, Nin was dead—assassinated. Guess it doesn't pay to go up against Stalin."

❋ ❋ ❋

Now, sitting in the truck, I remembered that conversation and worried for my friend. I realized then that Seth had fallen in with some dangerous people. But, I also knew that Seth wouldn't be deterred once he had his mind made up.

We didn't talk about the subject of Nin and Stalin again. Seth had eaten his breakfast in silence and we continued walking, in silence, to the waiting trucks. Seth usually sat next to me, but this morning, he jumped on the truck first and huddled in a front corner. I didn't realize then that he was trying to shield me, to protect me. It just seemed odd to me at the time.

I tried to push it out of my mind as the truck convoy pulled into an open field next to the road. We could hear a *whoomp, whoomp* sound in the distance.

"Artillery," someone muttered.

"Zaragoza, comrades, we are going to Zaragoza," and we—the newest soldiers—looked around at each other with shrugs. We had no idea where we were or where Zaragoza might be.

"Franco is breaking through and the Basque have surrendered. We are the only ones standing between Franco and Madrid. Comrades, we will walk from here to Zaragoza."

We quietly shouldered our gear and rifles and started to shuffle down a long, winding road into the valley ahead. We could see a town in the valley and high rocky walls on either side; even to the untrained eye, we recognized it as a perfect bottleneck to stop the advancing Nationalists. We also saw that it would be a damnable place to be trapped if we were over-run.

Seth fell back and walked alongside me now. The two of us didn't need to talk much, but I was puzzled by his manner.

"Is it still about...you know...what you were saying last night?"

Seth held up his hand for silence, but said nothing, turning away to hide what I thought looked like tears in his eyes. When we stopped for water, he still didn't say a word to me. Finally, as they were reassembling to continue the hike to Zaragoza, Seth suddenly embraced me and whispered, "We believed, didn't we? I'm not sorry, remember that."

I was stunned and didn't know what to say, so I said nothing. There was too much going on beneath his silence, and I didn't like being shut out. I had only one friend in this world right now, and I didn't want to lose him.

As we walked on, I realized Seth had slipped an envelope into my jacket pocket. I didn't say anything then, I just shoved it deeper into my pocket and kept going.

When we reached the valley floor, all thoughts of order quickly vanished into complete and total pandemonium. Someone shouted, orders were issued, and counter-orders were issued by another voice. Everywhere we turned there were shells falling and men dying, crying out in pain and agony. Suddenly, my gun was in my hands and I was firing blindly into the enemy.

From where I stood, it looked hopeless to me. The enemy kept advancing, despite our rifle fire. My rifle started to feel warm in my hands. Seth suddenly stood up and shouted, "Follow me, men!"

Pride in my friend swelled inside me as he organized an impromptu counterattack on the advancing Nationalists. He motioned at me to stay put.

"Keep up the rifle fire," he yelled.

He had spotted a piece of higher ground, and along with twenty-three other men, mounted a fierce defensive of the lone roadway coming through the town. The fighting raged as Seth and his men held off hundreds of enemy troops.

I watched him from where I crouched. I saw Seth shudder as a bullet found its mark in his left arm. He looked back at me, grinning like a man possessed. He shouted, "I'm o.k.!" and turned to keep on fighting.

His bravery kept the Nationalists at bay. Those heroes bought us time that day. On signal, our company of Brigadistas, hopelessly outnumbered, began our retreat back up the same road we had not long ago walked down with such bravery and hope. I was panting when I finally got to the top of the ridge, stopped, and looked back down.

I could still see Seth and the others on a small hill and they looked like ants in the distance. The sounds of ricocheting bullets and machine guns echoed into the vanishing light.

Someone handed me binoculars, but in the gloom of the approaching dusk, I couldn't make out much as the gunfire slowly began to sputter and stop. Nothing moved on that little hill below us.

My head sagged. I had never felt as alone in my life as I did at that moment. I was still in a daze as I sat next to my bedroll, looking up at the stars and thinking about Vermont. I dozed, never quite sure if I truly slept that night.

"Fuck me," I heard the familiar voice from somewhere in the fog of my restless sleep, "that sure was something."

It was Seth, out of breath, but walking into the lantern light. I hadn't realized how much time had gone by, and the sun was starting to glimmer just below the horizon.

I was euphoric. I had never expected to see my friend again. I wanted to feel him to make sure he was real, but I couldn't move.

Seth was excited and couldn't stop talking even though he was seriously out of breath. "We climbed straight up the fucking side of the mountain and they must still be wondering where we disappeared to. One of the guys with us was from here and showed us the way up."

I rubbed my eyes in disbelief, not trusting that my friend was truly standing in front of me. I lunged out of my bed and we hugged, alternating between laughing and crying.

"You, there," came a voice from the side. The voice didn't have a friendly sound. "Stand where you are and don't move."

I saw a man standing in the early morning darkness. He wore a leather jacket and fedora. He waved his hand in a presumptuous manner and I saw three armed men appear, stepping into the light towards Seth. Two of the men took an arm each, and the third confiscated Seth's rifle, the one he had used to hold off the Nationalist army just hours ago.

"You are under arrest," he said, waving a paper in front of Seth.

"What for..." I started to demand.

Seth spoke softly but the power of his words was like an artillery blast.

He turned to me and said, "Walk away, Alec, you are not a part of this." His face had hardened in a way I'd never seen, his eyes glaring at me like I was a stranger.

I looked at the pistols the men pointed and backed off. What could I do? I have asked myself that question for so many years now, and even to this day, I still can't find an adequate answer. I simply stood, transfixed, and watched as the men pinned Seth's arms behind him and began to march him off.

"No Pasarán!" Seth suddenly shouted defiantly, "Remember why we are here!" I watched them walking Seth along the road until they had walked around a bend in the road and were no longer visible. That was when I heard the sound of three shots ringing out in quick succession, the sound shattering the morning breeze. A covey of small birds sprang up, flushed from a nearby ditch.

I didn't have to be told to know what had just transpired. I realized what had gone horribly wrong, and a seething anger gripped me. *If I ever find you, you bastard,* I vowed, branding a memory of the NKVD agent in the leather jacket in my brain.

I walked slowly around that bend in the road, knowing what I would find. A small car raced away and Seth's bullet-ridden body was sprawled on the hallowed Spanish soil, his blood pooling into the dust under his body. His eyes were filled with rage at his own death. My tears fell, mixing with Seth's blood to sanctify the soil on that site high above Zaragoza.

✳ ✳ ✳

Michael was utterly silent. He realized no words were sufficient to help the man sitting across from him.

"That's how they treated heroes," Alec said. "For the first time in my journey, I started to question being there."

Michael drove back to his motel room after saying goodnight to Alec. He passed the neon sign advertising cold beer and pulled his car into the gravel parking lot, turned off the key and set the parking brake.

"Boilermaker," he said to the barkeep when he sat down at the bar. Michael sat staring at the glass in front of him for a long time, and finally, he laid down money on the bar and left the glass, untouched, on the bar.

Chapter 23
Love Found in Unlikely Places

I was drunk, very drunk. I was no stranger to drink and always prided myself in never losing self-control. As drunk as I tried to be, it still wasn't enough.

I wiped spilled wine from my chin and cheeks. *The bastard ordered it, and they shot Seth.* I tipped a bottle of wine, tilting it almost vertical to drain the last dregs. I looked down as a stain of that harsh peasant wine spread on my undershirt. I was sleeveless in the hot sun, and I let my arm drop and hand open. I dropped the bottle alongside another bottle, equally emptied. I just sat there and stared at them, my mind lost in a confused fog.

I needed to walk to a place of solitude, far from my resting comrades. I could hear others passing by on the edge of my drunken haze. They tried to offer consolation. "Fuck off," was my only reply. They took my advice and left me alone.

It must have been a combination of the heat and wine. When I tried to get to my feet, I was wobbly, but finally pushed myself up. Picking up three empty bottles, I wondered when I had lost count. I walked over to a stone wall near where I had been sitting. I kept my balance with difficulty. The hot sun seemed to spiral overhead, beating down on me. Red wine and a hot sun make for a bad drunk.

Placing the bottles carefully on the wall, at least as carefully as I could in my condition, I walked back to my pack, gear and rifle. I picked up the rifle and took three cartridges out of a pouch.

Looking at my hand, I thought, *one bottle for each of those bullets in Seth's head; one bottle for each of the executioners in leather coats.* Revenge was not a dish I wanted to serve cold, and I vowed to find the bastards, somehow.

I aimed the rifle, my eyes swimming with tears and drink. The rifle seemed unsteady in my hands at first. Suddenly, I summoned up the imagining of Seth's dying. It came to me with a terrible clarity. My finger tightened on the trigger and three shots shattered each one of the empty bottles in quick succession.

I shouldered my pack and rifle and pulled out a cigarette, staggering back to my resting comrades. No one asked me any questions, understanding that dangerous look in my eyes.

As I reached the other men, I turned to watch a truck slowly moving down the road, clouds of dust spraying into the summer heat. Behind that truck, I saw four other trucks following. At last, the lead truck came to a stop, brakes complaining with a harsh grinding sound.

When the dust found a place to settle, a woman in blue coveralls stepped out of the cab and my life changed forever. I watched her put a foot up on the running board to retie her boot, and when she straightened, pulled a cloth out of an upper pocket and rubbed the sweat from her face. She turned around and looked directly at me.

I returned her look with an intensity that made her uneasy. I had my pack over one shoulder and was carrying my rifle casually in my right hand. She would later tell me that she had never seen such intensity in someone's eyes before. But, that was much later.

I watched as she turned back to the truck and reached into the cab, pulling a clipboard from the seat.

She turned and shouted, "Up and in you lazy bastards, your ride is here!"

Her voice let slip one of the many accents I was growing accustomed to hearing in the International Brigade. However, I couldn't place the accent, and simply waited there, sweating and swaying in the sun.

I had heard something else in her voice when she shouted—the sound of humor, a voice that conveyed sympathy and understanding. We men took no exception to her comment about being lazy bastards. We had heard that time and again from much lesser people.

I didn't know why at the time, but for some reason, she turned to me. I was still staring wordlessly at her when she said, "You can ride up in the cab if you want."

I may have nodded, but could find no reason for her offer. She shrugged and turned away.

She told me once, she had sensed my agony that day, and somehow knew I was trying to make sense of something beyond my comprehension. She also knew the seat in the cab, even with worn padding, was better than sitting on the planks of wood in the back.

Motioning to the other men, she walked back and lowered the tailgate, then signaled them to climb in. "Hurry, comrades, the enemy is close."

I walked around and opened the passenger-side door to the cab and climbed up, not realizing when I made that climb, I had just found someone who would guide me back from my desolation.

"My name is Tamarah, but call me Marah, please," she said, as she climbed in and pulled out the choke and turned the ignition switch.

I still couldn't identify the accent.

Nothing happened when she turned the switch.

"Gayn cacken ofn yam," she muttered as the other trucks were starting, belching acrid clouds of smoke. I eventually learned it was her favorite Yiddish oath: *go shit in the ocean.*

On the next try, Marah was finally successful in starting the truck. "Filthy beast," she said. She looked over and peered at me, recognizing a look she had seen too often in men before.

She pushed her right foot down on the accelerator and we lurched forward, the truck shuddering up the slope in the lowest gear. Once over the top, she was able to shift into a higher gear and the truck ceased its whining and grumbling. She started to sing, a soft sound that was as delicate as morning dew and as sweet as sugar on her lips.

I roused from my trance and turned at the sound of her voice. I think I was truly aware for the first time that I was sitting next to a woman—a woman who was driving a truck, in Spain of all places.

Marah was looking at the road ahead, but sensing my stare without turning her head, she said, "Whatever it was it must have been terrible." She made no attempt to pry the story from me.

I remained silent until I finally asked, "What's that song you're singing? It feels so melancholy."

"It's a story about returning to rebuild an 'old-new' homeland. It's about Eretz Yisrael—promised by God to the children of Israel. My father was a Zionist and believed it meant uprooting us and committing our family to an old-new homeland. We moved to Palestine. I was three at the time." She smiled at the memory.

"Your accent?"

"Ah. I guess you could say it's a funny mixture of Polish, Yiddish, Spanish and English."

"Why is the song so melancholy?"

"Who wouldn't be melancholy? Leaving everything behind and marching into the unknown. My mother could never adapt. She would always talk about the family she left behind, knowing she would never see them again. I think it was a broken heart that killed her, but the doctor said it was cancer." She shrugged and added, "Melancholy is in our blood, after all we've been through."

"It's lovely," was all I could think to say, looking out the window to hide my inadequacy.

"Ha! And tell me you don't know what it feels like? You left it all behind, American. Will you ever see your family again?"

"I won't see Seth again," was all I could say.

After a few minutes of agonizing silence, I turned back to Marah and said softly, "Sing it again, please."

She tossed her head and laughed and started singing again. It was a different song this time, a song of rebirth and joy. I didn't understand the words, but I could feel their meaning.

"This is for you, my soldier," she said when she finished the song, and she began to sing another. It was a song in Polish, "The story of a brave man fighting for liberty and freedom," she explained when she was done.

"The brave ones are already dead or dying," I said, bitterness suddenly lacing my voice. "The rest of us are just trying to survive."

Marah sensed it would be best not to respond and reached for something under the seat without taking her eyes off the road ahead. The truck lurched perilously close to the edge of the road, but she quickly recovered control. In her hand was a crude bottle, and she handed it to me and waited for me to open the wine. It was peasant wine, the name they gave to wine in unsophisticated bottles, intended for drink rather than show.

"Open it."

Since I drank three bottles of the stuff earlier, I now hesitated. I struggled with the cork and she finally reached over and took the bottle out of my hand.

"Here, the peasant way," she said, and smashed the neck of the bottle on the window edge, but it didn't break.

The truck lurch as she handed it back.

"What the fuck are you doing," someone yelled from the back, "trying to get us killed? There are plenty of bastards out there willing to do that without your help!"

She grinned, "Ignore them. Go ahead, open it."

I lifted my kit and took out a pocketknife. It clinked on the barrel of the pistol I was still carried in my pack and I glanced furtively at her to see if she had noticed. She hadn't.

I had also learned the trick of opening peasant wine. I cracked the neck of the bottle on the window ledge, breaking the neck away. Careful with the jagged edge, I crossed the arm holding the bottle over my other arm, imitating a waiter in a fancy restaurant.

"Madame," I said, feeling a small smile finally returning, uninvited, to my face.

She tossed her chin up and imitated a snooty woman of high society, "Thank you, my dear man."

Then she took a long—a *very* long—drink, and I was glad to see she didn't take her eyes off the road while she did. When she handed the bottle back, I tilted it up to drink and recalled the three bottles from earlier that morning, and I paused.

I looked over at Marah, suddenly aware of an attraction to this woman with long, dark hair, her songs slowly lifting me out of despair. With a grin, I took a slow and very long drink from the bottle, matching her.

Our convoy of trucks finally reached a stretch of level roadway. "Maybe another hour, maybe a bit more," she said.

My budding attraction to this woman with the intriguing accent somehow helped me begin to veil the memory of Seth's brutal death in my mind. I didn't think it was possible to ever truly forget, but for now, it seemed she was holding out a lifeline and offering a hand to help me step into the future.

As crazy as it seemed at the time, I felt that I was falling hopelessly in love, something that had never happened to me before. The concept of loving a woman, in fact, had never really occurred to me, this single-minded man from Vermont. I had always been too busy thinking of causes.

"By the way," the sudden sound of her voice brought me up short, "Are you ever going to tell me what your name is?"

Suddenly timid, I mumbled, "Alec, my name is Alec."

"And," she said, "Tell me about this man, Alec, sitting in my truck."

"Well," I thought for a moment, wondering what I could say about myself, "I can't sing. That's for sure."

I laughed at myself, but I noticed her quick-tempered response to my joke and decided it would be best to tell her something more substantive.

"I was born Alec Ferguson. I come from Vermont and came to Spain to make a difference. My father, Ian, never had a chance like this."

We sat in the truck and passed the wine back and forth. I wondered about Marah mixing the wine with her driving, but she seemed well in control.

"More," she demanded, "tell me some more."

By the time the truck convoy reached the staging area, we had shared our dreams and talked about our families, deciding that our fathers were more alike than different. We talked about being a part of the International Brigade. I told her about joining the Mac-Paps.

"I think I'm more Canadian than American," I told her. Then, I did something I had never done before with anyone other than Seth and showed her my identity cards with the maple leaf insignia.

She told me that she had come because of a man named Kurt Goldstein. "I heard him tell his story and wanted to be a part of a company of Jewish volunteers, part of a battalion that was named after Naftali Botwin, a Polish Jew. I—"

I handed her the bottle again and interrupted, saying, "I heard there have been over five hundred Jews from Palestine that have joined us here."

She held her head with pride and added, "And there is that business with the Nazis—" Suddenly, she stomped hard on the floor pedal and the truck squealed to a stop, the brakes grinding metal on metal. We had driven through an opening where trucks were circled in a courtyard and someone was starting to shout orders, directing men to disperse.

"Get settled and there will be food in an hour!" someone yelled.

"More rice and beans," someone grumbled from the back.

"Do they ever serve anything else?"

I picked up my rifle and kit from the floor of the cab and hesitated, not knowing what to say or do. I didn't want to lose her now. With Seth gone, I had no one.

Without warning, she leaned over and kissed me lightly on the cheek. I can still feel the touch. She leaned in and whispered, "I have another bottle and a nice place to walk," and winking, told me where we could meet.

Blushing lightly, I jumped down from the truck and walked towards my assigned billet, smiling like a satisfied cat. My comrades seemed quite surprised by the sudden change in my mood.

"It must have been nice riding up front with that looker, eh?"

I ignored the comment on the outside; but on the inside, I felt an enormous pleasure growing. It was a feeling that even Seth's recent murder could not diminish. I knew he would have understood. *Go for it, comrade*, I heard him say.

✳ ✳ ✳

As Alec ended the session, he touched his cheek and Michael somehow knew he was feeling that touch, a woman's kiss, on his face.

Chapter 24
My Tamarah, My Love

There was no denying it, even if I wanted to. For the first time in my life, I felt an unshakable love for someone other than my parents. My feelings for Seth had come close, and I will forever think of him as my brother. But nothing matched this feeling for Marah.

Was I surprised at the speed with which this new-found love happened? If hours could be broken down into minutes, and minutes into seconds, the length of time it took to fall in love with Marah could be measured in miniscule portions of seconds. She had done the impossible, allowing me to live with the memory of Seth's dying.

Normally a cautious man, I gave myself totally to the emotions I was feeling. I was like a man diving off a high-diving board. Once my feet left the board, a kind of gravity took over and I was totally committed to the dive.

That night, we walked far from the encampment, enjoying the fading sunlight until we were both sitting on a stone wall at the edge of an olive grove.

"I can get a motorcycle," Marah said, "and the coast isn't that far, maybe five or six hours." She took out a crude map and pointed to a place called Vinaros.

"The way you drive," I laughed, "more like fifteen minutes."

She turned a glare in my direction, "And you want to complain. The faster we get there..." leaving the rest to my imagination.

Neither of us could believe our good fortune. We wondered if it was going to be like a Chinese fortuneteller who would offer you good fortune and then give you a bad fortune to keep it all in balance. We wanted only the good, thank-you.

We asked our officer if we could have some time off. He gave us a stern look and said, "Five days, no more."

As we walked away, we heard him laugh and say to his aide, "Let them enjoy some time. This bloody Spanish mess is a nightmare by any measure. Besides, she's a real looker, eh?"

"I will get the motorcycle and we can leave at first light," she said to me, and raced off toward the motor pool.

✻ ✻ ✻

The next morning, I heard a rooster crowing in the distance. I sat up on my bedroll and rubbed my eyes awake. My kit was packed and ready, and picking it all up, I walked to the latrine and then over to the washbasin to shave.

Carrying my kit and my rifle slung over my shoulder, I walked to the road running alongside the encampment. Camp routine was slowly taking shape, as men stumbled out of tents and sleeping bags. I watched it from the road, a sense of anticipation overriding any need I might have for breakfast.

Standing in the growing light, I heard it first—the growl of the motorcycle as it came around a curve from behind a small berm. A cloud of dust rose up from behind the bike until it looked like an advancing tornado.

I watched Marah as she deftly skidded to a stop, inches from my feet. Her head was wrapped in a leather flying helmet, goggles pulled down over her eyes and her face was covered with grit. She pushed the goggles up and I couldn't help laughing at her raccoon eyes.

"And what's so fucking funny?" she asked as she tossed the right end of the silk scarf back over her shoulder.

"You just look like a dusty flying ace without an airplane," I said, trying unsuccessfully to keep a straight face.

She reached back, opened a compartment on the sidecar and pointed to put my kit into the compartment. That done, I settled into the seat, my rifle between my legs and over my right shoulder. She handed me a package wrapped in waxed paper, "Some cheese and bread. I knew you wouldn't stop for breakfast," she added with a dusty grin, teeth showing bright amid the dirt on her face.

As she started to withdraw her hand, she softly touched my cheek, sending an electric jolt through me.

Just as I was about to say 'thanks,' my head snapped back as the motorcycle lurched ahead. Marah had engaged the gears and twisted the throttle wide open, sending the bike into high speed as we raced down the dirt road until we came to a paved highway. A look of pure pleasure spread over her face, the wind pinching the flesh of her cheeks back on her face.

"Here, you can navigate," she yelled over the noise, handing me a map. It was clearly marked in Russian.

"Where did you get this?" I asked. Suddenly, I was nervous, "No one is permitted to have maps, just the-"

"You are dense sometimes, aren't you? When I'm not driving a truck, I'm a motorcycle courier. We need maps, silly."

I looked at the paper in my hands and for the first time, I saw my small part of the Spanish war and world spread out on a piece of paper. I spotted the place I had come ashore from the freighter, or thought I did anyway, and traced the line from that spot to the fortress.

"No wonder it was such a hard walk to the castle," I yelled over the motor.

"Just tell me where to turn," she yelled back, gesturing to the map.

I felt the wind in my face and my eyes were starting to water. Seeing my discomfort, Marah reached into a saddlebag and handed me a set of goggles. I didn't usually allow myself flights of fantasy, but I suddenly imagined myself in the cockpit of a plane.

I was startled out of this momentary daydream when I saw Marah lifting a wine skin from her shoulder and skillfully arching a stream of wine towards her mouth. The motorcycle took a nervous wobble as she drank and I yelled, "What the... watch it Marah!"

Her laugh sounded almost demonic in the rushing wind, as she casually pitched the wineskin to me. I was starting to have doubts about her skill as a driver and her attention to driving. But, I was enjoying the moment. Looking at the map, I suggested a turn as we crested a mountain. We could see Alcaniz in the distance. The view of the small city below was breathtaking.

Marah pulled the bike onto the side of the road, "Time for a stretch."

"Time to make my last will and testament, is more like it—the way you are driving."

She ignored the jibe and got off the motorcycle, stretching her body in the morning sun.

"Look at that view," she said. The view was truly magnificent, but I was not looking at the town before us. "If we ignore the war, Spain looks beautiful from this distance."

A sense of sorrow settled over me as I remembered how I had come to be in this place. I thought about Seth and felt a burning rage return, a rage about the man who had killed him. *What had he done to deserve it?* My eyes clouded over with the hatred I could not suppress, and I didn't notice the accompanying shudder in my body.

Suddenly, she was there for me once again, her hand softly on my shoulder, stroking down my back and soothing my rage. I turned to her and told her about the rousing words of *La*

Pasionara. I told her about the people along the way, offering their soft encouraging words of "No Pasarán."

My coming here was much, much more than Seth and dying.

As I told Marah this, I accepted all of my doubts, anxieties and rage. I knew that in meeting Tamarah, it had all been worth it, and I wanted to spend the rest of my life with her.

Standing there, I reached and turned her head toward me, and with a softness that surprised even me, I tilted her chin upwards. I can still see her stretching up on her toes as we kissed. Everything in my life had merely been leading up to this moment.

We dropped to the ground with our awakened desire, and in one life-defining moment, we completed our union on that isolated mountain top, oblivious to the world and war around us, oblivious to the dust and gravel beneath us.

When we were finished, I started to say, "I love you more than-"

"Shh," she said, "no talking, let's remember this always." We lay wrapped in a blanket alongside the motorcycle.

Later, we dressed, and Marah started the motorcycle with no further words. She was smiling a lot now, and driving at a more sedate speed. We were almost hysterical, laughing as we tossed the wineskin back and forth.

✳ ✳ ✳

I was in love and this was the perfect place for us. Vinaros was a beautiful town on the shore of the Mediterranean. We could see all the brilliant shades of blue and green reflected on the water as we descended into the town. It was a place of magic for two lovers.

The first morning, we sat in a small beach side *taberna*, enjoying the view of the sea. We took off our boots and stepped across the sand to wade ankle-deep in the soothing water.

Except for my stinking boat ride from Galveston, I had only seen the ocean from a distance. Rowing ashore in the dark, I had little use to look back and enjoy the ocean. Now, I marveled at this very personal encounter. Marah watched me, smiling at my sense of discovery—I was like a child.

In the distance, we could see movement where the water met the sky. A ferry or boat of some kind inched its way across the horizon, until we watched as it finally fell off the edge of the earth.

Arriving the night before, we had ignored sleep as we continued to explore the new feelings between us. There was the sexual intimacy to be sure, but it was much more than that. The physical was simply a manifestation of how we cemented our private bond. Beyond the sexual, there was the complete joining of two souls into one.

Without sleep, yet feeling very much awake, we took an early morning stroll through the town, enjoying hot coffee and *pan dulce* at the local bakery, the sign overhead advertising the village *panadería*. The woman behind the counter smiled at the lovers across the counter. I whispered to Marah that she was secretly remembering her first love.

That had been earlier, and now at the *taberna*, we negotiated our way through a lunch order. When it came to the language, Marah had a command of Spanish that was only slightly better than mine, but she took the lead.

The barkeep entered into the negotiation with his few words of English, the three of us laughing our way through the effort. With much pointing and fractured language, we agreed on a drink and watched him pour red peasant wine into a jar, adding a liqueur and some brandy. We watched him squeeze oranges into the mixture. He sliced what remained, dropping the pieces in as well. He did the same with some lemons and slices of apple. He seemed to wave his hand over the mixture like a magician and dropped some more ingredients in the pitcher and with a laugh, dropped in some chunks of ice and set the pitcher on the counter in front of us.

Placing two glasses on the counter, he poured the mixture into each and motioned us to drink. "*Sangria*," he said, "Drink and enjoy."

I held up my hand and pointed to another glass. When the glass was on the counter, I poured the drink mixture into the glass, sliding it towards the bartender.

"*Qué es su nombre?*" I asked.

"Alejandro."

"*Salúd, riqueza y amor!*" I said, not sure if I had it right.

"And the time to enjoy them," the barman replied in halting English, lifting his glass and smiling broadly.

I slipped my arm around Marah and decided I had never felt as complete in my entire life, and we had a whole five days ahead of us to feel this way.

"I'm starving," Marah said. "What's good?"

"Ah, señora," he said. "We are a simple *taberna*, but people come from far away for our paella," pointing over his shoulder, "and Yvette makes the very best."

A young woman was already heaping large portions of the feast into bowls.

✳ ✳ ✳

The days passed all too swiftly. We walked the streets and countryside and soon, people recognized us and nodded as they passed.

"Buenos días," we would say, and the reply was always, "Y No Pasarán."

I felt a compulsion to start each day wading in the ocean. On the second day I think it was, we noticed a sign: *Fotógrafo*. We looked at each other and opened the door. It was dimly lit and an old man stood behind the counter.

"Habla ingles?" I asked.

The man simply smiled and shook his head to answer no.

"Wait here" I said, and raced out the door. In a moment, I returned, pulling a grinning Alejandro.

"Tell him we want our picture taken," and Alejandro translated.

"We have to have it before we leave," I said.

Alejandro explained, and I was sure he was adding that the two of us were very much in love. The old man laughed and led us to the back of the shop. Alejandro watched as the photographer posed us, asking us to raise our arms in a salute.

"No Pasarán," the old man said as he draped the hood over his head, adjusting the lens. He knew why we were in his country.

The photographer said something in rapid Spanish to Alejandro. It was far too fast for my understanding. Alejandro turned and told us our photographs would be ready in exactly three days.

"There is no charge, my friends, Alejandro added.

✳ ✳ ✳

Too soon, it was time to leave, time to return to the reality of the encampment and war. Marah and I looked back as we were leaving. Our special town had, indeed, been a magical place, and each of us had photographs in our pockets, a remembrance of that special time.

"Was it our honeymoon?" Marah asked, almost to herself.

She engaged the gears and the motorcycle eased forward. I noticed she was driving at a slow pace this time. I looked over at her. *I am the luckiest man in the world*, I thought, recognizing how cliché it would sound, telling that to someone.

※ ※ ※

Michael was still holding the letter, the one Alec had written to tell his parents about his love for Tamarah. He knew the interview session was over and silently handed the letter back to Alec. He had an uneasy feeling about the stories to come, as he picked up his recorder and notebook and silently walked away.

Chapter 25
Harrison's Career-Ending Moves

Harrison, even in the best of moods, was a man that most avoided. Today, he was in a truly foul mood. He was not accustomed to being on the losing end and failing to capture a suspect, especially one like this.

He kept chewing his memory, unable to spot the problem. He was sure he had set the trap this time. He wanted to blame it on the bartender, someone leaking information from the inside, but he knew he had to accept responsibility.

When the driver saw Harrison's face in the rear view mirror, he wisely knew he would be best-served driving and keeping his mouth shut.

The metal skin of the Lockheed Vega was shimmering as the plane waited in the Texas sun. The afternoon heat was nothing compared to the heat radiating from Harrison. He opened and closed his hand around the crumpled telegram. *How could they?*

Harrison rolled the telegram into a sweaty ball, its contents memorized: *You have been officially removed from this case; return to New York at once.* He opened the door and stepped out of the car.

Harrison finally unclenched his fist as the plane took off. He realized how tightly he had been holding the telegram in his hand and began to rub it to stimulate the circulation.

In the cockpit today was a different pilot, an unsmiling man who simply stared ahead after instructing Harrison to strap his shoulder harness. Without another word to his passenger, the pilot pointed the plane toward Teterboro Airport.

Harrison, so excited flying to Galveston, now dreaded this flight back to New Jersey. *Even he knows,* thought Harrison about the pilot.

The plane reached cruising altitude quickly and with the benefit of a strong tail wind, was soon flying over the eastern Pennsylvania hills, tilting slightly to the left as the pilot made an adjustment.

Sensing they were near, Harrison looked out the window on the starboard side and glimpsed the familiar outline of New York City. The pilot pushed the plane into a sharp descent, much to the aggravation of Harrison's stomach, and the wheels were soon touching down on the tarmac. Harrison looked out the small window at the sign, *Teterboro,* emblazoned on the sides of the control tower and reception building.

As the plane came to a final stop, the pilot waved and signaled the ground crew that he was turning off the engine. He looked back at Harrison, and without getting up from his seat, motioned him off the plane. Yes, it was a much different ride than the one to Galveston had been, just a few days ago.

Harrison opened the door and carefully placed his feet on the ladder that had been pushed up to the opening. The ladder felt spindly and inadequate for such a giant of a man, but it didn't collapse.

At the bottom of the ladder stood two men dressed in the Pinkerton style: dark, two-piece suits with jackets loose enough to conceal shoulder holsters. They both wore identical fedora hats and twin, unforgiving looks. They quietly moved to either side as one said, "We will be happy to carry your bags, sir."

And just as happy to take me out to a remote field...

"I can manage," Harrison said gruffly, but the man in the fedora took his case anyway.

As the car pulled out of the airport gate, the driver made a sharp left turn, away from New York City. Harrison gave a surprised turn and glanced over his shoulder at the receding skyline. He fought a momentary panic as he imagined a sinister intent in their unexpected change in direction. They were not headed toward the agency's public offices in the city.

Instead of crossing the George Washington Bridge, they turned and headed west through Hackensack and Paterson. Further along, only twenty-five miles from the airport, the car finally turned into the parking lot of the private Pinkerton Headquarters in Parisspany, New Jersey. The directors preferred this place, constructed away from curious eyes. It was the perfect place to direct the undercover political policing for the United States of America.

The sign simply said, *Pinkerton's Annex Number 1.* Inside the gate, the car hummed over smooth gravel, the wheels softly crunching over the ground oyster shells in the lot. At the rear of the main structure, the driver made a sharp turn and a door ahead opened smoothly. Once through the door, they went down a steep ramp into an underground parking lot. Harrison shivered with a chill that had nothing to do with the drop in temperature.

"This way, sir," one of them said, as he held the door open. The other one led Harrison to an elevator door, the other following closely behind. Harrison noticed they had left his belongings in the car. *What did that mean?*

When they were inside the elevator, the taller of the two inserted a key and pushed the button for the top floor. Nothing was said on the quiet ride to the top.

The elevator door opened onto a private entryway, the chill of Harrison's mood matched by the cold look of the marble flooring. The rich, wood-paneled walls did nothing to warm the sterile reception. Glass doors opened to a reception area with no receptionist. Their footsteps echoed eerily in the empty space.

"Enter," a voice boomed from an inner office, a deep voice from a surprisingly small man sitting behind a desk. There was no disputing the note of authority underneath; it belonged to none other than the Assistant Director himself.

Harrison was startled—gob smacked, more precisely. His father would have used that colloquial term. He noted there was not a single chair in the office except the one occupied behind the desk. This was not an office to entertain visitors.

He stood in front of the desk, shifting his weight from foot to foot and waited what seemed an eternity for the man to speak. The chill Harrison felt before now plunged into a deep-freeze. He realized the man behind the desk, while listed with the quiet title of Head of Administration, was, in fact, the real power that directed Pinkerton's. Mr. Randolph was known to anyone unfortunate to cross him as *the laughing stranger*. The term was not a reference to his good humor.

Harrison suddenly felt like the farmer who heard a rattle while walking in the tall grass, knowing the snake was in the act of striking, and knowing before he put his foot down that it was already too late. Now, his fear had a substantial basis in fact, as he stared at the man sitting with the sun directly behind him. Harrison could make out the hair on the top of his head, thinning and wispy, and he sensed his own silent, hysterical laugh starting to form in the pit of his stomach.

He had a sudden impulse to lean down and blow on that thinning hair, to watch it flick back over the man's bald spot. In reality, what he really felt like doing was to lean down, grasp this little man around the neck and crack it as if he were snapping a pod of sugar peas. But, Harrison was mindful of the two very serious-looking men standing on either side of him, who had very serious-looking guns within easy reach.

All Harrison could do was to wait; bracing himself for the hard news headed his way. Harrison watched the man look up suddenly at him from his paperwork, but couldn't see his eyes, the brilliance of the sunlight from the window behind the man kept his features dim and shadowed. Harrison suspected the timing of his audience had been predetermined to provide such an effect for Randolph.

Finally, the man's head tilted down and Harrison saw that he was looking at a file. Harrison waited and knew the man already knew every detail–he most likely had the entire file memorized. Harrison, reading upside down, could see that it was his own personnel file.

"*We*," accenting the word, "have a serious problem here. How does one of our leading field agents go from the head of the class to *this*?" He pointed to Harrison's file.

Harrison knew it was not really a question.

"I can make it simple, Agent Harrison, or should I say, *former* Agent Harrison."

Harrison was seething, but kept his silence.

"You had a guardian in Inspector McParland, didn't you?" Again, it was not a question.

Harrison waited.

"McParland died nearly twenty years ago, however. Heart, I heard. It's just as well," the stranger said bluntly, speaking of a man Harrison had considered almost a father. "Today, Pinkerton's needs a delicate touch to work behind the scenes, not a sledge hammer. McParland and the secret unit he built...how do you say it...was not the type to lead us in our 1938 direction. He used you as his own personal blunt instrument; subtle is not a trait we would assign to you. Your usefulness to Pinkerton's is over."

Harrison started to protest, but Randolph held up a hand.

"You have been chasing a ghost, blinded by your hatred of Ian Ferguson. He is not the man who killed our agent in Montreal. He was in a cabin in Vermont at the time, something that wasn't all that difficult to discover, had you not been so short-sighted in your efforts. It's as simple as looking at income taxes. He files his faithfully, and we have access to those tax records. His address is on the record. A stringer from New York was able to verify his location at the time of the murder."

Harrison was dumb-founded. "How do we have access to tax records?" Again, he was abruptly cut off.

"Our Canadian stringer on that train to Montreal made the first mistake. It wasn't Ian that our Canadian agent spotted on that train to Montreal. That ignoramus mistook Ferguson's son for the father. Sure, they may look alike, but it was the son, Alec, on that train."

Harrison accepted that his best tactic now was to simply listen.

"That agent made the first—and for him, fatal—mistake, and then you just added to the problem by losing your objectivity. You started chasing the illusion." He sighed, disgusted. "No matter, in any event, you even managed to miss the son all along the way."

His voice melted into a silky whisper as he leaned closer to Harrison, as though to tell him a secret, "How could you? You couldn't catch him because you were blinded by your obsession with laborists instead of looking towards our true enemies, the ones on puppet strings, with the puppeteer, Joseph Stalin, in Moscow. Sadly, the men who work for him are much smarter than you are." He stopped and leaned back in his chair, finally expecting a response.

"So," Harrison said finally, "you are throwing me out after forty years of service."

Randolph ignored the statement, however, "Which brings me to the women."

Harrison's chill was complete—a frozen block of ice in his heart.

"It seems that some very unhealthy things happen to women in the places you are assigned. We have a new department, our Office of Technical Analysis. One of the analysts spotted a pattern. Whenever you were in a location for a period of time, there was always a case of a woman seriously injured... or worse. Would you like me to go on?"

This time it was a question, and Harrison simply shook his head no.

"You are lucky. We do take care of our own; none of this was reported to the police. However, if you decide, in any way, to challenge my decision, all of this will be reported to each jurisdiction."

Harrison was frozen to the spot as the man asked, "Do you understand?"

Harrison was speechless, his face grey and drawn. Finally, the *laughing stranger* repeated the question, "Do you understand?"

Harrison realized that an answer was demanded and said a quiet, "Yes," and after a pause, "sir."

"You will get a modest pension and be listed on our records as a consultant. Consider yourself lucky I let you live. Now, get out of my sight. You, to put a fine point to it, are disgusting. Your behavior has put a blot on the reputation of this fine organization."

One of the men gently touched Harrison on the shoulder, but it felt more like an electric shock and he jumped involuntarily. They backed out of the room, returned to the waiting elevator, and dropped slowly to the parking level.

"I think you should seriously consider not harming any more women," the man on his right whispered, so very close to his ear that Harrison could feel his warm breath.

Just consider being much more careful, Harrison thought. He had a serious urge to find just such a victim tonight to release the rage inside him.

Chapter 26
Teruel: Beginning of the End
December 2, 1937

It was unusually warm that particular morning, especially for a day in December. It had started out with a warm wind from the south, and the temperature continued on an upward climb.

Our camp, a simple cluster of tents in an olive grove really, was on a plateau near the road between Teruel and Castralvo. It wasn't a road of consequence, but it snaked through an area that was shaped like a bowl created by the mountain and high hills surrounding it.

I recall walking to the edge of the camp and looking to the north. I could make out the intersecting highways and rail line that dissected Teruel in the distance. I recognized the importance this small place held for both sides.

"Camarada de buenos días," a passing man said and nodded.

"And may the rest of the day go well, comrade," I finished the greeting in English, suddenly amazed to realize how easily I moved from language to language now.

I walked back to the washing rack, listening to the rumors, each cluster of men with their own version of the truth as they saw it.

"The Francoists are getting close, coming down the valley from the north."

"They are getting more and more equipment, thanks to Hitler and Mussolini, the dogs."

"Even when Mola-"

"We still have a lot of fight," but no one took that rumor seriously.

The rumors, I thought, *are as plentiful as the insects we sleep with.*

In every army there is always someone who sounds like he really knows what is going on. This morning, in our small camp south of Teruel, it was no different. A man to my right stood listening as a truck drove past slowly. Mounted on the top were large loudspeakers. A man with a microphone was in the passenger's seat.

"Comrades, we are ready for the fight!" we heard blaring from the truck speakers. I saw several men look at each other, skepticism on their faces.

"Comrades," the speakers blared again, "this may be the most important battle yet. We will not give in. Each man and woman must do their part."

"And what do they think we've been doing?" the man to my right said back to the speakers. He was the sergeant in charge of our unit, and we knew to listen to him.

I was jostled to a stop as a group of men crowded around the sergeant, listening to him talk about what really lay ahead for us.

"Sure, if you look at any map," he said, "we still occupy a part of Spain, especially in the south and east. Yeah, there is that small pocket in the north on the border with France, but so what?"

"What about Madrid?" one of the men asked.

"Forget Madrid. We almost pulled it off," the sergeant said, "but we don't have any seaports to get supplies in there.

The French and British and the League of Nations all turn their blind eyes to the German and Italian supplies coming in."

"They do more than that, comrades," another man said. "They actively try to block supplies and men getting here to *our* side. They do everything to stop volunteers like us. They do the same for the supplies we need."

"Then what are we supposed to do, quit?"

"Just the opposite," the sergeant said. "We are like a wounded dog. Just when they think it's safe to pet us, they will be in for a nasty surprise."

The propaganda truck pulled slowly away toward the next cluster of tents down the road, and the words calling them to action grew more distant.

I was still trying to shake off an uneasy sleep and thought I had heard enough. Just as I was turning to continue on to the washing rack, I heard the first explosion. I turned back to the north so fast, I almost fell over. You don't need training to develop that first instinct to seek shelter. But, I knew enough at that point to realize it was far enough in the distance to be only mildly dangerous...yet.

"Here we go, comrades," someone said with a Texas drawl, "the fox is in the hen house now!"

I didn't need binoculars to see the columns of smoke rising in the valley north and west of Teruel. Suddenly, we heard what had to be the beginnings of a serious barrage. Explosion after explosion resulted in huge puffs of smoke showing where each shell was landing. The sergeant in charge went into his tent and ran back with binoculars. He gazed intently, and the men waited to judge his reaction. His face displayed no emotion. Finally, he shook his head, not a good sign, and started to pass the binoculars around.

"We had best get ourselves ready," he said quietly.

I finally got my turn to look through the glasses. The shells were landing on the north side of Teruel, and I could see fragments of buildings shattering with the raining artillery. I could see brave Brigadistas running for any shelter they could find. I saw the mismatched uniforms jostling for some remnant of organization, pointing obsolete guns at the well-armed and disciplined forces gradually inching toward them.

I looked down at them, my brave comrades, setting up barricades on the road leading to the city, but when I looked further up the road, I saw a steadily advancing column of Francoists.

I knew in my heart it was hopeless for us.

Worse, I could also see motorized weapons carriers among the columns. Helmeted commanders stood on them ordering men ahead, ready to blast their way through our barricades.

I was about the hand the glasses back when I heard planes flying overhead. I looked up. There were three of them, so low I could see the faces of the pilots clearly through the binoculars. One blonde pilot looked down at our camp, but kept flying on. I would swear later he was smiling and waving to us. They were Hienkels, the biplanes used by the German volunteers.

I watched in horror as the planes continued toward the town and started to strafe the hapless men in the city. That's all it took. It was the final straw for our side, and I saw the men racing to pull out, retreating to safety.

I don't blame you, I said to myself and handed the glasses to the next man waiting.

"Unlucky bastards," I heard him say, "It will be our turn soon enough."

What else could I do? I walked on and carried my helmet to the washing rack. I filled it with water and set it over the flame on the stove next to the rack. I longed for the shower truck, but this would have to do. I started to lather some soap and begin the crude shaving as I heard the propaganda truck passing again.

"Tomorrow we launch a major offensive. We will drive them back out of Teruel."

I tried to think of an appropriately sarcastic retort, but instead, used the remaining hot water in my helmet to wash my face and under my arms. I washed my feet and put on clean socks, turned and dumped the leftover water into a waiting oil drum. Nothing was going to dampen my spirits that day. Tamarah was scheduled to drive a convoy to us today.

I tried to put the propaganda truck out of my thoughts and wondered where she was, when she would be back with the convoy. I smiled at the thought of her, but remained worried for her safety, especially with those planes flying overhead.

When I was as clean as I knew I would ever be, I returned to my tent. I opened my pack, reassured when I could feel the cold steel of the pistol. Had it really been only a few months ago when someone passed it to me in Montreal?

That gun had become my touchstone. Touching it reminded me again of Seth and the bastards who had killed him. *If I ever see them again, I will be using this,* I vowed again, thinking about those men in leather coats, their faces burned into my memory for all eternity.

I reached past the gun and pulled out a leather pouch, looking very much the worse for wear now. I took out my precious photographs and remembered our time together, the time I had spent with Tamarah on the Spanish coast. I looked at the one of Tamarah and me hoisting glasses of sangria, toasting our good luck at being together. The other three were reminders of how truly happy I was to be with her. It was a feeling of total contentment.

I remembered our whispered conversations in bed after our love making, careful to tiptoe our way through discussions about any future.

"I just figured," I had said to her one night, "that you would want us to go to Canada or America when this is all over."

"Are the streets really paved with gold?" Her tone was teasing as she grinned at me in the dark. "Of course I want to go, but not until the paving is finished." I remember her hand on my cheek to reassure me she was joking.

Finally, she had told me, "I would like to take you to my home, Palestine. My father is a bear of a man and he would like you even if you aren't," she paused, "a Jew. It wouldn't matter to him, I think, because he would see the warrior in you. And if my mother were still alive, she would have both of you men wrapped with her apron strings," she laughed, throwing her head back in her infectious manner.

She talked often about her home being the 'Promised Land' that would marry history with the future. "It's a land of the future and it's tied with thousands of years of history and mystery."

I suddenly remembered how quiet we had been on the ride back from our leave. Once we were back, we took every opportunity to grab some wine and cheese and walk to the perimeter of our camp with our bedrolls. The other men respected our privacy, however envious they might have been.

I was thinking about that when nearby, explosions snatched my attention back to the present and I carefully stowed the photographs. Without waiting for orders, I slipped my pack over my shoulder after putting my soft hat into a pocket. I put my steel helmet on, picked up my rifle and walked back to the assembly area.

There were no trucks to be seen yet.

"It may be a long walk, comrades."

As we formed up and started out, wordlessly now, we headed toward the sound of the fighting. What else was there to do?

✷ ✷ ✷

As the interview ended, Michael sat back and looked at Alec, a man who seemed to be sagging as he told his story.

"The next part is..." and Alec stopped.

Whatever he had been ready to say, he seemed to change his mind, "This next part has to wait until tomorrow. Turn the fucking recorder off."

With that, Alec stood up and walked down the hall. Michael knew he would have to wait for tomorrow's session. He didn't think he was going to enjoy it.

Chapter 27
Harrison in Spain
November, 1937

In New York, it had been much colder than usual in the city. Harrison turned up the collar of his overcoat to ward off the chill. He walked from the warmth of the waiting area down to a dock pointing like a finger out into the frigid waters of the bay. At the end of the dock was a waiting Boeing 314 clipper, the Yankee Clipper.

It was a magnificent looking seaplane, but that mattered little to Harrison. He patted his pocket with the letter of invitation from Major Flunther, a senior officer in the German Army.

Would Mr. Harrison care to observe Franco's troops in action? the letter asked. Included were the necessary travel papers and *expenses related to such travel.*

On board the plane, Harrison settled back into the leather seat and studied the timetable he had removed from the seat pocket. He would be in Lisbon in a mere twenty-nine hours. A tri-motor passenger plane, a Junkers Ju 52, would be waiting to transport him to the front lines from there.

"Would you care for a drink, sir?"

Harrison waved the steward away. With a mighty roar of the engines revving for take-off, the pilot pushed to full-throttle, and the plane began the take-off, moving slowly at first, then it skimmed over the whitecaps of the bay.

The water seemed to hold onto the plane, to somehow deny its ability to fly until finally, the huge plane freed itself from the water's grasp. Jouncing soon gave way to the suppleness of the waiting wind currents.

Harrison slept little on the clipper. He couldn't block the drone of the motors from his mind. When he slept at all, it was fitful. None of the other forty passengers seemed troubled by the noise, laughing and joking as they shared drinks and conversation. Harrison ignored them and kept to himself.

The four Wright Cyclone engines kept the plane at a steady 183 mph, and he could see the whitecaps on the ocean far below when he looked out his window.

He had been impatient as the plane lifted off in New York and then turned north.

"Why are we going north?" he asked the passing steward.

"We are flying to Newfoundland in Canada," the reply.

"Why Newfoundland, Harrison yelled over the engine noise. "I thought we flew direct to Lisbon," Harrison demanded.

The steward patiently explained the globe and pointed out the need for refueling in Newfoundland before flying on to Southampton. Harrison sat back, still confused by the plane going north in order to go east.

Finally, when they reached England, there was a brief stopover in Southampton before the clipper took off again and turned south for a final leg to Lisbon.

The dreary winter weather of the North Atlantic had not prepared Harrison for his first view of Portugal. The sunlight was dazzling. The houses were layered up a hill; they were terraced and each painted a different pastel color. The brilliant blue sky provided a superb backdrop to the scene.

Harrison, however, didn't have the inclination to enjoy the view and was pleased when they landed and he saw a car sitting next to the passenger terminal. He knew it was waiting for him.

A thin man in a grey pin-striped suit stepped out of the car, looking at a photograph, and then looking up as if to verify Harrison was the man he was supposed to meet.

"Herr Harrison?" he said softly as he bowed slightly.

"Yeah."

The man with the German accent stiffened at the crudeness of Harrison's reply.

"Please, this way, sir. We have made arrangement that will facilitate your way through customs," and he signaled the driver to retrieve the luggage from the steward approaching the vehicle.

"These must be yours," he said, pointing as the steward set some bags next to Harrison. The steward didn't look unhappy to be rid of his passenger.

Once he was through customs and had been welcomed to Portugal, he was soon sitting in the back of the embassy limousine. Harrison was amused that the car was British instead of German.

"All the arrangements have been made. Your plane to Spain leaves in two days. You will be met upon your arrival. Tonight there will be a cocktail party at our embassy. Your escort, if it is not me, will meet you at the hotel and provide any further information you might need."

Harrison frowned and felt a growing unease. Maybe it was from the recent travel, but Harrison hated functions that involved cocktails. "I'm not sure-"

"Nonsense, it is in your honor, you just have to be present. All other details have been arranged."

Harrison nodded.

Later in his hotel room, soaking in a large, enamel tub, he thought as he rubbed the bar of soap over his huge arms, *I wonder what it will be like there in Spain?*

He leaned back and at least no longer had to put up with that sniveling, condescending man at the airport, oozing fake sincerity.

The same man met him later that night, however, in the hotel lobby.

"How was your dinner, Herr Harrison?" he asked in his heavily accented English.

"I couldn't get a decent steak," Harrison said with sincerity. "The potatoes were...not the way I like them." Harrison was definitely not a diplomat; there were no mincing words in his presence.

He walked into the reception hall at the German Embassy. The party was not an especially large one. It was an all-male gathering and most of the men were in uniform. In fact, Harrison had never seen so many different kinds of uniforms. Each seemed to have a different color, and they looked like they were outdoing each other in the number of medals pinned on the jackets. It reminded him of his earlier trip to Germany. *These people sure like their uniforms.*

His only attempt at culture before this night had been to attend a performance of a Gilbert and Sullivan opera. Tonight reminded him of the characters on that stage.

But, this opera wasn't comical.

A man in a stark, black uniform walked up to Harrison and put his hand casually on Harrison's arm. "Let's get some air, shall we," indicating as he pushed open the double doors to the balcony.

"You don't look any more comfortable that I feel," he said to Harrison.

That brought a slight smile to Harrison's face. "Is it that obvious?"

"Only to me," the man said. He held out his hand, "My name is Kessler, Fritz Kessler. You may call me Fritz, if you like," and smiled.

"People just call me Harrison now. It used to be Mr. Samuel T. Harrison, but I'm kinda used to Harrison now."

"Certainly," the German said with a slight bow.

"For the record," Harrison said, "my role at Pinkerton's is...how should I put this...limited these days."

"We know about what happened," Fritz said. "No matter," waiving his hand in dismissal. "We may have a role for you to consider before you leave." His face was the perfect reflection of an enigma. Harrison wondered how they could possibly know.

"I just don't want any misunderstanding," he added, "That's all."

Fritz leaned in and lowered his voice, "We don't have a lot of time to talk. There is much to see in Spain. When you see just how powerful we are, we want you to talk to the right people when you are back in America."

The German stood back and pulled out a cigarette. With the other hand, he reached into his jacket and pulled out a holder. He carefully placed the cigarette in the holder and lighted it with a casual move. He stood with the holder clenched between his teeth, exactly the way President Roosevelt was often pictured.

"We have arranged for you to see it firsthand, raw power at its finest."

He took Harrison back into the room and announced to the other men, "Our American guest is tired from his flight. I am going to take him back to the hotel. Please continue to help yourself," gesturing toward the food and drink. The other men didn't seem to object. In fact, they grew more animated as Harrison and Fritz left, as though free to finally talk amongst themselves.

The next morning, Harrison and his luggage were delivered by the embassy limousine to a nearby airfield. The location was identified as a strictly private field by a black and white sign. Serious-looking men with automatic weapons guarded the entrance, and the field was crowded with planes of all descriptions, all carrying the German black and white cross on their sides and the swastika on their tails.

Men in uniforms scurried about and Harrison saw some of them loading crates into a waiting Junkers. Fritz was standing next to the yawning loading door with a clipboard in hand.

"Ah, my good man Harrison. You are just who we were waiting for. These are the last of the cargo to be loaded," and he waved his hand vaguely. Harrison noted that Fritz was no longer in uniform, but wearing a full-length leather coat and a fedora on his head. The men all seemed submissive in his presence.

"Gestapo," he overheard one man whisper to another, and they avoided eye contact with Harrison.

Fritz led Harrison up the metal steps sloped against the fuselage. Inside the plane, Harrison adjusted his vision to the dimness and saw cargo strapped to the sides, leaving barely enough room to walk between the crates. He noted the distinctive outline of weapons, but didn't comment. Just behind the door to the cockpit, there were two leather seats side by side. They were turned around so that Fritz and Harrison had their backs to the cockpit, looking back over the cargo.

"Amazing, eh," Fritz said, "how much they can pack into a plane these days?"

They could hear one of the crew members closing the cargo door, making sure it was secured. He saluted Fritz as he walked past them to his place in the cockpit.

"Close the cockpit door behind you," Fritz said to the departing back.

"Jawhol," was the instant response, and the cockpit door clicked shut. Harrison imagined the man's heels clicking and his hand extended into a *heil*!

The three motors started one by one, and soon the plane was taxiing. The throttles engaged and Harrison felt the plane begin to move, gathering speed. He clenched his fists on the side of the seat until the blood practically drained from his hands. He held his breath until the heavily laden plane finally reached lift speed. The wheels started to bounce and then smoothness settled over the plane, but Harrison could feel the plane straining for altitude.

Fritz laughed, "No worry, my good friend, Hitler wouldn't let one of his precious planes be overloaded.

Harrison knew better than to laugh at this deprecating comment. He remembered from his earlier trip to Germany that only insiders were ever permitted a jest at Hitler's expense.

Fritz opened an envelope. "We have the information you requested. There is more than one Ferguson, but we think we know the one you want, an Alec Ferguson?"

"How did you-"

"It was easy, my American friend. This tidy little war is over for all practical purposes. We have more spies on the other side than we need. The rats are scurrying for whatever money gets handed around." A snide leer crossed his face before he continued, "We hear this man probably came on a ship from Texas. He was bloodied in a battle near Aragon. That was a few months back, in August."

"By bloodied, you mean hurt?"

"No, I should have said 'blooded' in battle. He went from being a recruit to being a real soldier. They may be a band of rabble, but they fight like a pack of hyenas."

Harrison waited for more.

"He marches with an infantry company. We know they are in the hills south of Teruel. The fighting there has been vicious. Those bastards fight and fight. First, we took the city from them. I'm sorry, I meant to say Franco's army took the city," he said with a slight smile. "I'm so used to saying *we.* Frankly, the Nationalists wouldn't be anywhere without us."

"You have provided much, from what I hear," Harrison said.

"We sent men, equipment and money. We have given them the latest and best men and machines. You should see the grins on the faces of our fine Condor Legion airmen. The newsreels back home are proving to the German people just how powerful we are on land, and especially in the air."

He talked over the noise of the engines, "Women have been known to swoon merely watching our blonde warriors on the newsreels."

"And the Italians," Harrison asked.

Fritz snorted, "All they brought to Spain was their strutting. They are particularly good at strutting."

The plane bounced unexpectedly on an air current. The door to the cockpit opened and the copilot apologized for the turbulence, saying they would be crossing the mountains soon and to strap their harnesses until it got better. He closed the door again and Harrison noted how men seemed to defer to his new friend sitting to his side.

"Let's get back to your request, Harrison. I have arranged for a tour. You will be touring the battlefield at a place called Teruel. Imagine, you and Mr. Ferguson—together at last." He laughed so hard he started to cough and took out a handkerchief to politely cover his mouth. When he stopped coughing, Fritz pulled out his cigarette holder and a pack of cigarettes once again. Harrison noticed this time that it was an American brand. "The best," Fritz commented, as he lit up and smoked in the languid European manner.

The events of the next two days swirled like a tornado in Harrison's world. He was driven to the front line with Fritz always at his side. They ended up on a hill about three kilometers southeast of Teruel, where a rail line snaked through the valley below, and another hill rose beyond the track, further south and east.

Fritz barked, "Bring us binoculars!" and two pair appeared as if the men knew in advance he would ask for them. Handing one to Harrison, he said, "Look at the hill on the other side of the track."

Harrison raised the glasses and adjusted the focus.

"If I may," a soldier said to Harrison. He took the glasses and showed him how to adjust the focus more. When Harrison looked again, he was amazed at the detail he could see and marveled at the Germans' lensmaking talents.

Across the expanse, he clearly saw men in peaked caps, uniforms that weren't congruous, and a line of new trucks. He could hear the artillery roaring behind him and saw puffs of smoke from shells landing in the distance. They whistled overhead as more shells rained down on the unfortunate bastards in the distance. He noticed that none of it seemed to unsettle Fritz, who continued to look through his glasses.

Finally, he said, "Look," and pointed. "There, the man standing by the truck. He seems to be in charge." Fritz looked down at a photograph and nodded. "I'm not sure, but that may be your man."

Harrison pushed the glasses to his face so quickly he caused a small cut to the side of his nose. There, he saw a man come into view. There was no doubt in his mind. It was the spitting image of Ian Ferguson. *No*, he reminded himself, *not Ian*. He was looking at the man who had started this whole nasty episode in his life. He was looking at a man that could also, perhaps, restart his career. He could see Alec through the lens. He turned with a sneer to Fritz.

Reading his thoughts, Fritz said, "We will try. We have it arranged." They tried indeed. There was no shortage of volunteers who seemed ready to impress the steely-eyed man in the leather coat.

The men standing around planning the next move all seemed like experienced veterans to Harrison. They were organizing a special raid on the hill across the valley. He didn't know this was orchestrated especially for him.

"Would you like to go with us?" one of the men turned to Harrison and asked.

Harrison leapt at the opportunity. He suddenly felt very old next to these soldiers, but he more than made up for that with supercharged adrenaline. They offered him a pistol, but he pulled his own from his shoulder holster. "This is all I need," he said, touching the gun lovingly.

When it was time, they marched hard. First down the slope, and then crossing the rail line, they waited for bullets to come flying toward them. The careful march up the slope on the other side of the track was eerily quiet, however.

Harrison's worst suspicions were soon confirmed. He had been developing a growing sense of dread and uselessness. When they reached the top of the other slope, the only thing in evidence was piles of discarded and unneeded detritus. It was a familiar sight, the look of ground deserted by an army. Alec Ferguson was nowhere in sight, and Harrison grudgingly accepted that his last opportunity to capture his adversary had slipped through his fingers once again, into the Spanish night.

Back in Lisbon, he told Fritz that he was grateful for the opportunity, and he was.

"We are looking for good things from you when you are back in America," Fritz had said with a casual wave good-bye.

On the long flight home, Harrison contented himself thinking about his new role for the Gestapo. Fritz had officially handed him commission papers. In his pocket, Harrison had a lot of money, with orders for his return to the United States. One of the last things Fritz had said was, "Someone will contact you soon. They will provide you with a radio and a code. We are most interested in what this man, Roosevelt, is all about."

The drone of the Yankee Clipper had the opposite effect on Harrison during the return trip. Instead of anxious anticipation keeping him awake, he slept soundly on this return trip and dreamed about a young waitress he knew back in the Bronx. He thought about giving her a visit when he got home.

Fuck you, Randolph, he smiled to himself dreamily, as the plane started its majestic descent.

Chapter 28
Tamarah's New Truck
February, 1938

I had seen Tamarah's highs and lows and had comforted her when she was feeling down and disillusioned. When she was feeling elated, I willingly shared her enthusiasm, delighting in her eagerness to stand up for what she believed to be true.

That said, I had never seen her as excited as she was this particular morning. Her enthusiasm radiated with an almost untamed abandon. I had awoken that morning to a cold wind blowing up the valley from the direction of Teruel. I held a metal cup of hot, steaming coffee, warming my hands as I carefully sipped the dark brew.

Say what you will about the food, we do get good coffee.

I knew she was coming before she arrived. There was no mistaking the sound of her arrival. The deep, throaty roar of truck motors preceded the arrival of her convoy.

What was different about the sound today? I wondered. I was puzzled. It wasn't the wheezing sound of old trucks. No, I heard something else—the sound of *serious* trucks.

I saw the first one as it crested the hill to my right. The morning sun was just rising and the trucks emerged from out of the sun's glare. As they came to a stop, I saw her in the first truck, the lead driver's flag fluttering from the fender of her truck.

"Look! It's a brand new truck!" she shouted to me, stepping to the running board and then jumping to the ground. She pointed to the flag. "And, just look at that." She turned down the sleeves and held out her arm; new chevrons had been hastily sewn on.

"Comrade Sergeant to you," she said with a laugh. "You may salute me, if you wish." She untied her bandana, wiping grime from her face and ran up to me. We kissed and hugged, and I held her as long as I could, until she finally pulled away. I felt an electric excitement coursing through her.

"How did this happen, your new truck?" I asked. I didn't even try to hide my smile. "And those chevrons, how did that come about?"

"We finally managed to land a ship at Valencia. It got through the international blockade. Those brave men on the ship managed to get through. I will never forget the name of that battered ship, the Oreposa." She was beaming.

She stopped when she saw the look on my face.

"What did you say? What was the name of that ship?"

"The Oreposa," she repeated, the smile falling from her face in confusion at my reaction.

"Did the captain have flaming red hair and a beard?"

"That was the ship that brought you to Spain, wasn't it?" It was not really a question; she remembered the story of my passage to Spain.

She paused, carefully choosing her words. "They tried to get underway as soon as she was unloaded. Three of Franco's gunboats raced up and cornered the ship, just offshore." Her eyes filled with tears. "We watched it all, helpless to do anything. I couldn't turn away. The shelling was brutal, and that wonderful old ship rocked with each explosion and just couldn't take it anymore. We could see the fires on her deck and black smoke started to pour out of a huge gash in the side. Then, she just turned and sank. Just like that!" snapping her fingers for effect.

"There were no survivors," she continued, "Some fishermen risked their lives to go out. They looked all night and the next morning. Then they had to run back to escape the patrol boats."

I took the news hard. It had been miserable hiding in the hold of that ship, but I was determined not to show it, even to her. *It just keeps getting worse*, I thought, wondering why I felt such loss. It was, after all, just a rusty old boat. But, I also had the memory of the brave men on that rusty old boat, men who had risked it all.

I shook my head at the image. *How many more?* I wondered.

"Tell me about your new truck," I turned and said, brushing away thoughts of the ship.

Her enthusiasm came rushing back. "Damn, you should have been there, Alec! I wish you could have seen it."

She was interrupted by a crowd gathering around the new trucks. The curiosity about these brand new Soviet trucks carried a tone of cynicism.

"Kinda late to be giving us new shit like this now, eh?" That came from a Canuck that I knew, a young lad from Manitoba.

She couldn't be put off, however. "You should have been there," Tamarah repeated, turning back to me, "We drove to Valencia in our old trucks. It took us forever. Three out of our fourteen trucks simply gave up on the way. We had to push them off the road and leave them. There was no use even trying to repair them."

She frowned slightly, "One of them was my old truck. I rode with comrade Fiddler. He's a terrible driver. He can't help but grind the gears, and more than once I had my hand on the door, ready to jump."

I had heard her complain to me about him before and I just nodded.

"I just couldn't bring myself to criticize him. He's so tired, just like the rest of us. Anyway, when we got to Valencia, we drove straight out to the docks and parked alongside a warehouse. I started to light up a cigarette when a guy ran up and yelled at me. He yelled something about all the high-octane fuel. Well, he didn't have to tell me twice. We slept in our trucks that night." The words poured out of her in an energized rush.

"When the sun came up, we could see that old ship. There was a gantry lifting up a truck and started to swing it to the dock. Hanging from the arm of that gantry was the prettiest truck I had ever seen. Oh, I know it was built Soviet-ugly, but it was beautiful to me."

She brushed a fly away from her face, "It was shiny, the windows were all taped over, and the gantry dropped it on the dock with a clunk. I couldn't stop myself," she laughed, "I just ran up and put my arms over the hood and gave it a huge kiss."

"Not like our kisses," she laughed throatily, touching my arm.

"I sure hope not," I smirked, brow raised.

"You should have seen the other drivers. All the men started to laugh. I didn't even care. Then a man stepped out of the office. I knew him right away. We all did. We came to attention, our arms extended in salute. It was Comrade Tovarich, the head of all trucks and convoys. I could see the two red stars on his collar. He took off his hat and when I saw his brow, I could tell he was very tired."

As she told me about Tovarich and the new trucks, I watched, unable to contain my delight for her.

"Tovarich started to laugh at me," she said, "and so did the other men. I knew it wasn't an unpleasant laugh coming from him. Alec, I can still see him standing there, sweeping his arm around. Then he did something that startled me. He walked over to me and said that he had heard of my work. Can you imagine, he had heard of my work?"

She wiped her hair back and said, "He told me the new truck was mine and called me Comrade Tamarah." Her eyes sparkled as she spoke. "In fact," she lowered her voice a bit, "he told me that *all* the trucks were mine to command." She paused as she watched my shocked expression. "Then, he added that I had been appointed the new convoy commander. He pointed to the men as he said that, and every single one of those drivers was stunned. Well, they certainly stopped laughing at me then!"

I put my arms around her and asked, "Am I permitted to kiss a convoy commander?"

She pointed to the flag on her truck, "You have to ask for permission first," and then we kissed long and hard.

I watched her as we let go of each other. She patted my arm again and turned, shouting to the men, "Comrades, we need to unload these trucks at once." There was a new charge of authority in her voice.

While she busied herself at being a convoy commander, I walked away. I was trying to focus on thoughts that were whispering into my consciousness.

In spite of my pleasure at seeing her with the new trucks, I started to worry about what was happening with the war. I had finally admitted to myself that I had some dangerous thoughts about the war swirling around us. In less than a year's time, the continuing collapse of our positions was alarming to anyone following the news.

The propagandists are telling us what they have to say. They tell us we only have to fight harder. It was something they had to say, but we all knew better.

This latest battle alone was a sign of how things were unraveling. We were putting up a good fight. We kept trading positions with the enemy, but I knew it couldn't go on. Attrition was taking a toll on our side. Franco's army just kept getting stronger, with more and newer equipment.

It's going to take more than nine new trucks. That reality hurt all the more, knowing how much they meant to Tamarah. She had even painted a name on the side of her truck, dedicating it to one of her heroes, Emma Goldman.

As I walked, I thought about my enthusiasm when I first marched up to the fortress. At last, I was going to be a proud member of the Mac-Paps. I was going to make a difference. It seemed so long ago; my naivety evaporated with what had passed for training. The rest of my enthusiasm was sapped when we were sent, unprepared, into that first battle.

Now, as I watched Tamarah unloading her truck, I couldn't quell the despair I still felt over the utterly senseless death of my friend Seth.

No, I shouted silently, *it was much more than just a death— he was assassinated. He was murdered by those henchmen in leather coats. He was shot for believing in something, something that had not been cast in the NKVD mold.*

I knew the real power strings led back to Joseph Stalin. We all had seen the pictures of him, unsmiling, as he stood on some podium, almost waving to men and women parading before him.

I tried to stay focused on my real reason for being here. It was much more than the struggle between right and left, Hitler and Stalin. We Brigadistas were champions of real men and women, the farmers, workers, and children. We believed we were helping them in their struggle against the rich and powerful, who had kept them under their thumb far too long.

But, such rhetoric sounded hollow to me now.

Worst of all, I realized we were being handed another setback here in Spain, in Teruel. I knew it was just a matter of time. I could count. The numbers for Franco were increasing while the numbers for our side were rapidly depleting. For the first time, I openly admitted to myself that it might be over; the end was in sight. We had fought our best fight. And we had lost.

I walked to a hill overlooking the camp and looked back at the line of new trucks. They looked so military. But, what good would nine new trucks really do in the grand scheme of things? I was truly heartbroken for my Tamarah.

No Pasarán. It had been a long time since anyone had shouted that. The very sound of it now, sounded hollow to my ears.

I need to talk to Tamarah soon. Would it be Palestine or America? Whichever destination we chose, we needed to make up our minds and our plans soon. *This can't go on and we have to make a decision.*

I did my best to shrug off my ennui, knowing it would do no good to share it with Tamarah while she was basking in her enthusiasm.

I started to walk back down the hill to the camp. My feet were sore from marching in ill-fitting boots. One foot, my left one, had a sore that wouldn't heal. I tried to ignore it by joking to myself about a heel needing to heal, but it was a painful joke at best. I knew many of the others carried similar woes of pain and discomfort, or worse. We all seemed to carry our misery without complaining. *What good does it do to complain?*

My spirits lifted as I walked back into the camp. I heard her voice behind me. She was talking and surrounded by a group of men and yelling at me to join them. Many just wanted to be near a pretty woman. She chose to believe they were interested in the details of her truck.

"It was built in Russia," she said, as if that was all anyone needed to know. "Look," she said pointing, "some of the workers painted their signature on it. It's a ZIS-6. We can get speeds up to fifty-five kmh. Can you believe it? Coming back to camp, it practically climbed hills by itself!"

"I've heard of this truck," a man said. "Someone saw one just like it with tubes on it, large tubes."

"The Katyusha rocket launcher," she said knowingly. "You know what they call it? I saw it on the side of a truck in Valencia. орган Сталина in Russian. In English it means Stalin's Organ. It fires rockets, looking and sounding like a gruesome pipe organ."

I wondered where she learned all of this

"It all depends on which of Stalin's organs you're being fucked with," a man sneered, and several others nudged each other at the dangerous statement.

"I didn't see any Katyusha rockets here at this battle," another man spat out in his disgust. "What good are they on some dock in Valencia?"

Many of the men shifted their footing, visibly uneasy with these ill-advised remarks and looked around, wary that men in leather coats and fedora hats might snatch them away for being unpatriotic.

The disgusted man added, "We get new, shiny trucks to bring us what, comrade?

"Only some food for your belly and bullets for your guns," she snapped.

In her irritation, I sensed this wasn't the time to discuss thoughts about our leaving. *There will soon come a time.*

Chapter 29
Tamarah—Comrade Hero

I was standing on the hill when I felt it.

Odd, I thought, *it's almost like someone is looking at me.*

I had turned away from the trucks and was gazing over the valley to the opposite side. I looked around and none of my men seemed to be paying any attention to me. So, why was I feeling like someone was looking at me?

I smiled when I thought back to how surprised Tamarah had been with my own promotion to sergeant. I waited until well into the evening and her trucks had been unloaded.

"Who's in charge now?" I had laughed. "In fact," I said, "my promotion came first. I think I outrank you by a few minutes," and grinned at her changing face. I could tell she was happy for my promotion, even though I still had my own dark doubts about it.

Now, we stood by the side of her truck and looked across the valley. Even with the naked eye, I could see the enemy. I think I pointed them out to her.

I walked over to the artillery officer and asked him if I could look through his spotting glasses. They were mounted on a tripod and all I had to do was put my eyes against the rubber rims. The office told me they had been made in the Soviet Union and were an exact copy of the Ziess German lenses.

I saw them, the enemy, clearly across the way. I could see men passing out equipment, I could see some eating, and I could see some men kicking a soccer ball. *They even have time and energy for games.* I shuddered at the thought.

I wasn't surprised to recognize the German uniforms many were wearing. I saw one particular group of men with glasses, their glasses staring back at me. Was it my imagination, or were they really looking at me? They stood apart from the other soldiers and two of the men were dressed in suits. One of the men I saw was huge, and I swear the man was looking directly at me.

He's wearing a leather coat, same as the man next to him. Doesn't matter which side, men in leather coats are the dangerous ones, and I silently resolved again to find those men who killed Seth. I knew it was something I had to do somehow, before I left Spain forever.

My arms were starting to get tired as I shrugged and turned away from the glasses. The sight of those men soon left my mind. I had other things to do, and I was responsible now that I was in charge. I was unsure of myself, but I couldn't let the men see me looking worried.

"I have to go," Tamarah said quietly. We hugged briefly and I watched her walk back toward the trucks. An immense feeling of melancholy washed over me and I shrugged it away.

Looking at my watch, I took a whistle out of my pocket and signaled for the men to assemble.

"We have our orders," I said, not wanting the weariness creeping into my words, but unable to keep it completely from them. "Just as soon as it gets dark, we are going to load up the next trucks and get the hell out of here. This fight is over for us."

"No!" someone shouted, and I gave him a sharp look.

"No arguments," I said, as I held up my hand, palm outward. "Comrade Tamarah and her drivers will get us out of this hell hole. We can't let anyone see us preparing to leave. Use the remaining daylight to take inventory and have what you need ready to grab when I give the order."

I reached deep inside for the strength to give the orders with clarity and authority. "As soon as it's dark enough, we will quickly get on the trucks and leave nothing behind that's of any use to our enemy. We will see how fast these Soviet trucks of Tamarah's can go, eh?"

One of the men, from Poland, said with dripping sarcasm, "Can we leave the lice and rats for the enemy, too?"

Some, but not all of the men, laughed.

Tamarah listened to this and stood at attention, looking proud. It may have been a withdrawal, but her trucks would do their job.

"Did you hear that, comrade drivers? These men are depending on us." She glanced at me and nodded, "We are ready, comrade Sergeant," and she actually saluted me. I rubbed away the pain from my forehead. It was my almost constant companion now.

"Comrade Convoy Leader-"

"Yes,sir," she beamed.

"I can see your trucks are ready," and I smiled back.

It was a Sunday afternoon and I had watched over the preparations. Now the men were doing as they had been told. They slowly and quietly performed an inventory—in one pile the things they would take, and in another, the things they would simply abandon.

I was pleased. We didn't lack in bravery, ready to take a stand where we could, but I was relieved that we were abandoning this place. There was no winning to be had for us here, only more death.

To anyone observing and I knew there were men across the valley doing just that, my men looked like they were preparing for battle. *Well, they can have this damn place. They won't find us here by morning.*

"Comrade Sergeant," a young man said. He was new and fresh from what passed for training. "Are we not going to fight?"

I struggled to keep the weariness and sense of betrayal out of my voice. "Son, we have had the fight kicked out of us too many times."

"But-"

I held my hand up to stop him. I knew he wanted his chance. He had made it here, all the way from the south of Africa.

"You will get your chance, but tonight, we live for another day. Treasure that and write it in your diary. Someday you will understand what I'm telling you now."

"Sergeant," another voice rang out.

"What is it?" I answered.

"The sunlight is almost gone. The men are ready."

I looked at my watch and nodded. "In thirty minutes," I said, "start moving towards the trucks. Walk slowly, as if we are going for chow."

I could hear Tamarah and her drivers. One by one, they were getting in their trucks, each door closing quietly. After a few minutes, one lone truck started up. Right then, I was very happy with these new trucks. The old ones would have wheezed their loud coughing across the valley floor and easily been heard on the other side.

I was pleased that Tamarah had known to instruct each man to start their trucks at random times. The enemy might not notice that they were all being started if it were done one at a time. I should have known she would know exactly what to do.

I crossed my fingers for luck and walked towards the trucks, satisfied when all the men had boarded. As the last truck quietly idled, Tamarah came up behind me and put her arms around me, hugging me from behind. I turned to her and we embraced.

"See you in Valencia," she whispered, just before I tilted her chin up to me. Our kiss was long and passionate, and we paid no attention to the envious glances from the men who had slowly made their way to the trucks.

"Ready when you are comrade," I said as I stepped back to salute her.

"No Pasarán," she said, probably on impulse.

I gave a scornful snort at the emptiness of the phrase and turned toward the enemy somewhere in the growing darkness. *Fuck it,* I thought.

"O.k., men. Let's get the hell out of here."

I heard the tailgates lowered on each truck and was pleased as I watched the men boarding the truck, barely a sound to give away our escape.

I was so proud of Tamarah, too. She was like a hurricane of activity, flitting from driver to driver, making sure they each understood their instructions. I heard her complimenting them and knew she could rely on her experienced drivers to get us to safety. She had planned it so each truck would start out at random times, again to avoid creating a convoy sound. Each driver knew they would drive by the growing moonlight, without headlamps, to a rendezvous point several kilometers down the road.

There, we would join up and race out of this shithole.

Tamarah, as the lead driver, started her truck, gears engaging smoothly, and though the truck may have looked square and lacking in style, it was powerful, and she drove into the darkness with her precious cargo of escaping veteran Brigadistas. Many, myself included, were weeping openly as the trucks started to leave.

I made sure I was the last man remaining in the camp. When all but the last truck had disappeared into the inky darkness, I went around and lit candles, lanterns and flashlights. They were placed strategically around the abandoned campsite, an illusion of occupation. For fun, I even started a small campfire, throwing abandoned ammunition crates on the flames.

I finally stepped onto the running board next to Tamarah and nodded. Her truck lurched forward and one man started to sing softly. He had a beautiful baritone voice, the words in Spanish. It was the *Himno de la Internacional.* Soon, others joined in, each in their own language, applying their native tongue to the *Internationale.*

I couldn't hold back the tears as I listened. Even though I considered myself a horrible singer, I soon joined in. As the singing slowly faded away, the truck kept moving until we could see small flickers of lights ahead.

"That must be the convoy, I hope," Tamarah whispered.

Then we saw the welcoming signal.

I had done it; I had managed to help pull off a full-scale retreat under the very noses of our enemy. It may not have been a victory, but it was far better than the certain disaster awaiting us on that lonely ridge in the morning.

Our small convoy arrived in Valencia just as the morning sky made its transition from dark to gray, then to the slate blue and orange of a morning on the coast of Spain.

Tamarah and her drivers moved their trucks into a large warehouse and started the maintenance necessary before they could seek needed rest. The drivers were obviously sagging under the weariness and tension of driving through the dark, a part of that drive with nothing but moonlight to show them the way.

My men and I were directed to a large table that had been set up in a courtyard. Soon, we were enjoying the first real breakfast we had seen in weeks.

"We did it," I heard Tamarah's voice from behind me.

"We did it," I confirmed, as I shoveled in a large spoonful of eggs.

"We just got more orders," she said wearily, "They need our trucks again. We have to hurry; there is another group to pull out. I don't know how we can do it, we are all so tired. But we will manage," she said this with more conviction than her face indicated.

We hugged quickly and I walked with her to the trucks and watched them prepare to depart. This time, the trucks all started at once, and with a wave from Tamarah, they all lurched into motion and soon disappeared on a road leading northwest out of our new camp.

I found a table under an olive tree and spread my blanket on top. I climbed up, closed my eyes, and was thinking about Tamarah, smiling as I dreamed.

I hope she can stay awake at the wheel of her truck.

That was my last thought before sleep fell heavy upon me. It was a deep and dreamless sleep, a sleep I hadn't experienced since my promotion to sergeant and before the useless battles we had fought in retreat.

What was it? I tried to focus as I realized I was being roughly awakened. No, not roughly, it just seemed like it.

"Alec," a voice said.

Who the hell calls me Alec anymore?

"Comrade Sergeant Alec?" a man said in Spanish accented English.

I sat upright, combing my fingers through my hair, "Yes?"

"The officer there, he wants to see you," and he pointed to a man standing in the doorway. I remember I clamored off the table with some semblance of dignity and did my best to stand straight and walk towards the man. In reality, it was probably more like the walk of a man who had been drinking too much. No matter, no one paid any attention to it or made any comment.

The officer didn't say anything to me, but gestured to an empty room. Once inside, he closed the door quietly behind him and turned to me. He seemed to be thinking of the words he needed.

Finally, he started, "We all knew about you two..." and he stopped, his mouth moving, but no sound coming out. He shuffled his feet and looked at the ground

"We all...we all thought..." and he stopped again.

The officer ran a dirty sleeve over his eyes and nose, wiping away his sadness. That was when I knew. I felt it with an awful clarity, feeling it physically before it even registered in my brain. I suddenly turned and started to vomit, started my keening.

"No, oh my God! No!"

No!

No!

No!"

I struggled for breath. "How?" I somehow managed to ask between the sobs.

"Three dive bombers appeared out of nowhere. There was nothing anyone could do."

"Tamarah?" I rasped.

"She's dead, comrade. The lead truck was their first target. She died a hero's death. She will most certainly get a medal."

I erupted at his words and turned on the officer who was now backing up against the door. Suddenly fearful for his safety, he was looking for a way out.

"*No*," I said, so softly the officer could barely hear me. "A true hero's death would have come to her in old age, while she was telling stories to our grandchildren. A *true* hero's death would have been to know all *this* had been for a good cause, which was all worth it!"

My rage burned itself into white-hot grief.

I abruptly realized I would never see Tamarah again, and I suddenly saw her waving to me from her truck earlier that day.

As soon as I imagined that, the image of her waving blurred into my tears.

Seth and now Tamarah, I shuddered at the thought. They were now both a part of this sacred land forever.

Chapter 30

Harrison in Vermont

Something bothered Harrison on the flight back to New York, trying to get comfortable in the leather seat of the Yankee Clipper. Finding comfort in any seat wasn't easy for a man his size.

As darkness approached and the steward made up the berth, he was uncomfortable in the bed designed with smaller people in mind. But, he had learned over the years that few beds had been intended for someone his size.

He continued to curse himself at the memory of storming the hill in Spain, only to find an empty camp. He understood the reality, but he had so imagined his joy at finally capturing the man he had been chasing for so long. Instead, Alec Ferguson and the others had vanished. *The man is an illusionist,* Harrison thought to himself, *disappearing into clouds of vapor.*

He tried his best to sleep, but the image of Alec Ferguson kept floating back into his consciousness. He listened to the drone of the engines, turning on his side first to the bulkhead, and then towards the aisle.

"May I help, sir?" the attendant was checking on his passengers. Harrison merely grunted and turned back away.

His bad humor increased as each mile passed on the trip back to New York. At some point over the Atlantic, his emotions rose past simply a bad mood and turned into a white-hot rage.

He rolled to his side in the cramped berth and started to pummel the mattress, imagining each pounding of his fist was really landing on the face of a helpless Ferguson.

Finally, in the growing light of dawn, Harrison stood and watched as the steward pushed the bunk into the wall. As the man moved on, Harrison sat in the waiting seat and pulled the seat belt tightly across his lap. The plane descended through layers of rough winds and Harrison looked out the window at whitecaps on the water below. The plane made a sharp turn to the right and entered a cove shielded by a breakwater. There were small whitecaps, but the plane continued down and finally slammed against the waves, embraced by the caress of the water, and turned away from the wind, approaching the landing facilities and passenger terminal. Harrison made a pledge to himself—his flying days were over.

His luggage stowed in the trunk of the taxi, Harrison reached into his pocket for the envelope he had been given by his German handler, and reread the instructions, smiling at the missive:

1. Maintain your employment with Pinkerton's Detective Agency.
2. Report to the Bund offices in New York.
3. Begin reorganization of the Eastern operations at once.
4. Follow strict instructions on radio operations.
5. Contact your cover as instructed.

❇ ❇ ❇

Harrison's first days back at Pinkerton's were uneventful. They were all too happy to have him sit at a desk shuffling papers from the *in basket* to the *out basket*, without much happening in between. He was the model of insignificance and that suited his purpose just fine.

People around him soon realized it was in their best interest to ignore him. Before long, any invitations for coffee or lunch dwindled away, and the others went about their work as if he weren't even there. There was one woman, nevertheless, who seemed to hold his attention. She caught him looking at her in a peculiar way. She would never know how lucky she was not to be added to his list of victims, but she shuddered at the office gossip when the full story was passed around the agency, with the lurid descriptions of his treatment of certain women.

He knew he had to be cautious. He had been warned. Still, he was more interested in her job—custodian of files. He waited with the patience of a hunter, knowing the information he was really after was in the hundreds of thousands of files in the cavernous warehouse behind her desk.

Fuck Pinkerton's and fuck the Germans.

The single driving force in Harrison's life was to find Ian Ferguson. He had missed the son, but Ian Ferguson was the name that had been on his personal most-wanted list ever since the Haymarket Riots. Ian Ferguson was the man truly responsible for the assassination of the undercover Pinkerton detective, a man recruited by Harrison himself. He made a vow to take his revenge on the father and track down the son later, no matter how long it might take.

Like his son, Ian Ferguson was a ghost, an apparition that would appear somewhere, and then be gone in a flash. The man was like a chimera, and the mere thought of him drove Harrison into a fury beyond reckoning.

And now, he knew the complete file on Ian Ferguson was on a shelf somewhere behind the desk of Marsha Clamb, who spelled her name with a 'b' at the end. Without her, the file stayed just out of Harrison's reach.

Harrison decided he would be very nice to Miss Marsha Clamb, though playing nice was not something that came naturally. It had never been a part of his repertoire of tactics that he used on his victims. He made a stop-off at a florist on the way in to work one morning; it was a Thursday, a day of no particular meaning. It was the day he would find the key to the file he needed.

His first instinct was to buy the largest bouquet he could find. Then he thought about Marsha Clamb. *Funny name,* he thought, *just like her—kinda plain but not unattractive.* He realized she might feel overwhelmed with a large display, given for no apparent reason. He didn't need her suspicious because of grandiosity.

He looked around the shop and spotted a small pot. It was a live plant, the clerk explained, "Your girl will be able to keep it for a long time. Miniature roses, they are."

Harrison ignored the 'girlfriend' reference and knew it would be the perfect introduction. He didn't give a damn what kind of plant it was, it just looked elegant and understated, exactly right for Marsha Clamb.

He had guessed correctly; Marsha looked up in amazement when the man with the huge hands and normally gruff façade gently placed the plant on her desk with a crooked smile on his face. He didn't say a word, just kept the smile as he turned and walked to his desk across the room, keeping his back to her.

He was amused when he looked over later to see them, pot and all, in a ceramic turquoise vase, sitting prominently on the corner of her desk. *Women,* he thought, *always seemed to have things like a vase on hand, just in case.*

Harrison, after all, was still a detective, trained in the art of observation and surveillance, and he used those skills with Marsha Clamb to his advantage now.

He did give some thought to what he would like to do to her after this was all over, but for now, he needed her for a different purpose. She was the caretaker of the files and he knew the files for the Ferguson's, both father and son, were neatly hidden away somewhere in that huge warehouse behind her desk.

If he couldn't get to the son in person, he would see what the file said about the father. He blamed himself for the failure to capture the son, even if the raid had been planned by the Germans. He should have kept looking—never let that little shit of a boy out of his sight. Now his eyes turned to the father.

He knew Ian Ferguson was the real prize, the man who had ordered George Menge killed after the Haymarket disaster. Menge had been recruited to work undercover for Pinkerton's and Harrison had been his handler.

Bastard, thought Harrison. *You will pay.*

Then it would be the son's turn.

His patience with Marsha paid off the following day. When he sat down at his desk, he noticed a small envelope on the top right hand corner, tidy handwriting thanking him for the "lovely tea roses." His face had an evil smirk as he slipped the envelope into his pocket and strolled over to her desk.

It only took one day over a week for Harrison's plan to work. By that time, Marsha was looking at him the way someone in love will do. He played on that look. He suggested they return to his place one night after a long and very romantic dinner. The warmth of the wine helped smooth the way for Harrison.

When the moment presented itself, Harrison invited her back to his apartment. But, as they stood at the restaurant door, he paused, patting his pockets and said he must have left his keys back at the office.

They were alone when they entered the office complex. Harrison did not have permission for entry after closing time, but he had guessed correctly that Marsha did.

He wasn't wrong.

She was flush with wine and more as they made their way to their work area. Once they entered the office space, Harrison pretended to find his keys and then embraced her. With a long kiss and a passion that wasn't hard to fake, they looked around the empty room and Harrison showed a remarkable tenderness as they made love, clothes strewn and desk items pushed aside.

With a promise of more to follow, she stood up and looked back over her shoulder as she walked to the washroom. This was the moment Harrison planned for all along. He knew exactly where she kept her security key and made a quick impression of it using the modeling clay he had brought with him. He also needed a security code and knew she kept the code under the front drawer. He pulled it out and recorded the code, replacing the drawer just before she returned.

When she came back into the room, he was sitting back in her chair with his feet on her desk, a sly grin on his face as he imagined what he would really like to do with her, once this was all over.

* * *

It was easy for Harrison, once he had what he needed. The following Saturday, he used her key and security code and bribed his way past the weekend security guard. Once in the file room, he located the files of both father and son. He took them both, just in case.

Today, he was mostly interested in the father. He made copies of both files in his tedious handwriting. When he finished, he made sure to return the original files to their respective places in the file room, exactly as he had found them.

Back at his apartment, he set the son's file aside and started to read about Ian Ferguson. He realized that he was looking at data from the master file. The working files he had been given over the years had never included this much background information. He frowned and thought that curious.

With this information, he realized that he could have easily located and dealt with the laborist traitor. He wondered why the information had been held back from him. Surely, it must have been McParland's idea.

Why would McPartland have done that?

He tried to think about other reasons this might have been withheld from him over the years, and finally, he shrugged the thought away, a victim of his own incuriosity.

He had the information now. What he had was an address. All he had left to do was obtain a map to Beebe Plain in Vermont.

Chapter 31
It's over in Spain

On September 21, 1938, President Juan Negrin issued orders for the International Brigades to be withdrawn. Over half of the Canadian volunteers, 721 out of 1,448, had been killed. Alec remembered women, children and old men weeping and singing the Internationale, Viva La Quint Brigada, No Pasarán and other patriotic songs.

The Brigadistas marched out under an umbrella of fists raised high in the international salute.

✳ ✳ ✳

I remember my last battle well, along with the many rumors surrounding it. We had a saying: *shit will always roll downhill.* Those on the losing side always seemed to get fucked. It was not going to be any different in my last battle, here in Catalonia. My dreams were well and truly shattered, so it didn't matter much to me anymore.

Franco had ordered his "promenades" and the reprisals were already underway. No one had to say that they would get worse.

Where could we go for sanctuary? The church was no place of safety; in fact, the church openly sanctioned the reprisals, seeing them as a way to punish the godless communists, leading them back to their belief, or straight to hell—it didn't matter to them which one.

I had to face a reality. I just couldn't go on anymore. Whatever passion I had for the cause was gone now. Seth was dead. Tamarah was dead. *I* was dead.

Most worrisome to me, I had not heard from my parents, not one word. I had a funny feeling about them, but I continued to shrug the feeling off. It didn't work. I could not shrug off the strange sense that my mother was crying out to me. I knew that the stress of our battles often shaped our fantasies, thoughts bordering on hallucinations. They often crept into our wakefulness when we were tired and hungry.

Had the rest of the world really abandoned us? With each new development in Europe, we knew their eyes were being drawn elsewhere. That madman, Hitler, was the main reason. Sure, Mussolini was a man who strutted like a peacock, but Hitler didn't strut; he stomped on everyone's throats instead. We heard the echoing cadence of German jackboots in Spain.

I'm not sure of the exact time, but I recall it was a Wednesday or a Thursday. We were in the middle of a fight, damned bloody one I tell you. The Black Arrows–Franco's special storm troopers–were across the road from us, behind a small range of rolling hills.

That morning at daylight, their artillery started, loud booming rolls, like thunder. We had learned to count the seconds from the first booming of the gun until the shells started to drop out of the sky like lethal rain. We could hear the trumpets of the Black Arrows and their raunchy yells, and we knew they were starting up and would soon be cresting the hills, straight at us. It would be relentless.

As if on cue, five Stuka dive bombers appeared in the blue sky. Starting as small dots, they soon grew in size and one by one, they turned on their sides and started diving. We were told to ignore the sirens mounted under their wings. That was simply a device some German psychologist thought of to terrify the intended victims as they delivered their deadly cargo. Well, it worked. We were terrified. No one was ashamed to admit it.

After their bombs blew holes in our defenses, they turned around and came in again to fly down our lines, strafing those men unlucky enough to get caught in the open.

I thought it couldn't get any worse.

That was when I heard the tanks. The distinctive clanking of their steel treads forcing those dreadful beasts ahead. We had been putting up a courageous fight, but we all looked at each other then with blank faces, realizing the hopelessness of the situation.

We quit counting the dead and dying. I remember feeling cold in spite of the autumn heat. I had developed a tremor and that was worrisome. My right hand wouldn't stop shaking. I did my best to prop up and encourage the men in my platoon, but they shrugged their disbelief. We all knew it was time.

Then a messenger arrived and handed me the orders, *All International Volunteers are ordered to make way to Barcelona and from there, on to France. Your gallant efforts will live forever.*

I still have that paper. But that day, I couldn't read it through the tears. I knew it was finally over and I was ashamed to realize I felt relieved.

There were no trucks or transportation of any kind now. So, we walked. We walked all the way back to Barcelona. There, we walked through brave Catalonians giving us a hero's farewell, knowing that for them, the fight was over.

We volunteers kept walking, and walked until we were near the French border. The Pyrenees stood before me like a wall, as if the French had put them there to keep me out.

We were no longer marching or walking in large units. Young boys and girls were acting as our guides, leading each of our small groups on twisting paths. We climbed higher and started to feel the cold burning our exposed flesh.

My boots were worn thin and every time I stepped on patches of snow, my feet felt the insult. We climbed higher until my breath was coming in small, smoky gasps, but we couldn't stop or rest. The Francoists were not far behind us, and the French border guards were in front. At times, I felt like I was in a giant vise, waiting for it to clamp the life out of me. Vermont seemed very small and far away, and I began to doubt I would ever feel the gentle woods and hills of my home again.

Every time we would meet another group, the rumors would become more elaborate. "Did you hear, Franco is building concentration camps?"

"I heard one has already been built in Ebro."

"They don't need camps; they just line up the Brigadistas and shoot on sight, not even bothering to bury the dead."

I did my best to ignore them, but couldn't...not completely. Sitting around fires at night the debate would heat up.

"How will the French treat us?"

"I'm going to Mexico," one man said, in his heavily accented English.

Our last guide, a young girl, seventeen perhaps, told us, "The French bastards," she said spitting out the words, "are building internment camps, too. Your only hope is to find the right guide. Otherwise, *ustedes son jodidos*, you're fucked. That's what we have heard."

There was total silence after her words. We simply pulled our blankets over our shoulders and slept where we were sitting. If I had ever felt more alone, I couldn't remember when. I tried to keep warm by thinking of my parents, but the coldness of the memories of Seth and Tamarah kept intruding.

If mountains can look angry, the Pyrenees did to me that night—treeless arrows of rock pointing into the darkness, home to millions of stars. The girl, our guide, knelt by the fire on that last night in Spain, holding a tin of coffee over the coals. Standing, she turned to us saying, "It's time."

We rolled our blankets and some of the men tried to cover their embarrassment at relieving themselves just out of the light of the fire. They kept their backs to our guide and when they had finished pissing, they turned back to the fire, quietly prepared to follow her into the new morning.

As we descended the northern slopes, the air grew marginally warmer, enough to bring a bit of cheer to our band of veterans. Our guide led us to a fence and stopped. She pointed, "Just over that hill is a river. Follow the river north. When you get to the village, look for a house with a sagging roof. Stay back in the woods until dark," she said, and waved good-bye with tears in her eyes.

Wiping her eyes, she hugged each of us as we prepared to step over the fence, "When you see two lamps in the window, you will know it's clear. Go to the door and Henri will show you the..."

Her voice faded and she began sobbing. Through her tears she whispered, "No Pasarán" to each of us as we stepped over the barbed strands of the fence.

It was a night for our last tears to fall in the dust, as we finally left Spain behind us.

Chapter 32
Unfinished Business in Vermont

"I need a map," Harrison yelled through the window, over the wind.

The gas attendant finished filling the tank and tipped his hat. "That will be $6.50 for the gas and I can bring you a map. What state?"

"Vermont," Harrison said as he pulled the paper with the address out of his pocket. When he had refueled, he pulled the car ahead to the edge of the roadway and stopped. Pausing to check traffic, he drove off with the map until he came to a rest area. He studied the map and calculated his route. He was getting an early start and looked at his watch.

Hmmm, seven or eight hours, maybe longer, he thought. *If I drive straight through,* looking at his watch again, *I might make it to that little town by late afternoon. Enough time to get directions.*

He was tired and excited. In fact, he was more tired than he realized, as he felt his head starting to nod. His adrenaline had kept him going until now, when he jerked upright. A pair of headlights suddenly appeared from around a curve in the road ahead, bearing straight toward him. He quickly pulled back into his own lane.

He looked down at the passenger seat, three empty containers of coffee. It still wasn't enough. Spotting a side road, he pulled over and turned off the car. *This is taking longer than I thought. I need to sleep and this will have to wait until tomorrow.* He fell asleep listening to the pinging of the motor as it cooled off in the cold Vermont darkness.

It was the sound of a dropping branch, a wild animal perhaps, that woke him. No, it was the crunch of tires pulling alongside.

"Problem, sir?"

Harrison looked past the man standing at the window and saw the emblem of the state police on the side of the car.

"No, officer," he said in his most sincere voice, "I was getting sleepy and wanted to rest before anyone got hurt."

The officer looked at him for what seemed like a long time. Harrison felt the cold metal of the gun under his leg, reassured. The officer finally nodded and without another word walked back to his car, started it up, slowly backed the patrol car onto the highway and sped off into the night with one last and very long look back at Harrison. The trooper ended his long career five years later, never knowing how close he came to death that morning.

Harrison loosened his grip on the pistol resting between his legs on the seat. He slowly uncurled his hand and picked up the gun, putting it back in his shoulder holster. He was getting close, and nothing was going to stop him now, not even some yokel cop in the Vermont woods.

Feeling annoyed and more awake, Harrison started the car and sat listening to the satisfying hum of the engine. He took pride in maintaining his car and engine in pristine condition. He put his right foot lightly on the gas pedal, pushing the clutch pedal in with his left foot in a practiced way. He shifted into first gear and eased his left foot off the clutch, as he accelerated with his right.

Looking up, he saw a sign. He had been parked on a side road—Jules Road. The sign indicated he was at a crossroads near his destination. He turned right on Beebe Road, and as he picked up speed, he saw the outline of the small town ahead,

Beebe Plain, less than a mile from the side road where he had spent the night.

Driving slowly into town, he watched two men crossing the road, dressed in overalls and straw hats to complete the rural wardrobe. His eyes followed them to the general store on the left and slowly turned into an open space by the gas pump.

As he got out of his car and stretched, a young man got up from a chair on the porch and raced out to the car.

"Gas, mister?"

"As much as it will take," Harrison shot back.

"Not from around here, eh?" It wasn't a question particularly. "Going into Canada?"

Harrison watched as two other men walked up the steps to sit under the roof overhanging the porch of the store. They looked at Harrison without looking. Then, another man with an apron joined them. The three men just watched as the boy finished with the gas. Harrison could not read the meaning on their faces, but sensed suspicion.

"People don't talk much around here," Harrison said to the boy at the pump.

The men on the porch heard him. "When we have something to say, stranger, we say it." It was the voice of the grocer, who had walked off the porch.

"We don't get many visitors in these parts, and very few people use this road to get into Canada anymore." The man looked into Harrison's car, the only sign of curiosity he gave.

Harrison pulled a piece of paper out of his pocket and pushed his hat back on his head. "Know where this is?" he asked, hoping the man could read.

"Yep."

Harrison waited but the man didn't offer anything further.

"Care to tell me how to get there?"

"You know who lives there, do you?"

"We go back, Mr. Ferguson and me," Harrison said.

That seemed to satisfy something for the man in the apron. "I never heard him mention someone like you, dressed the way you are," his suspicion once more returning.

Harrison was about to give up.

"I do work for Ian," the boy said. "Take the road you just passed," he pointed back. "That would be North Derby Road. It sort of snakes along the border between Vermont and Canada. Over the fence, on your right, is Canada. Not supposed to cross that," he added.

"How far," Harrison asked, "do I follow the road?"

"Take that road about a mile, maybe a mile and a half. There will be a rundown farm on your left, just past the sharp curves. Turn in at the laneway just before you get there. You will see it on your left, just past the John's River."

The boy hesitated when he saw the grocer glaring at him, but went on anyway, feeling important.

"Take that lane back through two clearings. In the last clearing there will be a road bearing left. It will take you deep into the woods. You have to ford the river this time of year. It could be kind of deep with all the rain we've had."

"Hope he does know you," the grocer said as he wiped his hands on his apron. "Ian has some nasty dogs back there," and the two men on the porch nodded.

Fuck you, old man, Harrison thought, *I never saw a dog that could outrun a bullet.*

The boy's eyes grew wide as he saw the gun and holster when Harrison reached for his wallet to pay for the gas. He decided not to comment on it, but couldn't wait to tell the others as soon as Harrison drove off.

"Damn you kid, you say too much," and the grocer took on a worried look and went back into the store and the telephone.

Vermont can heat up quickly on an early August morning, and as soon as Harrison turned onto North Derby Road, he pulled over and took off his coat and hat. He rolled up his shirt sleeves and he could feel the sweat starting to pool under his armpits.

He rolled down all the windows and looked at the road ahead. Deep forest spread out off to his left and the advertised Canadian border fence ran along to his right. He bumped over a bridge, *John's River*, he imagined. *More like John's fucking muddy creek.* As he turned the sharp curve and slowed down, he was greeted by a skinny cow looking at him over the fence. It was the saddest looking cow he had ever seen and he almost laughed, but didn't.

He could sense a nearness to Ian as he turned into the laneway. It was a double-track lane, the kind found in the country. There were two ruts of dirt with a wide shred of grass between them. It was bumpy and the long grass brushed the underside of the car with a loud whisper.

He drove until he came to a canopy of trees and finally emerged into the first clearing beyond. He continued on until he came to the second clearing and spotted a dim set of tracks leading off the left. *Must be the way*, he thought.

He drove the car into the brush until he was well out of sight. Then, he got out of the car and walked around to the trunk. Opening it, he pulled out a shotgun and a box of shells, and calmly loaded the gun, putting extra shells into his pocket.

He was sweating heavily, in spite of the coolness of the forest around him. He reached in and pulled out a handgun. It was the luger he had been given on his visit to Spain.

"Our gift to an American friend," the German had said.

Now It will be my gift to my fucking commie friend, Harrison vowed, *with a bullet from the other end.* Harrison smiled at the thought.

He had doubted that Ian Ferguson had dogs, but Harrison was taking great care anyway, and was panting in the noontime heat as he finally saw the A-frame building through some branches.

He stopped and listened for the sounds of a dog—nothing.

Then he saw her, Alec's mother, walking out with a basket of clothes. He listened as she quietly sang, attaching laundry to the line with wooden pins.

This just keeps getting better, he almost said aloud. He sneered, realizing his day would be complete, and breathed out a loud gasp when he saw Ian Ferguson walk out the door with a cup of coffee in his hand, wiping his forehead and looking up at the cloudless noonday sky. He could tell the two were talking, but he was too far away to hear.

Harrison waited until he felt it had been long enough, and suddenly burst through the branches. With several quick strides, he walked past the woman and knocked her to the ground, holding the shotgun in a manner that suggested to Ian that he and his wife were trapped.

Harrison was annoyed, and his annoyance turned to rage when he realized that Ian wasn't acting intimidated. His stance was one of acceptance.

"This has been a long time coming," Ian said, without a sign of emotion. He looked down at his wife and she caught his signal and stayed on the ground, watching the moment unfold.

"This is what your last day looks like," Harrison said, raising the shotgun slowly.

Ian shrugged and that was enough. It set something off in Harrison. He looked maniacal as he pulled the trigger, the blast of buckshot almost cutting Ian's body in half. He fired the second shell into Ian's lifeless body and calmly reloaded as he heard the woman screaming, "No, please!"

He didn't stop but kept walking toward Ian. He reloaded and pulled the trigger again, watching the body twitching on the porch, blood pooling rapidly on the unfinished wood. Harrison reloaded and put more needless shells into the body; he almost felt an urge to ejaculate as he turned back to the woman, who was trying to pick herself up off the ground. Harrison dropped the shotgun and pulled out a knife. *This will be amusing.* Holding it casually, he advanced toward the woman.

When he was finished with her, she was completely naked, severe cuts over her entire body. She was dying slowly. Harrison made sure of that. The medical examiner would later say she was almost unrecognizable. After the killings, Harrison placed her mangled body so that she was straddled, obscenely, over Ian's face. He wanted to leave a message.

Harrison walked to the well and washed the blood away and finally dressed again, pulling his pants up over his bloodied underwear. His last thought of this afternoon affair was that it had been the most exhilarating sexual experience he had ever known, and his nemesis was finally where he belonged.

He got back to his car and instead of driving back toward Beebe Plain, he bounced over the laneway and back to North Derby Road. There he turned left, heading towards Lake Magog and back to New York. Harrison had no illusions that he had somehow fooled the grocer. The man certainly would have tried to notify both Ian and the police.

Then he heard them. He smiled at the sound of the sirens coming from Beebe Plain. Satisfied he had finally closed the case, he put Ian Ferguson out of his mind forever.

Chapter 33
French Connections

I remember looking around with wariness as we crossed the border into France. In spite of these dire warnings, my crossing was uneventful.

There must have been thirty or thirty-five of us walking mostly in single file. A few men walked side by side, and if they talked, it was mostly in quiet conversation. There was no singing or shouting of rousing slogans. Our feet seemed to plant themselves one after the other in a defeated cadence. Our shoulders slumped forward, heads bent low with the weariness we felt.

We were told our reception in France would depend on the politics of the people we would meet; look for a man in working clothes, we were told. Then someone said the police were good at disguising themselves as workers, another risk we faced.

I was carrying my rucksack over my right shoulder; my bedroll was wrapped with a leather strap draped over my left. I looked down at my boots. It had been raining and I could feel the water seeping into my boot. The sole of the right boot was starting to separate at the toe and was flapping as I walked. Despite the wretched circumstances, I started to laugh; my shoe looked like a wee, yapping dog, panting down the path.

When we got to the first village, I made my decision, for better or worse, to head off on my own. It was instinct. The authorities would be looking for groups of men who didn't fit in, I thought. Would I have better luck on my own? I thought so.

Before darkness set in, I stopped, pretending to tie my laces until the men walked well ahead of me. I watched them continue walking around a bend in the road and over a hill. I straightened up and leaned against a fence rail. As the last man disappeared over the crest of a hill, I turned back to a fork to the left. I had seen it, barely noticeable, and hoped it was a road headed in a northwesterly direction. I had made my decision. I would travel at night and find some type of shelter to hide in during the day.

I got back to the road just as the waning light faded to black. I looked up and smiled; the big dipper was clearly visible in the night sky.

Our last day in Spain had been spent in a village appropriately named Encamp. Seeing the irony of the name of our last bivouac, I would have renamed it "Decamp" for all I cared.

Now, across the border in France, I had dropped out of the group just south of a village called Saint-Girons. Pretty sure that was the name, anyway. It had been a brutal walk from Encamp, a walk that took over three days of marching. I looked it up later, a distance of 132 kilometers, mostly mountainous terrain.

No one complained on the trek. We were all well used to walking. Tamarah and her trucks were luxuries when we were being moved in a hurry, but, like armies everywhere, we mostly walked, and walked, and walked...

From a distance, Saint-Girons looked like a pretty little town, intersected by a river. On the west bank, another river connected. I never bothered to learn their names.

I stood on the hill just to the southwest of Saint-Girons; my eyes focused on one of the most welcome sights I could have imagined. I spotted train tracks winding along one river and I almost yelped when I saw they pointed in my direction.

If the lessons of the great depression taught me anything, it was how to "ride the rails." I imagined it was no different in France, and it was not. I could see the police walking the tracks, and on cue, when they passed out of sight, I spotted two or three shadows running out of a copse of trees and jumping on a train that was gathering speed. *Just like home*, I thought with a smile.

Watching, I tried to ignore my hunger. I hadn't eaten in over twenty-four hours now, and I knew I would not last long without nourishment. I sat and watched the trains coming, stopping, and then moving on. They all stopped in the village train yard, but not for long. One or two cars may have been detached or added, but soon the train was underway once again.

I vowed to be on one at first light, hungry or not.

I was crouched in a large growth of underbrush when I saw a farmer walking by. He was whistling and carrying two pails, milk slopping over the tops of both as he walked. He was whistling a familiar tune, the *Internationale*, his beret askew on his head.

I made a quick decision and stood up. I didn't yell or anything to startle him, but I could tell he saw me in the near darkness. He walked a bit further and stopped. He set the pail down that he had been holding in his right hand. He slipped that hand into his pocket and simply looked at me, waiting for some explanation. I held up my hands with a universal shrug that I hoped was not threatening.

He looked at me long and hard. He couldn't help but notice my clothes, the uniform of an ex-Brigadista. Then he said something in French. It was too fast for my comprehension of the language. Back home, near the Quebec border, it may have been passable or barely adequate. Looking at my puzzled look, his face changed. He switched into Spanish.

"Brigadista," it wasn't a question.

I nodded in the affirmative.

I knew it was a moment of reckoning. He would either turn me in, or not. It was up to him, so I waited.

"It's over, I hear," he said in Spanish.

"*Sí, ha terminado,*" I said. Yes, it is finished.

Our mutual skill in Spanish was limited. I must confess that despite my time in Spain, this Frenchman's command of the language was better than was mine. But, as I started to relax, the tension seeped from my shoulders.

"Come," he said with a motion, picking up the pail, "walk with me."

I picked up my bedroll and rucksack and walked out of the brush. His eyes filled with sympathy when he saw my condition.

"I live alone," he said, "My wife died and who the fuck knows where my children are these days. But I have a small farm and we won't go hungry," he pointed us ahead. I will always remember him and I can still see his weathered face clearly, judging what seemed to be a week's growth of graying beard.

I had to duck to get though the cottage door, but the inside felt warm and inviting. He heated a pot of stew. It had been a long time since I had seen food like that. It was the same type of stew my mother was famous for. There were hearty portions of meat and beans. He cut carrots and other vegetables with nimble hands, stopping in his cutting only to lift a glass of wine.

I offered to help and he waved me away, "There is a well and wash basin outside, go and wash yourself,"

We talked into the night in our horrible Spanish, but we somehow managed to understand one another. He told me he had no one left to talk politics. It was too risky anymore. "If I had been younger, I would have gone with you," he said.

"We could have used your help," I said, pleasing him greatly.

I was asleep the next morning when I heard a knock on the door and felt an immediate, electric shock of tension. The knocking became banging.

"*Attente! Attente!*" I heard someone say.

I opened the curtain on the bedroom door just enough to watch. Two policemen with flowing capes were standing at the door, and they had an animated conversation in French that I was hopeless to follow, hearing only "Brigadistas and Communists."

They finally left and Henri turned, "Come on out, I know you were watching."

"What-"

"You need to watch your back, *mon ami*," he said. Some of the police look stupid, and a few really are. But, the ones you have to watch out for are the ones who are clever to a fault."

With that, he poured me a cup of steaming coffee and then added a generous amount of brandy.

"They said a large group of men were captured on the main road last night. They were caught just east of here. The dimwitted policeman said they were rats that had deserted a sinking ship in Spain. He seemed to enjoy it as some kind of joke."

I told Henri about my decision to go my way alone and he agreed, "You would have been arrested as well."

"What will happen to them?" I asked.

"Our new government is like a whore, sleeping with the Germans," he spit out disdainfully. "We French are building internment camps, more like the concentration camps we hear are being built in Spain."

He took a sip of his coffee, "Even worse, a lot of men arrested are simply being sent back to Spain. The rumor is that those men are never seen again—they disappear into thin air, eh?"

"You could have turned me in," I said. "Wouldn't you get a reward?"

"My reward," he looked at me, "my reward for turning you in would mean that I would never be able to look in a mirror again. Look," he said, "I may be a plain peasant farmer, but

I know what is going on. You soldiers had it right. You went to Spain for the best of reasons and got sold out for it."

He looked over my shoulder into some middle distance. I was tempted to look back to see what he was looking at, but knew what he was seeing wasn't in this room.

"My reward will be helping a brave man like you on his way," he smiled. "My *compagnon* of so many years would have said 'Oui, mon amour.' She would have understood and approved," a tear formed in his eye as he thought back to some time in his past.

We spent that day repairing my clothes, and he was able to nail my sole back onto the boot. I walked down to a stream and spent a long time in the water, my clothes lying on the bank to dry out. It was a cold, fast-moving stream. I relished the cold water and it reminded me of other rivers just like it, back in Vermont.

Mom, Dad, I promised, *I miss you and will be home soon.*

That night, Henri and I wrapped enough food for my journey, we hoped. We wrapped salami in waxed paper. We wrapped cheese in a fine mesh cloth. The provisions would mean that I could travel without a fire. He walked to a cupboard and pulled out two bottles covered with dust.

"These were for a special occasion," he said, "Mama passed before whatever occasion we might have been saving them for. I think this occasion will do," and he handed them to me. My rucksack was bulging, but I was determined to find room for the bottles, nodding my appreciation.

There was another thing Henri and I shared. We talked without talking; sharing many of our thoughts without a sound. A part of me wanted to stay with Henri and the warmth of his hearth, but I didn't want any more names on my growing list of dead friends. I knew he was risking everything in helping me. When it was time to leave, we embraced in the European manner that men use, unembarrassed with the emotion and touch.

I looked back as I walked away, but Henri had turned away and was suddenly busying himself with some wood that needed chopping. I smiled when I noticed he had somehow channeled his strength and was splitting some very large logs with the axe, raising it over his head and slamming his emotions down on the wood.

As I had guessed, the train proved to be an easy ride. It was the same the world over. I ran alongside a slow moving train and jumped into a yawning opening. Inside, it was dim, and once the train was rattling its way down the track, I started to relax.

When it was lunchtime, I opened my first packet of lunch. There was a note, in English. I was stunned and realized it must have taken Henri much of the night to write it.

I have a cousin, maybe not really a cousin, in Ares. We both share the name Henri. He walks the same way that you and I do, if you know what I mean. If he is still alive, he might be able to help you. He has a boat—look for the name 'le point du compass.'

My cheeks and chin were flooded with tears as I folded the note and put it in the special pocket of my rucksack, next to the photographs of Tamarah.

✶ ✶ ✶

I later learned it was over 311 kilometers from Saint-Girons to Ares on the west coast of France. It would have taken days of walking, but trains were my friends. I soon left the mountains behind and passed through lush farms and along pristine rivers.

I rode the train northwest until it stopped in a rail yard. Then I walked to yet another train. I finally jumped off that last train before entering Gabarret. From there, I walked through lowlands. I was becoming best friends with the big dipper. It seemed like weeks, if not months, had passed since leaving Spain, and yet I knew it had not been long.

One day, as the sun was bidding farewell to the land, I found myself standing to look at a wharf in Ares. I walked along the wharf until I saw a name on the transom of a boat; a surly looking man in a heavy woolen sweater was bent over, the stench of fish wafted up to me.

"Henri?" I asked.

Chapter 34
The Long Voyage Home

When I saw Henri look up, I knew without thinking, he was a man I could trust.

Men who make their living on the sea have a similar look; the same independent air shared with farmers. They are all men knowing and understanding hard work for small reward.

Henri might suffer government regulations and men of authority when he was in port, but that tolerance evaporated with the first spray of salt water sloughing back over the bow of the boat.

This Henri, my new Henri, was a paragon of surliness. He sneered and grunted and I somehow knew it was mostly an act for my part. As my mother would say, "Don't judge too quickly, the proof is in the pudding."

After our introductions, this Henri waved me on board. It didn't feel at all welcoming, but I stepped down and felt the boat tremble and bob as I put one foot down on the gunwale and then jumped onto the deck.

He disappeared into the wheelhouse and I could see him open a locker. He threw a bulky sweater and rain slicker in my general direction. "*Ici*, you will need these soon enough."

I tried to resist, but he grabbed my belongings. "We don't want you looking conspicuous," he growled as he took my rucksack and stuffed it in a locker, out of sight.

His English was passable and he said, "*Je passe* enough time with the bloody *Anglais*," he said, rubbing two languages together at once. I learned it was a common trait for those whose commerce in these waters depended on knowing both languages.

As I had guessed, his disdain for shore people left him as soon as he untied from the pilings. He had made his decision about me and we were on the way. As the boat turned to the northwest, we passed a rock breakwater and my stomach flip-flopped as the first swell started to lift the boat up and then gently set it back down. At least that was the way it felt to my stomach. I glanced over at Henri, his hand resting casually on the wheel. He was humming a song known only to him. He looked at me and grinned.

"I appoint you *Capitaine en Second*, my first mate," he roared at his joke. "You have only two duties, but they are crucial," he laughed.

I waited for my duties.

"For one, you are to keep me awake at all times. I have to tell you, the sea may be a quick cure for a hangover, but I don't want to fall asleep. It was after two in the morning when I left Michelle's bed. Luckily, her husband wasn't in it with us," and he started to cough as he laughed even harder.

He did have an infectious laugh.

"What is my other job?" I asked, joining him in his laughter.

"That locker," he pointed back, "has a pot and some coffee. You might have to clean the mugs though. I'm not sure when they were last cleaned. I like my coffee very strong. That's your other duty."

"*Oui, mon Capitaine*," I said and saluted, with the wrong arm. We often did that in Spain to show our contempt for military discipline.

I wasn't sure of my footing as I retreated to the locker. I balanced as best I could. Through the window ahead, I looked with alarm at a very large swell coming from the north. To my dismay, I could see many larger swells following. They were marching toward us—like Franco's Blackshirts. We seemed to be heading right toward them and Capitaine Henri seemed decidedly unconcerned.

I could hear him snorting as I struggled to maintain my footing, first sliding into a bulkhead on my left, and then falling into a doorframe on my right.

Somehow, I figured out how to light the small stove, pleased with myself for not having to ask *mon Capitaine* for instructions. When the flame was adjusted, I reached up and unlocked a small compartment and found the coffee. Henri had devised an ingenious contraption for making coffee in rough waters, seas that seemed to be growing more monstrous to me with each passing minute.

His design allowed me to place the coffee pot on the stove, fill it with water and add the coffee–three extra scoops to make sure it was good and strong–and then fasten a collar that went around the pot. The collar had small wires stretching in four directions. It kept the pot securely in place in spite of the worst the sea could offer...I hoped.

The coffee was soon ready and I saw four mugs hanging overhead. I took one off the peg and looked at it. I was used to filthy living conditions in Spain, but this mug looked beyond anything I could remember from there.

What the hell, I thought, and poured anyway. It was the consistency of mud, but I handed it to the outstretched hand of the skipper. The second mug was no cleaner and I poured coffee for myself, taking my first gulp, and smiled. It was hot, strong and tasted wonderful.

"Damn," Henri said, "the best coffee I have ever had!" I felt bizarrely pleased at the compliment.

I spent the rest of the journey hanging onto a handle on the front ledge of the wheelhouse, amazed that our boat seemed to shrug off the giant swells; they seemed gigantic to *me* anyway. My consolation was that I somehow refused to give in to *mal-de-mer*. It wasn't nearly as bad as being stuck in a stinking hole beneath the deck.

Henri continued to act as though the waves and weather were nothing, and I could see the nonchalant shrug that Frenchmen were so good at. He finally suggested I might want to try and sleep, but we both knew that wasn't meant to be. I stayed by his side like a loyal puppy until the day turned into night, and was ready once again to turn back into day.

I was never sure when the swells started to subside. It was like a headache—one moment there and the next moment gone, without knowing when the transition had taken place.

We had turned more westerly, and Henri told me we were on the edge of the abyss. He pointed and said, "The ocean drops there, *une mer sans fond*, a bottomless sea. The fish love it on the edge of the abyss, plenty of food for them. That is where we will fish for a while, just in case a patrol boat spots us.

He taught me how to throw a net and pull it in. Most of the time, we pulled in nets that were teeming with fish and the weight in hauling them aboard was grueling work. We fished for over eighteen hours straight, with only one break for some of my great coffee. "It's the best damned coffee, ever," Henri swore.

My back was hurting from the strain and yet, there was a healing of sorts. My mind, for the first time in weeks, was free from the memories of Spain. I simply threw a net and then pulled on the line, over and over and over again. Yes, it was healing in its way.

Finally, Henry said, "It is time to get permission from the gutless authorities. This time, we unload in Brest. We won't be there long."

I started to question him, but he held up a hand to stop me, "You will be my deaf cousin," and started to laugh at his idea. His laugh turned into loud guffaws that almost led him to choke.

It only took two hours to unload our catch, as I silently watched the man at the scales count out the money, handing it to Henri. The two men exchanged knowing glances in my direction and nodded to each other while they turned to look in the direction of two armed men in uniform.

The uniforms were the same as the ones at the cottage door, back at the first Henri's farm. Today's Henri told the policemen we were returning to Ares and added he had a nice warm woman and bed waiting. The two men looked at him with lifeless eyes and didn't care about Henri, his bed, or his woman. They were done with their duty and walked off, unmindful of my deafness.

"Fair seas," the man at the scales said to us as he helped cast off the lines. Henri nodded and our boat throttled to life until we were well offshore, out of sight to those on land.

The swells from the northwest were as unfriendly as the days before, but Henri turned the boat to starboard and thrust his chin forward, "*L'Angleterre*, England, is that way."

I was almost getting used to the swells when I became aware that they were no longer as pronounced. Henri seemed to read my mind and told me, "We are finally getting some protection from the *Anglais*," he laughed. "The bloody island may be good for something after all. It is shielding us from the winds now."

Ahead, I could make out the form of a coastline through a misty rain that had developed. Then, what seemed to me like an apparition, loomed out of the mist and another boat was suddenly off to our starboard side. It seemed motionless on the water.

"They are hove to," Henri explained as if I would know what that meant. I pretended I did and just kept my ignorance to myself.

A signal light blinked from the boat and Henri reached for a lantern hanging over his head, swinging on a cord. He switched it on and flashed a signal back.

"There you go my friend. They will show you the way now. Pay no attention to my attempts at humor; the *Anglais* you are about to meet are good people. Do what they say. I am honored to have played a small part in your drama."

I had lost so much in Spain. The world lost so much in Spain. Nevertheless, I was suddenly aware I had found something important despite all my losses—a band of brothers that had helped me on my way to Spain and was now helping me back to Vermont.

I was terrified about jumping between the two boats, thinking about the bottomless abyss beneath me. I threw my kit over and almost closed my eyes before jumping. Everyone had a great laugh at my expense when my feet hit the slithery deck of the other boat and I landed on my ass. Thus, I was introduced to the *Lady Edith*. Her deck was covered with slimy fish scales and guts as I slid into the far bulkhead with an ungainly sprawl. I picked myself up with as much dignity as I could manage after such a landing, and waved back to Henri and gave him my best wrong-handed salute.

"No Pasarán!" he shouted back through the increasing rain, and I heard the roar of his engine as the boat sulked into the mist and out of my sight.

I turned to look at two smiling people, a man and a woman. "This here's the *Lady Edith*," he said pointing to the boat, "And this here's the Lady Edith." He put an arm around the woman's shoulder. "Over fifteen years with the same boat and Lord knows how long with this lovely lady." Laughing, he turned the boat towards the coastline.

"Welcome back, soldier," the woman said quietly into my ear.

Chapter 35
England to Canada

On this new boat, I looked at Edith, a hard-looking woman with a voice as soft as a snowflake, as she handed me a cup of hot and very strong coffee. I was starting to think that strong coffee was a bond far greater than politics or philosophy.

"There's no sugar or milk on *Lady Edith*. Arnie...that's Arnold there," she pointed to the tall man hunched over the steering wheel, "Me husband says coffee was meant to be drunk black, so black it is."

I nodded my thanks and gratefully sipped the coffee. It was like the syrup I had served to Henri, but she heard no complaints from me. It was a style of coffee I had learned to appreciate during my time in Spain.

With a blinding flash, like sudden lightning on a dark night, the memories of those left behind screamed at me, and I turned away from Edith to hide my unexpected tears.

"It won't be long now," Arnold said over the wind. Edith looked at me with understanding.

We had been underway for some hours when I could finally make out the growing form of land on the horizon.

"I am going to time it so we are coming in after the customs man has left for his first pint of the night. He always does that before he goes home for dinner. We are supposed to put in at Flushing, there," pointing to our port side, "But after dinner, the fool is done for the day and we can just go right on in."

Edith joined in with a knowing chuckle.

I watched as Arnie pointed out the sightings we were passing.

"That's Sain Anthony-in-Meneage on our port side now; soon you will see Durgan on the starboard side. Won't be long now," he said, casually adjusting the wheel.

"That's Helford Village up ahead," the *Lady Edith* steadily carrying us further up the Helford River. It was a rapid incoming tide, and I admired Arnie as he maneuvered with a practiced hand, guiding *Lady Edith* between the sloping hills on either side. Then, he made a final turn to port towards a basin in an arm of the river.

"Edith, love," he said offhandedly, "when we dock, would you please take our friend here and show him where the shower is. We can meet at the Shipwright's Arms when he doesn't smell like French fish." Laughter filled the boat.

I knew it wasn't only the 'French fish' that he smelled. The stink on me was from miles of walking, hours of hauling nets and the guts and scales stuck to me as I had slid aboard the *Lady Edith*. I must have reeked.

Once in the shower, I savored the feeling of clean. As I toweled off, I found to my delight, a fresh set of clothes laid out on a table. I remember how glad I was for that heavy jersey sweater to ward off the chill as I walked to the pub, especially one that was clean.

Helford Village was a small place on an arm of the river. It was like small villages and towns anywhere. Arnie and Edith had a small cottage near the dock, where I had showered and changed.

I walked around the end of the basin and followed directions to a gravel path, until I spotted the sign for the Shipwright's Arms. A bright red sign with yellow lettering beckoned me along a path. Heavy marine rope sagged from post to post along my right side. The buildings looked old, very old, nothing like Vermont or Canada.

I saw the jutting end of what looked like some type of storage shed off to my right as I walked. Turning a corner, I saw the side of another building just beyond, with another sign with an arrow pointing to the right. I wended my way around the corners and soon entered the pub. The sound of laughter and clinking glass filled the room, and the fireplace gave off enough warmth that I was soon wishing I wasn't wearing a heavy sweater after all.

I looked around at the faces in the pub, expecting suspicious glares toward a stranger. I was fearful of any politics of the day.

I need not have worried.

"This is him," Arnie said as he wrapped a welcoming arm around me. They all raised their glasses in welcome and quickly crowded around.

"What was it like?"

"We have heard so many stories."

"It won't be long before we, too, are fighting the Germans," someone added, "Just listen to Winston."

"I don't always agree with Churchill," another added, "but he is right about the Krauts."

They all nodded in agreement to that, and I felt my shoulders fall, not realizing how much tension I was carrying with me. My reluctance to talk about Spain gradually gave way to their curiosity when I recognized it was genuine.

"No high regard for the rich and famous hereabouts," one man roared. It was evident that he had consumed more than one pint, but his sentiments were not clouded by his slurred speech.

"Had me a job in Liverpool," he said, "until the bankers closed down the yards. Damn near starved. Now I'm back with me mum and dad and all we have to eat are the fish we catch and the vegetables we can raise. I'm damned glad to have that much, I can tell you. No point in complaining, mind you."

It was a long speech and he had to take a long swig to catch up with his thoughts.

"Commies they called us," he added after a drink, "Fucking bastards only wake up when you hold a gun to their head."

The other men all yelled, "Hear, hear."

Then he looked straight at me and said, "And that was just what you did lad. You held a gun to the bastards' heads. It may not have worked, but it did get their attention for a while. Good for you," and he walked over and held me in an embrace that was more like a bear hug.

"Up the Canadians," someone shouted and I felt embarrassed by my subterfuge, but accepted the cheer.

Another man said, "We lost someone from nearby. He went to Spain and we never heard another word until it got back to us he was..." his voice trailed off. The room grew quiet at the remembering.

Perhaps the feeling of small town kinship was so familiar to me that a memory of Vermont and my parents suddenly washed over me as I basked in the warmth of this fellowship. No doubt this feeling was helped along by the third pint I had just finished.

With home on my mind, I pulled the man aside. I knew he might have helpful information for me.

"Liverpool, you said?"

"Aye," he said back.

"I hear boats from Liverpool go to North America, to Canada," starting me on another leg of my journey.

That bear of a man, I can still remember his bushy beard, not only told me how to get to Liverpool, he insisted on coming along and showing me the way personally.

"Name's Reginald, Reg to you. I can show you who and what to look out for," he said knowingly, "I know someone there who will help you if it's me doing the asking."

I added Arnie and Edith to the list of people I said good-bye to along the way. It was something I was getting used to, but it wasn't getting any easier. I remember what my father had said before I left, "There are some willing to risk all, even their own safety, to help you. They are the true believers," he had told me.

I knew now the truth of what he had tried to tell me back then.

I thought often about my parents as I made my way to Liverpool. I was longing to spend time with them and enjoy the tranquility of their little corner of Vermont.

In Liverpool, I was introduced to yet another fellow-traveler.

"You will be on the manifest as crew, but all you have to do is eat and sleep. It looks like you could use the rest," the small, balding man said, as he led me up a gangway in the darkness of the middle-night.

The days and nights somehow passed on the voyage to Montreal. The freighter was old and slow. I learned much later that it was rumored to have been torpedoed, and I can't even remember its name. I do remember watching the Ile d'Anticosti, after we had passed Glace Bay and entered the St. Lawrence River. Quebec City looked majestic looming over us as we glided our way upriver to Montreal.

I tell you, it was easy to slip on and off ships in those days, and lucky it was. I had heard the official policy was to make it hard on us to get home. Brigadista veterans weren't welcomed with open arms back home. In fact, we were branded as *undesirable* by the government.

I slipped off the freighter under cover of darkness. As I was leaving, the captain, that same small, balding man, slipped me an envelope with some money, "Your ticket home, wherever that is, my friend."

It wasn't much, but it was enough for a ticket, and it wasn't long before I was on a train and once again leaving Montreal behind, Hamilton ahead. This time, I was on the train legit. The drama of my earlier trip from Montreal to Hamilton seemed so long ago now, and this trip passed without incident.

I still kept a wary eye out for undercover police or Pinkerton's agents. I soon found out that in Hamilton, like elsewhere, returning Brigadistas were branded as agitators and worse. With that sentiment and the lingering effects of the Great Depression, it was all working against me. There were no jobs, period.

Then one day, and I remember that day so clearly, I was in a pub. I can still remember the name, the *Lucky Shamrock*, on Barton Street. I usually drank my beer in silence, preferring my drink over companionship these days. But that night, I sat with some men and was having an animated discussion, if you want to call it that, when the bartender suddenly yelled over the noise, "Shut up!"

He turned the radio up and we heard a reedy voice coming through the speakers, "Today, Churchill is once again warning that war with Germany is inevitable."

"Blame that on Chamberlain," someone hissed the name.

Canada was a part of a world poised on the brink of war with Germany. I can still remember the quiet that fell on the room that night. I had an uneasy feeling that this was not good news for me. I laid some money on the bar, nodded to the bartender, and left to walk home.

I was staying in a dingy room, lucky to spread out my money for even one meal a day. Some days, I was able to get something to eat at the union hall. It wasn't much, mind you. It was enough, however, to keep me going.

Then it happened, as I knew it would. One night there was a knock on the door of my room. I knew by the sound that it was not a friendly knock. Two stern-looking men wearing long overcoats to ward off the November chill flashed badges, "RCMP," one said, while the other one stood alertly to the side.

"Grab your stuff."

"Am I under arrest?"

"Should be," he said, as the other one lit a cigarette. With that, they started walking me along the street to the train station. Soon we were on a train to Niagara Falls, and not for a honeymoon, I knew. The two men made sure I was not in a position to jump or run.

Once the train huffed into Niagara Falls and pulled into the station on Bridge Street, it felt like I was in handcuffs, visible for all to see. The passengers seemed to know I was a prisoner of some kind and kept their distance. I remember one mother pulling her son away in disgust, hearing her whisper the word, "Communist." I felt especially miserable at the way that little boy looked at me.

I was marched between the two men to the center of the whirlpool bridge, the rail tracks on the level overhead. At the center of the bridge, one handed me my pack.

"Got us a real war and we don't want your kind in Canada. Go home and stay there." I was just glad they hadn't searched my pack and found my pistol.

I remember walking to the inspection station on the U. S. side. It was clear from my reception that I wasn't any more welcome on that side of the border, but when I showed them my birth certificate one mumbled, "I guess we can't keep you out, even though I sure want to." That was my welcome home.

Home, I remember thinking, *where is home anymore?*

Once off the bridge, I turned right and walked along Main Street to Portage Road, where someone directed me to the bus depot. At the ticket window, I counted out my remaining money. I asked the clerk how far I could get on that. He told me I had just enough for a bus to Schenectady, and started handing me the tickets I needed.

I was unconcerned. I knew a walk from Schenectady to my home in Vermont was a mere stroll compared to what I had been through already.

On the bus, I settled back in my seat and cradled my kit, glad not to have anyone in the seat next to me. I put my head back and anticipated the reunion with my parents.

Chapter 36
An Awful Truth

I still remember that night on the bus ride, especially the smell. It's surprising how clearly some memories come back to me. There was the tang of the leather seats. And there was the sound, the *whoosh*, of the airbrakes as the bus finally pulled into the ramp of the Schenectady bus terminal. It was an overnight ride from Niagara Falls, my invitation to some needed sleep. I barely noticed our stops at the small towns along the way.

As I stepped off the bus with my meager belongings, I reached into a pocket and counted out some hidden money. Maybe there was just enough to buy some food along the way. I still had my canteen from Spain, and I knew water would be readily available.

There was no one to welcome me to Schenectady, as I longingly watched passengers greeted with embraces and kisses from loved ones. To them, I was just another weary traveler walking though the terminal and out the door to the street.

I spotted a gas station, just as the attendant was turning on the lights. I walked over and asked if he could show me a map. I had a general idea of direction, but wanted to keep my walk as short as possible.

My excitement mounted at the thought seeing my parents, and I almost used some of my money to call ahead. There wasn't enough for both food *and* a call, however.

Oh well, I thought, *there will be plenty of time for talking when I get home.* I was looking forward to sitting at the kitchen table, just like we did before I left. Maybe my father would have a bottle ready to share.

The man who had opened the gas station looked sleepy but was friendly. He looked in a drawer, pulled out a map, and stretched it out on the counter. When I told him my reasons for looking at the map, he looked at me as if I had just stepped out of a comic book. "You're going to walk...all the way to North Vermont?"

I pointed to a place on the map. "There it is," my finger on the map, "a piece of cake," I said, enjoying a conversation in the New England accent.

What I didn't tell him was that it was, indeed, a mere stroll for someone who had trekked up and down the mountains in Spain and walked across France. I didn't tell him that it took only a few boat rides to get to Canada and I didn't tell him that it was only a couple of train rides and a bus ride to get to his station.

Walking home would be a...what...like a walk in the park, as the expression went.

I was still looking intently at the map when I heard that familiar *ding*, and the gas jockey walked out to a car that had just pulled up to the pumps. I looked up from the map and watched through the grimy window. A man got out of the car, stretched, and stood off to the side waiting for his car to be fuelled. He followed the attendant in and waited while the young man walked behind the cash register.

"That'll be $2.75. You don't need any oil."

The driver handed over a five-dollar bill, and when the gas jockey started to hand back the change he said, "Can you believe it? That guy," pointing at me, "is going to walk to Vermont, damn near the Canadian border."

"Where in Vermont?" the driver asked me.

I grinned, "Beebe Plain," knowing that neither one of them probably had a clue where it was. "A couple of steps from the front porch there and you cross the Canadian border," I added to give them some reference.

The man looked at me closely and finally seemed to make some sort of a decision. "Not much of that part of Vermont I don't know. I'm going to Burlington," and paused, "I could use some company."

"I don't have money..."

He held up a hand, "Just helping me stay awake is pay enough," he laughed, and I remembered that same request from Capitaine Henri.

I looked at the map as he waited for my reply.

Its seventy more miles from Burlington to Beebe Plain and home, I judged. That was something I could easily handle, and smiled to myself as I said, "Sure, I'd appreciate it."

In the car, he told me his name was Albert, "Bert is what people usually call me."

Bert was a talker, I can tell you. But he wasn't nosey and didn't try to pry the past out of me. It was obvious we shared opposing views of the day's politics, but we both agreed the Depression had hurt everyone, everyone except the people with real wealth.

He was a salesman, he said.

"Sure, I'm getting more orders now. I sell cloth and there is a company in Burlington that makes uniforms for the army. They are getting more business these days. That stuff in Europe is something, huh? Tell you what, let me buy you a coffee and some doughnuts, there's a place right up here. What do you say to that?"

Before I could say "no, thanks," he had stopped alongside a parked car and smoothly backed into the open parking space behind. I didn't want to leave my kit in the car, but he assured me it would be safe.

I remember Bert fondly. Later, we argued some about politics, but stayed away from any real controversy, by unspoken agreement, I always felt.

We finally left for Burlington mid-morning. The drive was slower in those days before interstate highways were put in place. We passed through the small town of Warrensburg and it was a beautiful drive as we passed a sign for the entrance to the Adirondack Park Preserve.

I knew Bert was curious about me. He kept looking at my kit that I kept clutched in my lap. He was in the cloth business and I guessed he suspected it was military of some sort. But he didn't pry, and I told him I hadn't seen my parents in a long time and was looking forward to a reunion.

"The Depression," I said. "A lot of us have had to go where we think the jobs are, only to find out there aren't any. We have all had to go places and do things we don't want to. Still, it's getting better..." I shrugged, unsure of what else to say.

He agreed, "I worked in a laundry until the sales started to pick up again. Lost a lot of weight in the steam heat," he laughed. "It didn't hurt though. It was actually good for me," he said and patted his stomach.

"I'm going to stay in shape now."

I thought about the four doughnuts he had just finished and the extra sugar he had put in his coffee, but kept that thought to myself.

There wasn't a lot of traffic as we curved our way through the preserve and finally pulled into the small village of Essex, on the New York side of Lake Champlain. We both laughed as we saw the ferry leaving the dock without us, bound for the Vermont side of the lake, near Cedar Branch.

"Just our luck to miss the boat, eh," Burt said.

A man was standing by the car. He sounded as if he surely had moved to this side of the lake from Vermont, judging by his broad accent.

"Won't get there for a spell," he chuckled, "It's half an hour over, half-hour there, another half-hour back." He was Vermont-thrifty with his words.

Bert and I got out and stretched our legs. It was a warm day for this time of year, and we enjoyed the healing sense you often get around water. We rolled up our pant legs, took off our shoes and let our feet dangle in the water.

"When did you last see them?"

It took me awhile to understand his question. I thought back, "April, last year. Seems like forever."

"Were you close?"

I had never really considered that.

"Yes...and no," pausing between those two words. I tried to decipher just how I felt. I had never tried to explain it before.

"My father was gone a lot. He was a man of a certain mystery. I know I respected him. He instilled a fierce independence in me. He always said I had to stand for myself in a world that didn't give a damn about the common man, not really."

"But, were you close? I wish I had been with my father," he sighed.

"I think so," I finally said. "I know he is the only person who will understand what the past year-and-a-half has really been like, whether it was worth it or not."

"And your mother? What about her?"

"She was the softness of a candle's flame compared to the diamond hardness of my father." I smiled as I described her. "She could be tough, and had to be to survive her history. We were close without many words. I just...sort of...knew," I had a sudden image of her in her overalls, brushing her hair out of her eyes.

The ferry returned and we were soon on our way again. It was getting dark when we finally got to Burlington. We passed the train station and I had a sudden impulse, "Drop me off here."

Bert pulled over to the curb, and as I got out he said, "I didn't want to pry, but you have a look of sadness about you, friend. Whatever lies ahead, I wish you the best. God knows we all need it in these damnable times."

I watched as the car pulled away and realized I was watching yet another link disappearing, a link between my past and my future.

I walked back to the train station. I knew it was one place I could find a bench and spend the night without drawing much attention. There were four or five people scattered around the dimly lit waiting room, and I can remember the sights, sounds and smells. A pot-bellied coal stove was in the center of the waiting room. The nights could be cold, even in summer in these parts. The ticket man would come out from behind the wicket from time to time and stir the embers, adding more coal if he needed to.

The room seemed almost overly warm that night, and there was a smell of sweat and heated woolens filling the air. Occasionally, an ember in the stove would hiss and pop, and smoke would fill the room with the acrid scent of burning.

The people waiting all seemed to find a spot apart from each other, each seeking some modicum of privacy, as the station man further dimmed the lights saying, "First train's out at 6:30," and walked back behind his cage.

No one paid any attention to me and I was asleep within minutes.

One of the problems with sleeping on a hard bench in a lonely waiting room is waking up sore and poorly rested. That was what I remember most about that morning when I woke up.

I only had about thirty hours of walking ahead of me, and I would soon walk any soreness out of my body. *Ten hours a day, maybe more,* I thought; find a place to sleep along the way and I would finally be home.

I counted out my money, enough for a cup of coffee. I knew I needed strength for the walk ahead. I still had a small amount of money in the watch pocket of my pants. Counting it out in the palm of my hand, I was pleased to see that I had saved enough for something to eat. I walked across the street to a small coffee shop and settled on a bowl of oatmeal and lots of sugar.

"Here you go," the man said, sliding the bowl of cereal to me. He wiped his hands on his apron stained with the history of the many meals he had served up in his small diner.

I nodded my thanks and ate in silence. I was thinking about my parents and how long it had been. I felt I should call ahead and let them know, but I was anticipating their surprise. I didn't know if they had a phone anyway. I recalled the last letter from them, something about electricity coming to their farm. Father had said it was one of the good things Roosevelt was doing for the country, electrifying the rural areas. He had written that it might not be long before they had a telephone, but he wasn't holding his breath.

The start of my walk was uneventful, without ceremony. I could sense home, and it kept me going. I remember pausing on the bridge at Newport, the southern tip of Lake Memphremagog. It seems like a distant memory, that I had left from the northern tip of that lake for the train ride to Montreal.

Before long, I was walking along Western Avenue and watched as the signs informed travelers that the road had now turned into Darling Hill Road. My pace quickened; two more hours and I would be turning north on Beebe Road, almost home. Even with the leaves long gone from the trees this part of Vermont still had a green look to it.

If I had known what was waiting at home, would I have turned right and walked away, never to return? I have often thought about that, not knowing.

Instead, I turned left and walked on, the familiar sight of Beebe Plain growing larger the closer I walked. Everything I was carrying suddenly seemed lighter and my pace increased, almost to a run.

Beebe Plain was never a large place, unlike its sister village just across the Canadian border. I remember looking forward to stopping at the store. Would Mr. Carson still be there, behind the counter, quietly chatting with the old timers sitting around the coal stove? I wanted to tell those familiar people what I had been through. I wanted to tell them how bittersweet it had really been.

I pushed that aside and walked up the steps to the store, the spring on the door stretched as I pushed it open and the door made contact with the small bell overhead, ringing my entrance. Carson looked up and put his hand up to his mouth. He was never one to say much, tightfisted with words he was, but he looked speechless.

I heard chairs squawking on the floor as three men turned to see what he was looking at. Their silence was profound in warning, but I didn't hear the distress in that silence. I only recall standing there wondering about my reception. They had all been supportive of my adventure. My father had written about their interest and concern. And now they looked, what? I couldn't exactly tell.

Finally, Carson said, almost in a whisper, "Oh, my God, we had no idea where you were. We would have..."

The other men all stood up and took off their hats, looking at me with something I couldn't identify.

Mr. Carson wasn't a large man, but he seemed to shrink as he tried to talk. I was puzzled by the tears I saw on his face. I never thought of him as sentimental.

Suddenly I sensed something was horribly wrong. I wanted to close my eyes and ears and back out of the door. I wanted to turn and run. I wish I had.

He came around the counter and the other men came up to me. *What is happening?* I thought.

"Have you been home lad?"

"No," I said, "Why, what..."

"There is no easy way, so here it is in the Vermont way, straight from the shoulder. They are dead."

His bluntness was appropriate, as I look back in this telling.

"Were they sick, an accident, what?" My throat swelled and I felt like I was choking, strangling from the horrible grief building inside.

"You don't know do you?" he said hesitantly. A growing sense of dread gripped me in its tight embrace.

"Tell me, Carlson," I shouted, almost hysterical, "what do you want to tell me?"

It seemed I was not yet finished with my tour of hell.

I felt it, a hot emotion, living up to hell's reputation. Yes, Spain was hot, more hot than cold, even in the mountains. But, the hell I am telling you about now is the hell of utter loss. My list of those lost was long, and I tried not to think about it, tried not to tally my list. It had started with that strange little detective in Montreal. Then there was Seth. Finally, Tamarah's name was added. Surely, I had paid all my dues?

Now, I was hearing about my parents. My father dead and sprawled on the porch, my mother obscenely positioned on top of him, and their home left in charcoal pitted ruins.

Carson was the unofficial 'sheriff and coroner,' and his heartbreak was obvious as he told me the story.

"I saw the bastard, I'm sure. He stopped here for directions. If only..."

He paused, but continued on, "I was a part of your father's network. No need to keep it secret now. I should have..." He was unable to continue.

I felt my rage and something worse, starting to grow in my gut. I reached for my pistol in my bag, unsure of just what I would do with it. I started for the door, to run to the house, to see for myself.

But the strong hands of those caring Vermont men held me, held me close in a protective embrace.

"We will go with you, son. It's best that way. You don't need to see the place alone.

Welcome home, Alec, I thought, as my body began to shudder. What more could ever happen to me after this?

We all got in Carlson's car and drove as close as we could. Then, we started walking to the cabin, each foot resolutely ahead of the other. Step by step.

Chapter 37
Unspeakable

Walking back to the highway from my parent's home, a car pulled alongside. My eyes were blinded by tears as I heard a woman's tender voice saying, "Get in. This is no time for walking."

But that was after. We walked from the old laneway to the house. We walked until I could see it, the blackened remains of my parent's home. Those kind men were there to help me, I knew, but I suddenly told them all to leave. There must have been a tone in my voice, maybe the tone of combat command.

After they were out of sight, stillness returned, a hushed silence about the place. Ribs of timber and blackened wood piled in a jumble were all that remained. I walked into the ruins and started to see things. In spite of the recent rainy weather, I could see remnants of their living days.

I don't know what drew my attention to the metal. It was on my left. Maybe the sun happened to cast a rare ray of light on it at the same instant I glanced in that direction.

No, my sight wasn't fooled. There it was, I remember; it was definitely some kind of metal. I pulled some boards away; one of them catching on a pile of cloth that I suddenly realized had been part of my mother's wardrobe. Before going on, I had to stop until I could choke back my ache.

Turning back to the metal box, I saw it was larger than I originally thought. I pulled it into open view. It was starting to cloud over, and I felt rain starting to drift slowly down in a fine mist. I carried the box to a place under a large tree and sat back, the box on my lap. I remember thinking whoever it was that had made his terrible visit; it definitely hadn't been about money or robbery of any kind.

I broke the small lock and opened the box. The lock had only been symbolic. I knew my father didn't expect it to keep the contents safe from theft.

As I lifted the lid I could see, carefully tied in string, all of my letters. Underneath the letters were clippings, newspaper accounts they must have thought applied to me somehow.

Beneath all that was a photograph; it was Tamarah. My mother's handwriting had made a note that it was her new daughter. When I looked up at the sky spinning overhead, my view was through a prism of tears.

Further down was a note, carefully folded. I recognized my father's hand.

I have always been so impressed with you, son. You went where I couldn't, and God only knows the outcome for you.

I have given you all that I know to give and I am proud that we have walked together like men. The rich and vainglorious strive to leave their wealth, to pass it on, to keep it in their family. That stands for everything I detest about wealth. The real wealth is in our faith, faith that a new world will be better because we passed by.

There is something, however. Carlson has been more than a friend. He and I have worked together for years. It was no accident we ended up here. If anything ever happens to me, to your mother and me, arrangements have been made for him to give you something he has been holding in safekeeping for me.

Your letters have meant so much...

I couldn't read any further and put the letters, the photograph, and my father's note in my kit and tried to stand up. I think the weight of the last two years came crashing down on my shoulders at that moment. I rolled over on my hands and knees and started screaming, howling at a world that was bearing all of its weight down on me.

I wretched and wept until only dryness was left. My insides felt drained, the vomit and tears puking out my emotions. I lay like that until the rain turned cold. I did nothing to protect myself from the weather and simply closed my eyes to everything. In that moment, I wanted to die.

Through that night, I thought of Seth, remembering his devilish smile as we handed out flyers to the steelworkers in Hamilton. It seemed like a lifetime ago. Then I remembered Seth, riddled with bullets, a needless casualty.

I turned on the wet ground and in my grief, reached out for Tamarah, to touch her and to hold her close. But when I reached for her, there was no one there, just the wet, cold night air. I had no tears left, just the feeling of an empty, gaping hole, vast and bottomless.

At some point during the night, I sat up and reached into my kit. There it was, cold to the touch, my pistol. I pulled it out and snapped it open. I never believed in unloaded guns, and there were bullets in each chamber. I stared at the gun and closed it shut with a snap. *Was it time?* I thought. *Had I paid enough dues?*

Just as a band of light glimmered over the trees, I started to shiver uncontrollably. Some voice, deep inside my head, started to speak to me of the things yet to be done.

I finally pushed myself up, picked up my kit and started to walk back into Beebe Plain, my boots squishing in the wet grass and mud.

✳ ✳ ✳

Mr. Carlson looked up knowingly as I came through the door, the bell signaling my arrival with its usual *ding*. Unlike yesterday, he was alone in the store. He motioned me through the door, to his rooms in the back of the store.

"There," he said, pointing to the shower. "Get yourself out of those wet clothes, now." His voice carried the authority of too many sergeants I had known.

I think I slept until late that night. I awoke to Carlson sitting patiently in a chair alongside the bed. He smiled and said, "It's about time. I was beginning to wonder if you would ever wake up, getting ready to call Mr. Reedy over Derby way."

Mr. Reedy was the undertaker. But, I knew it was his way of teasing.

"Saved some leftovers," he said, as he walked out the door and returned with a tray filled with sandwiches and a bottle of beer. "Tain't fancy," and he watched me devour the meal and finish the drink.

We talked through the night. I slept the next day and then we talked through that night as well. I unburdened myself on poor Mr. Carlson, telling him about Seth and Tamarah. I told him of the many who had helped me along the way, never expecting any thanks for their efforts.

"Your mother was so happy for you when she heard about that woman, Tamarah," Mr. Carlson said. "She even carried a picture of her."

I nodded and showed him the photograph I had found in the box.

"That'd be the one," he said, nodding.

Then he told me about my father, things I had guessed at, and many things I would never have imagined.

"He was a giant for being such a short man," he said, "not unlike you. You two were a lot more alike than you may realize. But, he knew his time had passed."

The last night, Mr. Carlson went to a closet and pulled out a suitcase. In the suitcase was a complete wardrobe. "It was his getaway case," Mr. Carlson said. If he needed to leave in a hurry, it was always ready to go.

"There's more," he said, as he reached under the clothes to show me. There was an envelope, unmarked and sealed with a waxed hallmark. "Open it," he told me.

I took out my folding knife and carefully slipped the blade up the spine of the envelope. My eyes widened. Inside was more money than I had ever seen in one place.

"There's a lot," Mr. Carlson confirmed, "It's yours now."

"For what?"

"For a lifetime of devotion," he said. "It represents his devotion to a cause, devotion to your mother and devotion to you."

Then he showed me another surprise. He slid his hand down the inside of the lid of the suitcase and I remember hearing a loud click as a panel opened. My father, a man who managed to surprise me even after his death, had left two complete sets of identification.

I looked at the photos on the identification and started to say something.

Mr. Carlson smiled and shrugged, "You two sure looked a lot alike didn't you?"

His words were starting to sink in. At the end of this awful part of my long journey, I now had a ticket to the next leg.

I walked out the room, into the closed store, and over to the shelf holding the liqueur for sale. I looked until I found the most expensive bottle of single malt scotch in his inventory. It was my father's favorite. I carried it back into living room and reached inside the envelope. I laid out more than enough for the bottle and Mr. Carlson and I did our best to drink the past away.

"To Ian," he said.

"To Ian," I replied, clinking cheap jelly glasses together.

I looked in the envelopes at the two sets of identity. I let one drop from my hand and looked at the one remaining. I looked at a name, Mitchell Sheridan. I turned a driver's license over and stared at it. It had a different name, but it was my photograph.

It looked authentic. Along with that, were all the papers establishing Mitchell Sheridan as a Canadian born in Goderich, Ontario. My shock was complete when I realized my father had left the identity for me and not himself. It was my age on all the records. I had no idea where he got the photographs of me, but there they were. The envelope contained, among other forms of identification, a Canadian passport, driver's license and union membership card. My father's final gift was a new skin over old bones. It was like being born anew.

With the all the heartache I was feeling at that time, I don't remember much about crossing the border once more or the train rides back to Hamilton. I was now an old hand at crossing borders. How many times and how many countries? I used the money to travel in style this time.

If there was one advantage to approaching war, it meant that it was imperative to produce lots of steel. Some of it turned into sheet metal, and it took me no time to land a job working sheet metal at a plant in Hamilton.

With my new identity, no one questioned my name or nationality. The plant was not alone in welcoming any able-bodied man who wanted to work.

I was still Alec Ferguson under it all, and it didn't take long to start handing out pamphlets again.

"Come on fellows. We can put our energy into better working conditions and still be patriotic."

One day, after I had worked there for some time, the plant superintendant called me into his office. He motioned for me to close the door and the noise of the factory was muffled behind the glass windows looking out over the floor.

It must be something about my union work, I thought.

I think I remember one of the guys on the floor looking up, probably wondering what I was doing up there. It was usually not good news to get called up here.

"I have to tell you," the super said, "you are a hard worker and a quick learner."

He waited for that to sink in and said, "We need men with talents like yours. We are opening another plant. The owners have asked me to send up some good people to help set it up and run things right. I hate to lose you here, but we have more orders than we can handle and even more coming in. Interested?"

"What part of Hamilton?" I asked, wondering about moving.

"It's not Hamilton, but it's not far. It's in Guelph."

"Where the hell is that?" I think I said. I had never heard of it—Guelph.

"It's strange you don't seem to know much about the local geography do you?"

My nerve endings started to tingle with the threat to my real identity unfolding. He leaned over the desk and motioned for me to lean in so he could whisper. "I've known about you. A friend of mine pointed you out and said you were active a couple of years back."

I shifted uncomfortably, but said nothing.

"I always wondered. You looked familiar somehow. That was when my friend said you have a different name now, but he was sure."

He waited for me to respond, and when I didn't, he went on, "Did you ever know a man named Seth?"

I started to protest, but he grinned and said, "I thought so. Don't worry; your secrets are safe with me."

"And, I knew your father, as well."

This was too much for me. Even with my new name, I couldn't escape my heritage. I would always be Ian's son.

The manager went on, "Well, Guelph has some curious history. It might interest you to know that the Communist Party of Canada had its very first meeting in Guelph. You just might find some friends there and feel right at home."

It was funny to hear this from a manager.

"A lot of us have not given up," he said. "We're just waiting for the right time."

He ignored any further attempts at denial and handed me a letter of introduction to the plant supervisor. The address was on Elizabeth Street in Guelph.

"It's not far from downtown," he said, watching me read the letter. "Good luck, whoever you are."

With that, I moved on—on toward the end of my story.

Chapter 38
Peace and Quiet: O.K., Not Peace, But At Least Quiet

What followed was a time of peace for me, but not necessarily quiet. When I had slipped back across the border, all of the rumors about war were being whispered from ear to ear. I wanted to tell people that there was reason to be afraid. I had seen the influence of the fanatical Germans up close in Spain.

By 1939, all it took was a look at a map to see Germany reaching its tentacles like an octopus, reaching into every corner of Europe. That pesky island off the coast of France may have been comprised of men who called themselves Irish, Scots, Welshmen, miners, shipbuilders, farmers and more, but it was proving to be a pesky particle in the eye of German domination.

The rumors followed me to Guelph, a quiet town that was a reflection of the quiet nature in its rural setting. But, looking more closely, I could see something beyond that rural scene— the influence of industry. The growing hunger for things military meant factories were gearing up to feed that hunger.

Sandwiched in among dry cleaners, grocers and dry goods stores were quiet looking buildings, buildings innocuous in appearance. I remember walking by one of those nondescript buildings. I stopped someone coming out and asked what went on there.

"We make small, machined little round things."

He suddenly looked cautiously around. "I ain't supposed to-"

He stopped when a man in a suit yelled something from a window in the building, and two men in army uniforms ran out and waved their rifles.

"You'd best be moving along," one said.

Those little round things, I later found out, were specialized ball bearings. Almost invisible to the naked eye, they were vital to some sort of weapon-aiming device. This was confided to me by a man as we discussed unions over drinks at a tavern.

Then, on my birthday on August 25, 1939, the newspaper headline story told about units of the Canadian Militia being called out, "to defend vital locations throughout Canada in light of the deepening crisis in Europe," at least according to the news stories.

Then, on September 1, I was just starting at work when someone yelled, "Turn on the radio!" We all gathered around and listened to the reader describing the German invasion of Poland.

"That's it," someone said quietly. "We're in it now."

The next day, I read a newspaper story. The Canadian Active Service Force, a corps of two divisions, was mobilized. You can imagine the buzz at work. We had all stopped working, and even the manager had joined us. The plant manager actually came out of his little glass office. I remember watching him in his crisp, white shirt and bright red suspenders. He had his sleeves rolled up to his elbows and was wearing a visor. He walked over and joined us in listening.

"This is it boys," he said, "Turn on the radio, there is going to be an important announcement."

I can still hear the words in my mind as clear as anything. I knew what war was like, even if people wanted to pretend that Spain hadn't been real. The tears and blood in the Spanish dust were real enough, I can tell you. Now, the flow of blood would start in earnest.

Someone started to fiddle with the tuning dial on the Hammond radio, and we all yelled at him to leave it alone. Finally, an announcer told us that the CBC was interrupting its programming for a bulletin from the British Prime Minister in London. The signal faded slightly, but we could hear the words clearly. We all looked at each other with that sense of history, that sense of knowing we needed to remember this moment forever.

Then, Chamberlain began:

I am speaking to you from the Cabinet Room at 10 Downing Street.

This morning, the British Ambassador in Berlin handed the German government a final note stating that unless we heard from them by 11.00 a.m. that they were prepared at once to withdraw their troops from Poland, a state of war would exist between us.

I have to tell you that no such undertaking has been received, and that consequently, this country is at war with Germany.

I can tell you, we were all in a state of shock, even though we had been expecting something like this. Some of the men said they were ready to walk to the recruiting office at once.

"Where do we go?"

"Must be down at the armory, you know, the one down by the tracks."

But, as eager as we were, the Canadian Parliament debated for three days, debating on whether Canada should participate in the war or not. There was a loud outcry from many people who still carried the emotional scars of the Great War. They said we had no business going to war. But, after three days, we read that Mackenzie King's cabinet had sent a letter to the king asking for a declaration of war.

It was hard for someone who was not really Canadian to follow all the protocol, but apparently, King George, not Mackenzie, finally gave his approval. I read the proclamation wondering just who the First Baron Tweedsmuir was. He turned out to be the Governor General.

The entire protocol aside, on September 10th, they issued the proclamation that we were officially at war. I thought of myself as Canadian by that time. I was a part of the "we" even though I was a fake, here in Canada simply by virtue of the deceit of counterfeit identity papers.

Shortly after dark on that first night of war, the city of Guelph began to test the air raid sirens. Terrified residents ran into the streets looking up into the darkness. Apparently, the authorities forgot to inform us there would be a test. People milling around the darkened street were all too aware of German bombings. They had seen so many newsreels not to know. Someone tried to point out the illogic of German planes reaching Guelph in Ontario, but he was a lone voice that night.

I felt the fear more acutely because that sound of sirens had been ingrained into me in Spain. The newsreels of Stuka dive-bombers with their screaming sirens were on the minds of people as they mingled in the streets, soon to be told it was only a test.

At work the next day, the plant manager called all of the supervisors into his office and told us to be ready for a special shipment coming up from Detroit. There was going to be a train designated specifically for Guelph.

The next morning, it was on a siding, next to a row of warehouses and loading docks. The engine sat gasping steam, almost like it was tired from its race from Detroit to Guelph. I remember being surprised at the number of men who appeared suddenly in this sleepy little town and started offloading all sorts of boxes. I recognized the boxes from my time in Spain and knew they were packed with weapons and ammunitions. Toward the end of the train, there were several flatcars of tanks that started, with treads creaking, to roll down from the flatcar.

Someone directed our group to a car and told us to unload our plant's materials and "get the hell out of the way," as the person in charge had said. The side streets were all blocked off and a cordon of soldiers had appeared overnight to guard the entire unloading process.

Boxes vanished into waiting trucks and they started, one by one, coughing to life and then disappeared with their cargo. I couldn't help but think of Tamarah and the efficiency of her truckers, who had done as much as these men, and as quickly, with far less help.

It was only later we learned why Canada had waited for one week after the United Kingdom and France declared war on Germany. Between September 1st and September 11th, Canada used its neutral status to purchase $20 million worth of arms from the still neutral United States. Then, it was time for Canada to march off to war.

When I heard about that later, it was the first time I could remember appreciating that the United States was finally ready to take a stand against fascism. Maybe this president Roosevelt was going to do the right thing after all.

I think I was having an identity crisis about that time. I felt very Canadian, in spite of my birthright. I knew that I was in the country without approval, and I knew what it was like to be marched across the bridge at Niagara Falls by the RCMP detectives.

Still, I felt the tug when men around me started lining up at the recruitment office. It wasn't long before there were men in uniform marching around in small units or walking to and from the Armory carrying rifles.

I knew I had to do something, and finally took my place in line at the recruiting table, waiting my turn. As I stood in line, my mind drifted back to a line on the stairs in Toronto so long ago. I had been enlisting for a Spanish adventure and I had to rub my eyes to clear the memories. The image of Seth and his grinning face as we both celebrated that day in Toronto rose up before me. I looked around at the other men in line and wondered how many of them would end up like Seth and Tamarah.

I filled out my application for the infantry and was finally pushed and prodded and carefully examined by the doctors. Then, to my surprise, they told me they saw something on the x-ray. Apparently, there was a shadow; something they said looked like tuberculosis. It turned out to be the residue of some fever. A doctor said it left scarring that was going to disqualify me from the army.

"We need war production now," an officer finally said as he looked at my crestfallen face. He was sympathetic to my disappointment, but didn't change his mind.

Part of me had been worried that my impetuousness would lead to my being uncovered as a fraudulent Canadian. But, the fever of patriotism, even to this fake Canadian, was rampant.

I always wondered if the company who owned the plant where I worked didn't have a hand in it somehow. Did the authorities know more about my real identity than I realized?

I decided such thinking constituted informal paranoia.

Years later, at my retirement, there was a hint of the owners' intervention in one of the toasts raised in my honor that day: "Here's to Mitch, a great plant superintendent we almost lost to the army," he laughed.

I didn't ask him what he meant.

Instead of marching off to war again, I bought a small bungalow. I could walk to and from the factory on Elizabeth

Street. Walking home, I enjoyed the familiar surroundings as I passed under the railroad bridge overhead to turn right and walk up a steep hill.

My bungalow wasn't anything like the mansions on top of the hill to my left. I couldn't help but feel the resentment. I knew some of those people were getting even wealthier because of the war. I still had enough of my father in me to feel intense dislike about their profiteering.

Walking a bit further along the ridge, I finally got to my modest home. It wasn't much, but over time I kept adding improvements.

Each morning I would enjoy my strong coffee, skip breakfast, and begin my walk down the steep hill. I would walk again under the railroad bridge to the factory. I did that day after day, rising through the ranks to finally become the plant manager.

After Tamarah, there was no other woman in my life; there would never be. Truthfully, it wasn't a hard commitment to keep. The only adornment I ever had or needed on my night table was her fading photograph. Visible in the photograph was that smile, permanently etched in my memory—my Tamarah, my love.

Chapter 39
Harrison Has a Birthday

Harrison's slide into obscurity was almost complete by the time his 63rd birthday rolled around. People passing him in the street were still stepping aside, sensing something inherently grotesque about him, but he was a shell.

The night of his birthday wasn't a happy occasion. Harrison couldn't deny the date. It was his birthday. He looked at the calendar and the math was inescapable. It was 1943 and he turned 63.

He was also unhappy about the unfinished business with Alec Ferguson. It was an obsession that devoured his soul like a cancer. He was rereading a letter for the fourth time. Some twit in personnel had written, informing him that the Pinkerton's policy manual was abundantly clear on the matter; he was being put out to pasture, a year overdue.

They called it retirement.

He knew there were some who never thought he would make it to the end with the agency. Even in the disgrace and anonymity of his useless job, he still thought of himself as a Pinkerton's man. Now that they were taking even that away, he wondered what he would do next.

He read the letter while sitting in his office in the warehouse, shuffling through papers. *Making sure everyone has enough paperclips,* he thought.

"We take care of our own, even assholes like you," some senior manager had said. "If it were up to me, I would have turned you over to the police, but..." The manager had shrugged his shoulders and walked away, letting the threat linger on the air.

Harrison ended up transferred to the logistics division, *to be a glorified supply clerk*, he would say to himself. His job now was sending out supplies to the detectives in the field, who were doing the field work he would never see again.

It was an exciting time to become a Pinkerton's detective, now that the U.S. was at war. The government was only too happy to have help in tracking down spies and saboteurs. Harrison would sometimes have a bitter smile, knowing that the detectives were now hunting down the shadows of a German network that had, at one time, included him. He had covered all traces of his work for the Germans, however, and was never suspected.

The night of his birthday, he had left his rooming house to sit alone at a tavern in the bowery. It was a desolate tavern in one of the bleakest parts of the area. Everything had the appearance of a grainy black and white silent movie, and he drank steadily into the night.

He ordered the barmaid to line up shot glasses of bourbon on the table of his booth. *Old and ugly*, he thought, as he looked at her, although in reality, she was neither. His fantasy of what he would like to do to her turned inward, bringing a jolt of near self-destruction. She brought a bottle of beer, placed it next to the shot glasses and watched while he picked up the first shot glass, pouring it down in one swallow, and chasing it with a long drink of beer.

"Bring me more, more," he said, as he slammed the empty beer bottle down. She walked away shaking her head and brought back four bottles, unopened, placing them on the table. She didn't wait for a reply and went off to serve other customers. He had to laugh to himself. There were only two other customers and they were either drunk, or half-asleep. It was hard to tell in the gloom. She only knew that she didn't want to be around the huge stranger, the heat of his rage reaching out to curl around her.

The man behind the bar paid no attention to any of this and pretended to wash glasses that probably had not seen soap and water since prohibition. It was that kind of place.

Harrison never knew precisely when he finally stopped drinking. He was only dimly aware of standing and staggering out the back door.

"Hey, fuck, you haven't paid!" the bartender yelled.

Harrison held up his hand in warning.

Once on the sidewalk, Harrison started to vomit until there was only a dry retching left. He wiped the foulness off his mouth with his sleeve and walked back in. He fumbled for some money and finally left some bills on the table, not even taking the time to count it. He knew it was more than enough.

What the hell, he thought, *Happy Fucking Birthday to me.*

Harrison had been a man who could consume great quantities of alcohol and walk a straight line, even able to aim his pistol with accuracy. But that was then, and tonight his age was an enemy, catching up to him as he staggered along the sidewalk, lurching from light post to fence, grabbing support along the way. He stopped part way down the street, feeling a strong need to vomit again, but there was nothing left. He rubbed his forehead and kept stumbling his way home.

Alone in his room, he thought again about the phone call the day before. A contact in records still had some sympathy for the case Harrison could never close. He had a brief moment of clarity as he remembered what he had done in Vermont, smiling at the memory of helping Alec's mother to her end. Alec Ferguson was still a loose end for the old detective, but his contact in records said they had a new lead.

"You still interested in that Ferguson fella?" the caller had asked.

Harrison's head had snapped to attention at the question. "Yes," he agreed.

"Don't know what there is to it, but I just came across a record of an interview, some guy in Vermont who had a grocery store there."

Harrison suddenly remembered a name: Carlson.

"Who? When?"

"I was just putting some files away when I saw the name Ferguson noted on the margin. A field agent interviewed this guy on an unrelated matter in late 1941, maybe 1942. Here it is, February 20, 1942."

"What about Ferguson?" Harrison almost crushed the phone in his hand.

"Hold your water. It seems like this Ferguson went back to Canada, snuck across the border with bogus identification. The grocer mentioned one of the names. I did some cross-checking with a name the grocer had mentioned. There is someone in Canada using the name the grocer mentioned. It might relate to one of those fake identities."

Holding the phone tight to his ear, Harrison could hardly control himself with this information. He had written down the name and wondered where in the hell *Guelph* was in Canada.

"Don't tell anyone who you heard it from," the records clerk mumbled, "Nobody really cares about any of this anymore, but if someone noticed that I looked at the file...well, I hope it's worth it," and Harrison heard the buzzing of a disconnected phone.

The morning after his birthday celebration, Harrison awoke to an impressive hangover, swallowed a large handful of aspirin, and was working on his third cup of strong coffee.

He walked to a corner diner near his apartment and shook his head with a clear 'no' when the waitress asked him if he wanted breakfast.

"Toast, plain," and waved her away.

He rubbed his temples harshly and tried unsuccessfully not to think about Alec Ferguson. He was sure the information was useless, but he couldn't help it. He started making plans. He was no longer an armed Pinkerton's detective, but that didn't mean he was *un*armed, not by any means. And, once a detective...

What he was missing, however, was other resources that had been once available to him, resources he once took for granted. One of those was the field intelligence and the other cash; both were necessary if he wanted to confront Alec Ferguson, once and for all.

This was going to be unofficial, very unofficial. He sat in the diner developing a plan as he choked down the toast, and finally arrived at a decision—Alec Ferguson would meet the same fate as his parents. It would be a slow and very painful ending for all the years of suffering that one man had caused in his life. It was time to put closure on the murder of that Pinkerton's detective in Quebec so long ago now.

Harrison always believed Alec had killed the man in Quebec. Alec Ferguson was a laborists and a killer. Harrison didn't know which was worse.

Without help, Harrison developed his own intelligence. He went to his steamer trunk, unlocked the lid and retrieved a large envelop overstuff with papers. It was his file on Alec Ferguson, the one he had copied from the files long ago.

He studied the information accumulated over the years. He was glad he had saved it all, finding the photograph he was looking for. It was a photo of Alec. He turned it over and noted the date. *Six years old, now,* he thought, *it will have to do.*

He also took out a picture of the father, Ian Ferguson. He put them both in separate envelopes and continued with his preparations. He retrieved and opened a small metal box. It contained what he called his 'pension plan.' It was merely some of the cash he had saved from his Nazi pay. It wasn't much, but it would get him to Guelph and back.

He started to feel better and was glad it was Saturday. He wouldn't have been able to do this sort of work with a serious hangover. He picked up his box of carving tools and carried it to the kitchen table. He picked out a record, a Vivaldi recording, and started to carve a miniature. As usual, the activity helped him control his fixation and focus on a plan.

Later, he laid down the latest carving and left his apartment. Instead of dwelling on his hangover, he thought about the work left to be done, as he walked to the New York Library. Inside the cavernous building, he was directed to the reference section where he located a map of Canada. Harrison was not a man used to libraries, and he finally walked over to a woman behind the desk.

"Where," he asked, his booming voice echoing, "Where can I find out about Canada and some place called Guelph?"

"Shush," she said as she turned around and pulled a book off the shelf behind her chair. Turning back, she started leafing through the book and finally whispered, "It's in Ontario."

"Can you show me?" he had lowered his voice to match hers and tried to smile, not sure if he was succeeding.

"There," she said. Her finger was resting on a dot.

Harrison eyed the map and noted that it wasn't far from Buffalo. He ran his finger over the map and drew an imaginary line from Buffalo to Guelph. It wasn't far at all.

She watched his finger tracing the line and said, "Oh my, Niagara Falls. You have to see it."

He didn't respond to her enthusiasm and simply grunted something like a thank-you, turned, and walked out of the library. He knew where he was going now, and he felt like a detective again.

Back at his apartment, he packed his suitcase, slipping his holstered pistol between layers of clothes. Then, expecting a search as he crossed the border, he slipped it behind a false wall on the end of the suitcase. Leftover from his days with Pinkerton's, it was designed for hiding things from border guards and other curious eyes. He looked around his small, dismal room and walked out with the sensation he would never see it again.

He walked to the subway stop and rode to a station with an escalator leading up to the New York City bus depot. He carried his suitcase and walked up to the ticket agent. "Buffalo," he instructed, feeling it was all that needed to be said.

After an hour or so, he boarded and settled onto the bus. He wouldn't allow himself to sleep. He quit counting the stops the bus made until he finally saw a sign welcoming the bus and its passengers to Buffalo. The last time Harrison was in Canada, his position with Pinkerton's had smoothed the way, and he didn't have to submit to the indignity of a border inspection.

He was grumpy today, as he answered the questions and was among bus passengers that were travelling from Buffalo to Hamilton. He could see mist rising to the right as the bus drove up the highway.

"The mist from Niagara Falls," someone noted.

He thought about the librarian for a moment, telling him to visit Niagara Falls, and then he returned to thinking about Alec Ferguson, now living under a different name in Guelph.

The bus station in Hamilton was like bus stations anywhere. Some people waiting impatiently, and others who seemed to accept their wait with indifference.

The ride from Hamilton to Guelph was an old bus that chugged up a long grade as it left the shore of Lake Ontario and climbed the escarpment towards Guelph. It was a narrow road with little traffic this particular morning, but the bus had to stop several times, as military convoys roared past. Tarpaulin-covered trucks flashed their camouflage colors as they raced past.

The bus finally arrived in Guelph, passing what looked like a college campus of some sort. The bus drove down a hill and crossed a river. Then, the driver shifted into low gear as the bus made the approach to another hill, passing an armory bristling with military activity. After crossing under railroad tracks, the bus made a final turn and wheezed to a stop at a small terminal. It was a very old bus, probably called out of retirement by the war.

Stepping off the bus, Harrison looked up at a sign and started to walk. *McDonnell Street*, according to the sign, and he spotted a flashing neon hotel sign. He walked in that direction and started humming. It was a tuneless song and a couple walking by sensed the evil in the sound of it, and would later remember feeling a chill as this ugly man walked by.

"I actually shivered," she would later recall.

At the hotel, Harrison counted out the money for a week's stay, and was promised more clean sheets if he stayed a second week. He walked up to the third floor and the room looked just like the dismal room he had abandoned in New York.

He didn't care. He simply put his suitcase on the bed and walked back down the stairs to the bar. *It's odd*, he thought, *to see the sign at the bar entry. Men only*, it read. *My kind of bar*, he decided, as he pushed the swinging door.

"Beer," he said.

When the bartender slid the stein across the bar, Harrison asked, "Do you know where this place is?" He slid a paper with the name of a factory across to the bartender. The barkeep told him it was a factory on Elizabeth Street and drew Harrison a brief map on a napkin.

Chapter 40
Star Crossed, but Hardly Lovers

Looking back, I realize that I didn't wake up that day aware it would be an extraordinary day. Everything that had happened in my life, up until that day, had been no more than a dress rehearsal. Everything that followed would forever live in the shadows of that day. As is often the case, special events have inauspicious beginnings. Some may tell you they had a premonition or a sense of impending expectation for some cataclysmic event. Not me. I believe that premonition is something we are only aware of after the fact, not before. We trick our mind into thinking otherwise. I can tell you that I remember no such feeling about that day.

Since that day, however, I have never been able to forget it, etched forever on top of all my other memories. It's as though the day's events were captured on tape, a tape that loops back upon itself without end. I can replay it anytime in my mind with the clarity of a video recording. At times, I manage to push the memory of that day aside for a while, but it often sneaks back into my awareness while I sleep, even to this day.

On that day in October, my alarm went off, as usual, at 5:45. That was the usual start to a work morning. I never resisted waking and sat up on the side of the bed, feeling the chill of the morning. I slipped my feet into my slippers and walked out to the kitchen. I put the kettle on for some tea and made toast while the water was heating up. That was my breakfast, tea and toast. When I felt like taking my breakfast over the top, I would open some marmalade and splurge.

After breakfast, it was my custom to toilet and dress for work. With my promotion to plant manager came the expectation of appearances. In spite of my new title, I tried to remain on the side of the common workingman. Now that I was in management, it was an incongruity that never escaped me.

That particular day, I had on my crisp, white shirt, bow tie and red suspenders. It seemed to be the uniform of a plant manager in 1943. Wearing my jacket to acknowledge the cool, late October temperature, I took my usual morning stroll down the steep hill to the factory. Nothing felt out of the ordinary, and I clearly remember the lightness in my step on that morning.

I nodded my good mornings to the clerks as I walked through the outer office. Just as I was opening the door to the factory floor, a clerk put a hand on my shoulder and motioned me to the side.

"There's someone—a man—came in and asked about you."

I had always secretly worried that a day of reckoning would come. Now, I wondered whether the RCMP or someone in authority had discovered my identity. I was immediately on high alert.

"No one had any idea who he is and he didn't offer any identification," but the clerk added, "He's huge."

I turned and walked to the window and parted the curtains slightly with my finger, just enough to peek out, and could see no one there. I turned, walking through the door, and went out to the plant floor. Ignoring any uneasiness, I busied myself with my morning walk around, snaking through the bustle and noise of the stamping machines. I was always at home among the workers and resisted time in my office behind the windows.

About an hour later, the clerk came out to the plant floor and once more tugged at my sleeve and yelled into my ear above the noise of the machinery, "He's out front now, just standing there!"

I pushed her aside and raced out to the front office and the window. There was nobody there, just an empty street with a bus slowly driving by.

"Are you sure?" I asked the clerk, who had followed me.

"I...I thought so. Maybe it was just a coincidence."

I watched through the window for a few minutes. Rose, that was her name, the name of the clerk, brought me a cup of tea. I finished it while I scanned the street.

While I finished the tea, I didn't see anything out of the ordinary. I walked out on the street, looked both directions, and saw no sign of anyone other than an old woman walking a dog. I put it all out of my mind and concentrated for the rest of the morning on our production quota.

I walked around the block at lunchtime, telling myself it was for the fresh air. I was really on the lookout for suspicious looking men, especially big ones.

I managed to once more put it out of my mind by the time I walked home; convinced it was the product of a vivid imagination. As I walked up to my house, there was something out of the ordinary, I realize now as I look back.

People today have no idea what it was like during wartime. During the war, there weren't many cars on the road. Tires and gas were strictly rationed, and that meant we all tended to walk or take the bus.

What was unusual that day was a car parked just past my driveway. Though it was unusual, it didn't register with me at the time. It was one of those things we sometimes see without really seeing, if you know what I mean.

As I turned to the steps of my porch, I noticed the front door slightly ajar. It had become quite windy, not uncommon at that time of the year. The weather forecast had been for strong winds and dropping temperatures. I chastised myself for not properly shutting the door that morning when I left for work.

First, there had been a car, and then the door slightly open. Still, neither one of those facts set off any alarms for me. Instead, I walked through the door and made sure it was tightly closed behind me. I took off my jacket and carefully put it on a hanger. That was when I first noticed something, a smell.

What is it? I remember wondering.

Then I recognized it, the unmistakable odor of a cigar.

As I walked into the kitchen, he was sitting there. I remember waiting for him to flash a badge of some sort. He looked up at me with something approaching a smile, but not quite making it. I recognized it as a look of satisfaction.

My God, the man reeked. His musky scent even overwhelmed the cigar he had clutched in his teeth.

He sat with the bottle of my favorite scotch uncapped in his left hand. Glen Garioch, it was. His right hand was under the table and when he pulled it out, I saw an enormous pistol. I had seen lugers just like it in Spain and had a sudden epiphany, realizing that RCMP detectives didn't carry Lugers.

When I tried to strike a pose of composure, I looked down and saw two photographs on the table. I saw my photo and my eyes locked on the other one—my father, Ian. He nonchalantly used the luger as a pointer, tapping each picture. "Ian Ferguson," he said, tapping my father's photograph. "Bang, bang, you're dead." It was the voice of pure evil.

I was frozen in fear, expecting the gunshot that would end my life. I didn't have to be told that this was the man who had killed my parents. I saw it in him. He was going to do the same to me. All I could hope for was to find out why, before he killed me.

"Alec Ferguson," he said, tapping my photograph. "Bang, bang, and soon to join your father," he laughed. It had a sound more evil than I would have thought possible.

In all my time in Spain, I had never completely lost my nerve, even when I probably should have. It wasn't a fact of bravery, really. I just accepted these kinds of events as my fate. But, looking at this man, I felt the wetness as my piss released without intention, a dark patch spreading down the front of my slacks. This brought on even more wicked laughter.

You would think I would have been embarrassed, but I knew it was a natural reaction to primal fear. I had seen it too many times on the front lines to think twice about it.

When I could take a breath, I finally asked, "Who...who are you?"

"I'm your worst nightmare, my friend."

"Friend, that's an odd word. Do I know you? Am I supposed to know you?"

"Have you ever been to Vermont?" he suddenly said, and for me, this confirmed everything. I felt a shudder. *This is their killer.*

He saw the understanding unfolding on my face and this time, his smile of pleasure looked genuine.

"Tomorrow morning we take a ride. It would give me pleasure to kill you now, but I need you alive—for the moment."

I was feeling an equal mixture of fear, loathing and curiosity. I had no choice with that luger in his hand. He held it in a casual manner, but I had spent a lot of time around men with guns, and I recognized his practiced hand.

I looked around.

"It's no use," he said, "You are what, two or three steps to the door? I can bring you down as soon as you move."

I knew he was right.

He waved his pistol and motioned me over to a wall. "Lean against the wall and spread your feet," it was the voice of a detective.

I did as I was told. He ran a hand under my arms, around my pockets and up and down the legs of my pants. Finally, convinced I was unarmed, he reached up and yanked my left arm behind my back. I fell, face first into the wall. He yanked my right arm behind my back as my chest pressed against the wall, my cheek flattened against my teeth.

With a practiced motion, he had the handcuffs on. "I haven't done that in a long time," he said with something approaching satisfaction. He turned me and marched me out into the small living room and pushed me back onto the sofa.

"We leave at first light," he said. "We have a whole night to get acquainted," he sneered.

I kept my silence.

"Oh, I know all about you Alec Ferguson, or Mitch whoever-you-want-to-be."

So, he knew who I really was. I was somehow not surprised that my fears had finally been realized.

"Let me tell you a story."

He finished my bottle of scotch during the tale. It had been nearly full when he started and he showed no real signs of impairment when he finished it. Maybe a slight, occasional slurring, but that was the only indication. I remember regretting that I didn't have any close friends who might drop by and discover my plight. But years of living alone with my privacy afforded no such luxury. Instead, I listened to his story without really wanting to.

"My name is Harrison, Samuel T. Harrison, to be exact," and he held up a shield.

I saw *Pinkerton's* arching over a badge number. The number was ninety-three. I will never forget that number.

He launched, uninvited, into an incredible story. I some-how had the feeling that this was a man who didn't talk much, but he unburdened himself of his entire history that night. He talked about Montreal, Toronto and Galveston. He talked about setting traps hoping to catch me.

He described in great detail how he had killed my parents. He laughed, telling me how much he enjoyed killing my mother and the indignity he caused. He drank my scotch and laughed when I kicked at him, uselessly, with my legs. The handcuffs behind my back made it a futile gesture on my part.

Then he told me why. He started at the beginning. He said it was my father who had started it all, ordering the assassi-nation of Harrison's man, a man he had recruited to be Pinker-ton's spy in the Chicago circle of anarchists. His spy had been one of my father's friends, recruited or coerced into becoming an informant for Pinkerton's. I knew the story had some merit, but I always heard the story from my father's point of view. It all depended on whose story was being told, I guess.

Harrison talked about his search for my father over the years, and how Ian had always eluded him, vanishing like smoke. He told me about almost catching him in New York, when my father vanished with a new wife and baby. "You," he said and waved the gun in my direction. "I didn't realize he had gone to Vermont, taking you with him. Quite the clever man, your father was."

Then he connected the dots to my part of the puzzle.

"1937 and Montreal," Harrison scratched his chin, "One of our Pinkerton's detectives was killed in Montreal. He was found with an ice pick sticking in his ribs, and his pistol was missing."

I remember my uneasy feeling as the memory of those men in Montreal slipping me a gun flooded back. I had always had a feeling about the pistol that I had carried to Spain and back.

"You are one slippery eel," he said, "We almost had you in Toronto, you and some bastard named Seth. Thought we didn't know, eh?" He told me how he had set a trap in Toronto and then learned we had evaporated into thin air, only to resurface in Galveston, Texas.

"I always wondered how you managed that," he said.

When it was obvious I wasn't going to tell him how we got out of Galveston, he told me how he had missed Seth and me in Texas. Then he told me an unbelievable story about Spain. I shuddered visibly when he told me details about the near capture that confirmed my memories about that day on the Catalonian hilltop. It had been a raid specifically designed to capture *me*. I was more incredulous as the minutes passed.

He even confessed his rise and fall, talking about a career with the mighty Pinkerton's Detective Agency. He rambled on and told me about his father, a real bastard of a man. He told me about his own undercover work as part of some secret unit inside Pinkerton's. He talked about a man name McParland, but I was not really following his ramblings at that point. I was engrossed with the psychotic man in front of me, wondering how I would ever be able to get myself out of this situation. After everything I had been through, this seemed like a real fuck of a way to die.

He seemed convinced his career would be resurrected with my arrest and conviction. He was a bit unclear about what crime I might be convicted for, but it didn't seem to matter much to him. He certainly knew I was in Canada illegally, and that alone would get me tossed out of the country once again.

The end of his confession coincided with his finishing my bottle of scotch. With that, he stood up, looming over me.

That was when he detailed my parent's final moments once more. If anyone has ever experienced despair, they might just have an inkling of what coursed through me at that retelling. I know I had never hated anyone as much as I did at that moment, not before or since.

He walked over to me and slammed the barrel of the pistol across the left side of my face, cutting the skin across my cheek. I could taste the blood from the cut as it drained down past my lips to my chin.

"That taste of blood is only the beginning," he said with a leer. "There's nothing in the rule book that says how alive you have to be when I take you in."

But, he didn't do any further harm, although I suspected he wanted to. He simply pulled the belt out of his pant loops and strapped my legs securely together.

I was in an uncomfortable position, lying halfway back to one side, my legs draped over the edge of the seat cushion, but he paid no mind.

"Tomorrow, we have a big day ahead of us," he grinned, as he took one of the cushions off the sofa and threw it on the floor, using it as a makeshift pillow. He stretched out on the carpet and within moments, I was listening to the sounds of his racking snores, rising and falling throughout my sleepless night.

I tried to think of a plan, some sort of escape. I had never felt more alone in my life. My parents were dead, Seth was dead and Tamarah was dead. There was no one left to come to my rescue this time.

I must have slept some, but if I did, it was not restful. I think I just wondered and waited through the long night. In my waiting, I could see the faces of my mother and father. I could see the faces of Seth and Tamarah. I could see the faces of all those who had helped me on my incredible journey.

Where was someone now?

I cried tears for Spain. I cried tears for all of my lost friends. Mostly, I cried tears for myself.

Chapter 41
The View from Rattlesnake Point

You might wonder how I could have slept at all. This dangerous man had made no effort at my comfort. I was tied securely in an uncomfortable position and still fell asleep sometime toward morning.

I was startled awake by the sudden cessation of his snoring. A delicious silence filled the air and I was tempted to embrace more needed sleep. That's when it all rushed back to me, my predicament clear.

My eyes flickered open. The large man was sitting erect with no visible signs of the after effects of my scotch.

What was he doing? I wondered.

I realized he was carving. His huge hands were skillful, and I admit that I was amazed at the detail of the miniature in his hand. He was whistling, and I realized it sounded familiar and classical. None of that lessened my dread, however.

He finally laid his carving down, looked around, and with a glance at his watch said, "It's time, asshole."

Before we left, he made no effort to clean himself. With no attempt to close the bathroom door, I was treated to the loud stream of his piss into the toilet water. Without bothering to flush, he came out through the door, zipping his fly and rubbing his hands on his pants. His breath preceded him and it was not pleasant.

I told him I had to use the toilet.

"I don't think it makes any difference for you today if you piss yourself again or not," he laughed.

He told me to stretch my legs out, careful to stay out of any kicking range. He took off the cuffs first, and I rubbed my wrists where the metal had dug into my flesh. He unfastened the belt he had wrapped around my ankles and threaded it back through the loops of his pants while he watched me walk into the toilet.

"Don't close the door," he warned me.

After I washed my hands, I reached for the cabinet to get my toothbrush.

"Leave the cabinet closed," another warning, "Your dental health is the least of your worries right now," he said. My additional plea for a toothbrush went unanswered.

I did my best to rub my teeth clean with my finger. It was better than nothing. I knew the smell of my urine-stained pants contributed to my general malaise, but it was still no match for the smell that emanated from that monster waiting in the living room. It was clear he wanted to leave under cover of darkness and he hurried me towards the door.

"Please," I said, motioning to my backpack in the alcove by the door. I had always left it there as a reminder. It was my constant companion on my Spanish adventure. It held the few mementos that really mattered and it was never out of my mind.

"Let me take it, please." I actually begged.

I will never know what prompted him to agree, probably putting it in the same category as a condemned man's last meal.

"Take the fucking thing, what do I care."

He carefully fastened the handcuffs to my hands, in front of my body this time. I continued to rub the soreness from my wrists, ignoring the ache in my shoulders. I leaned down and finally managed to pick up the backpack, carrying it with me to the car. It felt heavy, but it gave me a sense of reassurance. *At least I can die with my memories*, I thought.

Harrison looked watchfully up and down the street and hurried me to the car. We walked to the street side of the car, and he opened the rear door. It was a Ford sedan and the back door opened from the front angle. We used to call it a suicide door, a reminder never to open it while the car was travelling at high speed.

He grabbed my pack and threw it in on the floor behind the passenger seat, and shoved me onto the back seat without ceremony. While I was lying there, he hurried around and opened the door on the right side of the car, and tried to fasten my hands to the door handle.

"Don't get up," he said, "or you're a dead man," he grumbled, realizing he could not secure my hands to the door handle.

Was it a mistake I could use?

Any civilian car on the road in 1943 was sure to attract attention, and driving with a man in the back seat would look suspicious, for sure. He told me to stay down and out of sight. He finally shut all the doors and locked the back doors. It was a useless gesture on his part, but must have given him some sense of control.

I saw a faint hint of sunlight just over the trees. It was still dark enough to need headlights, but streetlights were still a rarity in this neighborhood. No one really expected German bombers to appear over Guelph anymore, but we all acted as though they might. It helped us to believe we were a part of the war effort.

I could tell he was looking at a map. I could see through the gap between the front seat backs. He ran a flashlight over it, and after studying it for some time, he seemed satisfied. He turned the ignition and started the car.

I found out later that he had used his Pinkerton's credentials to "borrow" the car from a local police detective. I tasted the bitter irony as he told me that while I lay there in the back seat.

Since moving here, I had spent a lot of time exploring the countryside around Guelph. Walking came naturally to me after all the walking I had done in my life. I also had a bicycle that I used to ride great distances, often camping overnight alongside the back roads during my time off. A co-worker had also used some of his precious rationed gas to drive me around the area one weekend. He was proud to show me where his family lived. He had told me all about an escarpment that started in New York, passed through our area, wending up over Lake Superior and ending somewhere in Wisconsin. When I asked him what an escarpment was, he laughed and said, "You might think of it as a large cliff."

He told me it ran through Hamilton, and I remembered how we referred to it there as *the mountain* when I lived there. From down in lower Hamilton, it looked like a mountain, but its top stretched out to the south for miles, flat as a pancake.

All this gave me a vague sense of where this guy, Harrison, was taking me. I could get my head up high enough every now and again to see where we were headed, before he would yell, "Get your fucking head down!"

In the growing light, he drove us south out of Guelph and turned left. I could tell we were passing the small village of Arkel. He drove through until we came to the end of that road. Now he had to make a decision: it was either left or right.

He looked at the map and tried to mutter the pronunciation of Nassegweya Sideroad. That was when it became clear to me he was avoiding any major roads leading to Toronto.

Why would turn me in? I wondered. I knew he wanted to kill me, to mutilate me as he had my parents. I felt it emanating from him as sure as heat from a fire.

He muttered his confusion as he looked at passing road signs. "Damn, every one of these is called a sideroad something or other." I knew he wasn't really talking to me.

He was finally forced to turn right at another intersection, and as we crested a hill, he saw a highway ahead. The congestion was a sharp contrast to the back roads we had been travelling. I was just able to lift my head enough to keep some bearings. As we approached the highway ahead, I could sense his growing uneasiness. That was when I sensed I might need to test my slight advantage.

It was apparent that he was afraid of something. But what?

He had flashed that badge, but it dawned on me that if he really wanted me in custody, he would have taken me to the police station in Guelph, unless Pinkerton's had an office in Toronto he wanted to use. That still didn't make sense to me.

I felt the first glimmer of hope. I was dog-tired, but my mind brushed away the fog of pain and hatred. Something about his story last night finally registered. He was a discredited Pinkerton's agent whose only authority came out of the barrel of his German Luger. It wasn't much, but I started to think, the glimmer of a plan forming.

While I was scheming, he seemed to make a decision; when there was a break in the traffic, he suddenly accelerated across the road. As we left the traffic of the highway behind, there was another sign. We were on Appleby Line Road and had just crossed over the railroad tracks. He raced and bumped over the tracks and past a crossing guard, who was frantically waving a warning lantern and cursing us as we sped by. The screeching whistle of a fast-moving train joined the guard's warning.

As the car bumped over the tracks, I found myself almost wedged in place. Harrison pushed the car to its limit, and left the guard and train behind as we started up a sharp incline in the road. I had been here before. This was where my friend had taken me on that outing one day, to a place called Rattlesnake Point.

I realized that whatever Harrison had been trying to do in attaching me to the door handle, it hadn't worked. A feeling of relief was my reward for turning and easing the pressure point on my right buttock. I moved my hands back and forth along the floor and my right hand touched the rough webbing of my backpack, lodged under me between the seats. With some effort, I moved as slowly as I could, peering up at the driver to make sure he didn't see me move. I moved my hands up along the pack until I could feel the flap.

With lightning bolt clarity, I remembered the pistol. I don't know how I had forgotten it until now. I had carried it all this time, reluctant to part with it somehow. How could I reach it now, at the bottom of the pack?

Harrison shifted to a lower gear as the car climbed the slope. It was steeper than he expected.

I kept working my hands slowly until I had the flap open. My shoulders were aching, but I remained as motionless as possible while my hands dug into the pack and finally touched metal. I kept straining the muscles in my arms until I had it in my grasp, trying to pull it out. I almost lost my grip twice, but finally, it was lying on the floor just under my right thigh.

I had never believed in unloaded guns. If you had one, it was meant to be loaded. I was no longer in Spain, but I could never make myself unload that gun. Now, however, even loaded, it felt useless.

My arm brushed something else. It was a box—a cigar box. I felt the top and opened it. I could feel the carving he had been working on with my fingers. Then my hand felt the cold, sharp edge of a carving knife. I wrapped my fingers around it and quietly closed the box.

"Where the fuck!" he shouted to no one in particular. He pulled the car over, clearly at a loss for what to do next. He looked back, and I recognized the look on his face. I had seen that same look on the faces of those men in leather jackets, the men who had killed Seth. Harrison wasn't wearing a leather coat, but he might as well have been. He was going to kill me. I could see it in his eyes.

"I was going to take you back and turn you in, but what's the use," he said. "Nobody gives a damn anymore." With those words, my impending execution was fixed. He got out of the car and opened the back door on the driver's side.

I can't begin to describe the surprise on his face when I drew my right knee up to my chin and pushed with my leg.

I used my one opportunity.

He reached in to restrain me and with a sudden move, I plunged the carving blade into his wrist. I could feel it lodge against bone, and the huge man screamed. I knew his scream was involuntary. It was unearthly.

He stepped back and pulled the blade. It had been dangling from his arm. His eyes were wide with rage and he seemed to ignore the pain and turned back toward me. I can still see the look of disbelief on his face as he stared at the pistol in my hands.

I don't remember aiming. It was a moment of self-preservation, and I pulled the trigger without thinking. The sound echoed in the car and the acrid smell of gunpowder blossomed.

People who have seen gunfights in the movies think the man getting shot suddenly clutches his chest and falls backwards. Harrison did neither. His eyes simply opened in recognition and he lurched forward, falling over my left foot. A large red stain appeared on his right shoulder. Had it been enough?

I used my other foot to kick him off, finally feeling the car shift as the weight of his body slipped to the ground and off the running board.

In what seemed like hours, but was probably only minutes, I managed to struggle out of the car. There was no one around. I saw a farmhouse in the distance, but no sign of anyone running toward the sound of a gunshot.

I felt in his pockets, ignoring the variety of stinks rising from his body. It was truly awful. On top of the foul odor his body had emanated from the moment I smelled him in my apartment, his bladder and sphincter had both released a mixture of gas, piss and shit. That's something else you don't see in the movies; people sometimes shit and piss themselves when they have been shot.

That was certainly the case with Harrison. He moaned slightly as I fished his pockets until I located the key to my handcuffs. I stepped back. He was still alive.

It wasn't easy. You concede a lot of dexterity when your hands are cuffed together, but once rid of them; I was finally a free man. I stretched and walked to the edge of the woods to relieve myself.

Even in this remote place, I respected my modesty. I turned away from the parking area and was just finishing, when I heard an unearthly scream behind me. Turning, I saw the giant stumbling towards me. It was a terrifying scene even when I knew I had a gun in my waistband. I pulled the gun out as quickly as I could and realized how perilously close he was.

Instead of shooting, I sensed he was handicapped by his wounds. I turned and ran. I ran as fast as I could with his pounding footsteps lumbering behind me. He was crashing his way through the underbrush, branches snapping off in his passing.

I finally stopped when I reached the edge of the escarpment. The fertile farmland stretched out far beyond, fields neatly patterned, glowing golden in the October sunlight.

I looked down the rocky ledge and could see straight down to the bottom, hundreds of feet below. Outcroppings of rock signaled this as the edge of the Niagara Escarpment.

Trapped, I'd had enough.

I was filled with a terrible resolve and could go no further; in fact, I decided in that moment that it was ending here, one way or another. It was a murderous emotion welling up inside of me. My parents, Seth, and especially Tamarah, had all paid a terrible price to men like this.

Harrison lurched toward me, but his footsteps were unsteady and his eyes had developed a terrible glaze of pain, rage and murder. He was a dying man who didn't quite appreciate it yet.

I recognized it for what it was. He almost made it to me, when he stopped and suddenly sat down with a thud.

"So close."

I swear those were his final words. No final duel to the death, no witty last words. Just those two words.

I struggled until I was able to drag him to the edge of that drop. I forced his head back until his eyes looked out over the view, but I think I knew he wasn't really seeing it.

I thought about my mother. I remembered my father. I thought of Seth, and I had a glimpse of Tamarah's beautiful face, black hair framing the porcelain white of her visage.

Finally, for all of them, and for me, I set the gun aside and simply gave him a slight push, watching his body tumble, bouncing from rock to rock and breaking tree branches, until it reached the bottom.

Did I feel elation? Did I feel any sense of revenge?

The only thing I felt was a hope for some type of closure, I guess. The rest of that day I remember far less clearly.

I'm sure my mind retreated to a place of safety where it wouldn't have to remember. It has stayed in that place until now.

I looked out over the vista and Lake Ontario in the distance. I knew that my running days were finally over. This was my home now, and the past was finally in the past.

I walked back to the parking area. I remember starting the car. I drove back to the road and continued south on Appleby Line Road. I braked through a twisting series of curves until

I made my way down the escarpment to Derry Road. I must have turned west, because I do remember coming to a church at Guelph Line Road. It was a magnificent stone church, common to this part of Ontario. I can still see the sign for St. George Anglican Church. I parked the car in the empty lot and went inside the church—they were never locked in those days. There was no one around as I took a seat in the back row.

It's strange to think about now. All of my upbringing and experience had been a denial of the need for religion; my father was convinced it was an "opiate for the masses." But, there I was, sitting alone in that church, asking for forgiveness. And, on their behalf, I asked for all those I loved to be welcomed to a peaceful heaven.

I learned an old saying during my time in Spain: there are no atheists in foxholes. I had heard brave men and women crying out to God for protection when we were under barrage. For the first time in my life, I experienced a complete feeling of indescribable emotion wash over me. I was praying, praying for forgiveness, praying for peace in my soul.

Then, something almost magical engulfed me, as I stood up and walked back to the car. I felt completely released from my misery to finish my life in peace.

As I walked to the car, an older priest walked out of the manse next to the church. "Good morning, friend."

I somehow knew he meant it. "Thank you, Father," and I meant it back.

What happened to the car? I drove it back to Guelph and left it parked at the train station. If the owner ever questioned the damage and the mixture of bodily fluid stains, I never heard.

Chapter 42
Every Story Needs an End...Or Does It?

There was a long silence after Alec finished telling Michael about the stone church. He sat back in the chair, suddenly looking like a very old man. Michael had never really thought of him as old until that moment.

Michael started to ask a question, for follow-up, he said.

The man sitting across from him shook his head from side to side. "No more. I have held this story inside for so long. Now it's over." He paused. "I know it wasn't what you really wanted to hear, what you hoped to find."

Michael tried to protest.

"Looking back, I realize it was a time when nothing was really all that clear, and the years since haven't made it any more so," Alec admitted.

When it became apparent to Michael that Alec was well and truly finished, the reporter reached down and turned his recorder off.

"Will we talk again, tomorrow?" the reporter asked.

"No one cares about the ramblings of this old man. Was it even true?" he teased with a sly look. "It meant a lot to me, your patience. Will anyone care? No, I doubt it. I think the time for talking is over."

Michael knew a truth that he didn't share with Alec. He *would* write the story, regardless of whether anyone truly cared.

It was something he felt compelled to do. He somehow felt it was like his story now, too.

In truth, he knew few might ever bother to read it, and even fewer might even care if they did. It was a story covered in dust, a story from a time long forgotten. It was a story with a theme that history had tried to erase, denying it ever happening.

Who gives a damn? Michael admitted to himself.

Was there a civil war in Spain? Yes, but there wasn't anything civil about it. He knew historians were once more beginning to shine the light of history on it, but it only mattered to a few old rusty relics in academic departments.

Franco had won...or had he?

The Brigadistas had lost...or had they?

All anyone had to do was to choose a side and describe what happened. Michael knew from his research that there was a bitter reckoning after the war, especially for those brave Basque and Catalonian fighters who had felt so right and so noble in their cause. Old scores were settled by the Francoists.

Thousands were imprisoned and worse, after the war was over. People who think the Germans invented concentration camps should note well that Franco's side used them to "rehabilitate" the Reds to the "Catholic way."

That rehabilitation, for thousands of the unnamed men and women of Spain, meant graves that would never be identified. Poets, musicians, husbands and sons, all took turns lining hastily dug gravesites in the Spanish soil.

All Michael had to do was hear news about today's Basque Separatists to know the echoes of that war were still rippling in the Spanish dust. Michael knew all of this, even as he silently pledged to Alec that he would write the story, regardless of who might read it or care.

As Michael had watched that last time, Alec sighed, stood up abruptly, and walked away carrying his precious memories. That was the last time Michael, the reporter, ever talked to him. He vowed to make regular visits, to stay in touch, of course. It was a vow, forgotten all too quickly.

He returned to Toronto to write his story. When it was finished, it created some interest in certain circles and even realized some modicum of critical acclaim.

"But, it's not really history," the historians claimed.

"It's not literature," the book snobs retorted, turning up their noses.

As the story skidded into obscurity, Michael's career took the twists and turns that careers often do. But, he could only try to outrun destiny.

❄ ❄ ❄

Michael turned on his computer one morning to check his e-mails. He was almost ready to delete one he suspected of being spam. It was from someone calling herself "missvermont@homewood.com"

It was the "Vermont" that snatched at his attention. He opened the e-mail and read:

Dear Michael:
I still have your card. That nice man you interviewed a while back, Mitchell, died yesterday. We are all so sad.
He left something that looks like an old backpack. He told me to let you know if anything ever happened to him, you know, like dying.

❄ ❄ ❄

Michael didn't need a map this time, as he made the drive to the care center. Walking in, he glanced over to the alcove, so familiar to him still, and somehow expected to see Alec sitting there.

Michael thanked the receptionist, who still remembered him. She even tried to flirt with him again. He realized that they both looked older now.

He resisted the urge to open and look at the knapsack and boxes that had been willed to him. He carried them to the car and consigned them to the trunk.

Later, back to Toronto, he rummaged through the pack and laid Alec's treasures out on his table. There they were again—the photographs. Michael held them up to the light, looking carefully at the young man and woman, noting the many details in the background.

He carefully lifted out and handled the pistol, remembering the warning that it was never unloaded. Snapping the pistol open, Michael decided it was finally time to remove the bullets one by one. He had a sudden laugh, glad his prize hadn't been searched at the border crossing. When he was sure the gun was finally unloaded, he laid it aside and continued inspecting the pack's contents.

Identification cards and a carefully folded uniform shirt and pants were on display next to the photographs. Michael took the uniform cap out and put it on his own head, walking over the mirror. He looked at it on his head and, on impulse, saluted. He noticed the image in the mirror and laughed. It looked like his twin was giving him a left-hand salute, and he remembered what Alec had said about that in his story.

The last item he retrieved was a card. Carefully printed on the card was something written in Spanish.

"Con patienza y salivita el elefante se coja l'armagite."

Michael tried a translation website and could make out something about an elephant. It didn't make much sense.

Finally, he promised a woman acquaintance dinner and a nice bottle of wine if she would help him translate. She was on the faculty of the Spanish Department at the university.

Over dinner that night, she told him.

"It's Catalan, a slogan that was used during the civil war," looking sad, she continued, "They knew from the time Franco and his army invaded that it was going to be an uphill struggle for them," she explained.

Then she translated for him.

"With patience and saliva the elephant can fuck the ant. There might be a more polite way to say it, but, there it is."

She stopped when she saw his tears, his tears washing away the dust of time.